FORBIDDEN BEING

Written & Illustrated by

SALEM HASKINS

To those that built me up, cradled my descent,
and nurtured my growth, may you find solace
with minimal sacrifice.

Content Warning

The following story you're about to read is not for the faint of heart and articulates the author's repressed experiences in a fictional format; things left unspoken, exaggerated for entertainment some may find relatable, triggering, or disturbing.

As such, the author has outlined the following content warnings for your consideration. Please read them before continuing.

This book contains passages that may rile emotions of helplessness, pain, and more if emotionally unprepared could affect the reader's mental state.

The literature contains:
Possession and physical entities
Religious and political conspiracy, conflict, denial, and abandonment
Pagan practices
Attributes to a caste system
Attempted homicide and imagery of suicide or self harm
Domestic assault, kidnapping, and child abuse
Descriptions of strangulation and suffocation
Miscommunication and manipulation
Discrimination and ableism
Favoritism and victimization
Vampirism and cannibalism
Gender oppression
Violent and graphic imagery (body horror)
Drug use and swearing
Diverse nontraditional characters
Some actions might be associated with bestiality

This is a work of fiction not intended to inspire revolt, revolution, or overthrow of any governing body or religion. It is intended to open the mind to self-evaluation and reflection for healing and developmental purposes.

REMEMBER IT IS IMPORTANT TO BREATHE.

If you feel overburdened by any of these potential triggers, please stop and take a breather before continuing. Your mental health matters.

CONTENTS

Theo's Playlist

CHAPTER 0

The Guilty Conscience of a Non-hero

Death is inevitable for all those who stand against God. And for one man,.if 'man' was a proper term for the empyreal being, death was a saving grace which came in the shape of a woman. Immortal, he knew death's dance as their fates frequently twisted throughout time. The last attempt 30 years ago left the world in devastation.

Today, humanity celebrated the survival through memorial while he avoided demise through dilapidation. As the colony rejoiced, he disciplined himself with the consequences of life, scampering the edge of society to evade the hunter's gaze of a vengeful queen he offended millennia ago. For his safety, he waited for the feastivites to begin before leaving.

In the meantime, the television in his presence chimed with a live broadcast of the opening ceremony.

"Now, a word from Lord Raymond Sambuca," the host handed off.

"Good evening, dearest citizens of the Oasis. And thank you for joining me on this momentous occasion, for today we memorialize the horrors that plagued our home this day 30 years ago."

As the official spoke, the man imagined scrolling white words spackled across a teleprompter conveniently provided. From the viewer's experience, the official lacked the creativity to formulate aspiring words. He analyzed Raymond Sambuca's ceremonial appearance. The advertisement of state on this day inadvertently displayed the political morale of the Oasis. Groomed and ornate, Raymond appeared more royal than usual. Even his bronze skin was amplified to be more righteous than the name Sambuca was capable of being. It was all unnatural. His behavior wasn't very different. Fingers crossed on the iconic mahogany desk, a prideful expression plastered on the official's face, yet his posture sent mixed signals: straight spine and drooping shoulders.

From his canter, the Lord recognized the integrity of his citizens and the unfortunate circumstances surrounding them. For this occasion, Raymond was "Keeper of Man" instead of the usual "Warden of Beasts."

"On this day, April 28th, we honor the men and women whose courage and sacrifice laid the foundation for human survival. Corralled to an ancient city, perfectly isolated from all sources of darkness, the birth of the megalopolis became a horrific epic."

The viewer scoffed. Unmoved by the charade, he switched the channel. He refused to hear the tale be recited by a heretic. However, he couldn't escape it. Every channel capitalized on the holiday and delivered similar renditions of the same script. News anchors, talk shows, and commercials televised the broadcast. Channels flew by.

"Beach —"

"Heroes —"

"Newfound capitol —"

"Vampire mutants —"

Each word cataloged the calamity at Arnireth, a light orb rig in the Mare Nostrum seabed, miles from the Oasis but close enough to be fearful of resurgence. He groaned. After so many years, the tale was inscribed in his brain.

"The seas caved and conceived evil anthropomorphic entities, the Malum Saltus. Darkness swallowed the light, and showered the lands with wickedness," recited News Anchor John.

The viewer knew them well.

Unlike humans, he had known this evil for centuries. As a knight of God and priest of Persia, he battled them, cursed them, ate them, and in some way, was even related to them. They were a part of nature that refused to stay hidden. Consequently, he was present when the veil on their existence fell and became known to modern society. Though it happened thirty years ago, the nightmare was still fresh in his mind.

Before the collapse of Arnireth, no one feared the water, shadows, or rural emptiness. Civilization flourished, covering the land with human activity and prosperity. That all changed once the sun peaked on the horizon.

An hour before the world died, Ana wandered the beach, basking in the day. Apricating, he devoured the sun radiating his skin and absorbed the healing breeze of ocean spray. The sand brushed beneath his feet. The sensual gratification of the place always alleviated his mind, a therapeutic redemption he often used as an escape.

To his surprise, he found his favorite spot crowded but didn't mind sharing it with those who enjoyed its splendors, and they didn't mind sharing it with him. A complete stranger, they beckoned him to their play, tossing a ball and then again with lunch, ignorant to his danger.

Eventually, Ana's march continued, leaving his new friends for endless scenery. Smiling at their play, he admired their splashing and chasing of waves. Blissful was an understatement. Their laughter and cheer were still in the distance when it happened.

When the event crashed upon them, the atmosphere did not warn them of the danger. There were no clouds, shift in the wind, smell, or sense of anything that called for Ana to protect them. There just was.

Then the dials aligned to the twelfth position and a second sun broke the watery horizon. Light towered and opened the gates of hell. Unsuspectingly, waves tumbled onto sand and ripped to shreds the first victims, the children of the family he broke bread with. The faces of the children, joyous and nescient, were instantaneously dismembered, embedding his memory with details he wished to forget.

The dark creatures' claws ran through innocent flesh and abandoned the corpses without taste or recognition, without any validation of life spent. The sight sickened him, not because death was indiscriminate, but because their genocide was weightless.

Effortless, like breathing air or drinking liquid. Mass annihilation was too fluid and unrestricted. The silent emerging disemboweled him as he was completely blind to the demon's signature vibrations.

He watched in horror as whimpering and playful screeches turned into desperate screams as the horde dispersed.

In seconds, the deluge of waste rusted the white sand and spray from victims showered the day with bloody rain. To his dismay, thousands more followed, more than he had ever seen, flowed into the city. For every soul slaughtered, a thousand emerged from the waters. He had to do something.

After all, he was accustomed to this monstrosity. He was capable of intervening. If he did not, more people would suffer and die agonizingly. Thus, he followed the horde into the city, narrowing the malum population as one man possibly could, only he wasn't a man, nor was he alone.

Others were fighting. Like him, they possessed the stripes of a different breed. Their elongated teeth clenched with growling screams and their incredible strength severed shadows apart cleanly. Weaponized with the power of nature, these inhuman beings held back hordes in time for evacuations.

Society witnessed their resistance; how different they were for the first time in history. Ultimately, the fate of humanity was left in their hands, all except for one — him.

Ana's fight was halted by the very creature leading the violence. The army of darkness was under the control of a silver-haired maiden he once cosseted, a ruler of his species, a queen he wronged, and she had her vengeful sight on him. At the time, no one questioned why she flooded the lands with vengeance. On that day, his brothers and sisters abandoned their mortal faces to save humanity from the scourge. Their only focus was the primal instinct of preservation. On that day, Ana could have been a hero had it not been for his queen and her murderous plot to destroy him. Instead, he vanished.

Customarily recited, the following lines of the epic were devoted to the fighters, not for a coward like him. "In the chaos of bloodshed, some souls were brave enough to face the horde. These men and women were not of the same breed as the humans fleeing. They stood for the greater good and abandoned anonymity to save humanity. Vampiric and tiger stripped, nature's guardians sacrificed secrecy to maintained the natural balance."

Another channel spoke on the event, "For as long as time, these forces have counteracted the other. Yet, it was this moment, the collapse of Arnireth, which threatened the vitality of our civilization. Humanity would not have persisted without the beings we call mutants. On this day, April 28th, we recognize the atrocity of Arnireth and its impact on the world. We appreciate our heroes. If it were not for their bravery, determination, and sacrifice, the world as we know it would have ceased to exist —"

"— would have ended."

"— destruction of humanity."

All the sources said the same thing.

The television suddenly went black. The annual repetition of propaganda fatigued Ana. He sighed. In the silence, his eye caught his reflection, twisted by the curvature of the glass.

Dark circles peered back at him. His paleness could no longer hide his grotesque existence nor the particular features that differentiated him from humanity. Stripes, dashes, marks, and dots; signs of mutation melanized across his skin like stretch marks, especially on his face. The lines and wrinkles caught the pigment well. He had plenty in the corner of his eyes and the outer edges of his cheeks. Hands quivered. Nowadays, relaxation was easier said than done.

A deep inhale filled his airways as he spoke internally, *Today is Memorial Day. There will be parties and festivals, blood rains, and supply raids; too much chaos to focus on one offender. Mutant kind will be everywhere with their identities bare. I'll be able to get out, blend in the crowds without confrontation and hopefully ease my mind.*

Memorial Day was the only day He could relax without the danger of a stake penetrating his heart, shredders tearing his skin, or Venator capture. He took the opportunity yearly to establish a new beginning, to rewind his ticking clock.

For starters, his psychosis required alleviating. He pined for energy and knew exactly where to get it. The eternal rose on his wrist granted him access to the largest event. However, attending meant encountering Leo, dealer of substances partial to his kind. Though reluctant, he had to see him at least once.

The news played again as he got ready. For the moment, the sound of nonsense propaganda and fake sentiments was better than silence. People spoke as if mutants had only been around for the last few years. In truth, they have guided humanity since before time was written.

Mutants have been cultural leaders, politicians, celebrities, warriors, authors, myths, and at one time, deities. Yet, since Arnireth and the rise of a governing power, staying mystical became more challenging.

When asked for their opinion, one mutant woman detailed the shift perfectly, saying, "We congregated to one area to protect the few humans remaining, our Oasis. With so many of us in one place, humanity flourished to the point society no longer required our strengths. Even more so when synthesis became an option for convenience. Species converged, no longer able to distinguish between human, synthetic, or mutant; a reality that grafts disdain among those still true to their nature."

"Thank you, Olivia." News Anchor Wyatt then turned to the camera. "Today we honor our heroes with our sacrifice. Be sure to give thanks through charity. Give an ounce or two. And remember, be safe."

Ana buttoned his collar, now listening intently as Raymond Sambuca provided the closing statements. "Now that the Oasis remains the only patch of green on the continent, people have begun to question, 'Where are our heroes today?'"

The man in the mirror couldn't contain a toothy smirk.

"Definitely not where you would expect."

CHAPTER 1

A Lion Chasing a Hummingbird

In typical Memorial Day fashion, people flocked to the western half of the Oasis, to Crescent City, the "home of mutation," to celebrate alongside the heroes. Among partying and indulgence, non-beings are subjected to the graces of mutant kind, a grateful sacrifice in a time of deserving. In the height of ration decline, the mutant population embraces the offerings of partygoers. They feed off the swirling energy of celebration, the charisma of drug induction, and of course, the blood of anyone.

It was a techno-noir to the observing, a calling to go wild and crazy to appease the dangerous animals of the kingdom. Many could not wait for the holiday. Many could and made their opinions known.

Parades blocked all major highways. People walked miles to the other side of the Oasis. The streets were packed with flamboyant charades and costumes of every type: festival, macabre, angelic, and more.

Feathers danced around hips and hairpins. Bedazzlement shimmered trails from prosthetic wounds and chariot beauties exposed their fake fangs. The masquerade shunned their faces to recognize mutant suffering, and in opposition, chained tigers walked alongside their owners, supporting the enforcement of their power.

Since the inauguration of the Oasis, it has been a tradition for all beings, human or mutant, to witness the festival spectacles and attractions of Crescent City. However, for one woman, a different feature astonished her, an outlander which her group celebrated over the excitement of the day.

"I can't believe your birthday falls on the same day as the Arnireth memorial. That's amazing!" A lady coiled her arm around the woman of interest.

"It's so paranormal," disgusted a friend behind them. She was practically green with superstition.

Furthest from the pack of women, Geda smirked. *Paranormal indeed.* It was also her birthday, but the group was unaware for a good reason. Strategically, the excitement was directed toward the newcomer.

"Nonetheless, we have to give you a proper welcome, to the sorority house and the city," leader Breanna mentioned.

Another member chimed, "There's no better time to be in the city than Memorial Day."

The group cut around the corner of a busy intersection.

"Have you seen a mutant?" one of the ladies asked the new girl, Kasey.

"I have. Many," she replied.

"Ooh! Right." Eyes meet another's in exaggeration, clearly unsympathetic to those living outside the Oasis. "Only vampires travel beyond the hills."

Dunes, Geda corrected internally.

"Vampires?" Kasey asked, falling into the stereotype others had for her (behind the times).Geda's eye twitched. Kasey's pretend of ignorance somehow worked on the others. And her disguise was too unique.

An accomplice, Geda saw right through it.

Honestly, the girl was from the mountains, just a stone's throw away from the Oasis, southeast of Crescent City. Though it was not unheard of for people to reside outside the colony, people still gasp at its mention.

Humans haven't ventured from the safety of the Oasis in generations, and those that do, rarely return. So when an outsider arrives, they are remarkably integrated. Aware, Kasey used her history to her advantage, almost as if she has done it before.

Without hesitation, the house welcomed her into their home and inner circle within two days. What more could she ask for?

"That poor girl." An emotional diva leaned to Geda.

Her space was violated by the woman. *Which one was this again? Leann?* Geda thought. Honestly, she couldn't remember half of the girls' names. Breanna, Tiffany, Leann, Kasey, and other words starting with the letter B. She didn't much care nor feel required to learn them.

"It must be tough for her," Leann continued.

"What do you mean?" Geda questioned.

"The outsiders. I bet they are told horror stories about the vampires and that's why they don't move to the city." Like most, the diva Leann was ignorant of why people voluntarily chose to live beyond the security of the Dunes.

The new girl overheard and intruded, "Actually, we outsiders hold mutants in high regard. In fact, I am here on a grant to become synthetic." The latter was a lie. Geda recognized that much, but again it worked on the others.

Breanna's eyes lit up. "Is that true?"

Kasey nodded.

"I begin my procedures in a couple of weeks."

"Aww! We were just getting to know you," Tiffany expressed, as if synthesis had high risk of death.

The leader twirled. "Then, let's go off with a bang!" changing their plans once again.

Through they had their differences, Kasey was beyond alluring to this house of intellectuals, irresistibly dripping with forbidden information. Knowing this, the persona maneuvered them into position like pieces on a board. In this instance, she catered to Breanna's obsession with mutants to get what she wanted.

"Have you ever experienced a mutant party?" Tiffany asked the new girl.

Kasey shook her head.

"You will today," Breanna stated with new direction.

They followed the ecstatic leader down the sidewalk.

"I assume you know where one will be?" Leann directed to Breanna.

"More like, I know where they all will be," Breanna corrected, "but an exclusive club is where it's at and this year, I know how to get into the largest one."

"How?" Tiffany was curious.

Breanna shot her fist into the air. "Why with me, of course. I received an invitation." On the back of her thumb was an outline of a pink rose, an implant.

"I see," Geda whispered.

They stopped in front of a building just off the main street and Breanna outstretched her arms under a pink neon sign spiraling with rosebuds that matched her implant. "Welcome to the Rose Garden, a nightlife establishment built for the vampires and honorable mutants. Whichever you call them, this will give you a glimpse of their world."

The young woman worked harder to embellish the rabbit hole she led them down. After all, it was her passion.

"Inside, it will rain down with blood. Lights flashing. Incense burning. Strangers groping with a venomous seduction. People will dance their guts out to relive some old-time glory. This is Crescent," she growled. "Welcome to the jungle."

Only the new girl was impressed. Across the way, Geda caught Kasey's smile against the rosy hue. This is what she was looking for.

Others saw Breanna's potential wasted on this fascination. "This is where you go every Sunday?" Leann judged.

"It's the only salvation I need," admitted Breanna.

"Then, perhaps we should see what the excitement is all about," agreed Tiffany.

"I thought Leo's club was for members only. You're not a mutant, are you?" Leann was suspicious. Even on Memorial Day, only those accompanying mutant members could enter, evident by the crowds around them. The average attendance was one male mutant to ten women.

"Don't worry. I have a contact on the inside," said Breanna.

"Who?" Geda asked.

Their leader blushed. "The bartender. We had a lovely night recently, and he gifted me a rose. A shame it's only a one-time use."

"You were smart to save it for today," Kasey mentioned.

As they waited in line, Tiffany's body could not be restrained. As the music bumped the building, she moved to the rhythm.

While others basked in the aesthetics of the falling sun and neon glow, Geda couldn't shake the sensation of being watched. She had felt it multiple times before. Her sight frequently scanned the skyline and empty alleyways. Yet, what she expected to find was missing. It made her uneasy.

"Hey!" Kasey bumped her arm. "Why are you so stiff, girl?" she asked.

Geda chuckled uncomfortably. "I've never done anything like this before," she admitted.

"Neither have I, but I'm sure it will be alright. Besides, you have me here." Kasey shrugged, nervous.

Geda smiled. "That's true." By now, Geda knew Kasey, or better yet the person behind her makeup, enough to feel safe next to her.

Even so, she had to remind herself, *Right. I just met this girl. I do not know her. I must not demonstrate any recognition of Kasey's true nature, or else my actions may unveil the hunter under the makeup. In this, I must be alone.*

The group approached the bouncer covered in thorn tattoos, and Breanna proudly displayed the rose emblem on her wrist. He acknowledged it. "Does your party need additional supplies before entering the Rose Garden?" he asked, holding up a vial.

Nostalgia.

Again, Breanna's eyes widened. Excited, she whipped back around to the group. "Do you want to get Nostalgic?" But, of course, what she was suggesting was blasphemous.

"Are you crazy?" Leann objected.

By that, Breanna had her answer. A bag landed in her hand.

"Nostalgia only works on vampires," Tiffany suggested.

"Is that so? Has it been proven? You'll never learn how it works until you try. Think about your thesis on mutant life. Will you settle for a lower grade by not experiencing something so influential to their existence? Plus, you will not get another opportunity to experience a Memorial Day like this," Breanna rebutted, a great argument leaning into the girl's research.

Convinced, Tiffany smiled and took from the supply. "Oh, why not? But don't think I will ever eat raw meat."

Breanna dropped a vial in everyone's palm. Geda peered down at the tube rolling in her fingertips. The serum was otherworldly, indescribably captivating. The contents glistened and twisted against the neon radiance. The color changed every second from recently being mixed. She now understood Nostalgia addiction. By simply peering into the oil spill, the drug practically called out to her.

"I'm not okay taking drugs," Geda resisted.

But, of course, Breanna stepped in. "The categorization of drug gives the substance poor connotation. It is not what you think it is. It will keep the fatigue away so you can wake up for class tomorrow," Breanna attempted to convince her.

Then Tiffany butted in, "And show you what you've lost along the way. That's why mutants take it, to reminisce."

Their ampoules pointed towards the sky. As the circle sedated themselves, Geda lingered on the decision. Statistically, one out of four people lose themselves in the illusions of Nostalgia.

Then a breath kissed her ear. "It's okay," Kasey whispered. Geda turned and met the auburn eyes so close to her own. "You should enjoy yourself tonight. Trust me. It will melt the guilt away and make fun feel real again. We just need to get inside, and I'll do the rest," she assured, sliding her vial into Geda's back pocket.

Geda wasn't sure how to respond to the persona but she did value the word of the woman beneath it. Again, Geda reminded herself of her place. For this mission, she was meant to be the catalyst of success and success required her sacrifice; the sacrifice of being absent, a part of the crowd. The drug went down with ease.

Once all had consumed the nectar, the garden gates opened.

"Let's go, girls! We have work to do," Kasey led the way. Her target finally within reach.

As she crossed the threshold, nothing stopped her from entering. Not the bouncers. Not the mutants. For the first time, she was finally inside the hive. Uninhibited, her perceptions did not deceive.

Purple tones and pink highlights smothered the greys of humanity weaved within the canvas of red. Rhythms and beats even vibrated a few sedated to sleep. Hands cradled their trance and fed off their romance. Fangs captivated the harmless. Like demonic hummingbirds, mutants were careful not to disrupt the petals, delicately licking the nectar from their victim's lips. And this was before the main event.

The others joined her side, amazed.

Inside was a maskless masquerade. Humans and mutants were the same, predator indistinguishable from prey. Though the group of women dawned wigs for the occasion, the congregation was a seamless union, unheard of by theorists.

Many fear the mutants, calling them worthless skin rippers and vampires. Their group, however, were allies of divinity; some would say victims of dark comforts. Regardless, they were eager to join. They faded right in.

Their leader pulled them through the crowd. "Come on, girls. We have to find a mutant for Kasey."

They squeezed through shifting openings between people. The wave waned in, retreated, and quickly returned to trap them momentarily. The hive was a living unit of twisting bodies and slow-dancing beauties of all shapes and all sizes, carefully tending the safeties of each and satisfying the aggressions that rested beneath. In passing, Geda carried the wetness of the body she brushed. When the waves parted, the gentleman detected her loneliness, wrapped a muscular arm around her, and pulled her in.

"No." She calmly rejected and he respectfully released her back into the current, back to her friends (Breanna, Tiffany, Leann, and others starting with the letter B.)

"Wait, where is Kasey?" Geda searched for her.

Not far from the entrance, Kasey stared motionless, fixated like a cat on her target. "I've found one," she said. Their gazes were directed to the balcony above.

"Him?" Tiffany questioned, pointing to a silhouette admiring the performance from the second-floor lounge.

"That's the club owner, Leo," said Breanna. "You don't want him."

"More like he doesn't want you," added Leann. The snotty women chuckled. "You aren't exactly his preference," she explained, meaning he enjoyed the company of men.

Kasey smiled. "I'm sure I can convince him."

Geda caught the twinkle in her eye as a nasty plot come to fruition. When Kasey stepped forward, Geda stopped her.

"Wait! What do you want me to do?" she asked.

Kasey returned with a loving touch down Geda's cheek and said, "Nothing. You have accomplished your mission. You got me inside. Now I will be able to accomplish mine."

"A mission of a lifetime," they shared in unison.

"That's right. The hardest part is over. Enjoy yourself. Go have fun with your friends," Kasey suggested, but they weren't her friends. This woman was. Submissive to her order, Geda released her, and "Kasey" vanished into the crowd of unfamiliar faces with ease.

At that moment, a sudden shift in music altered everything. The air was sucked from Geda's chest as the Nostalgia landed. Her head spun, twirled, and jotted. Gravity became heavy like water; from the sea, a ghastly figure appeared on the shore. A dark shadow pulled itself from cohesion. The creature captured her eye.

"Hey, are you coming? It's about to begin." Muffled, Tiffany tugged on her, but Geda was frozen.

"Wait," she whispered, mesmerized by the being now ascending the iron steps.

Tuxedoed with dark hair, his elegance stood out from the trash she was in. His fair complexion was lined with dark curls she could not forget. Unlike the others, he did not hide his mutanity.

"Who is that?" Geda gasped.

"What does it matter? Let's go. It's about to begin." Geda gave in with little thought and regrouped with her housemates. Whereas the gentleman entered the lounge to satiate his hardships. Sighing, he found a place at the bar surrounded by others like him.

"What will it be, sir?" the bartender inquired.

Looking at the bottle displays, the man couldn't decide. "What's your oldest bottle of scotch?" he asked.

The young man behind the counter scoffed, "Just a 3 year."

Ah! That's right, he almost forgot. *People don't keep nice things anymore, not since the collapse.* After which, society consumed all the luxuries of life, fearful a tomorrow wouldn't arrive. *Can I blame them?* he questioned internally. Looking at the sparse glass shelves that once held decadent bottles and foreign elegance, picked explicitly for mutant therapy, he had his answer. *Yes.*

"Give me a Negroni or Sazerac," he ordered.

"No specifics?" The bartender was confused.

The customer shrugged. "Surprise me."

"Yes, sir." And the bartender got to work.

As the man waited, eyes lingered as people passed. A couple gasped at his appearance, but he wasn't ashamed.

"There are more people here every year, huh?" the bartender mentioned.

"Mason, are you trying to make small talk?" grumbled the man.

The young man was caught off guard by the gentleman's directness. He was unsure what to do until the man responded, explaining, "You'll lose business."

Mason chuckled. "No, sir. I don't believe that. The great Ana at my bar? Ha! I'll get loads of requests."

This poor kid doesn't know, Ana thought. *I am an omen to these people.* "Yes," he eye-balled the room. "Nothing but synthetics."

Synthetics dressed in high fashion. Ladies in dazzling gowns. Strapless and sex-driven, they ruined their faces acknowledging him. The men accompanying them were even more reluctant and pathetic. They judged him for his inability to hide his mutant signs when they themselves had no right to the honor of mutanity.

Ana swallowed the daggers they gave, for each one was a hypocrite, prancing around like they deserved the services provided with the celebration. But, in truth, there were no heroes here.

An amateur could distinguish those who claimed a name from those given one. True saviors intentionally retained their battle scars as a reminder in case they forget. These porcelain dolls were unmarked. He remained judged by scums. They were not so different from him.

In the lounge, people debated politics and war. The hushed counterarguments bloomed a pain in Ana's mind. Aside from the whispers of gossip, multiple voices could be heard over the classical ambiance. One of which belonged to Leo, the club owner, introducing a set of newcomers to the ongoings of the mutant lifestyle. In his fingertips rolled a tube of the mutant drug.

"They say Nostalgia represents a deep wound. However, in Greek, it means a painful yearning to what you miss most."

Intrigued, the new blood partook in Leo's offer while his companion accepted the rose brand. After all, only a rosed mutant can enter the garden and devour its abundance. Leo's eyes then met Ana's, which initiated an unwanted confrontation.

Ana sighed. He had hoped to avoid it, but at the same time, he couldn't help but watch him. Leo was graceful, chiseled, and firm. He was a rolling stone, continuously moving.

In opposition, he planted his roots here after the collapse. His influence could be seen throughout the city, frequently thrashing his limbs over the dividing river. Ana corrected himself; Leo was a wisteria.

Ana returned his attention to the bar where Mason rushed his drink. His hands were unsteady as the clock ticked down to show time. *What's got him so worked up?* he wondered. *Oh! Sazerac in a martini glass.*

"Cheers, sir." The bartender slid the glass across the wood. The young man got to work on another order.

"Thank you, Mason." Ana's long fingers lifted the glass from the tiny white napkin and escaped the scene, avoiding the confrontation in progress but mainly to run from his own "kind." In all, he sought relief in the flamboyant charade, where talks of mutantity were nullified by human interlude and music.

Through the balcony doors, he passed into the modern age and the essence of party goers washed over him. Like waves, the crowd danced to the artist on stage.

Lights flickered and swirled. The air was energized by citizens expressing themselves. Dancing, drinking, and drugs. A tingle crept upon his cheeks and he devoured the worldly pleasures from a distance; a distance he was obliged to keep.

This is why he came tonight, to revitalize something within him that died, something that has been gone since he abandoned the world thirty years ago. Oh, how the world has moved on!

Never again can he be a part of it. After all, he is the reason it was nearly destroyed.

Removed from the pack, he refuses to be stitched back in. He remains a man motionless in a hurricane determined to take him and, in the process, destroy everything around him.

For Ana, the only pleasures in life are those who see him for who he is, surround him with openness, and welcome him unconditionally. So, for now and forever, for life to continue, he will remain a mutant in a static state, insensitive to time's current, haunted by his mistakes. His silent sacrifice. Or so he reminded himself.

"Mason," greeted Leo, brushing his hand.

"He's here," the bartender informed.

"I know. I have seen the cruel expressions."

"After all this time, they still blame him for what happened?" Mason was sympathetic but did not understand.

"It's not as simple as that. Others judge, unaware of what the massacre was, a hecatomb for his demise. They only see him as the summoner, thus subject him to cruelty," explained Leo.

Mason retracted his hand. "He is just through there," he motioned to the balcony.

Leo took the liberty of joining the observer. Unlike the others, he respected his friend's seclusion considering all he had been through. Through the ornate double doors, Leo found Ana leaning on the balcony railing, soaking in the rays of humanity. "It's time for the show to begin," he said.

Ana didn't respond to his ample warning.

"It's going to get messy. Would you care to stay inside?" he offered.

"Not tonight," Ana said cold-heartedly.

"Very well." Sympathetic, the owner placed a hand on his comrade's back. "I can see your struggle, Ana. We all can. If you need anything, call me." He lingered momentarily. Without a reply, Leo went back inside.

Ana's brow tightened. The tense confrontation he had prepared for was left unsatisfied. Instead, he was left with a lingering warm spot at his acnestis, the touch of concern, Leo's concern.

Knowing this may be the last time, sorrow bellowed through his nostrils, forcefully refraining from following his friend. *Do not go after him. Do not ask him for forgiveness,* he told himself over and over again until the doors behind him latched. With a barrier between them, Ana could relax. Besides, it was time. With a simple button, the bartender initiated the long-awaited ceremony.

A buzz sounded. The back door unlocked in time for 'Kasey' to welcome a small team of armored men.

"What took you so long?" groaned Agent Tuwile, aggravated by the wait.

"I had to disable security," she explained as the intruders stepped over unconscious men on the ground. Her gasping breath was evidence of a brutal fight and her rush to meet them.

"I'm surprised it actually worked," admitted Agent Sabre. A change in the muffled music caused the crowd to roar; the perfect cover. "Enough chitchat. We have a job to do," he led. The two men got to work.

As her team infiltrated the building, 'Kasey' took a moment to clear her senses of the nostalgic aroma and called in to her superior. "We are in," she informed over the phone.

"Good. It would seem the source was reliable," a deep male voice returned.

"Of course," she agreed, previously doubtful. "You should know that agent 7541 provided the resource for entry."

This was a detail Lord Raymond was surprised to find out. "Geda? Did she choose to take part in such violence? Ah, she's growing too fast." His fatherly concern was apparent.

"I assure you, sir. Her only mission was to provide a key. Anything more, she was told to stand down," she highlighted.

Raymond released a sigh, a sign of vulnerability he showed only a select few. "I am pleased to hear that, Sasha. I have another request for you. Once things are done, leave a breadcrumb for a specific someone."

"Who?" she asked but answered the question herself.

Raymond replied, "Ana. The queen is still searching for him. I doubt he is aware of her return."

"She's back?"

"Yes." He sighed again. "And prepared to destroy the world again if he is not careful."

"What makes you think he is here?" Sasha asked.

"He always is. Besides, our informant confirmed it. Give the letter to the bartender. If he has any spit of ambition left after his betrayal, he will do the rest for us."

She was doubtful. "If he doesn't?" she challenged.

Raymond chuckled. "Then, we will understand what metal he is really made of and deal with him properly."

"Understood, sir," she said and ended the call.

Sasha remained in the alley, wiping away her disguise as Kasey. The two identities were almost indistinguishable. The only significance was the scar on her cheek; Kasey's was missing.

Then, seemingly out of nowhere, a drop of water touched her skin. *Rain?* She looked to the night sky and found dense ambiance blocking starlight. The humidity was on her skin, but she was currently blind to the smell. Her mind wondered, bending on the edge of nostalgia, but she quickly shook into strategy.

She focused. *Raymond is planning his game. We have Ana within range, but it is Leo we are after.* Then she recalled Leo had never been captured before, making this is about more than the queen. *This is a publicity stunt for Raymond to gain more power.*

Raymond holds the location of Ana over the queen as leverage. Capturing Leo gains the Lord reputation throughout the city and instills insecurity among the Separatists he struggles to control. The planted breadcrumb will warn Ana about the queen's return and create enough fear in him to unearth the religious master Raymond seeks to smother.

It's genius, Sasha thought. *Raymond seeks to win, and if everything goes accordingly, he will.*

Setting everything off her mind, Sasha returned inside, aware of the scandalous action she was about to commit for her beliefs. But she didn't care so long as she was the one to drive the blade through the heart of the old master.

Inside, the synths whirled on the stage, signaling the main event. Breanna spotted Geda's confusion and said, "This is why we came tonight. It's going to rain!"

It's been ages since it last rained in the Oasis. Companies often imitate the process as a reminder of the natural phenomenon. Yet, the rain that nourishes the Rose Garden is unlike anything nature could replicate. That is until the collapse of Arnireth when the Malum Saltus met the mutants in battle.

Blood rain was once a sign of impending doom. Now, it quenches the thankful.

Red drops fell onto Ana's haggard hand. He looked up at the sprinklers a few feet above him. "Any second, now." Prepared for its contents, he closed his eyes and prayed the rain would release him from his ailments. "I have lived and died multiple times," he whispered. "May I live with death until it takes my final breath?"

Thus, the rain came. Red, it fanned from the sprinkler heads and crashed upon everything, metal and flesh alike. Sins were washed away under the blood rain and some were committed.

The annual "cleansing" was also a time for feeding. All around, fangs slipped under the skin of the unsuspected. The gore was too much for some to handle, but not for Geda.

She danced, calm within its drench.

As the red stained her skin, she twirled in her own direction, soaking in the false carnage. She found safety among the gorging mutants. Something about them was nostalgic.

With the blood sliding through her fingers, a sense of belonging existed in her consciousness. Releasing her inner sanctum, she let them in.

Again, aromatics filled her senses. As Nostalgia numbed her mind, they jumped to her rhythm. Their touch embraced her, cradled her worship and guided her expression. Exposed, she understood the limit of their possession and never went past it. For the moment, it was all about her.

"More, more," she sang along to the artist on stage. For her, it was a controllable euphoria. The same could not be said for others.

Unfortunately, the shower was short-lived, ceasing before the song was over. Yet, the crowd didn't seem to care.

Seduced, the aqueous coagulated in the smearing rubs. Body heat humidified the air with stench. It was exultation.

Above, Ana basked in the tame violence. He inhaled their essences, draining the air of all redeemable qualities and energy until he had his fill. The appeal violated his mind with dark thoughts and temporarily satisfied the corners of his mind. However, it wasn't enough. It's never enough.

High from the supply, his collar dripped with the substance. His color-washed suit resonated madder red finish. The white angelic robes now quenched vermilion. Although his shell was alive with the music, his mind, on the other hand, teetered on the edge of defeat.

Gluttonous, this year it would take an extortionate amount of effort to diminish the effects of his prolonged deprivation, which generally subsided with a gentle touch. Something was going on. He had gone too far with his intention that he might not recover. Ana needed help.

He downed his glass. Palliative and languished. With no cure for his symptoms, he fell onto the music hammock and rested his fatigue on the tempo. He prayed for effectiveness. Something had to elevate him to the man he used to be.

Then, he tasted it. His tongue flicked at the bitter taste of his drink. There was something in it. Citrus? "Nostalgia," he recognized the savory sourness. "The bartender spiked my drink."

Realistically, the young man had put it in everything. The drug was carbonation to drinks, seasoning to food, and even the refreshing rain. Dancers were drowning in the substance. He smelt it, citrus and vanilla.

The lovely aroma stifled the breath and paved a pathway for psychedelic possession. It was the relief he wanted, achieved by a method he did not for it had a tendency to birth demons from memories.

Staring through the crystal film of his glass, Ana's eye caught a glimmer of his ghostly past. In the sea of sanguine, cotton hair spilled from a disguise and triggered his mind. The familiarly dreadful color shot through him like a stake to the heart. Breath left him. The Nostalgic shard hit and reopened the wound of disaster, the memories of Malum conception.

It's her, he recognized. *The queen.*

Red-skinned, she caught the scent of him.

Their eyes met.

Quick survival instincts nullified all symptoms. Fearful, Ana's heart found its rhythm. It pumped, spiked adrenaline. He took a step to retreat as doubtful thoughts flooded his reason.

She has found me, he repeated subconsciously. *She has seen me. It's all over.* He wheezed, breathlessly.

Everything was red, along with the sirens in his head.

What more must I do? He broke.

Dread permeated his gut. His world was spinning and the walls were closing in. Has he been slacking in this cat-and-mouse game? The queen has not gotten this close since the collapse of Arnireth.

Against his doubts, the queen did not move to claim him. Instead, a wig of faded hue replaced the paleness of his bane. The childish smile that emerged from her face refuted his presumption of evil.

Instantly, the cold weight melted from his chest.

That was not the queen. He breathed, repeating, *that was not her,* accompanied by a joyful giggle. He couldn't have been more pleased, but he was left with uncertainty.

But I do know her, he admitted. Unusually familiar, he watched her rejoin her friends.

A human? How? Why did she have such an effect on me?

Baffled, he had to know more. His nostrils flared, taking in a deep inhale. He had to remember her. As he dug deeper, the lovely aroma of citrus and vanilla was no longer present. Instead, Ana's senses were filled with the scent of wild figs, a signature of the queen.

His heart froze again. *I knew I sensed her.* He put up his defenses, this time controllably as the Nostalgia had already peaked. The smell was growing stronger by the second.

I must leave, he told himself.

He glanced at the crowd for a lasting image of the strange

girl, but she was missing. She had weaved herself among the bodies, no longer noticeable.

Abruptly, Ana's eye witnessed a distress signal among the bouncers. They marched to the rear exit, mentally prepared for a fight, supporting the evidence Ana detected.

It's now or never.

Again, Ana started to leave when something snagged his mind. *Wait! Leo! She would be after him as well.* He couldn't leave without warning him of the queen's arrival. After all, Leo would do the same for him.

He slipped back into the lounge. Unexpectedly, the club owner, Leo, was nowhere to be found. In fact, no one was.

"Where is everybody?" he wondered. Then he got a sinking feeling the commotion earlier with the bouncers was related to Leo's absence.

Staining the classic art deco red as he went, Ana rushed to the back lower levels. Pipes spewed steam and tinged his skin as he ran through the back corridors. Just before the exit, he found the remnants of a commotion. The floor pooled with blood, possibly due to a malfunction of the sprinkler system. Then, beyond the steam, he found unconscious guards surrounding a disarrayed bartender.

An attack! His heart dropped, confirming his suspicions and feared the worse. Ana ran to Mason. "Mason, are you okay?"

The young man didn't reply. Ana quickly found he didn't need an answer. The foul smell of the queen permeated from him. He recoiled. *He has had dealings with the queen.* Ana's sharp eyes narrowed and his anger began to spool. "Where is Leo?" he growled.

Mason finally looked up at him and responded with a dry throat and tears in his eyes. "They took him."

"Who?" Ana demanded to know.

Human, Mason dropped into his hands in defeat. Unlike his lover and the man shaking him, he was weak against the invading force. So much so the bartender would rather not say how he failed. Instead, he handed Ana the business card given to him.

Across its face were the last words a mutant wanted to see: "C.O.V." The Central Organization of Venators.

"Imprisonment?" Ana detested.

"He volunteered in the place of those inside," Mason explained but the reality of those words were unreal to Ana. Leo would never leave his ship voluntarily, especially not for the petty souls inside.

Ana coughed harder, chocking on the increasing scent. The smell was coming from outside, along with multiple voices. Dangerously curious, Ana left Mason to grieve. As Leo's lover, this had to be hard for the young man.

Stepping into the alley, the last remnants of a convoy could be seen leaving the scene. "C.O.V." labeled, the armored trucks matched the card.

Bystanders began their gossip. "Did Leo have chains on?" one asked.

"Who cares? He's gone now," replied another. The selfish were concerned for their own safety.

Meanwhile, a bouncer sadly remarked, "I can't believe he's gone." Yet from the state of their knuckles and face, Ana could tell Leo was taken with little resistance.

Something crunched beneath Ana's foot. *A glass vial?* he guessed. Now in long shards, the object resembled the vials of Nostalgia. He bent down to investigate when an insufferable scent crashed into his nose, nearly knocking him over.

Ugh! They brought with them the scent of the queen. He gagged. *This must be the source of the distraction,* Ana thought. He had been fooled. He honestly thought she was here, that she was back.

Then, he realized the pavement was wet. It had rained, a typically absent phenomenon. To confirm his sanity, he tumbled a pebble over, registering it with his fingertips. Water replaced it. It had rained. Unusual, the last cloud seeding was a couple weeks ago, too late to see the effects now.

And the queen, though within her capabilities, is not known to express her energy in this way. Still, the witch is unpredictable. *It has to be her, he detested.* Ana sighed.

The dreadful evidence was there. He couldn't deny it. She is back and at the worse moment for him. He couldn't clear his head or ease his pain tonight; only more was added. The worst part of it all, Leo had been taken.

The card prodded his side. He pulled it from his pocket. "C.O.V." was embossed on the front. He flipped it over. On the back, he found a personal message. "I will have you, next."

He winced, pressing his palm into his eye. "How do I escape you?" he whispered.

Unexpectedly, Ana was pulled to his feet by the back of his collar and turned to face a beastly man, the front bouncer with thorn tattoos. "Hey! I'm talking to you!" he yelled. His grip made the fabric cry. "You are the reason why Leo was imprisoned," he snarled.

Ana grew concerned when his feet left the ground. He was in no position to fight. "Now, wait one moment," Ana insisted.

"It was you and don't deny it!" a woman screamed at him from the gossip group.

A crowd merged for the show. "You are a disgrace! I don't understand why no one has done anything about you. Tonight that changes!"

"Yeah!" The crowd cheered as the bouncer reared back his elbow. Ana braced as contact was made.

CHAPTER 2

Anthropology 4514: Death & Dying

Dude!" exaggerated a man, elbowing his friend sitting in the chair to his right.

"Hmm?" Recovering from the night before, Ana raised his eyebrows in response, but remained fixated on his paper, vigorously scribbling, determined to finish work left undone.

His friend dropped a heavy bag on the floor, displaying the aggression of a morning class. Others slinked into the auditorium with a similar attitude, regretting signing up for an early college schedule.

Theo continued, "You didn't tell me you were going out last night." He pointed out.

A mistake on Ana's part. He should have said something to his guardian, but the night of celebration was the disguise he desired to get business done, to set things in motion. Regardless, Theo deserved an answer.

Ana stopped and materialized a response. "I do recall you saying if I interrupted your study time, then you would, and I quote, 'defile my water and rebottle it for consumption.' Do you know how expensive this water is? Hmm?" Brows raised, the mutant waited for a comeback.

The young man's mind was processing his thoughts, trying to determine if his response was authentic. He also noticed the subtle movement of the straw and was taken aback by how someone so troubled could still find comfort by just drinking coconut water.

It was amazing to witness, given his mentor's horrendous condition. Yet, at the moment, jealousy barked at Ana's intentional display of momentary recovery, a freedom Theo would not feel for some time. His mind was bent by last night's drink.

"Oh, you're fine," grumbled the young man as he pulled out his books and took his seat. "Besides, I would have gone with you," he pointed at Ana's face, "and we would have avoided getting that pretty shiner." Ana brushed him away. The incident last night left a nasty bruise around his eye.

Flipping through the pages, Theo had clearly adapted Ana's signature practice of replacing every chapter with song titles. "Now, you have two black eyes," he added. "Now, your normal."

Ana smiled. From birth, he was cursed with heterochromia, one blue eye and one dark eye. To Theo's amusement, he was now uniform with the blue eye baring the mark of aggression.

"I heard about what happened last night," continued Theo.

"What do you mean?" Ana returned to work and attempted to avoid the conversation. However, he could sense from Theo's tone that he was about to receive a lecture.

Theo lowered to a whisper, "Leo got captured. You were cutting it a little close there, weren't you?"

He could tell Ana wasn't paying attention. Again, he nudged him with the back of his wrist while gifting him an earbud for musical relaxation. "You have a black eye and there's blood all over the bathroom. I was concerned. I couldn't tell what was yours and what wasn't."

Ana took the earbud. "It was a blood rave."

"And you bathed in it?"

Ana simply nodded.

Theo could tell something was off. There was something he didn't want to speak about. "Did it at least help?" Theo asked.

"Not as much as I hoped," replied Ana. He honestly couldn't differentiate now from the day before.

"Did you speak with Leo?" But, again, Ana understandably ignored the question and Theo left the subject alone. He was just glad Ana was okay.

Theo prepared for the lecture as more people filled the room. Melody chipped away the edges of Ana's stress, but the increasing batches of conversations throughout the room pressurized his ears.

His head began to throb. The pain traveled through his eyes and rooted in the center of his mind. Shortness of breath appeared, then anxiety began to surface. Ana took a deep breath to prevent triggering any further symptoms.

The assignment before him was seemingly endless. He was getting nowhere with it and chose to abandon it. Calming down was more important. He found it soothing to rest against the cold brick wall and, as usual, Theo gave him comfort with a lingering shoulder grip.

As it drew closer to class time, people flooded the room. The aisles were packed with young adults searching for familiar faces. The news broadcaster had detailed a record high was set for Gibbous University, saying, "Statistics report a 15% increase of incoming students from last semester."

They had become part of this demographic. Rooms suffered to meet the demanding capacity. Professors were expected to teach beyond their capabilities, yet another limited resource. Just another day in the Oasis.

"There's certainly more than I expected." Theo's eyes scanned over everyone. From row N of section D, they had a good vantage point of the crowd.

To cope, Ana took another deep breath. A familiar scent touched his nose, a whiff of citrus, vanilla, and — *is that rosemary?*

Recognition bloomed a shard of nostalgia and brittle danger. *Getae*, he reminisced. Memory of yesterday's ghost cut through his frontal lobe but was shortly broken by Theo nudging him out of the collective trance.

"Hey, Ana. Ana. Ana."

"Yeah?" Ana opened his eyes.

Theo pulled him closer, wrapping him with introduction. He pointed. "That," referencing the gentleman walking past their aisle, "is the heir to the Order, Darin Sambuca, Lord Raymond Sambuca's son."

"Is that so?" Ana squinted to see the resemblance. There was none beyond skin tone. Tall, slender, thin hair, and sharp eyes. He had seen the gentleman around Gibbous several times without giving it much thought. Yet, surprisingly, the young man held seniority. Ana could now perceive the commanding stance he possessed. Persecution resided in his shoulders like a toxin, ready to strike at any defiance of his father's policy. Ana kept that in mind.

"I want to get to know him. I have heard rumors about his skills. If what they say is true, he could be useful to the team," said Theo. "Plus, knowing him will give us an advantage over the Order and maybe even the queen. Hey, are you listening?"

He wasn't. Ana's eyes found the group of women following Darin. One, in particular, left him breathless.

"What are you…?" Theo tracked his gaze and found the source of disruption. "Oh."

"It's her." The words spilled from Ana's lips.

Her, the dangerous aroma belonged to her. He was sure of it, but seeing this creature physically beseeched all reality. It amplified doubt of his crazy. Still, seeing this woman was confirmation what he encountered last night was not an illusion or the murderous queen. It must have been this woman. In a way, he felt at ease.

This woman, he savored.

With hair paler than skin, she was the familiar of his bane, the reincarnation of the evil he coronated, yet wrapped in the flesh of an older memory. Though similar, Queen Sarolt was revered for her savage magnificence and serpentine seduction, while this girl was not.

This girl was seasoned with time. Her blood pulsed a hardier genetic. Resilient, she reminded him of a much older, kinder, and primitive soul, someone he once knew.

"It can't be," Ana whispered.

Unlike the angels surrounding her, this girl was beyond ordinary according to modern standards. Pale, fragile, and somewhat unsavory, she was nothing special. Yet, to him, this creature was once everything. Their touch was engulfed by flames during their time together, consuming the beauty that was now before him. He could feel the bygone heat arise in his palms, debating the possibilities of her appearance.

Before, Ana simply convinced himself that the ghost dancing in the flashing lights was just a memory, resurfacing from the mixture of drugs and his chronic condition. But, contrary to belief, this girl was fleshy and whole, a symbol returning to the roots of his mutation.

She is not her, he reminded himself not to fall for the illusion again. *She is not the being that claimed you. Though they share a resemblance, I must not make the same mistake I did with the queen. I must stay away.*

Ana released the breath he held. Sweat began to form on his brow.

"Are you alright?" Theo became thoroughly concerned. He has never seen him like this.

Restraining himself, Ana nodded.

"Is it my idea about Darin?" Theo asked.

Ana cleared his throat enough for a whisper to occur. "No. In fact, I think it's a good idea." Scars of the flames resurfaced on his body, an old memory. He was losing control. He conjured yet another deep breath.

Theo took note of them. "Then, what is it?"

Ana's gaze returned to the subject and Theo followed his sight to a girl taking her seat beside Darin. "Her?"

"What is she doing here?" Ana questioned, sliding down in his chair.

"I assume we have a class with her and her friends." People continued to fill the room uncomfortably beyond available seats. "And four hundred other people," grunted Theo. "Why are you hiding?"

Clearly, Ana was having a crisis. Reincarnated, their paths always crossed for worse, never for better. With the queen determined to gather his head, there could not have been a worse time for the destinies of two familiars to intertwine.

Ana already knew what was going to happen. With this girl, he will be called to fulfill the duty to his master. As much as he objected, refusing his master's commands would lead to a lifetime of suffering far worse than the torments he already faces.

No doubt the queen will exploit this newfound weakness for he is inevitably defenseless in the girl's presence. His teeth clenched, just thinking about it. It was in that moment he vowed to avoid her completely.

"Do you know her?" Theo asked.

Ana could say yes and how, but now was not the time to alert Theo to the familiar. If he did, it would take nothing for him to pull his blade and sacrifice her without alerting his master of her return, all to save Ana heartache. With that said, every being had a purpose, and with the resurgence of her spirit, he wondered what hers was.

"Something like that," Ana replied.

Theo was experienced with this unspecific expression. After all, he was the one who had a way with the ladies. "When was the last time you two spoke?" he asked.

"Years."

"Oh, it's that bad," Theo exacerbated. "Maybe she won't remember anything."

"She won't. It's been so long." Ana was confident about that.

"Then, what do you have to worry about?"

Again, Ana clenched his teeth. If only he knew.

During their discussion, the professor leading the seminar took his place on stage. As usual, he started the semester with an introduction.

"Good morning. Some of you may recognize me from past lectures, and others may not. Either way, introductions are in order. My name is Yaromir Currant. You will address me as Professor Currant and nothing more."

"Yeah? Your sister calls you Yara!" a student foolishly yelled from the crowd.

The professor released an audible sigh. He led a simpler life now than before, but the change was not enough to disassociate him from his old career. Until yesterday, very few people knew about his unfavorable past, but thanks to his sister's increasing popularity, it seemed like everyone was aware.

After his sister's successful capture of Leo, he woke to her devoted fan base ridiculing him for his historical shortcomings.

Nevertheless, he reinforced, "We are not friends. Some of you have clearly forgotten that." He glared in Darin's direction. "Moving forward then, welcome to Anthropology 4514."

"Sir!" an admiring student jumped up. "Is it true that you once worked for Joytech?"

Defeated, Professor Currant lowered his script. *Gah!* he groaned internally. *They usually don't pry this much into my life, but, with the Rose Garden uproar, I guess people have done their research.*

Checking his phone for the time, 8:02 am, the latest news caught his eye: "Rose Garden Bartender Named as Seperatist Leader in light of Leo's capture." However, he lingered, staring at his background image, an old family photo, scanned after years of damage, depicted four smiling faces. His happy family, two adults and two children, a girl and him. The photo was taken before the girl got the scar on her cheek.

"I was hoping I had more time," Ana released. At this point, he was speaking to himself a little too loud. Glances were made to his position.

"You're fine," Theo reassured.

"Anastas!" The professor called his name, silencing him.

Ana froze. Outside of the aggressive warning, the professor's appearance surprised him. It was unusual to find Currant, a priest, in everyday clothing; unholy.

Amused by Ana's expression, Theo lowered his tone to a faint whisper. "I can't believe you are all worked up over a girl." Their shoulders bumped.

"Do not tell Marcy about this," Ana demanded. "I don't want her lecturing me or advocating any potential relationship."

Theo surrendered, remembering the last lecture he received from Marcy. "Okay. I won't," he assured, holding a finger over his mouth.

Professor Currant continued to quiet the room. "Darin!" The rustling settled down from his bolstering voice. After several seconds, he had full control. Recognizing several familiar faces, he smiled and continued, "Welcome to the Anthropology of Death and Dying. Let's begin."

With a remote click, a large white screen was lowered from the ceiling and illuminated for the presentation.

"Death," the professor began, "is an inevitable reality of all beings, even for our immortal-style heroes we call mutants. Death is defined as the cessation of all biological life-sustaining functions of organisms, including, but not specific to, the brain and brainstem function. Spiritual ramification after death is highly debated among cultures. Certain rituals have been catered for the transition to ensure the spirit gets the most out of the afterlife, rituals like inhumation, entombment, cremation, or excarnation.

"Not only will we dive deep into the practices of death in this class, but also the cultural significance surrounding the occasion. We will analyze documented cases, the physiology of dying, and the psychological impact of death. In short, death is more than just dying. But, before I dive too deep into the subject, I must warn you," a crooked smile crossed Professor Currant's face.

"If you are squeamish or intolerable to gore in any way, which if you are, then how do you even live in the Oasis," he joked and quickly reverted to his original seriousness, "I am going to ask you to leave. Go on. There's the door."

No one moved. Most likely because no one thought he was serious. "Just be aware, you have been warned."

Upon clicking a button, a disturbing image of a burned human appeared on the screen. Blistered, fresh, and black.

Gasps sprinkled the audience.

Professor Currant out spoke them, "My presentations include forensic evidence. This is a very tame example of what I will be showing. If you can't handle this introduction, please leave."

Again, Currant scanned each face, reading their sensitivity. "I will not have anyone throwing up in here," he threatened, but instead spotted determined faces and curious spirits accustomed to the carnage and ready to understand the topic.

Good, praised Currant. *At this rate, the next generation may be strong enough to handle what is to come.*

He continued, "Can anyone tell me how this person died?" It took a minute for students to come forward but finally one student did.

A hand raise in section B.

"Yes, you."

"Is it human or mutant?" one asked.

"Does it matter?" he rebutted. The student was dumbfounded. He explained, "Although mutants possess incredible abilities, they are still susceptible to the same causes of mortality as us fragile humans. Next, you." He pointed to the hand in section C, row K.

"They were burned," Darin called out.

Currant nodded, "You could say that given the body's appearance. The poor soul could have died from another cause, such as a disease that required a mass burning or a heart attack that initiated a house fire when they fell. But I don't teach forensics here, so for now, let's all agree this person died by fire. Why? What significance does this have with the corpse? You don't just die by fire. We don't combust."

"Sacrifice," blurted a female voice.

"Who said it?" He scanned the crowd. Next to Darin, a hand raise slightly. Currant snapped, "You are correct. Sacrifice!"

Then he realized who the woman was.

Pale complexion, albino and rigid. She resembled a textbook deity. As her identity registered in his brain, his speech slowed, contemplating the connection. "Some cultures believe that the soul had to perish for good to exist."

The sudden change got Ana's attention. Evidently, Currant comprehended what the innocent surrounding the pale lady did not. *What do you see, priest?* Ana speculated.

Then Currant's eyes met his. Within his gaze, a sense of familiarity was present. *Tell me*, Ana begged silently but Currant went on a tangent instead.

"Alternatively, to some cultures, sacrificing one's life for prosperity is seen as a worthwhile pursuit. This idea is called martyrdom."

"Martyrdom?" Ana was hoping to get something good out of him but his answer left him deflated.

Scribbling in his notes, an important reminder spontaneously crossed Theo's mind. "Oh! By the way, your fridge broke."

"What!" Ana expelled, already agitated.

Theo nodded at the absurdity. "I did my best but didn't have time to fix it this morning. I was almost late."

"Ha!" Ana shot up from his seat, cursing a little too loud.

Rags separated from the roll into sheets, cleaning the murder scene their apartment had become. With his messy tux on the bathroom floor and the blood dripping from the fridge, Ana was beyond frazzled.

He stood on the precipice of change, unsteady by the winds he felt at the cliff's edge, and molecularly untethered by internal turmoil. He released a crying sigh. What followed was a flow of air that realigned his mind.

Martyrdom, he considered. *Currant mentioned it specifically for me.*

Years ago, strategies on how to undermine the queen's support were proposed, and one suggestion involved Ana making the ultimate sacrifice. But the question remains of the familiar albino lady and what part she will play in his demise. Only time would tell.

Ana stood, disposed of the nasty rags, and placed the thawed meat packets in the sink. It would be a few days before a new freezer could be delivered. His gut twisted, looking at all the food he would have to consume. He was already planning the most efficient feeding schedule based on the meat's longevity and his symptomatic patterns when the door opened.

Theo entered and immediately noticed his emotional state. "Are you okay?" Ana silently nodded. "Class ended early. I don't know how they expect Currant to teach like this," he said, dropping his bag on his bed. He motioned to the mess. "I thought what I did this morning would stop the spread," referring to the paper towel dam he constructed before nearly missing class, but the fortifications had oversaturated while they were away.

"It helped," said Ana, appreciative of the effort.

"So, what's wrong?"

"I have a feeling Bog will request a meeting with us soon. Do you want a steak?" he offered, taking the rawness from the packages.

But Theo was already switching his books out for gear. "No. I have to get to the field. The Decider is tonight. Coach is really hammering us this month. He's tired of losing."

Ana stopped the preparation, looked down at the red meat, and took a bite. But before he could swallow, Theo stopped and spilled, "I'm missing something. Before the lecture, I thought your reaction was very uncharacteristic especially regarding a lady you have never mentioned before. But for Currant to stumble? Nah, his soul nearly left his body after learning her name. Who is this chick? What power does she have over the two of you?"

"What is the girl's name?"

"Geda."

Ana nearly choked. "Well," he cleared his throat, "that's why." His paleness amplified. *It is her. Death certainly has appeared before me.* Blood settled to his feet and he fell on the bed next to Theo. "Do you remember the lesson of familiars?"

"Yeah?" Ana gave him a look and waited for the information to sink in. Abruptly, Theo's mind exploded. "Oh! No!" He jumped to his feet. "No, no. Is she one of them?" he asked.

"Relax," Ana tried to calm him down. "We don't know that yet, but it is undeniable. They have the same name, same face."

Theo grabbed Ana's shoulders with all seriousness. "Do you have any idea what this means?"

"Ah, do you?" Ana challenged. "I will be asked to do the unthinkable."

"I know you won't do it. After what happened to Queen Sarolt, you took a vow, and master has honored your decision."

"You need to be ready for when he does not honor my choice. My refusal may very well cost us our lives." The seriousness settled between them.

"A familiar. Does this mean the Order will get involved?" asked Theo.

"It is a huge possibility. Nothing is confirmed yet. It's just..." Ana's thoughts were lost at the possibility of her existing. "It's too soon for another one to be born."

But why her? He desperately wanted to know.

Theo's excitement died when he tasted Ana's despondent aura. "How do you know?" he wondered.

"When you fall deeply in love with someone, lose them, and find them again later in life, you keep track of the intervals." Ana's cheek lifted, admitting such a thing.

Theo raised his brow. "Wait. If it's too soon for a reincarnation, is the current Geda and the previous Geda the same person?"

This stunned Ana. He hadn't consider that. "Are you implying they are the same creature? That's impossible."

"Unless she is a mutant like you?"

Ana shifted uncomfortably. Defiant, it made sense.

Theo persisted, "Who is Geda, anyway? She clearly meant something to you, yet this is the first I am hearing of her."

Ana was totally lost for words. "I never told you?" How has he not brought up the creature who won his devotion solely through determination? How has he not hinted at the being who possesses his endless thoughts? How? Perhaps the reason resides in their sudden disconnection. Expressing her would liberate what little he had left to cling onto.

"No," Theo whispered, "yet it all revolves around her."

Ana took a fearful breath. "Geda was mutant. She was the first of many to reject the church. A martyr of her beliefs, she intertwined me in her poisons, and they made a spectacle of her execution. There is no way she survived."

Or is there? announced an intrusive thought.

Shaking his head, Ana rejected the idea. "No. No. I don't want to accept that she survived after all this time." His voice lowered to a whisper, clearly talking to himself. "Besides, she didn't recognize me."

Or did she? his intuition spoke again.

Ana recalled the moment their eyes met. *Those eldritch eyes,* he recognized. There was intent behind them.

Theo witnessed his mental tumble and offered more support.

"Do vampires lose their memory?"

"Yeah, but I don't know." Ana had no answer. He was plagued by doubt.

Sympathetic to his denial, Theo couldn't help but smile. "I've never seen you like this before." Ana had a reputation for being intelligent, so to see him stumble was unfortunately remarkable.

Abruptly, Ana stood and grabbed his keys.

"Wait, where are you going?" Theo did not feel the conversation was finished.

"Work, but this cannot wait. I need to speak to Bog about this. He will know what to do."

"And when he asks you to do the unspeakable?"

"We will cross that bridge when it arrives," said Ana. As he went out the door, he noticed Theo wasn't moving. He peered back in and beckoned, "Don't you have a game?"

"Ah! Crap!" Theo jumped up and hurried, knowing he would likely be late again for another program.

CHAPTER 3

Imprisonment of the Separatist Leader

With hair iridescent of a silkworm, Queen Sarolt strode with haste. Visibly angry with her fists clenched and jaw tightened, everyone steered clear of her march. She had a reason to be irate. Just moments before, she intercepted hushed rumors in the passageway.

"Did you hear? Lord Raymond holds the Separatist leader in contempt for his actions against the Order. What was his name again?"

"Ah, Leo," replied the other man.

"What did he do?"

"He disrupted shipments coming from Joytech, particularly the Nostalgia crates."

"Huh, that's unusual. I thought Leo was an avid supporter of the drugs."

"You would think, but Raymond considered it as 'disturbing the system' and had him arrested."

"Wait. How were the Venators able to capture him? The queen has been trying for years. He was notorious for being inexpugnable."

"Apparently, someone he trusted turned him in."

"Unbelievable."

True or not, Sarolt had to see for herself.

The next door opened, and her senses were greeted by Leo's screams. As the electrically charged water sloshed from his container, pleasure formed upon her face. However, the cause of her elevation was indistinguishable between witnessing his unfortunate circumstance or his inability to escape. Either way, she was delighted.

"So then, it is true." Sarolt chuckled.

Surprised, the executioner ceased his torture. "My queen! I did not see you there."

The prisoner had a moment to breathe, though realistically he drowned. Submerged in a tank full of green acid, Leo was forced to inhale it. The liquid ate away at his flesh and singed the deepest regions of his lungs. There was no sanctuary from the dissolving feeling, an Order standard.

"I only just entered," she assured and admired the new specimen. The wicked royal came into Leo's view as the executioner stepped away from the tank. Dread suffocated him more than the acid he breathed in. "I heard an unbelievably good tale about how the great Lord Raymond arrested a garden snake under the disguise of the queen. How rude," she teased.

"Actually, the great Lord Raymond, as you put it, was under the disguise of an invited guest," Sasha bravely corrected. Sarolt's attention deviated to the other side of the room. There, Lord Raymond sat behind a tiny desk with Sasha by his side.

"I see," she said, admiring the setup. *This is the notorious chapel, the chandelier's base. Here, mutants receive corporal punishment and pray for death. I wonder if Leo will pray,* she wondered. *If I don't approach this carefully, it will be me that descends.*

"Continue," ordered Raymond. "Don't stop until I say so." The executioner did as he was told.

"Since when have the Lions done such prosaic tasks?" commented Sarolt.

Raymond looked over his glasses. "I was wondering when you would arrive. You have been gone for a while. I have fulfilled my end of the bargain, and still, you arrive without your army."

"Yes, the bargain," she remembered, peering back at Leo.

They had a deal. Raymond would give her Leo in exchange for her dark army. Of course, returning with her army was a much greater task, but worth it for the club owner. Leo has been evading her fangs for centuries, even more so in the last two decades. Ultimately, he was the gateway to finding her betrayer. Finding Leo meant finding Ana.

At one time, Ana and Leo were inseparable brethren. Records exist describing two men being in love. Passages embellished their commitment but many were just speculation. After all, words can get twisted.

Over time, Leo chose his path and strayed from God.

Lingering on balance between the Order's control and the church's protection, he thrived in a neutral environment as a Separatist. And on that fateful afternoon, on the 28th of April, it was Leo that pulled Ana from the bloody queen and hid him in the crevasses of what became Gibbous.

According to Sasha's uninjured state, it wasn't a challenge for them to retrieve Leo, which infuriated Sarolt. She has tried and failed numerous times to conquer the club owner, and Raymond accomplished it so effortlessly.

I wonder what else he is hiding, she considered.

Sarolt finally spoke up, "It is shameful of me to come crawling back with nothing accomplished, but I admit, I need your help."

"Just say the words," offered Raymond as he flipped through contract agreements.

As Sarolt revolved around Leo, her words were meant for Raymond. "It has been a little over ten years since his holy monarch stole the power of the cursed army and infected my commanding king with his impurities. The army that expands every year —"

Raymond interrupted, "I am aware that the dead fuel its numbers."

"And mutant kind," she reminded him, "are connected to the shadows below. If one is consumed by darkness and becomes an aggressor, the mutant will beacon for the army to follow."

Raymond nodded his head. "Which is why we do what we do. Over forty percent of the population is mutant, and increasing. Given the resources it takes to sustain humanity, life is easier once synthesized."

"Do your homemade vampires feel the heat?" The darkness.

"Unfortunately," Raymond admitted.

Sarolt found that amusing. "They are without the power of proper mutation yet suffer the same consequences. You will do anything to keep them alive."

Raymond hesitated. To "keep them alive" was the duty bestowed upon him by the True Queen in the final moments she was last seen alive, and he refuses to let that promise tarnish, even at the cost of royal teases.

"The holy monarch needs a king to possess the full power of my army, and I need a king to take that power back."

"A king?" Raymond speculated. "What about the one you created?"

Sarolt's face soured at the thought. "Casimir is barely flesh; even if he was whole, his blood is filthy, contaminated by the monarch. He has become a rabid dog, uncontrollable to his new master and incurable to his previous."

Raymond smiled. "You're admitting incompetence."

Sarolt made eye contact with Leo. His rage had calmed; the edges of his defenses soothed. She was amazed. In the acid, Leo was still beautiful to her. "I must know. How did you manage to capture him? Was it as they say, through betrayal?"

"Not on my behalf," Raymond reassured.

"I would hope not. Betrayal seems to be the easiest emotion expressed in this family. It has been ongoing since the Mother supposedly betrayed the True King, years ago. Unfortunately, the trend has continued with the children, especially those who remain close to the Father." The queen's hand brushed the glass prison, making Leo's skin crawl.

"You can thank 'Kasey' for coordinating it."

"Kasey, huh?" Sarolt glanced down at her name tag that clearly read 'Sasha.' "You used that name? Tsk." She judged the woman.

"No one would suspect it," defended Sasha.

"Indeed, and the scent of the queen? Where did you get that from?"

"Oh." Sasha reached into her pocket and handed the queen a tiny vial of red liquid. "The Royal Aroma, synthesized from your serum." Sarolt gave her a questionable look. The woman explained, "Dr. Jakobi requested that I test its weapons capabilities."

"And?"

"It is effective in large groups but unpredictable," Sasha informed. "I am not comfortable using this in public at such an early stage in development."

The vial juggled in Sarolt's hand. Its contents boiled from her glare. *That scoundrel! How dare he violate my property for his personal experiments!* She growled, "I will inform Jakobi of the results myself."

Sasha bowed as the queen stepped away.

"I am, however, glad you captured him." Sarolt's attention returned to the prisoner. "Now that we are finally face to face, he can lead me to the king I need, Ana." Leo recoiled. "I've always wanted this," the queen sneered at him.

"You mean, 'you've always wanted to be me'," Leo spat back.

Her brow raised with curiosity. "Oh?"

"You wanted to be special in Ana's eyes like I once was, but you never were. Now, you think you deserve revenge," Leo scoffed bravely. "You are not the first he betrayed for the Monarch."

"That's right!" she fired back. "He abandoned you to pursue me."

Even in the face of danger, Leo defended Ana. "Because he was ordered to! His selfishness in service kept him alive, and you must realize that. You must learn forgiveness like all the rest of us. It is the only way you can move on. It is the only way we can survive."

A part of him was correct. This endless war causes so much suffering, but sacrifice is inevitable. Eventually, there will be nothing left. Sarolt's fight was not exclusive to Ana but also with the True King, the ruler of this kingdom and the last holy monarch. To slice his throat, some will have to die for her to reach the heavens of his throne.

Regardless, Leo's attempt at sympathy made her feel attacked. Sarolt's cold eyes sharpened. "He did not claim you," she replied cold-heartedly. "You are a fool to believe my fight with the hierarchy is singularly for vengeance. Although we do have different approaches, Raymond and I share an overarching goal. Yes, my anger will be satisfied, but I do this for a higher purpose," she admitted.

"And what purpose is that?" Leo demanded to know.

The queen paused. Was Leo prepared to learn the truth of this war? She looked at Raymond for confirmation. The Lord shook his head slowly. He believed Leo was not prepared.

"You will learn the full story when you are wiser," Raymond replied.

The queen's pace was stopped by the executioner who readied the button. Leo's interrogation has just begun. Fear shot through his spine. He knew what was coming. "I am not a pawn!" Leo cried.

"You are now," she replied.

Leo fought his restraints. To have a conference with the queen meant death was guaranteed.

Sarolt started, "Tell me where to find Ana?"

He felt her voice in his brain. Leo understood what would happen if he refused. The tall man was ready to hit the button at the slightest hint of resistance. Yet, Leo couldn't sell out his friend. Tears formed in his eyes. "I will not tell you!" He braced.

The button was pressed.

A wave of electricity flowed through the green liquid, hitting Leo's brain. His body tensed and squirmed. His veins surfaced along with the stripes he kept hidden.

"Stop," Raymond ordered, and the torture was short.

Sarolt's nails rapped the glass tank, focusing his attention. The club owner returned the gesture with a spiteful glare.

"You will speak," she demanded.

"I would rather eat my tongue," Leo growled.

She laughed. "I can make that happen."

The button pressed again, and this time Leo couldn't keep the screams behind his teeth. He cried out at the top of his lungs, but the voltage kept coming. It lasted minutes.

Sasha waited anxiously for the sign to stop, but it did not come. Concerned glances met their superior, who was intently observing. Raymond waited until Leo couldn't scream anymore before giving the signal.

Finally, it went quiet.

"Stop," Raymond calmly called. The Lion immediately released the button, and Leo fell to the bottom of his bowl.

Sarolt kneeled to him. "You're not dead, are you? Your death will gain me no reward."

Leo looked up at her and cursed, "May your blood spill at the feet of the True King!"

Offended, Sarolt snapped. "Our 'master' seeks my bleed. He knows where to find me! Drop this fool into the spiral! Put him where he belongs before I end up killing him!"

The Lion executioner slapped a tag onto the tank.

Sasha touched the controls at the desk, and the floor opened. Six tanks displayed freshly caught mutants. Hydraulics tucked them out of the way for Leo to descend. In seconds, he was pulled into the chandelier prison and placed in a designated spot. There, in the spiraling core of Joytech, he will be displayed for all to behold.

Approaching shadows grabbed her attention. Unwanted company was headed their way.

"Where are you going?" Raymond asked the retreating royal.

"To take my anger elsewhere," replied Sarolt, leaving.

Not long after, the doors opened again and entered Darin Sambuca, Raymond's son. Without hesitation, he went to the Lion locking the seal on the floor.

"You there," he ordered. "I need an escort to Crescent. For some reason, you are the only official I can find in this mess. I don't know what Father does with his weapons, but they are never where I need them."

"That is because they are not yours to command," Raymond spoke up, previously unnoticed by his son.

The Lion got off the ground and waited for his Lord's orders, disregarding the one just thrown at him. The slender man was several inches taller than Darin. Had the boy not known a man more prominent, the stature of the Lion would intimidate him.

"Why do you need an escort to Crescent?" asked Raymond.

"We have a game at the arena," answered Darin. "It is the monthly Decider. So it's bound to get wild."

Raymond's brow narrowed. "You've not requested an escort before, nor have you ever participated in such sport. Why now?"

"I've made some friends. Unfortunately, they do not have the name Sambuca like I do. I would like them to be protected as well."

"Hmm." Raymond was surprised. *Perhaps he has changed,* he thought. He nodded. "Very well. You may have Lion Sabre escort your team, and if you so desire, even participate in the match." But as soon as he gave his consent, the Lord caught the mischievous smile Darin hid while eyeing the Lion beside him.

Disappointed, Raymond frowned. *That was his intention all along, to bolster the team's offense.* "Now leave this chapel," he ordered.

Sabre bowed, and the two departed.

Raymond closed the files on his desk when Sasha's hand fell onto his shoulder. "Sir, there is something else."

"Show me." She did. A touch on the device displayed footage from the raid, particularly Geda. "Oh, are those her informants?" He noted the women next to her.

"Yes, but more importantly," she slid her finger across the device, following Geda's gaze to a man on a higher balcony. "It would seem she has found a king."

A knot formed in his chest, recognizing the man in the picture. Black twisted hair, opaque stripes with a dual colored gaze. It was undeniable. "Anastas. What are the odds?" he expressed. "I was beginning to regret my promise to her, but as you can see, Darin has not changed. He doesn't care about his team. He is doing this to demonstrate his power."

Sasha disagreed. "Are you sure, sir? The boy is right. He has the name Sambuca. He does not suffer when Gibbous loses the monthly Decider like everyone else. So is it wrong of him to secure the win using his power and resources?"

Raymond was hesitant. "That is how it was perceived, but it will not end there, Sasha. What will he do with his share of the winnings? I know my son. Every action has a purpose. Eventually, he will do something he won't be able to come back from. It is an inevitable outcome of power. I'm just worried; how many people will he kill before that happens?"

"How many people did you kill before your crown first shattered?" she challenged.

Raymond laughed. "Many."

"And if he never falters?" A daring question to inquire the Lord's perspective.

"He will. She has found a king."

She could see his scheming. "What is your plan?"

"Do not interfere. Let nature take its course."

"I'm not sure I follow, sir," Sasha admitted, taking the device Raymond handed back.

"Geda believes our promise will grant her wish, and it will," he assured, "in a different way."

Mystic as always, Sasha bowed. "Then, I will take my leave, sir." There was something in the way Raymond said, "in a different way," that did not sit well with her. Though she may have orchestrated the heist, she had no intention of entangling her dear friend in Raymond's web, no less the interlude of the Royal War. It was coincidental how Geda chose him of all people, not knowing the dangerous position it put her in.

Sasha sighed. "Attachment continues to be my downfall."

Her steps tapped and her words echoed throughout the descending spiral to the only conscious prisoner of Joytech, Leo.

"Sasha? Sasha!" Leo called, squishing his face against the glass to see around the corner. Then, finally, the woman came into view. "Sasha, please," Leo begged. "You have to get me out of here."

Sasha continued walking. "I will not."

"Please. Someone has to protect Ana," he persisted.

She stopped. "Why should I?"

"We serve to save humanity. Ana is the only king left. If he is captured, Armageddon will ensue, and this world will be lost," he persisted.

"What would you have me do?" she asked, helplessly.

"Imprison him. Hide him here where the royals will least expect it," suggested Leo.

"We have tried that before, and the Order was nearly destroyed. Remember?"

"Ah, the Peacekeeper," Leo recalled.

Her chest squeezed. "Peacekeeper," she lingered and her shoulders relaxed. Her mind went back to the time of her awakening, back to when the beast danced to her anger and betrayed every surface of training branded into her bones.

Realizing her hunger for his assertiveness, she snuffed all absurd recollections of him from her mind.

She shook them loose, aware of the intentional implant to influence her. *Nice try, Leo. The Peacekeeper was a failed mission, no longer relevant,* she reminded herself.

"You don't need to worry about Ana." Returning to status quo, her tone was unappreciative. "If the queen hasn't found him yet, he still has a chance." She turned away. After such a cheap trick, she didn't give him the time of day.

"It is not her I'm worried about. It's the True King," Leo called out.

The Lioness didn't respond.

His yells echoed throughout the chamber down to the exit making his final remarks inescapable. "The two of them have reunited. Ana and the Father; the clever and the cunning; the Devil and the God."

Even afterward, it trembled her conscience.

CHAPTER 4

The Child King of Mutanity

To the east, in the heart of Gibbous City, rests a dainty restaurant called Marcy Joan's, famous for curries and gumbo. Owned and operated by an uninhibited Creole woman by the same name, people gathered around her tables for every occasion. However, Marcy's hospitality extended beyond the service of food. She was known for her kindness to strays.

Unwanted orphans or starving mutants, it did not matter. Her property was home to everyone, including Ana. Because of this, she has made it her duty to enforce a neutral territory. All allegiances were welcomed, and no one possessed power over the other. Even the queen had no control over Marcy's property.

Demand crowded the restaurant as the monthly deciding match kicked off between the dividing regions of the Oasis. Unfortunately for Ana, he was stuck serving the winning side.

"I am sorry for working you so hard, but the occasion calls for it," apologized the owner, chasing after him.

Ana sat plates down at a table. "Well, the team did win their first game against the Wildcats. So naturally, everyone wants to celebrate." He completely understood society's reaction.

"That isn't exactly what I mean," Marcy said, trying to keep up with him. "How are you moving so fast?" She could hardly maintain his pace.

Every month, a game is held at the Arena field in Crescent City. The Decider determines which half of the Oasis receives extra supplies. The sport was fair until you realized the Crescent City Wildcats were all mutants. The Gibbous City Falcons barely stood a chance. It was a wonder how they won this time.

That matter had clouded Ana's mind all night. After all, Theo participated in the games to hone his abilities as a guardian. Yet, he was still human, and every month he was subjected to the cruelty of entitlement. Theo would return beaten and broken but fulfilled regardless of victory. Ana wondered how damaged little Theo would be on a victorious night.

As the evening progressed, the victorious Falcons eventually made their grand entrance, prompting a community roar. True to form, the team members were visibly battered with bruises, scrapes, and cuts. One man had his arm wrapped in a cast. Another put his nose back in place, but they all smiled. As did everyone else. To his surprise, Theo was intact, skin flayed, but bones strong, and veins remained in their place. Ana was relieved.

More people entered, following and cheering for the team. To his dismay, Ana looked around the room. Unoccupied space was nonexistent. Elbows did more than rubbing.

Upon collision, people rejoiced, throwing their hands up, and spilling liquids without the concern of a mess.

As customers bumped into him, inconsiderate of his serving, Ana couldn't help but feel the nostalgia of the old taverns he visited during his crusades. It was heartwarming, yet his mind pondered on the pristine condition of the team. Although thankful, he grew curious and suspicious.

"We will be eating good tonight!" one man barked.

"I'm surprised your shins didn't snap in half," another man

slapped Theo on his back.

"Ha ha! Yeah. They nearly did," he replied. From the many cuts on his face, his body certainly took a beating. The young man's sight soon found Ana's. His dual gaze recognized his fight, a proud response the student always sought from his mentor, making Theo's smile even more brighter.

In celebration, Marcy found the team a table kindly offered up by local support. In passing, Ana caught the side eye of one of Theo's teammates, Darin. Clearly, Theo had been successful in recruiting him. Then he noticed the Lion among them. The team had Order support. Lions, the Order's most elite force trained to subdue mutants, ultimately attributed to their victory.

Upon seeing Ana, Darin wrinkled his nose. The boy carried tension against mutants. However, it was a look Ana was accustomed to.

I hope Theo understands what he is getting into, pondered Ana.

Smug, Darin slid into the booth without a mark on his body. His subtle clinging to Theo told Ana of his possessive characteristic, a sight he did not appreciate. The thought of someone taking his Theo from him made him audibly agitated.

"As if," he scoffed.

"What are you growling for, son? Disturbed by the loss of your kind?" a nearby gentleman asked.

"Just the attention, sir," Ana replied. In all fairness, Ana didn't understand the need for such violence when the situation could have been dictated differently. But if his companion found pride and honor using his abilities to help others, Ana was glad to assist.

"Order out!"

The evening rush eventually became a snail's pace. With bellies full, satisfied customers were sluggish to leave, just as Marcy intended.

"Won't you stay for dessert?" she jested, but the belching men had to refuse. Though they desired to savor the spices forever, their stomachs simply could not handle the load. When the time came, Theo said goodbye to his friends, picked up a towel, and got to work.

The moon soon rose over the metropolis skyline and brought forth the creatures of the night. With the night came an unexpected guest. The doorbell chimed. As the hostess, Marcy peaked at the entrance, but no one was there.

She peered over the front counter and found a lonely child about three feet tall waiting to be seated.

"Good evening, Marcy," greeted the small child.

Her heart lifted, as well as her voice. "Oh, my God! Bog! What are you doing here?" She trotted around the counter to welcome him with a hug. "I haven't seen you in so long."

"Yes," Bog grunted. Crushed, he struggled for an escape. "I've missed you too."

Thankfully, Theo saved him. "It has been a while, sir." He bowed. The towel in his hands was discolored from cleaning all the tables.

"Yes. Look at you!" Bog devoured him up and down. "You certainly have grown, little Theo." Of course, little Theo wasn't so little anymore. He was a grown man and swollen from the fight. Bog was pleased to see his training being put to good use. "Congratulations on your victory."

Theo bowed again in appreciation. "Thank you but you are here for Ana," he reminded.

Marcy paused, aware of Bog's connection to Anastas.

Theo was correct, but the boy couldn't admit he arrived only for his subordinate, especially not in front of Marcy. "And the food, of course," ushered Bog.

That was enough to please her.

Marcy motioned to the booths. "Find a seat, and I'll let him know you are here. I'm sure he will be pleased to see you. Theo, will you help me with something?"

"Of course," Theo agreed.

While Marcy and Theo disappeared into the kitchen, Bog crawled into a booth. Patiently waiting, he swung his legs, happy that this place hadn't changed since it opened ten years ago.

"Bog," greeted Ana, joining him in the booth. "Thank you for coming."

As usual, Marcy served the young child. A menu met the table, and she left them to their private conversation, giving the child time to order.

"I'm surprised," admitted Ana. "You have a lot to handle but arrived sooner than expected."

Bog picked up a menu. "The urgency in your voice was enough to summon me. Plus, you hardly call your father anymore. I get worried, you know."

However, Ana did not feel comfortable calling this small child "father" despite their relationship. Thinking, the paper of his straw rolled in his fingertips, analyzing how this conversation was going to go.

"Something must have happened. Is the organization bothering you again?" Bog asked, flipping to the next page.

"No," answered Ana. "Thankfully, the Order has kept their distance since the last incident."

Bog wasn't so thankful. "Yes. Your brother certainly made a mess."

"How long did it take you to recognize Theo?" Ana redirected.

"Hmm! Too long," he admitted. "I was thrown off guard by Marcy's strength." Ana's head instinctively tilted. It was unlike his master to forget a detail about his most cherished human.

Bog continued as if he had discovered it recently, "The amount of inhuman strength that woman possesses bewilders me." He laughed.

"Well, it has been a while since you joined us for dinner." Ana produced an excuse for his master's absence of an authoritarian personality.

"How long has it been since I last saw Theo?" asked Bog. "He has developed immensely."

Ana almost blushed. It was charming to think how much the boy had changed. "It's been eight years since he graduated from Guardian Hall. You congratulated him then, too."

"He was nine when he fell into your arms," Bog calculated.

Once again, an inaccurate statement unsettled Ana. "More like submitted as prey," he reassured. After all, their initial meeting was not as graceful as Bog described, considering it was he who ordered Ana to murder little Theo back in the day. His lack of detail piqued Ana's curiosity, unless of course, the child was fainting ignorance to be intentionally harmful. Ana would not put it past him.

Bog continued, "Nine plus two years in the Guardian Hall — which was surprisingly quick!"

Ana nodded. "Most spend their whole lives there. So, you understand why I didn't want to kill him," he added, knowing his superior wasn't listening.

"That makes him the same age as Geda."

Ana choked on his tea. "Agh! How do you know about her?"

"How do I not?" Bog smiled maliciously. "With a powerful name like that, a soul could reincarnate. I was looking for a reemergence, and I heard her name."

A chill touched Ana's skin. "I'm afraid a soul may have," he admitted.

"What do you mean?"

Ana was hesitant to tell. "Geda, she is completely identical, almost an exact copy to the last. Theo brought up a good point after I told him about … her. Is it possible for the original to be alive, hidden all this time?" Ana looked for validation that he wasn't completely crazy.

"No." The child shook his head. "She burned. No mutant can survive the severity of punishment I bestowed upon them. When I kill someone, they're not coming back."

Right. Ana could do without the reminder of his master's judgment or that he was proud of it. Unconvinced, Ana embellished the being for clarity. "I don't think you understand. She is Geda. Name, face, albinism. They are the same."

Bog's eyes narrowed. "How can you say that? You knew the original for three hours."

"Sometimes that's all it takes," Ana defended, unable to meet Bog's judgmental gaze. He sighed. "Perhaps I'm just seeing ghosts in faces I don't actually know."

"Perhaps." Bog discerned the longing in Ana's dual eye and sympathized with his pain. "I'll admit Geda's passing was a missed opportunity. I could have utilized her abilities, but it wouldn't have led me to claim you."

"In that aspect, Sarolt would have remained human and wouldn't be hunting me now," Ana interjected.

"No. You would already be dead, being born in the 5th century and Sarolt in the 11th." Sarcastically, Bog was right.

If Ana had not discovered the warrior goddess, Geda, he would have died long ago. Instead, he became captivated by the mystery he uncovered and quickly fell in love with a cursed being who had selfishly captured his eternal salvation.

In all honesty, Ana couldn't agree with his master. His eternal suffering was worth a few moments with the primitive warrior. Now, she has returned with new skin.

"Unless someone found a way to clone your 'beloved,' the woman who stumps you so is nothing more than a human with a resemblance to the past," Bog said.

"So, she is —"

"Normal," Bog made it clear. "She looks like Geda and nothing more."

Relief and disappointment painted Ana's face. *She is not her.* Yet within the following silence, Ana could not shake the defensive note he sensed in Bog's words, like he wanted her all to himself. "So, you were looking out for her. Why? It's too early for her rebirth. Besides, you promised me no more queens."

"I did, but I am concerned about her allegiance to the Order. They have not made the same promise. With their research, they may try."

"A synthetic queen?" Ana could not distinguish what offended him more, the harmful insinuations of their scientific possibilities (founded by specimen 1141, himself) or Bog's excitement to the challenge. It would be convenient for the royal if the Order produced queens to harvest rather than request his rebellious child to follow an order.

"Bring me beings potential of the queen's crown so that I may bleed them of their power," Bog demanded long ago. Ana's purpose remained fresh on his mind. Yet, unlike that blood-filled night, Bog's spirit no longer reflected the same tenacity Ana was forged to.

Inclusions were evident in his master's metal. *There.* Ana saw them clear as day. And it was all due to this human girl. Regardless of what his master would like to admit, Bog was planning around the girl. Suddenly, applying pressure became irresistible.

"Get to know this new Geda," encouraged Bog. "You will find that they are not the same. Trust me."

With that said, something he said stuck with Ana. *Cloned?* He recalled the circumstances surrounding Geda's death, her deface of a precious tablet, engraving her name in blood and whispering beautiful pagan words.

"Where is the Gammal tablet?" Ana asked.

Bog flipped the menu over, almost hiding behind it. "In Raymond's vaults," he answered, justifying his concerns.

The Order had two objectives. The first was to imitate the process of crowning a royal, wherein a king can turn a queen with his venom, and use this method to gain control over a queen. The second objective was to recreate the rejuvenating properties of queen's blood.

As usual, Ana's mind spun theories. *If, somehow, they were successful at their second goal, could they regenerate the blood-stained remains of a forgotten warrior?*

"No." Ana shook away his intrinsic thoughts. "She is not Geda. She's not her, and I cannot act like this is my second chance at happiness," he reminded himself.

The boy's puny eyes glared over the menu. "Are you sure?" he asked.

Ana squinted. "I won't repeat the same mistake I made before. I may see her face, but I'd rather maintain my distance," he reassured and intentionally threatened.

Bog smiled at his son's development. "I am confident in you, but Ana, eventually, we must face our past."

Ana didn't know what cryptic message his father was trying to convey. But, before he could ask, Marcy approached them with Bog's meal to go.

"Ah, Marcy!" cried the boy. "I didn't get to order."

She smiled. "My dear, you order the same thing every time."

The child blushed. "That may be, but it doesn't hurt to look."

Marcy chuckled. "You just come in, and I'll take good care of you."

"You are too kind, Marcy."

The hostess's heart melted, and Bog inched his way out of the booth.

"You know that comes out of my pay, right?" Ana pointed out.

The child turned. "Shall I give you a kiss?"

Ana scoffed. "How embarrassing?" The dining room attendants chuckled at the thought. However, Ana's soft laugh melted into a speculating glare.

Bog certainly has changed over the years. Ages ago, he became progressively ruthless while his stature shrank. The monarch took a more diminutive form to conserve his energy. What he lacked in manliness, he made up for in constructive deception. The almighty overlord of mutation in the form of a child, yet Ana still saw the ravaged man Bog once was.

Bog's small hands lifted his lunch from the table and reassured his friend, "Don't worry Ana. Your fate is not bound to repeat. So long as Sarolt stays at bay, you will survive another day."

Ana bowed. "Good evening, my Lord."

"Stay alive, Ana." The child spun on his heels, disappearing as fast as he arrived.

Alone, Ana processed what he learned. His consciousness shifted like waves in the ocean, swirling with anxiety and elation of discovery. It was calmly nauseating. An unusual facial cue lifted his ears as his mind twisted with strategic fantasies.

"What is this expression?" Theo asked. "I don't believe I know it from you."

"Hmm?" Called out, the emotion was instantly replaced with shame. "It is betrayal," Ana paraphrased.

Then it hit Theo. He had seen the same in other mutants, a wild stretch and wicked smile. Thankfully, Ana did not share the horrendous extremes in his subtlety. He did, however, share the persistent desire to act on it. He could fathomed his mentor's thoughts; for too long has he secretly conspired to dethrone his master. To openly act on it, would guarantee Ana a swift death. "Are you sure you want to go through with this? I know it's been a long-awaited decision. But —"

"Patterns have aligned for repetition, including notable absences while dangers persist. Meeting with him today only strengthened my interpretation. My suspicions are correct. Bog is relaxed for a terrible reason. We must know why. Though it may already be too late, I am curious if she is involved in any way." Geda.

Theo knew what Ana was afraid of. The fear of not being able to protect his loved ones from destruction or damnation was something they shared. And to think Ana withstood centuries of Bog's exploitation was stifling.

"We will need an Oasis worth of support. What do you suggest?" he asked.

Ana sat up straight. "We must bolster all security measures to ensure proper discipline and self-restraint. Bog's nature is passive and uses indirect but effective attacks."

"Should I abandon my chase on Darin?"

"Amplify it," ushered Ana. "We need a direct line to Raymond should anything sour."

This surprised Theo. "You want to use them?"

Ana sighed and rubbed his blue eye. "At the risk of my own safety? It is worth it. I need you to understand that what I'm asking will take everything, wring every morsel of morality, and potentially conscript you to an eternity of pathetic existence like myself."

"I knew what I was getting myself into when I met you."

"Does that scare you?"

"No," Theo replied.

"Let me know when it does. You are most vulnerable when you are afraid. It's only human, but Bog will use that to his advantage. In this endeavor, you will encounter many new things from me, good and evil. It will test your devotion but know this is our only chance at freedom," said Ana. As he stood from the booth, he stumbled at the flare-up of his mental condition.

"I've got you," Theo supported. The action jogged Ana's memory, amplifying his lacking confession. He had contacted his master to confide his troubles but still his condition remained undisclosed.

"I just remembered why I called him." Ana had been distracted by a fragment of opportunity and dismantled by his master's unusual behavior to tell of his poor health. Something within him halted expression, cowering in anticipation for what might come if he was honest, displaying his weakness, especially now that he was plotting.

Onerous, it couldn't be helped. Things were about to change regardless of his readiness. Despite the consequences, if he were to survive the chaos he weaved, Ana desperately needed help. If anyone had a plan, it would be Bog.

"I must be honest!" Ana chased after Bog. The child waited for him to catch up, to which he said, "I'm suffering with time convergence."

It suddenly became clear as Bog looked into his eyes. His welcoming smile faded with despair. "Unfortunately so, and during such a pivotal time."

Time convergence, a debilitating schizophrenia reaction, is a common symptom among mutants, occurring as their lives progress beyond usual standards. As they develop and age, mutated kind cannot feel time's current brisking by them. Through derealization, temporal experiences are left boundless and free-flowing.

As a result, psychological time can become undefined and erratic to the point the sufferer loses the ability to separate memory from reality. It becomes particularly challenging when occurrences start to recur, such as Geda's striking similarity to the individual formerly recognized by that name.

Whether it's a joyous occasion brought on by nostalgia or chaos induced turmoil, prolonged exposure to time convergence can alter the being's self-restraint and eventually become an aggressor and a beacon of darkness, a summoner of Malum. The illness caused by neglect (now unavoidable in the Oasis) is the unspoken consequence of their unbelievable power.

"Our hell in our paradise," Bog recited the common saying. On the contrary, there was nothing ordinary about Ana's condition. "How long has it been since you slept?"

"There was a short moment of forced slumber from my capture 10 years ago. Before that, I can't remember the last time I slept," Ana realized.

"That long, huh?" Bog fully understood Ana's hardship. Lifetimes overlapped as one reality. Bog, too, would often slip and see enemies among the gentle population. He considered the outcomes.

Typically, Ana did not seek help from others. If his genius intellect couldn't fix an issue, there wasn't a person who could. However, Ana's mind was slipping, and his survival technique left him far worse than intended. Initially, his neglect was controlled but the sleepless nights compounded his symptoms to the point that no remedy could stave away the damage. It was only a matter of time before the sickness ate away his brain, before he was powerless, for his wits were his power as a mutant.

"It's beyond time for your slumber. That much is clear." Bog's breath clouded in the pale streetlight.

"But if I do it now, she will find me and kill me in my sleep," Ana added, considering especially since his slumber could last centuries, there wasn't a place on this planet that could keep him safe from Sarolt. Confronting Bog with this was an even greater risk, but Ana needed something to conceal behind while Theo reinforced their reserves.

"Yes." The boy rubbed his chin. He, too, had a dangerous thought. "Before you die, I will prepare a chamber in the great capital of your lord. The church will accommodate you, and your body will be safe from that demon and those Order scientists."

Ana sighed with relief. "Thank you."

Bog, however, was not relieved. The primogenitor walked away, clearly ruffled by Ana's secret. "I wish I had known. I wish I had seen. I wish I had noticed," he grumbled. If only Ana hid his issue well. "My plans will need altering." Mumbling, Bog quickly faded from sight.

Ana remained on the cold street, wondering where this could go. There was a possibility he just signed his death certificate with his confession. He once agreed if he experienced extreme symptoms, they would utilize his slumber to bait Sarolt into a trap. If that remained his master's plan, he sought to use this to his advantage.

Ana smiled until a different suggestion left him with intrigue and duplicity. The path ahead was unpredictable but there was something he needed to verify regardless of his vow to stay away.

Geda.

CHAPTER 5

Albino Maiden

The crunching ground beneath my feet did not reflect my decision on this cold night, nor did the piercingly empty sky or thick clouds of sighs. Instead, these elements only echoed my selfish approach. I told myself to not go, to stay at a distance, but how could I hold myself from her? I had to know.

Geda. I understand they are not the same being, but I cannot deny that her existence may play a part in my demise. The sinful realization tantalizes my skin and pulls at the hair strands of my neck. It's something my standing collar cannot protect me from. I have to know. I have to see the catalyst that will become my death.

"Don't get too close."

As my distance shortened, I reminded myself not to fall into her magnetism. It would be tragic if things between us were allowed to repeat, if my ignorance led to her defeat. Perhaps the opposite will occur. Maybe her ignorance will tie me to the burning stake instead. All the more reason to stay away.

How can I? Even during the age before my claim, this girl was an enigma, not meant to exist, especially her physical properties. For the region, her hair was like dried wheat in the sun and flour in the moon. Her light skin redefined the complexion of her breed, and her eyes were drained of vibrancy. Paled grey with undertones of flushed pink resulted in lilac albinism; bunny eyes. Among the fibers of her irises were chips of reflection that, at the time, I did not recognize the mutation's sign, mesmerized and culled the nurturing.

When I was a youngling, she granted me the gentlest consideration while engraving her spirit into stone. Had I known my lady's intention, I would have assisted in her plot of destruction, bowed before the evil master, and given her everything my earthly body had to offer.

Geda, our inseparable tension formulated whispers among the shadows, shifted pelt into a hunter, and kissed the ear of the only man listening, the man who would become my holy Father and the man who would spread your ashes.

Do you remember?

No. This Geda means nothing to me. Though she shares your identity, the one living serves our enemy, the Order, now disguised as Joytech, a telecommunications company. Whatever her connection, I try to convince myself she is just a diluted existence, much like the synthetic mutants around me.

Many decide to mutate synthetically, infatuated by false power, only raising the expectation of standards. Our kind has become diluted like domestic animals. Very few vampires are big cats in this jungle, tigers in an Oasis. I may hunt my lesser in this forest, but she is the watering hole I cautiously approach as prey.

A part of me prays that she is a fake. But, Geda, I cannot bear to believe she could be you, the same being from so long ago; alive, in hiding, and dead to me. If so, would you have finished our deadly kiss if you had survived?

Shortly, I found her.

A dead sorority house sits on an empty street, unreasonably far from the college. Segregated from the Decider celebrations, the old building was nestled perfectly in a natural shawl. Inside rested the most intelligent of the campus, for they did not partake in the festivities. Instead, its occupants were buried in books or blankets.

Lace fluttered a window trim, indicating an unspoken invitation I took unwaveringly. With a leap, I met its aroma, bitter vanilla and geraniums. It was her. I'm effortlessly drawn to her. To remain undiscovered, I edged myself along the trim and peeked into the room.

Her bed, horizontal to my stalking, was closer than I anticipated, and, on its surface, she shivered, testing her retention of subject, a mutilation that chiseled the brain with discipline. Her murmurs spiked with the wind and became audible recollections of history notes. Jerks of religious conflicts struck a chord within me, just where I left her.

Behind her staggering sighs, items in the room quivered with the invasive breeze. Chimes clinked. Posters lifted. Paper bags full of geraniums hung dormant for the winter. She was acclimated to the cold, only quivering when her hair, beautifully leeched of color, tickled her skin. Cracking to be released, she squealed and I found myself crossing the threshold of her domain, following the harsh wind. She was inches away.

What am I doing?

My brain screamed but my heart was ashamed to speak.

I quickly retracted.

I was right. She is dangerous.

Her allure. Oh! How she seduced my senses, blinded my mind, and compelled me to fulfill my cacoethes. Siren.

I shouldn't be here.

Did she notice me? Swallowing my fear, I looked back inside.

She was no longer there. Instead, she resided comfortably in the warmth of her sheets. Her abuse got the best of her and luckily I remained anonymous. That was close. I got what I came for. I had a scope of her possessiveness. And her location.

Her, Geda, I must leave her be.

I must.

CHAPTER 6

Close Encounters with Her Kind

Weeks have passed since Ana's curiosity nearly bested him. The crisp air concentrated into snowfall, and nights grew longer than the day. With the cold comes the end of the semester.

Since then, Ana has maintained his persistence, enforcing distance from Geda. If she was around the corner, he took the opposite route. Each time she met his gaze, he looked elsewhere.

Soon, he will no longer be exposed to her danger, nor will he have to deliberately avoid her. Relieved, the settling awareness became slightly disheartening. A part of him enjoyed their game of touchless tag. As he studied for the final exam, the impression refused to leave him.

Among the crowded tables in the university library, Ana submerged himself in research, jumping back and forth between mummification practices of the Inca and acolyte scriptures of ancient guardians, recollections Theo took from Guardian Hall.

It was barely noon, and a pile of books separated him from the commoners giggling at the other end of the table. Laughter born from a budding romance or tormenting jokesters, he ignored them.

With both headphones bumping in his ears, Ana was in his element. The table was covered with pages filled with tiny text, arranged like an apotropaic ritual. Sips of coconut water exfoliated his mind to new ideas, and extensive readings grounded old heresies from his existence, especially those dating back to his mutation.

The antique texts unearthed languages not spoken in ages. He squinted at the spotty Latin, reading eroded text, "Pugnant sicut daemones. Daemones sumus. Mundus esse desinet." Translating, "They fight like demons... We are demons... The world will cease to exist," he whispered, "signed Zalmos, Gardian al Reginei Zarin?" The True Queen? It was rare to find a fragment of the missing deity.

Secluded from the masses, Ana was free to explore whatever he liked. That is until someone invaded his vibe. In front of him, books slammed on the table, causing him to jump. Aggravated, he looked up from the pages to see her, Geda of all people, interrupting the distance he struggled to keep.

It was always her pulling him closer. Disturbed, a growl was nearly audible with his sigh.

"Sorry," Geda mouthed.

Of all places she had to sit, he exclaimed internally while consolidating his study.

As she settled, Ana removed a headphone to evaluate his environment. Come to find out, the seat across from him was the only available spot in the library. The place was filled to the brim, but nobody was brave enough to sit across a mutant, especially not him. She was.

People started to speak. "Did you see who that was?"

"Her, of all people?"

"I would never."

The few beings that glanced at them with whispers and rumors on their lips received his full glare. Aware of their stares, Geda opened her notebook with a stressful sigh. She wouldn't have to sit here if she had arrived on time.

Damn Darin and his constant need for attention, she blamed. Of course, he had insisted on seeing her during practice. Now, there was little time to study for her exams.

When Ana's attention returned to their end of the table, he detected a few irregularities about her. There was a slight shake in her wrist as she wrote. The swish of her pen was no longer graceful but jagged and tense. Raw red cuticle edges signified her frantic well-being; she continued to pick at them. Including the perplexed tightness of her brow, the signs triggered Ana to dig deeper.

What bothered her so? he wondered.

Ana rested on his hand. Disguising his concern with a book, his focus combed her structure. She furiously took notes, a fitting approach to the history she studied. Even Ana curled his nose scanning her page, but other reasons were the cause of her frustrations. Geda was almost in tears when she arrived. Then, he saw it.

As she brushed her hair behind her ear, he noticed a spot of darkness, smeared along the baby hairs before the ear, a close consistency to the paint Theo would wear on game day.

Did a ball player cause you to cry? Did Theo hurt you? he wanted to ask but doing so would violate his chastity. Yet, seeing her like this made him defensive.

Abruptly, Geda jolted, checking her phone. "Oh, my gosh!" she expressed. Realizing the time, she scooped her books off the table and ran out.

Baffled, Ana's eyes followed her to the door. Just like that, she was gone.

What just happened? he asked, dumbfounded. *What did I do?*

He wanted answers but what remained was a quiet, cold space and an empty seat. Again, Ana was reminded of what it was like for her to vanish. Disappointment settled in. His eyes returned to the windows, hoping she had forgotten something. She didn't.

Outside, the sun had already fallen.

Wait! What time is it? he checked.

The time on Theo's music player read 5:03 pm. He had been here nearly six hours, and did not feel any second of it, even with the music. These are the dangers of being with her, enjoying her. She is the quintessence of his destruction.

He was deeply immersed in her company. Now, he, too, was late.

Halted by disbelief, he lingered. "It's getting worse," he admitted. He reached for his boxed water, but it, too, was missing, gone like the girl who took it.

CHAPTER 7

Serving Demise

Thirty minutes later, the rear exit to Marcy Joan's opened, and Ana's shift began. The heavy door slammed behind him, bumping him with encouragement. His mind said other-wise.

Clouded from the day, Ana shuffled to the coat rack and tied an apron around his waist. From the sounds dancing with his senses, the afternoon rush was over. Plates clanked as they were thrown in the sink, and Marcy had grown hoarse from calling out orders. Hopefully, no one noticed his late arrival.

Ana stepped through the kitchen carefully, mindful of the wet subway tiles. *The floors are already mopped,* he noted. *Marcy must have been on a rampage.* He recalled her insane multitasking tendency and felt guilty for being absent. However, it wouldn't have mattered.

In his current condition, he wasn't much help. His symptoms nullified any sense of comfort. He could barely focus, no less function. At this point, he expected his skin to sizzle, and his hands to constantly quiver. However, today was far worse.

It was as if he was going through withdrawal. From Geda? The heat of the burners damped his brow. Or was it from needing her? The simmering aroma of jambalaya and seafood salivated his pallet. Or was it from craving her?

Ana paused at the server rack plagued with thought. He could not get the girl off his mind, and the fight amplified his symptoms. He was exposed to her for hours, soaking in her rays and overindulging her existence.

Ana sucked in a breath. *In her company, I was unconscious of the demands of life and lost sense of everything.*

Their brisk time together had more of an impact on him than he anticipated. Recognizing this was groundbreaking.

Being with her was … liberating. Shame flushed his face, maniacally savoring the release. His body senselessly matched her wavelength and breath. Continuously diving back into his malnourishment, his body consumed all nutrients gathered from her proximity and desired more. He ached for her even though being with her meant decapitation.

For a second, he contemplated it. *It's almost worth it. Either way, I will be free from this pain,* he agreed but the intellectual within him refused.

No. He shook his head, gathered what was left of him, and focused. It was unlike him to do something so thoughtless. *I'm being reckless. I shouldn't get caught in lust,* Ana reminded himself. *It's time to get to work.*

Theo caught someone sneaking past him. "You're late," he said, recognizing the shadow.

Like a child bound to be disciplined, Ana sighed and sauntered into the kitchen to confront him. He could not hide anything from Theo. Immediately, he witnessed Ana's state: jittery composition, beading sweat, pale lips, a scratch on his forehead, not to mention the darkness that plagued his face.

"Is everything okay?" Theo calmly asked.

Ana was hesitant to respond. "I —"

Suddenly, the server door swung open with Marcy chatting on the phone. Her intent was directed to the chef, ignoring the poor soul as she passed.

Surprised, Ana quickly held his breath, concealing any feeble indications beneath the skin. Melanation vanished. Knowledge-able, it still boggled Theo to witness how someone can go from impoverished to invigorating in milliseconds. If only the cloak had the same effect on the mind.

He recalled his guardian teachings of how mutants show their mental state through the pores in their skin similar to chameleons. If it is bright, bold, or fulfilled, mutants will be very appealing. If it is anything but, it will show. These crea-tures can mask their mind and face by mustering a spark of concentration and controlling their breath.

He could almost hear his teacher say, "With that said, can you maintain a spark within a hurricane? No? It is safe to say a mutant's duration of cloaking abilities is defined by the storm of the mind and breath of one's heart."

Ana found the necessary breath, caught a spark behind his different colored eyes, and melted disorder from his face just as Marcy dropped off two tickets.

"These are to go," she said and turned to find Ana leaning against the table. "You're late."

Ana nodded shamefully. "Yeah."

Marcy didn't care. She was capable of doing everything in the restaurant herself. However, she was more concerned about his well-being. Not once has he been late, and with his trickling condition, she was left to wonder the worst.

Her hand caressed his cheek. "Whatever the reason, I'm glad you are looking better," she smiled.

At that moment, Ana realized what she had done. Marcy refused to recognize the darkness he was becoming. It was a test. Walking past him, she knew her opinion would influence him, forcing internal retention to resurface. After all, she was the closest thing he ever had to a mother; no offense to his actual mother. If his mother had the strength to move during their short time together, he was certain she would have been just as caring.

Ana felt it in his heart the day he was forced to leave his mother behind and again just now as Marcy left the kitchen, realizing his strengths had not yet abandoned him. It was the act of masking the darkness, an everyday thoughtless action. Without it, Ana would be a mindless aggressor.

Unfortunately, the spiraling descent of madness was more profound than the winding core of Joytech, and one day, he would reach the bottom. It's inevitable, but his actions today proved he was further from the bottom than expected, evident by the human face staring back at him in the stainless steel.

Chary of her anger, the energy he mustered to revert darkness into human flesh cleared all doubts. He didn't know he had it in him. Relieved, his mind lifted from the haze. No longer was it clouded with pointless thoughts, specifically of the mystery that was Geda.

"Astonishing!" Theo gasped every time at the false sense of security. *So, this was Ana before he was claimed?* Youthful and handsome, his mutant was most certainly God's favorite.

But peace is often short lived.

Releasing his breath, Ana wilted back into his usual self with unconcealed details. The difference between human flesh and the mutant shell was undeniably noticeable. Typically, for mutants, it wasn't.

A new reality struck Theo. Ana was like a pair of old jeans. Tattered with hardships, worn from a long life, now the threads of his mind were coming undone.

How can the body of a young man be so aged? Theo knew one day he would be without his favorite "worn jeans." The thought sickened him.

"Do that again," begged Theo.

"You'll have to give me a minute. I have to catch my breath."

"Oh." Theo extinguished his excitement. Perhaps he was asking too much of Ana.

"You have seen the ability before. It's nothing special," teased Ana. He was right. Cloak was the most common of all the abilities mutants have. Theo encountered it every day but coming from Ana, it was special.

"Not from you," Theo smiled.

Ana was flattered. "I'm not very good at it. I don't know how to do it right. I often forget I can."

"Should we practice?"

Ana considered his suggestion for a moment. He did enjoy testing his strengths with him. It's been a while since they sparred. Doing so now would be too risky. "No. It's a waste of energy. I need all I can get these days," answered Ana.

Theo dropped his shoulders. "That's true. So, why were you late? Did you have a problem?" he asked.

Ana took a moment to formulate an explanation without worrying his friend. "I was at the library studying for the test tomorrow and —"

"Wait, there's a test tomorrow?"

"Yes. Finals."

"Damn it! I've been so busy with practice I haven't had any time to study."

Ana could tell. Theo was leaner, more defined, and ready for the fight next week. He no longer possessed the soft childish good looks. Instead, he was rigid and manly. There was only a two percent reduction in body fat, but it changed his frame.

"Do you want to go study? My books are in the car. Why don't you take the night off to prepare?" he proposed.

"No. I'll be okay," assured Theo.

"Are you sure? I can handle the shift. Payback for making you cover for me."

"No. It's alright. Besides, I took good notes. I'll just look over them before the test tomorrow. I usually get a better grade doing that anyway."

Ana let the conversation end there and decided not to mention anything about the library incident or bug him for an update on their divergence. Theo had enough to worry about as is.

Finally, beeps went off on the rice cooker and Theo prepared four meals, ladling stew onto a scoop of rice. Chunks of meat and vegetables tumbled onto the grains and washed with the corresponding broth. The aroma was so intoxicating, it could make any satisfied man hungry again.

"There's only one table tonight," informed Theo.

"Regulars?" asked Ana.

Theo shook his head. "I haven't put my eyes on them," he said, sliding the entrées to Ana. The bell rang, completing the order.

Ana grabbed the plates and initiated his regular delivery routine. Stacked, the hot ceramics boiled deeper into his skin with every step. The kitchen door swung open with minimal effort and danced on its axis until he reached the only table with guests.

The place was unusually tranquil, given the hour. Aside from fragments of Marcy's loud voice, probably unbearable for the caller, the music elevated the atmosphere, typically a missed opportunity from how noisy the usually place gets. It was nice to be able to enjoy it for once.

Humming to the melody, Ana made it to the table with

minimal damage, put on a pleasing smile, and recited the usual pattern required for customer satisfaction. "Good evening, guys. My name is Ana, and I will be the server filling in for Marcy tonight." Mindlessly, the plates went to the proper individuals. He distributed napkin-wrapped utensils and took orders for cocktail refills.

"Aren't you the mutant from Currant's class?" a woman at the table interjected, breaking the trance he unknowingly held with an albino lady. Then he recognized her.

"Ah, Geda?" he exasperated in a soft tone. Embarrassment flushed his face realizing the two had been stuck in the silent stare for many seconds, utterly awkward to the many around them. *Where are my manners?* he thought.

Thankfully, even she was overwhelmed by his presence. "Um, hi," Geda replied.

His ear caught the conversation of their audience. "I love that Marcy employs mutants. It is one of my favorite things about this place," Breanna mentioned.

"Yes. It's awesome of her to care for such fragile creatures," Leann added, unenthusiastically.

Ana bit his tongue. He wanted to defend his status but could not deny that the word "fragile" was practically spelled across his forehead.

Geda, however, did not let it slide. "Stop," she requested.

Sloshed, Tiffany smacked the table cheerfully and insisted, "Do the thing!"

Their purpose of coming here resonated with Geda. "Oh! Right."

As she dug through her bag, Ana scanned the group. To his right, Breanna, the weird mutant fan, gave him dreamily, googly eyes that made his skin crawl. Next to her was Leann, an Order sympathizer. Her tension was uncalled for. Across from them and beside Geda was a chaotic drunk, Tiffany. In all, an eclectic pack of sorority girls. He wondered how Geda fit in with them. Truth was, she didn't.

"Here you go." Geda got his attention again, handing him a familiar small blue carton. "This is for you," she said.

Coconut water, he identified. He silently took her offering with a questionable expression.

She explained, "Earlier today, I was in such a hurry at the library. I took your water by mistake. You see, we use the same brand, so it was pretty instinctive. It was only right that I replace it and apologize. I'm sorry for disturbing you and I'm sorry if my inconsiderate action caused you any discomfort."

Ana was speechless. Looking at the box, his mouth fell open to thank her but out came no words. But, while Geda offered sincerity, her friends giggled. His suspicious glare moved from the box to them, and they immediately silenced.

Geda's hand met his wrist in the most gentle way, pulling his attention back to her; the numbers, 7541, prominent on her skin. "Being you are a mutant, please consider this replacement adequate compensation for the trouble I caused." She bowed her head, begging full pardon for her actions.

Ana's heart nearly stopped. *She knows what I am.* He was aware of his noticeable difference, but that fact that she knew made him vulnerable. He stumbled, not sure how to handle this. His mind screamed, *It's a trap,* while his heart was convinced otherwise.

"Ah, um." Again, he looked at her and back to the box. He then made his decision. *Whether this is genuine or a prank, just escape for now and decide later.* Agreeing with himself for now, Ana went along with it.

Slowly backing away, he continued his server routine. "That was very nice. Thank you, and let me know if you guys need anything." With a smile and two thumbs up, he disappeared through the door he previously came.

Ana returned to the kitchen. Prepared to confront a potential trap, he didn't realize he fell for another. As soon as he entered, Marcy exploded with high-pitched squeals and threw herself around his neck.

"Hey! Wait!" expressed Ana.

Catching him off guard, the black woman did a little dance in his arms. "My baby has a little girlfriend!" Her words were drawn out intentionally.

"Wait a minute! Will you chill?" Ana tried pushing her off him but she latched onto his shoulders and shook, disabling him more.

"I'm sorry. I just can't help it!"

Even Theo couldn't contain his emotion. An evil laugh chuckled from his center and echoed in the pot he was cleaning.

"So, you're to blame for this!" Ana pointed.

Theo couldn't deny the obvious. "I couldn't help it. She pulled the information from me. You know how she is, ol' spy's mistress' and all."

"So I paid him to set the whole thing up," added Marcy.

"I told Geda I work at Marcy's. She's never been so I suggested she stop by. You said she wasn't a familiar. Bog even confirmed it." Theo didn't see the harm.

"Still, we can't get close," highlighted Ana.

"When were you going to tell me, huh?" Marcy demanded to know.

"I wasn't," he replied. Unlike Ana, Theo was free to build a relationship with Geda, an unavoidable circumstance given she was always around Darin. "If things had gone my way, we would have never had an introduction," he added.

Marcy advocated for the opposite. "Progress," she whispered.

She stalked the girl from a sliver in the door frame. "There is a reason for everything, Anastas. Until you feel time, do not run from it," she lectured, watching Geda's every movement.

Her eyes combed the fine lines in the young lady's posture, facial cues, and overall behavior; she tripped over the girl's thin pale hair. They were complete opposites, Marcy and Geda. Geda was royal-like and conservative, yet fragments of fearlessness were ingrained in her vanilla veneer.

"She is perfect for my Ana."

"She is," he admitted, fearful Marcy was right. There was a reason for her existence. A dread permeated him, mixing with the beautiful generosity of the woman. He recognized the sensation. This was death, the death he would have to face for things to change. He sighed, remembering the object in his hands.

Suspected of foul play, he inspected his gift. It appeared to be a regular box of coconut milk, with the same blue identifying logo. He flipped it over. The same description, nutrition label, and ingredient list were on the back.

There has to be something. Ana was desperate for a sign he was right.

He twisted the cap, cracking the threaded seal, and the plastic tab remained intake. *The contents are safe.* His shoulders dropped disappointedly until an idea coerced his mind. *Unless* — He pulled the ring tab, completely opening and depressurizing the carton. There were no leaks. It was a standard unmodified box of vitality, after all.

No syringe was used. Ana sighed. He was looking for a reason to not like this girl. *Well, I already opened it. I might as well drink it.* But shaking the carton uncovered a more concerning detail.

An eye, the insignia of the Order, was printed on the bottom of the box. He glared at the mark. *Why is she receiving rations designated for mutant consumption?*

In her own world, Marcy quickly perked up. "I'll go make some tea. We need to celebrate this momentous occasion," leaving Ana to the new found horror.

Finished with the dishes, Theo joined Ana and saw his expression. "What's wrong? Has it been tampered with?" he asked.

Ana shook his head and met Theo's concerned gaze. "She is a mutant," he whimpered.

Stunned, Theo took the water. "What? Why do you say that?"

Ana put his weight against the table. "Geda just handed me this. The eye…."

Theo was dumbfounded. "Humans can't order mutant supplies. How did she get this?"

"Exactly." Ana wanted to throw the water across the room.

"Hmm." Theo thought of the possibilities. "Perhaps, she ordered it specifically for you. I mean, she does work at Joytech. Maybe she has connections."

This was news to Ana. "She does?" he asked, intrigued. "What else do you know?"

"Now you're interested?"

"I need to know."

Theo reluctantly obliged. "She has an internship with the history department."

"In the basement?" Ana highlighted.

"I guess, but…." No matter what he did, Theo couldn't redirect Ana from his determination. "Only she can provide the answer to speculation. Talk to her before you act irrationally."

"I intend to," Ana said without a doubt. "Is she still here?"

Theo cracked the door to get a peek. "No. They're gone." The group of friends had finished their meal, paid, and left during their conversation. Alone in the store, the crew in the back contemplated what to do.

"Theo," Ana called him in for reassurance. He came back like a loyal dog. "Do you see any sign of mutation when you are with her?"

Theo sighed again. He knew his answer wouldn't be good enough. "No. Honestly, the possibility never crossed my mind."

Ana bit at his thumb. "Hmm." His eyes glanced back at Theo.

"What?" The boy asked, wondering what he was brewing. "You should know I do not doubt your abilities as my guardian."

"Yes?"

"We must be direct. I will see her mutation myself."

Theo was surprised. "What? Are you sure? You were confident in your decision to stay away."

Ana spoke calmly. "You made a point earlier. I shouldn't assume anything until I know. I will have my answer tomorrow."

"Tomorrow? At school?"

Ana nodded.

"But we have finals."

Ana placed the carton of milk down and straightened. "Yes, but now I must know."

Grabbing a rag, Ana left to clean the table. Among the plates, flakes of rice, and pools of condensation, he found a folded receipt addressed to him in blue pen, "To the mutant from class 4514," followed by her name, "Geda," and nine digits.

He sighed. No matter how distant he was, she always found a way to interfere with his life. "This can't be avoided. Can it?"

The receipt was the only paper not thrown away.

The next day, the intersection of Haymore and Burley growled the approach of a beast. Heads turned in its direction and the impending arrival shivered many in the vicinity with distaste. The deep rumble of the engine far exceeded legal regulations. Yet, the police did not interfere. Concealed by mutinous creation, Ana was free to sail the Oasis pavements. He did so frequently to clear his mind but this time his mind was bent on getting answers.

Among the sea of adept drivers, his hands gripped the restraints of the beast, taming the machine's desire to fulfill its purpose. It's ferocity fuel by his own. As he arrived, the growl brushed Geda's spine.

She froze. Her eye caught the insignia of a devil upon the streamlined Challenger body as he passed. "He's here." Her lungs deflated.

Soon after leaving the restaurant, she realized the error of her actions. She gave a rebel mutant property of C.O.V. as a gift, a mistake that was bound to be confronted rather aggressively. Needless to say, she did not look forward to finals.

Sasha saw the concerned look on Geda's face and placed her hand on her shoulder, reinforcing her. "Don't worry. He is an old tiger and once sided with the Order, so his fangs have been clipped. If he bites, it will not be deadly." The scars on her face told of her experience with his aggressive kind. Sasha quickly remedied her civil inconsideration but the suggestion that he could strike did not calm Geda's nerves. "Refrain from quick movements," she advised.

Anonymously disguised as Kasey, the C.O.V. agent could visit the college. Though she was here to see her brother, Geda was thankful to have her expertise nearby; expertise that could be noted in her words.

Geda stopped her. "Sasha, have you dealt with him before?" she asked.

The agent was reluctant to answer. "Once. Come on. Don't be afraid to look a tiger in the mouth. The likelihood of him doing anything is slim. He is very much in control of himself." The Lioness led the innocent inside. With their arms intertwined, she added, "If anything happens, call out for me. I won't be far."

Reluctantly, Geda nodded, and the two departed.

Parked, Ana pulled the strap of his bag over his shoulder and juggled the keys into his pocket with a heavy sigh. The finals were today, which meant Geda was here too. He could finally calm the questions burning his mind.

Inside, the halls were crowded. A mix of emotions tangled his senses. Hysterical failures passed him, anxious individuals ticked in their seats, and hunger devoured those unprepared for the early expenditure of energy. He smirked at the ignorance.

Testing schedules were staggered as a result of seating compacity. Students waited for the opportunity to enter designated testing zones. Within them, he searched for her, Geda. Groups laughed in denial, slacking. *She would not be in there*, Ana considered and kept walking. Whispers to his left spread trashy gossip. He didn't even bother to look in that direction.

Then, he squeezed through a tight intersection, and found those studying last minute. *Ah! That's something she would do*, he recognized. He paused and scanned the lifeless faces. Nearly camouflaged, he found her soaking in last-minute details.

A silhouette suddenly shadowed her light and touched her sense of claustrophobia. Yet, when she looked up, Ana displayed nothing but kindness. "We need to speak," he softly remarked.

Nervousness clogged her breath. "Oh, okay," she replied, shoving her book into her bag.

Ana bent to her level and whispered, "Not here. Let's go somewhere else." For her sake, he didn't want anyone to overhear their conversation. He was already intruding on her focus. The last thing he wanted was for her reputation to blemish. If anyone overheard or simply read the question from his lips, she would be disgraced by the mere implication. The slightest incantation or inkling to surmise another of possessing mutation automatically declared the suspect of moral turpitude. Yet being synthetic was romanticized?

Ana looked for an appropriate place. Unfortunately, every corner was occupied, a complete absence of privacy. They could go outside, but they would miss the window to take the test. He even considered addressing the issue after testing but could not shake the possibility of not seeing her again. If he was going to do it, it would have to be now.

Hands grabbed him and pulled him in.

His heart nearly stopped. The divine capture, her audaciousness fueled the fire at his feet. *Our distance must be maintained!* he reminded himself, disappearing through the door behind her. Above was a sign that read "men's restroom."

"This isn't what I meant," he growled.

"It will do for now. What do you want to say?" she asserted, ready for this to be over.

Ana caught his breath. "There is something I must ask," he stated, taking a step closer.

"Is this about the water?" she suspected.

"It is."

She cleared her throat and started to jitter off a reason, "I am ….." but was inferior to the decreasing space between them.

The mutant held no hesitation, only fascination. His mind lingered on her familiar unscripted boldness fading behind her mask. She kept it clouded with uncertainty and professionalism, not realizing it was the source of her beauty, a natural deception. He chased after it.

Geda, however, held her ground. *I have nothing to be afraid of,* she reminded herself and spoke up. "I spend a lot of time at Joytech."

"Why?" Ana responded quickly. In his investigation, he demanded. It herded her.

"My parents manage C.O.V.'s public relations, and I am a part of the research team," she answered.

He recoiled. "Research team?" Was she a subject?

"Yes," said Geda. "I'm a history intern."

That answer wasn't good enough to justify the evidence. While his suspicions increased, she went on about her dreams of becoming a history curator for the Order. "There is so much knowledge we've lost, previously discovered but scattered in the mists of Arnirethic chaos."

Ana desired to care but nagging questions eroded him. He needed an answer. He thirsted for it to the point of survival. Finally, desperation had spoken for him.

"Are you a mutant?" The venom spilled from his tongue.

He had to know. Internally, he prayed, *She is not the same woman. After all this time … she cannot be. Please don't be.* His heart couldn't bear accepting her mutated existence.

"What?" Geda expressed but before she had time to fully grasp his question, she was in his embrace.

Before Geda knew it, the beast had captured her, cradled firmly as a meal to be devoured. His left arm cupped her from escape. His eyes of different hues stunned his witness, yet his exposure was gentle.

Then his touch spidered across her cheek, appraising her soul. The flower of her iris was as volatile as the sun's surface. Vessels stained her baby blue. Rouge, lilac, and periwinkle; colors were indistinguishable. These were not the eyes of a human. They were alien and undeniably lured him in. In their magnificence, he found no sign of crystalline fracture, an imperfection formed from mutation, and a beautiful morphology he lacked due to his heterochromia. With that said, his eyes were full of luster. They were vivid opposites, and she was adrift in their magnetism.

With his thumb, he sundered her lips, revealing average canines like his. Inches from her face, he noted an absence of raw consumption on her breath and the formation of his voracity. A sliver of redness had cracked under his touch.

In the closeness, Ana smelt the sweet sticky wetness upon her lips, the harbinger of temptation; her. Basking in her hydration would complete his newfound urges.

Finally, he surrendered. There was nothing to be found. She was who she was and nothing more. Defeated, he rested his head vulnerably on hers. Eyes shut, she was able to breathe.

The pull he fostered ceased her airflow, and the complexity of the violation bewildered her into comfortable submission. Shocked, she pushed against him until she realized he did not rest on her but against the wall of discipline.

Aware what he had done to prove his theory wrong, Ana draped his insecurities as an apology. "This was never meant to happen," he admitted.

The demeanor beneath him changed. Her resistant hold against him collapsed and instead gripped him with support. In place of the expected rejection, Geda comforted him. "I'm sorry as well. The gift was absent-minded."

His touch moved from her back to her shoulders, enforcing distance he neglected to keep. There, he felt the weight she carried. If she wasn't a mutant, he had to know, "Why do you drink it?" The coconut water.

"Because I like it," she answered simply.

He squinted, dumbfounded. "What? Really?" As she re-turn-ed with a nod, he could help but think, *Her pleasures are satisfied against regulation? She is undoubtedly loved by the Order.*

Inevitably, the door behind them squeaked open, invading their privacy. "Um!" they said, hesitant to enter completely.

Theo, Ana recognized.

"What are you doing?" asked a second unfamiliar voice, pushing Theo out of the way.

Instinctively, Geda grew tense and her eyes widened. *Darin!* He had seen her with another man, a mutant no less.

They turned to the intrusion.

Darin's brow narrowed.

Theo quickly perked up to break the tension. "Oh, good! You are both here. Spots have opened. It's time for us to take the final. Let's go. Let's go now." Theo directed them from secrecy.

In passing, Darin's possessive touch caught Geda's arm, an aggressive territorial display catered for Ana.

Ana noticed.

CHAPTER 9

A Deal with the Devil

For their exam, Professor Currant presented an argumentative statement and students were required to counter it with personal research. As usual, the amphitheater was filled to the brim. Suspiciously, a couple of seats were unoccupied, still writing utensils moved wickedly across pages on the table accompanying the empty chairs.

The poltergeist writing was only a tiny fraction of the room's focus and added to the hum of scribbles percussed by mostly right hands. Yet, one left-handed man, Ana, did not play a note. Instead, he lingered, clouded by thoughts. The pencil eraser tapped the edge of his lips. The wooden surface was beveled by deep gnaws.

After the intense confrontation, Ana's mind danced on the edge of mistake, and not far from him was the subject of his fascination, Geda. This time he did not keep his eyes from drifting in her direction. Often, she would meet his gaze, including the man at her side, Darin.

Theo growled as he wrote, frustrated by embarrassment. After all, an explanation was left for him to handle. Ana could see Theo was taking it hard. He felt bad for putting him in the situation. "Try not to think about it," he whispered or else Professor Currant would hear them and disqualify them.

"How can you say that?" Theo shot back. He took a deep breath and continued, "To find signs of mutation, you have to look deep into the suspect's eyes. I get that but the two of you were practically intertwined. It was like walking in on your parents."

Ana smirked. "It wasn't that bad."

"Tell Darin that. If I had known she was in there with you, I wouldn't have gone in. How do you think he feels seeing a mutant on his girl?"

Ana recalled the boy's public aggressiveness, how it was far more than she deserved. Then he considered how he could express himself in private. Theo watched a stripe melanize across his brow. *His girl? Geda?* Ana was thrown back, and a disgusting look morphed his face. "They are dating," he ruminated, looking at them.

Theo shook his head. "You really have been out of the loop."

"That was my intention."

"But now you want back in?" Theo challenged as a reminder of his promise to stay away

Ana didn't have a response. Instead, the two shared a stare before he finally spoke, "Don't worry. I'll be back in the shadows in no time."

"That isn't my concern," explained Theo. "What if Darin says something to his father, and Raymond gets involved? The last thing we need is the Order's interference."

Ana sighed. Theo was right. "Do not hate me, Theo. I had to know."

How could I? Theo answered internally as Ana apologetically picked lint from his overwashed sweatshirt. "Did you see anything?" he asked, curious if the trouble was worth it.

"There was —"

Abruptly, a strange man joined Ana's side, sliding into the empty seat on his right. His suave slipperiness was a little too friendly for Theo's liking, causing him to tense for a fight. His mutant, however, was desensitized. He clearly knew the man.

"Basiliscus," greeted Ana coldly.

"How rude! Anastas, you know to call me Leo in this day and age."

Theo recognized the name. It's the club owner, the Separatist representative. Remembering he had been imprisoned, Theo's hand wrapped around the blade on his belt. Ana caught his wrist, stopping him. "Ana!" he revolted quietly.

"Then show me you are free before speaking to me," Ana ordered Leo. "Last I heard you became Raymond's prisoner. I doubt you're free."

Leo's nail scraped the metal necklace hidden by his high collar. "It's a shame to have this barrier between us."

Ana's suspicions were correct. He placed an arm around Theo, preventing the guardian from jumping out of his chair and protecting him from Leo's intention. "What are you doing here?" he questioned.

Recognizing the game, Leo returned the bitterness. "I could ask you the same. Why is a vampire hiding among the innocence of society when only logic calls for rest?"

"I am here to learn," glared Ana, but Leo was more robust in this fight.

"About what? Anthropology? Archaeology? Really, has the hunt for Father's relics gone to your head? Oh, how is your head? Are you still a ticking time bomb? Haven't you had enough, being unstable and tip-toeing the line of death? Why is it that you have not rested where it is safest?"

It's code, Theo caught on.

The Seperatist eluded to how the church's actions were harmful, coming forth as a supporter of their scheme. *Do others see our motives?*

Leo held his arms open. His heart exposed, accepting it was tempting but the collar reminded Ana they were enemies. Yet, within Leo's harsh perception of reality, Anastas detected concern. "You've become sentimental without your drugs."

The sleazy man wound up a witty return but was interrupted by the ironic resemblance he shared with the boy at Ana's side. *Funny how things repeat.*

Impatient, Theo leaned past Ana. "What do you want?" he barked. The commotion went on long enough and continued to interrupt his focus.

Leo smirked, brushed the thoughts aside, and spilled valuable information. After all, his whole reason for coming here was to warn Ana, not to fight with him. "The organization is aware of your contact with Geda. They sent me to deliver a message."

Ana's eyes shot to her. Their gazes collided. From her expression, she recognized the man beside him. Then she read the words that fell from his lips.

"To make a deal with the Devil," Ana corrected.

"Yes."

Geda wasn't the only being aware of the intruder. Darin squeezed her hand, pulling her attention away from the mutants. "Father's work is in progress. You should focus on the lecture," he ushered.

Reluctantly, she complied, slowly shifting her body back to the proper position. The presentation continued on to the next example of precursor burial styles and sacrificial offerings, items that normally fueled her passion, but at the moment, her focus concentrated on the commotion swelling behind her.

"Did you call him?" she confronted Darin.

"No," he said. "They were already here when we arrived."

With each passing second, her anxiety grew along with the hankering need for an explanation. *Why was the prisoner here? And what did it have to do with Ana? And that look in his eyes,* she recognized. She had received it many times from her colleagues and heard the gossip behind it. *What did it have to do with me?*

Her pencil tapped faster. She had to know but the feeling of Darin's rough touch lingered on her skin, reminding her to behave. Geda nibbled on her cheek, strategizing. From here, there was nothing she could do. Then, she remembered she didn't arrive alone but with a highly qualified agent. If anyone knew what was going on, it would be Sasha. One quick message to her would satisfy her worries. However, when she reached for her phone, she found it missing.

Oh, no! Her phone wasn't on her but in the pocket of the man beside her. Getting it back would be easier said than done. If she was caught... *It's worth it.* Secretively, her hand slithered in that direction.

Thankfully, she wasn't the only creature in attendance bothered by Leo's presence. A poltergeist chair in section A materialized a vampiric being, bald with a septum piercing. Upon seeing the prisoner, his jaw fell open. His concealing breath was interrupted by fear. Without hesitation, the young man threw his hand up in a wave, getting the professor's attention.

"No time for questions," said Currant, brushing off the student until he heeded the unusually visible form of the typically invisible mutant. Currant met him with a questioning expression. The mutant answered, forming an eye symbol with his fingers and motioning to Ana.

There is a C.O.V. intruder, he understood and scanned the crowd as he lectured, searching for an agent crafting a silent situation. Instead, he found the missing club owner whispering in Ana's ear. *Raymond captured Leo and now claws at Ana even more.* Currant sighed. C.O.V. was bound to come for Ana eventually, to put him to sleep. He didn't expect them to attempt it so openly.

The priest had to be vigilant. As a member of the royal church, he swore to guard mutants against the unlawful misconduct of the corporation and to ensure a haven for mutant coexistence. This act of sending Leo in for negotiations was a breach of security. Should things escalate, he was prepared to interfere.

"I don't make deals with Raymond," insisted Ana.

"You will have to," Leo promised, pulling Ana closer. As breath rested on Ana's ear, whispers conveyed the desideratum spilling from the man's chest. "I wish you happiness and salvation, friend. Believe me. I can see by your eyes that she will grant you freedom."

Suddenly, the light turned red on Leo's collar, and his hair rose. Wariness glossed over his eyes as the static wave surged up Ana's arm. The collar's fatal punishment was charged and ready to be used should Leo not return to the desired communication path.

Immediately, Leo released Ana and changed to a serious tone. "Geda, she has been tagged," he said.

"Tagged?" Theo questioned under his breath.

"Of course she is." Ana's voice grew deep, along with his sizzling pit of resentment. This is not the first time the organization has culled individuals for "survival" or "research," tagging them for synthesization.

The reminder of the Order branding sparked Ana's dormant fury. Hellfire flared his cold eyes. The faint flickers of his old ways resonated in Leo's chest, hope followed by nostalgia.

Ana wasn't the same as he used to be, and what flame burned uncontrollable was quickly tamed, extinguished by inductive reasoning. He was still capable of wielding the ancient and fearsome determination he was once known for. At least it still existed. Leo was pleased.

"We can change that." Leo spun his web.

"At what cost?" snarled Ana.

"A life for hers."

Naturally, dubiety narrowed Ana's brow. "Whose life? Mine?" he asked.

Theo clung to his seat for it was not Leo that answered.

A faint voice became audible from Leo's earpiece, a graveled dialect Ana wished never to hear again, Raymond. Recognition of the sound opened old wounds.

Scars emerged from beneath. He recalled the pain like yesterday.

Red light activated, the messenger repeated verbatim.

"Geda's family manages the front operation of Joytech, a foundational business that funds the organization."

"You are smarter than that. I have my own informant. Get on with it." Ana did not need the pointless review.

"Her boyfriend," Raymond said in a particular way to get underneath Ana's skin, "is the heir to the Order and enforces all mutant life in this Oasis. When my son was called to fulfill his responsibilities, his arrogance made him unfit for the task. Needless to say, he is a burden that infects this company with depravity."

Ana scoffed. "Depravity? In comparison to your own sins? He must be demonic," he said sarcastically.

"We want him gone."

"You would have your own son killed?"

"Is your father any different?" highlighted Raymond. "I would do it myself if not for the legal repercussions. By acting in this favor, Geda's tag will be removed. She will be safe. And if she chooses, she may continue her career at Joytech without any disturbance. You have my word." It wasn't worth much.

Ana paused. "Does she know about the tag?"

"Yes," Raymond replied through Leo.

That explains why she drinks the water, realized Ana. *She is prepared for the transition when her tag is activated.* He questioned her psychology. *She serves with pride? Or is that how they educate them, to find honor in self-sacrifice?*

No. Ana recalled the desperation in Raymond's voice. *Raymond is concerned, almost fearful. He wants her freedom so much that he is willing to offer his son to death, all for her safety. Unbelievable. Who is this girl?*

Raymond broke his trance, adding, "Her tag is not mine."

"Why are you telling me this?" asked Ana. The Lord of the Order, enemy to his religion, openly admitted to a weakness. There must be a reason.

"You're right. I am smart. I know what you are doing, Anastas. I see your movements. And if I do, so does the True King. Consider my honesty compensation for our past grievances. I just want her safe. Do this and you will have my support when it is time."

Ana was silent for a noticeable time. This truth was a dangerous thing. He had presented a weakness that could topple the Order's culture but also fortify an allegiance strong enough to dismantle the mutant monarchy. Ana could finally be free. He simmered resentfully with Raymond's offer.

Ana deeply considered the opportunity. The Order was ready for the insurrection and fought for it daily. Support from the Devil would strengthen the Order more. If he failed against the True King, there would be a place for Theo to survive. If only he could forgive the abuser. An expression settled into Ana's facial muscles, reflecting the decision in his mind.

Theo couldn't believe it. *Is he actually considering it?* Understandably, the decision was a tough one to make. But, his position as guardian forced his bias.

Theo repeated a moral scripture. "The fate of life is not to be decided by the hands of man." Often learned young, this vow once invoked guardianship and bound them together as sword and sheath. Theo hoped the reminder would help Ana to stray from sin.

The Devil had two angels on his shoulders. Both warned of righteousness. Ana didn't have an answer. Killing the boy meant saving Geda from mutation but also return Raymond to full power. Letting the boy live keeps Raymond weak at the cost of Geda's humanity. Both options kept her susceptible to Bog's schemes. Which was the lesser evil?

The Separatist spoke for him. "Of course, you would like to consort with your officials." Leo shot a glance at Theo. "I will be in touch." He hesitated his departure to whisper one final thing in the Devil's ear. "By the way, the slice in her lip was not the product of her self-mutilation." In captivity, Leo had seen the couple's behavior. "But the creation of Darin's gentle touch." With that, Leo disappeared as fast as he came. And almost instantaneously, Ana had his answer.

Shocked, Theo searched for answers in his dual eyes. "Ana?"

Ana didn't answer. His mind twisted, clinging to the words Leo had implanted. The fate of his rivals was in his hands; it disgusted him. What would come of the man far more evil than the Devil if he did not intervene?

Upon being overthrown by his successor, Raymond, the cruel Grand Torturer and Emperor would vanish into obscurity as many savored his downfall. People would drool over his carcass and smash his bones to pieces until less than dust remained. Even his soul would not be free from the pain he inflicted.

However, the boy, Darin, would inevitably become his father and the Oasis would suffer a new type of reign as he learned how to be surviving monarch. Raymond's commitment to his word attributed to his long success. How long would it take for the Raven boy to learn that?. If he did not die today, he would cause his death tomorrow.

Then, what would come of the girl, Geda? Ana has seen the outcome before. Carefully not to relive those memories, he vanquished those thoughts. No matter what, it always ended in disaster.

The beast's gaze lingered on the couple, debating their fates when his eyes caught evidence of the Separatist's suggestion. Darin's grip on Geda's wrist tightened, halting her pickpocket. He witnessed her silent grimace and his heart twisted. The contortion of her brow hinted desperation and carried a desire to end him.

The boy tagged her. And this… is how he treats her?

The couple shared a passionate disdain for the other. Familiar, Ana recognized the inevitable outcome of her commitment. A dark mutation was bound to happen under Darin's care. How could he allow that to happen?

"You were right," Ana finally answered Theo. "I am going to throw it all away."

An hour later, the final was over. People left their seats to give Professor Currant their interpretations, supported by external research. The priest was pleased by the lengthy essays piling up. However, he would be disappointed by Theo's paper. It was barely a page, front to back. After the subtle chaos that transpired to his right, his mind was clouded with uncertainty.

Theo just sat there. He was still digesting the encounter. The young man looked at Ana, hoping he would say something, but he didn't. Instead, the mutant exhaled the breath he held. From Ana's expression, it was best if Theo refrained from speaking of the event.

Consequently, the choice Ana held defined a shift in power and highlighted who held majority power in the Order, the Raven boy Darin. Naturally, such a matter must be reported to his superior. Regardless of what Leo said, it was not Ana's choice to make but the congregation's. For the time being Ana needed to consort with his ambassador.

They waited patiently for everyone to leave before having a private meeting. Strangely anxious, Theo couldn't calm himself. With each passing second, a shock wave of magnitude proportions would crash over his meditation.

What is wrong with me? he questioned the quiver in his hand. He looked at Ana and recognized the aura exuding from him. The Devil was churning. Sweat kissed Theo's brow, and dread saturated his pores at the reminder of Ana's malevolence.

This fear is primal. I can feel it in my bones, and even deeper. This is Ana. Ha! I know the stories. I read them every day. I knew what I was getting into when I signed my name to you. I know to be afraid but this is on a different level.

As for Geda, she was unable to contact Sasha. Darin's grip remained locked between her fingers. Helpless, she was left wondering what transpired in seat N3 of section D. On her way out, she looked in Ana's direction, hoping to detect some remnants of their conversation. But when his glance collided with hers, it said nothing more than "walk away."

Only a select few remained in the auditorium when the doors closed. Amid the silence, Ana stood up and made his way to the stage, with Theo following closely behind.

Professor Currant threw his arms in a massive shrug, nearly showering the stage in loose essays. "What was that about?"

he asked. "I didn't know he was here until someone warned me. Had I known, he would have never gotten the chance."

"I thought you were trained to detect their presence?" Theo threw out.

"An agent's presence, I am but not a neutral mutant, especially not Leo," Currant pointed out. "Leo, the Separatist leader and master of poisons. The beast is only detectable by one man." His eyes moved to Ana. "I'm sure he saw him coming."

He did. Ana detected it the moment Leo set foot in the auditorium. His scent, the rich flavor of Rose Garden nectar, was woven into his fabrics and stained his skin. Unfortunately, the wonderful smell no longer remained. Instead, what he found did not put a smile on his face, a rugged scent of mulberries.

He turned to the source, eavesdropping in the shadows. "We have a problem," said Ana, directed to the eavesdropper. His voice carried the aggression of confrontation.

From the dark, a young boy emerged; his height barely reached the stage. "Oh, it's Bog!" Only one of the three men was surprised to see him. "I didn't know you came here." Theo rushed to assist the child's climb onto the stage.

"I followed the agent," Bog replied as he dusted himself off.

Currant glared with noticeable suspicion. "Which one? There were multiple here today."

The boy cleared his throat. "Honestly, I was following your sister, observing her condition. Raymond should really do something. Excluding the Lioness, if there was another agent in the proximity, I am right to assume they are here for Ana," he said, conquering the office chair on stage.

"And others," corrected Ana.

"What do you mean?" Currant questioned.

"They have tagged students," answered Theo.

Currant noted Ana's deep sigh. His eyes widened, realizing

the situation. "They tagged Geda?"

Ana nodded. "Yes."

Hand over mouth, Currant had to detach himself momentarily to process the severity of the case.

Bog simply rubbed his chin. "That is certainly not good. No, no. Indeed not."

Currant jumped back in with an intensity Theo wished to express. "Their intentions with that are clear!"

Ideas bloomed in Bog's eyes and Ana instantly refused. "No! It will not happen. I will not do it even if you asked."

Bog wanted to have faith in him but doubted. With the organization meddling, resistance was forlorn. "*You* won't have to," he said in return.

The conference continued with little explanation. Theo couldn't help but feel left out. Within it, he witnessed raging flames engulf Ana's angelic wings, the uncontrolled franticness of the stiff godly disciple Currant, and the concerning excitement in Bog's contemplation, all at the behest of one feeble girl, a similar reaction upon learning her name. Undoubtedly, she had a power of unbinding nature. It made no sense.

Frustrated, Theo broke through the conversation. "Hold on one minute! There is something that is not being said and it's making this very confusing."

Currant educated him with, "The organization has been notified of their interception and wishes to use it to their advantage. He can kill the heir to save Geda and ultimately be delivered to the murderous queen, or he can do nothing and watch as her genome alter to royal standards. Both are unacceptable."

"Or he can claim her," Bog interjected, touching a subject forbidden to Ana. Ana shot daggers in his direction. Bog explained, "I understand your feelings but currently, you are a ripe pawn for their machinations."

"It cannot be avoided." Ana dropped into the front row seats.

Currant continued, "After Ana's successful mistake of creation, the organization has been working diligently to simulate the results, to synthetically produce a queen. What if he could do it again?"

"You mean Sarolt?" Theo questioned.

"Yes. If you recall from your studies, female mutants are rare," added Bog.

"And only those claimed by a being of a specific lineage, a monarch, can produce a queen bee," quoted Theo.

"Only I, the last monarch, can accomplish such a feat. Very good," praised Bog. "When I orchestrated Sarolt's claim, I didn't expect such powerful results to be born from an act of rebellion, especially not from Ana's venom, but it worked. In his attempt to save her from being crowned by my hands, Ana doomed her with a selfish claim that resulted in an unintentional coronation. It was beyond successful. A lesser royal had created a higher being.

"The act was against the rules of nature and made my superiority unnecessary. It made Raymond blush and since then the Order has researched the circumstances of Sarolt's birth to manufacture their own queen. Originally, they suspected Ana was the defining variable. However, after so many violating experiments and inconclusive results, they were unsuccessful."

"Not entirely," informed Currant. "They learned how mutant hierarchy works on a biological and psychological level. They know queens wield the power of the mutated gene, while kings can pass the genes to others. And after years of research, C.O.V. can synthetically procreate, stocking the city with fakes."

Bog spoke over him. "The point is mutant society cannot resist the allure of royalty. If the Order can control a queen, they can control the population. Though they harbor her, the

Order can't collar Sarolt for she is too strong and unwilling. We suspect the Order is motivated to forge a new queen, one loyal to their cause."

The priest exhaled regret. "And they want to turn Geda."

"Why Geda?" Theo asked.

"If Ana wasn't the source for answers, then Sarolt's heritage is. Knowing it's genetic, scientists can use Sarolt's genetic pattern to locate the mutation signature in the remaining society."

"That is why Geda is so valuable to him," said Ana.

"The original Geda was a precursor of Queen Sarolt," added Bog. "Whether today's Geda shares the genetic lineage or not, the Order may think they can crown her with Ana's D.N.A."

"Can they?" Theo asked.

"Unlikely," Bog reassured, "but they can try and she will die in vain."

The sign of the cross motioned over the professor's chest.

"He offered me an out," Ana said under his breath.

"You did not take it, did you?" Bog growled.

Ana shook his head. "In return for her tag, I must assassinate the Raven boy."

Currant turned to the child, arguing against the consideration. "With majority power, Darin has been wasting the Order's resources trying to fulfill the genome goal. So long as we keep Ana safe, technically, he is beneficial to the church."

"I disagree," said Bog. "Darin is on the right path of discovery. There has to be more to the story than Raymond having a bad egg and him wanting to throw it out. That's not something he would do. That man has a use for everything, even the dead."

"It would help to know that it was Darin that tagged Geda," added Ana. "Raymond cannot remove it, let alone do anything with his son in the way."

The child gasped. "I had no idea this turmoil existed between father and son. Spies have reported no change in power, politics, or direction," said Bog delightfully.

"Then it is done in silence," Currant suspected.

"Ana, can you confirm what you said?" Bog asked.

"No, but my suspicions are strong," answered Ana.

Ana was swirling with thoughts, including Raymond's quick response for help. *There was something else about this girl that Raymond wanted to protect. Perhaps we are overthinking this,* he thought. *I'm sure he is aware of his son's rough nature. If it's something as simple as that, I understand dispatching the boy.*

Bog had been thinking amongst the discussion. "This boy is key. Eliminating him grants Raymond an unknown security."

"Is there no other way to prevent his sacrifice?" Theo questioned. He had become friends with Darin and Geda. Choosing between them at the risk of Ana was something he wished to avoid.

"Does it matter?" Ana heartlessly pointed out. He was suffering the outcome of the decision before a choice was made.

"How can you say that?" Theo challenged.

"If I do what is asked, which, no matter what is a trap, will they honor the deal? Will Geda be safe? How will you know? What's to say they won't try this again? If they have the potential, the Order will always choose power over any previous promise made."

Theo turned away. He refused to believe they had only two options. Then Ana's words settled within him. They were full of suspicion and doubt, warning him of his predicted outcome. But when Theo turned to Ana for answers, he was cut off by the child.

"As a progenitor, the organization has had its way with Anastas. Forcing his slumber to craft atrocities from his veins," consorted Bog. "After Ana destroys their hindrance, they may become unstoppable. They can easily pursue the genetic research and eventually claim Geda and become the new oligarchy. The organization has never been fair." This did nothing to dissolve Theo's previous consideration.

Deep in thought, Ana's hands tangled in his hair. He was at a critical point of no turning back. Theo felt his despair and he recited his vow, "I am your shield, the holster to the weapon that you are. To veil, subside, and defend is my purpose at your side. As your guardian, I have vowed to keep you from harm and from harming others. I am the boundary that divides mutant from human and the same in reverse. I will not witness your sacrifice without exploring alternative options."

The reminder of his devotion moved Ana. Theo's heartfelt expression extinguished his indecisiveness and paved a clear path to the end. Yet, Bog's orders prohibited any decision.

"The two of you will do nothing. Obviously, our Geda is heavily valued by Raymond. Whatever he is planning, it is not for amusement. Therefore, we must be vigilant and plan accordingly. Do not make any rash decisions until my investigation is complete. In the meantime, we must do everything we can to protect her. Theo, I will leave that to you."

"What?" A united roar came from Bog's subordinates.

"Why me?" asked Theo

"You are closer to her than any of us. Distract her," ordered Bog.

Currant wasn't okay with this. "His hands are already full caring for Anastas. Now, he must watch over Geda?"

"Ana is capable of handling himself," returned Bog. It's true. Ana should be able to. However, with the severity of his condition, Theo was his primary source of normalization. Ana couldn't help but feel abandoned.

I see where this is going. He must have detected my resistance. Ana sighed. *I shouldn't have told him about my condition. Now, he wants my death. Doing this, he will surely get it.*

Offended, Ana did not restrain his words. "Perhaps I should recruit the Peacekeeper's help instead." His chosen words triggered something within his master.

The childlike voice twisted into something much more profound. "You will do no such thing! This is not his business," Bog roared.

Ana stood his ground. "If it pertains to the queen, it pertains to him," he threatened back.

Theo butted in. "Stop it, you two! I can do this."

Bog gave Ana one final look. "I will look into the tags." And left.

Not pleased with how things went, Currant applied a gentler touch. "All we ask is to keep Geda close and Ana alive. Then, we will take over when the time comes."

"Currant, he is going to kill me."

The priest empathized, but did not have the words to console his brethren. However, everything he could have said was spoken in his lingering stare before leaving.

Theo turned to the frazzled mutant. "Is it okay to let Bog leave like that?"

Ana straightened from the chair. "He is upset that I suggested alternative help. That's all. He doesn't enjoy his plans being upturned."

"Along with the acquisitions you threw his way," added Theo.

"So you noticed, did you?" Ana smirked.

"Of course, I did, and so did he. I know how you felt but he is still a father figure to you, just as you are to me."

"Not anymore. Bog wants division to make me weaker, more compliant."

"And to protect Geda," added Theo.

Ana disagreed, "That is a front to protect his assets and to put us back in line."

"But Geda?"

"She is not in immediate danger; even if she was, she is submerged in C.O.V. relations. I am certain there is at least one person there with enough wits to know what's going on and can save her."

Both men sighed.

Ana reassured Theo with a hand on his shoulder. "We should get to work accommodating the new situation, and I need to get some sleep."

CHAPTER 10

Change of Heart

The Devil," repeated Geda. "He called himself the Devil," she said over the nearby grunts of sparring hunters. As usual, Sasha was listening but too focused to answer. The agent twisted and tumbled, wrestling for a win while training her protégé, Tuwile, not to get distracted.

Seated against the wall of the training area, Geda had no interest in the flipping gymnasts, though her glazed eyes watched them. Even abrasive rubs on the leather mats by her feet nullified all her thoughts except one. One was very prominent. The word 'devil' spilled from Ana's lips in reference to himself.

"Why?" she wondered.

"Devil?" questioned the agent Tuwile, gagging on Sasha's debilitating hold. With two submitting smacks, she released him.

"You were distracted. Do better," informed Sasha. "That's enough for today." The two agents respectfully bowed, having learned from the other, and went their separate way. Geda perked up.

Sasha was now free to answer her curiosity. "The beast got that name for turning away from the church," she said, heavy with breath. "Let's go."

Walking together, Geda interviewed as the Lioness continued her strict routine. "I thought the church was a haven for mutants." Drinking water, Sasha nodded. "What made him leave?"

Empty, the water bottle coughed into the agent's mouth. "Tsk. Mutants have provided various reasons but many say he was forced to commit sin," answered Sasha.

"Sin?" questioned Geda. Their voices now echoed in the locker room.

Sasha grabbed the fatigues from her locker. Careful curation altered her movement. She then turned and replied, "You see, mutants were not as they are today. They were once strict in their discipline. They were saints, until one day, manipulation overruled all morals." The locker door slammed. "Fallen Angel was the name screamed at him as he turned away from the royal church, and over time, it morphed into what it is today, Devil."

Geda's brow narrowed, trying to understand. "But what would cause someone so kind to be given such a sinister title?"

Kind? Ha. The Lioness almost laughed. Then, she remembered she had once asked the same question.

Sasha was hesitant to answer. After all, Geda was innocent, unaccustomed to vampire behavior, and unsullied by their indiscriminate violence.

She recognized the glimmer in Geda's eyes. She understood the fascination she had for Anastas. In fact, she was once in the same position with a similar man, but like every mutant, their story did not go so well. She debated whether to entertain or scare her. With that said, she knew her friend. When Geda desired something, she is determined to get it or at least understand it.

A heavy breeze left Sasha's chest as she joined Geda on the bench. She tried to summarize the complex nature of mutanity with human words. "Natural selection drives the survival of beasts. To live, they must be the strongest of their kind. Strengths, whatever they may be, compensate for their weaknesses and must overshadow the latter for any fracture in their metal could easily be exploited and cost their lives. A fragment of compassion meant certain death. Anastas has existed in the jungle since the fourth century and has survived by being the most clever. But when the angelic are deceived, even they turn away from heaven," said Sasha softly, plucking a brittle cord in the back of her voice.

As she explained, Geda saw the unembellished side of the agent. "I will not keep you from your curiosity, but consider how they have to survive before becoming attached. It is best to keep your distance. That man is understandably bitter towards the Order and you are one of us," she warned.

Geda took everything she said to heart. After all, she was more at home with this soldier than with her assigned family. For someone to honestly be concerned out of love rather than obligation was fulfilling to the soul.

"Sasha, will you teach me to defend myself against a mutant? You know, just in case," Geda requested.

The Lioness looked down at her calloused hands. The marks of hard work and dedication peeled thin from overuse and blistering. "That is beyond the scope of your internship," she regretfully answered. "But I can show you a thing or two should you ever need to defend yourself."

In the empty training room, Sasha detached the blade from her belt and began her instruction. "To overpower a beast, you must become a beast; that is a misconception we often say. Realistically, anyone can hinder a mutant powerless by attacking their weaknesses. A swift move is all you need to get to safety."

"If that is true, then why does C.O.V. employ soldiers of your caliber?"

"To kill. *You* simply need to stun." Sasha handed her the knife.

Knowing blood had stained its edge, Geda was hesitant to take it. Regardless, the knife's weight fell into her hands, and she had a newfound understanding of the Lioness's burden. Staring at the ornate blade, the jeweled hilt contoured the edge of her palm, and the guard hugged her hand perfectly like it was made for her grip.

Across the room, Sasha pulled a dummy from the rack for demonstration purposes. "Mutants are not so different from humans. Aside from their mentality, we are anatomically identical. That said, there is one feature that cannot be found on humans, and if you know where to aim, you will hit a place of great vulnerability every time." She bent down to color a spot on the foam. A large black area curved across the abdomen of the training partner.

"The diaphragm?" Geda wasn't expecting this place to be the weakness, perhaps the heart, brain, or groin.

"Good." Capping the marker, the agent put a hand on Geda's chest. "Do you know what it's like to lose your breath?"

"Yes."

"Do you know what happens to your body when the wind gets knocked out of you?"

Geda shook her head. "Not specifically."

"When humans take a hefty blow to the abdomen, our diaphragm spasms. We lose our breath and the sense of control over a basic life function. It feels like we are dying. Then, we panic, making things worse. When we lose our breath, our body utilizes other abdominal organs to compensate for the disruption, but we aren't aware of that during the chaos. No. All that's registering in our brain is the missing connection. The instability throws you overboard. I'm going to die," she emphasized.

"It's a terrible feeling," understood Geda.

"It's a feeling mutants cannot escape. It's constant. Some days are worse than others."

"How do they know any difference if this is normal?"

"They were once human."

They remember, Geda found.

"Mutants retain their human instincts. They long for a time filled with deep breaths and unrepressed clear-headedness. To them, breath is as valuable as blood, just as warmth is to us. This spot," she pointed to the dummy, "the seal of darkness, as they call it, is basically their source of mental clarity and homeostasis. Like tigers, vampires have stripes, a sign on their body indicating their 'level of madness.' It melanizes the skin and runs the length of the diaphragm.

"In ideal circumstances, the indication is absent; they can breathe and focus. But in today's world, no one can relax due to hunger, insufficient funds, harmful drugs, a broken heart, or even the lack of quality rest. If the seal appears across the abdomen, the vampire has lost his focus and control. If the mark spreads over the body in tiger formation" — she drew more lines resembling Ana's — "the mutant has become an aggressor. Aggressors can beacon, drawing Malum to their center and endangering all of the Oasis. My job is to apprehend these aggressors and protect them from beaconing."

Sasha turned to Geda. "Now, imagine you are a bystander walking to school when suddenly an aggressor cuts you off. I am not in the vicinity. What are you going to do?"

Geda looked at the blade. "Stab it."

"Where?"

"In the seal or diaphragm."

"Why?"

"To disrupt the breath?" guessed Geda.

Sasha nodded. "Every mutant struggles to maintain homeostasis. Breathing is the best form of control. It's remarkable what you can accomplish with the proper breath. That is one thing humans can learn from mutants, given a chance but that will never happen.

"Unfortunately, you can't knock the breath from a mutant's chest. The sacred connection to breathing has developed an unwavering chest cavity. Bullets will not collapse their lungs, and a fall will not deter the muscular diaphragm. To stop them, you must sever their connection to their center."

The agent made a stabbing motion at the dummy with the marker. "Attacking the seal or stabbing the diaphragm will cause a vampire's equilibrium to topple over and paralyze them with fear. They will focus all their energy on preventing the seal from appearing, making them significantly slower and weaker. Don't worry. An attack like this is not as damaging as it seems. Remember, mutants heal fast. You'll need to flee when your blade enters the belly. Even an unhealthy beast can recover from this in less than a day."

"I understand."

"Now, attack the aggressor."

Geda did. With a swift lunge, the blade entered the dummy smoother than she anticipated. Nothing halted the edge of her knife, no barrier of resistance. To her surprise, a red substance surged from the pressure point.

Blood! She gasped. As the blade exited, the liquid remained. The sight twisted her stomach.

The realization of her commitment made her quiver. Disturbingly, she discovered she was capable. Although it was not to Sasha's confidence standards, nothing inhibited her actions. Geda took a step back, weighing the experience.

The blade's design streamlined her power. Despite the weapon's age, the guard kept her fury from the blade's edge without a rattle or wobble. The evidence was in the grip. Her fingers danced over the ridges engraved from all the vengeful holds that once wielded the dagger. Again, the pattern slid between her fingers nicely. But the red. The red was evident.

Sasha broke the tension, saying, "It's always a little shaky the first time. But the next time you use it, you will be ready and it will be swifter."

Part of Geda's innocence felt damaged. "I hope there won't be a next time."

"You mean, 'I hope I don't have to use it on Ana'," Sasha corrected.

Geda nodded. That is precisely what she meant.

Sasha witnessed a death within Geda's gaze. She grabbed Geda's hand, pulling her attention from the blade. "To be a part of their lives, you must be able to shed blood either for them, with them, or against them. The choice is yours. Keep the blade so you have something to protect yourself with," she said, walking away.

"But this is your signature blade?" Geda refuted.

Sasha stopped. "I don't think I have a use for it anymore."

"Why do you say that?"

A smile lifted the Lioness's face. "The blade has chosen a different wielder. I can tell by the way you hold it. My grip is opposite. Yet, it fits you perfectly. Hopefully, that means I won't have to slay demons anymore."

Geda's grip on the knife tightened. "I don't intend to use this. I just wanted to know."

"Then, keep it safe for me, will you?"

"Of course." Geda held the blade close. "Wait! Where are you going?"

"It rained for the second time. We need to know why."

CHAPTER 11

The Return of God's Enforcer

During the long hours of night, shadows engulfed the valleys between buildings despite being lit by street-lights. Malum adventured from alleyways in search of restless and weak souls to feast from. The isles in which most resided were flooded with stillness. The only disturbance echoed from a cloaked figure refamiliarizing himself with the city.

Intersecting Hill Cross Avenue and Mammon Drive, this particular spot was sentimental to the hooded man. Here a cherished memory was formed; it was here he faced his greatest enemy. Their collision broke pavement. To his surprise, the scar had been recarved.

Reminiscing, he kneeled and brushed his hand across the groove, wet from the rain. Fresh, the mark was reopened a couple weeks ago, around the time of Leo's capture.

Sasha, he simmered. *Ah. I've been away for too long.* Unfortunately for him, the Lioness was not the only being suspecting his return.

Swiftly, shadowed silence was interrupted by the company of another, catching him off guard.

Stomp. Stomp! STOMP!

Running, quick steps appeared out of nowhere. Before he could react, the individual leaped over him, yanking anonymity from his body. Then, cloak in hand, the intruder bowed and greeted, "Welcome back, my Lord."

He recognized the feminine voice. *Amora.*

As she cautiously peered beyond her draping veil, he could see her wrinkled discipline, confirming her identity. Her bow tested his threat level. There were no clear indications of the attack being reciprocated, but the man's bright gaze amplified the darkness he carried. He did not welcome her. Instead, he judged her.

He knew not to be deceived by her narrow shoulders and senior appeal. He knew her geriatric flesh disguised her real potential. Realistically, she was more limber than he was. Her deception kept him on edge.

"A trap?" he suspected. "Did you make this mark?"

Instantly, Amora was offended. "I would never disrespect such a ritual. No. It was her," the Lioness, she assured. "We have been watching her."

"We?"

"Did you think we wouldn't notice?" A second feminine voice called from the rooftops.

Sarolt. The man knew that haunting voice from anywhere. He looked at the woman lounging on the building's ornate trim, mocking his easy capture.

Sarolt continued, "There has been no sky fall for the last ten years. Who else but you, Ariel, God's Peacekeeper? Only you would nurture the fields of the damned."

"So we followed the Lioness," said Amora, pointing to the mark. "Only she knows how to find you."

Ariel grit his teeth and barked back to the queen. "You! You tricked me. You sent me to sleep!"

Sarolt pouted. "Yes. Baby boy needed his nap. You were destroying everything so I took a page from your master's book. It's not my fault you slept so long, but if I had my way, it would have been longer," growled the queen.

Hearing it angered him. "I had to destroy my chamber to get out!" The Peacekeeper fought back.

"You woke up too early!" she defended herself. "If you had been a good boy and stayed, I would have unlocked the sanctuary for you."

"You did that to get me out of the way," the Peacekeeper suspected.

"Of course I did," confirmed Sarolt. "With you here, the True King will use your strength against me. We will be forced to fight. You are too kind to be destroyed by his selfishness. I would rather have you hidden than be at the center of the destruction."

"What have you done, Sarolt?" He had missed so much in the last ten years. Who knows all she had done? He feared it was irreparable.

She curled her fist. "This war is almost over. I'm so close to ending this revolt, dear brother. But now that you are here, you will surely be sent to stop me. If only you didn't fight for the wrong side." She intertwined his consciousness.

"You know why my loyalty resides with the True King. So long as nothing happens to Anastas, you have my support," he reminded.

"Yes, Priest Anastas. While you are here, I need you to do something for me," Sarolt added, inclining from her lounge.

He glared. "You may not have him."

The queen laughed, exposing her vicious teeth. "Peacekeeper, you have been gone too long. If he remained my top priority, all my efforts would be directed to unearthing him."

"Isn't that what you always wanted?"

Sarolt took a deep breath. "Contrary to my desires, Ana will need to live," she admitted.

The man was surprised.

She continued, "I fear the Monarch's next move will issue Armageddon. Our survival may very well depend on Ana's ferocity and determination. However, in his escape, he has become frail. Soon, the Devil will embrace death. Do what you can to strengthen him."

Ariel turned away. "He has a guardian."

To emphasize her point further, she swung her legs over the edge and descended to his level. "Keep him alive, drown him in the blood of virgins, tear the flesh of his victims into consumable pieces, and feed him the rage he's been harboring. You must encourage his bloodlust and fan the flames at his feet. Let the chains father placed upon him melt away with hellfire and unleash the beast he truly is," ordered Sarolt.

"The same could be said for yourself," Amora directed at Ariel.

Ariel stopped. "You are requesting me to tilt the game in your favor. I may despise our master, but I'm not dumb enough to cross him," he hissed. "What makes you think I will?"

Sarolt glared. "Right. You have a place, a role to play, and if you step out of line, you will suffer." That is the way of their master. "You will betray him one day of your own volition."

"What makes you think that?"

"With Armageddon comes ancient warriors to bring forth the forces of nature. The being first has been unveiled, Geda."

This got Ariel's attention. "Geda? The True Queen's dark general?"

"What's left of her. We must prepare for the remaining few. It is what your mother would do. So, naturally, you will follow her path." Sarolt's finger followed the striations in his shoulder, and her words teased him into an alliance.

"All this talk and you haven't gotten to the point." Amora grew impatient.

Sarolt did as suggested. "Very well. There is a weapon in the Order's arsenal attached to a Lion's belt. You know the one. It made that mark on the ground."

He did.

"According to Athena, the ceremonial dagger is called the king's blade and predates the primordial king. Who knew?" advertised the queen. "A weapon of that caliber, born from the royal's body, is being used to slay tigers, creatures of his kind. Think about the level of Malum corruption that artifact could possess. Can you retrieve it for me?"

He instantly refused. "That blade no longer belongs to the king. It is the iron heart of an agent. I will not take that from them."

"That dagger is the vector of victory."

"You don't get it! It does not matter who wins. The Malum Saltus will plague humanity. When that happens, who will be there to save them if we are killing each other? Our numbers have become too few to save them again." The Peacekeeper took his cloak back from Amora and walked away.

"And what will you do when that happens?" called the queen. "Will you confront your enemy or save humanity? The horde will not stop for her."

Ariel stopped. Her. His greatest enemy. The very mention of her stilled his heart. His torment pleased Sarolt. He turned back once more and said, "It is the darkness that should fear her, not the other way around." Then, he vanished.

CHAPTER 12

Ammon and the Body Shop

Days have passed since finals, since Geda's life was threatened, since Leo spoke for a desperate man, and Ana became more self-reliant. From then, not much has changed. Just as he said, Theo was capable of handling both missions fluidly. He often checks on Ana, provides help, and manages to keep him company. Without Theo's flexibility, their rebellion came to a standstill, just as Bog intended.

When he is away, Ana is at his worst. He did not realize how much he relied on the boy. It disgusted him. *Why did I do this to myself?* he whined. Then he remembered why.

When the darkness finally takes him, he has to be able to maintain control. He did this all in preparation. Still the conditioning was deadly; some would say stupid. A mountain stood in the way of their freedom but why conquer the hill if every path was more convenient? He was training for something no one would dare to consider but the outcome, if he succeeded, would be monumental.

But every great person faced their lowest before reaching great heights and Ana was now facing his. Considering his dependencies, he simmered with helpless rage, stricken by the noticeable emptiness. *Is this paternal loneliness or the true nature of my condition?*

In the 66th room on the sixth floor, Ana took shelter in his makeshift fortress, spending the day lounging on the top bunk, about a foot from the ceiling. Lights cycled aromatic hues from underneath, decompressing his stifled mind. At night, he runs the rooftops and alleys, leading the shadows far from his safety.

Dark and cramped, his crawl space barely had enough room for one. The claustrophobic pressure comfortably paralyzed him. Unlike humans, mutants relied on the reflex syncope provided by tight spaces. With it, Ana snoozed the days away, avoiding the symptoms.

Returning to the dorm, Theo was always cautious of Ana's well-being. He slowly cracked the door to peer in. "Ah, he's still sleeping," he remarked and slid into the room.

"Should we leave?" Geda whispered, following close behind.

"No. It's okay," said Theo, allowing her into their sanctuary.

Upon entering, her eyes dilated under violet colorations, and found the beast lounging far from the ground. Inquisitive, she secretly tiptoed closer toward the tiger's stillness while Theo rustled the room for his wallet.

The young man's heart was dreary from helplessness. There was nothing he could do to ease Ana's illness. After his master's decree, the man was left to fend for himself. And until they are permitted to act, Ana endures.

Eventually, Theo found his wallet among his unkempt sheets. Rustling the covers caused a small box to tumble out from where one end was tucked. Theo picked it up. *Oh, yeah! I had almost forgotten about this.* From the carved wood, he pulled out a necklace with a red charm, a drop of blood.

"Is he okay?" Geda asked.

Honestly, Theo couldn't say if he was or not. Ana was not

well, but comparatively, he was doing better than anyone would with the extremes of his condition. As long as he was breathing, he was surviving. Therefore, Ana was okay.

"He has been doing that a lot lately," Theo replied, watching her.

"Why?" Instinctively, she reached out to comfort the restless.

For her safety, he requested that she didn't. "He has to get some sleep, or he'll die."

Shocked, she retracted her inquisitive reach. "Should we do something else?" She was considerate, but it wasn't an option.

"No. I have to be here for him." It has been days since Theo had a moment to share with Ana. Handicapped, Ana hasn't been able to work, leaving Theo to cover two shifts. With practice and his duty to protect Geda, Ana has been vulnerable.

Theo unfolded a stool to meet Ana's level. His eyes barely cleared the edge of the mattress. A touch disturbed the surface of the tiger's flesh, and the beast's eyes broke open to a familiar face. Recognition of Theo warmed his freezing insides. "Hm," Ana hummed.

"Hey, you okay?" Theo asked.

"Yeah," Ana weakly replied.

"Should I make the call?" Theo offered but Ana shook his head before he could finish.

While they spoke, Geda took note of the number of meat packets and punctured cans of coconut milk cluttering the trash. All were consumed recently. Black bold writing on a red label, "**STOCK END**," told her everything. *He already devoured this month's supply and still, is like this?* she considered.

"Ah." Theo motioned behind him. "We made plans to go to the movies and wanted to see if you would come, but now, I see you are resting."

"We can do it here?" Ana suggested.

Theo looked at Geda.

She agreed, "Yeah."

"We could do it here," finalized Theo.

Her voice! Realizing they weren't alone, Ana's heavy eyes shot open. "Did you sneak her into the male dormitory?"

Theo hesitated. "Technically, she did that herself. I bumped into her on my way back."

"What?" Exhausted, Ana dropped back into the blanket, twisted, turned, bumped into the ceiling, and groaned.

"Here. Take this, just in case." Theo held up the chain. The red charm shimmered under the rotating hues. A blood retain, it was a last case scenario if ever Theo didn't return. Ana took it and Theo took the opportunity to leave before he could fully wake. "We will be back with a movie." He climbed down. "Do you need anything?"

"No," Ana moaned.

"Alright. We'll be back." Theo grabbed Geda, and the door closed behind them.

Ana released his breath. Darkness cradled him further, wrapping his flesh with the warmth of his mattress. "Geda," he released, sinking into the pillow of her name. His eyes fell on their own accord and his stomach began to ache.

Fluorescent lights buzzed above as Geda and Theo browsed the shelves at a local movie rental store. Aside from the slow peeps at the register, the place was dreadfully silent. From a distance of almost thirty feet, Geda caught the whispered conversation between the cashier and two customers at the counter.

"Gah, man! I had no idea how powerless the Separatists would be without our leader," one gentleman expressed.

"I know. I haven't had Nostalgia for days," the other shopper whined.

"Yes. The Rose Garden is wilting without Leo. Mason hasn't been the same and his grief is evident in his leadership."

"Or he is just a terrible leader," mumbled the cashier. He has heard it all.

"After what he did, I'm not going back."

"Speaking of, did you hear? Ariel is back!"

Also mutant, the cashier's eyes lit up with excitement.

"The Peacekeeper? That means we may have a chance after all!" the first customer plotted.

"Do you actually believe the Order is using Leo to control the Separatists?" the other refuted.

The cashier leaned in. "Does it matter?"

"That's right! Do you know what happened last time Raymond got on the Peacekeeper's bad side?" One of the gossipers imitated explosive noises, and three chuckles came from the blood-driven consumers.

Her attention on the conversation sharpened, completely leaving Theo's criticism of snacks behind.

"If we can get Ariel inside Joytech, he can do some damage like before."

"How are you going to do that? Need I remind you he is the True King's dog. He is too trained to break his duty," the other mutant refuted.

"The destruction ten years ago was not dictated by the highest power. He acted on his own," the other man pointed out.

"Understandably, he was pissed, but I'm sure he was severely reprimanded. Why do you think he's been gone all this time?"

The man behind the counter detected denial in that statement. "Either way, it is too early to plan anything," the cashier interjected.

"What are you implying?"

The cashier sighed, knowing the effort wasn't worth it. "The Order has Leo and the queen. What power would we have if we united?"

As expected, the masses brushed him off. "Pshaw! Stop talking about such nonsense! We don't need to be united. We need the Peacekeeper to end this. Only he has the power to destroy the True King."

"We can dream all day, but we must be ready to move at a moment's notice. So make sure your people are prepared and fully stocked."

The men grabbed their bags. "I've always dreamt of meeting the Peacekeeper." Together, they walked out of the store.

"You may be able to sooner than you think. The True King's death is upon us." And the customers headed their separate ways.

Amusing. Even the rebels want their monarch dethroned, like Raymond. Geda considered the cashier's unique perception. *But of course the people only unite under the circumstances of relatable suffering.* The more she was exposed to the life of paradise, the more she understood the Order's teachings.

"Death to the True King," that customer had cried out unrestricted, unafraid of the consequences of who may hear.

It is precisely as the Order said. The people want death, and they want it done their way. *All they see is death,* she recognized. The insufficient surplus (which leads to death) is caused by a man (Raymond) who wishes death upon a god-like being that governs all deadly creatures. Geda was far from impressed.

Death is nothing special, simply a means to an end. It is something Ana sleeps with every day. It cradles him and spoons his shell until his unconscious departure. He holds it close and dear, so much that death becomes jealous when the living is near.

After witnessing what had become of Theo's mutant, she was convinced the True King did not deserve the dynamic relationship Ana had with death but something more unique, more endless. Perhaps this is what Separatists meant when they whisper in greeting, "May death kiss our king," or when Raymond preaches, "the True King deserves all the sorrows he caused."

On the other side of the delusion was a reason to be loyal to the unloved deity, exemplified by the being constantly on her mind. Ana remains on the church's side after all this time, after all the pain and heartaches. Why? His self-torture crossed her thoughts and how she had no explanation for the behavior, only that it was and should be expected of him.

The Peacekeeper, held in such high regard by the people, is controlled by a strict command. Is Ana the same way? Is his pain connected to his duty to the church and the True King?

"Wait, Theo. Why has Ana been neglecting his sleep?" Geda asked, shifting their previous conversation, which she had no interest in, to a more serious topic.

It threw Theo off. "What do you mean?" he replied.

Geda attempted to map her thinking process. "Someone known for intelligence refrains from sleeping, an essential necessity, to the point of cessation. That seems contradictory. Surely there must be a reason why he keeps himself on the edge of death? Tell me. Does it have something to do with the True King?"

Theo froze. This girl had no connection to Ana or the church. Until now, she hadn't expressed any knowledge of Ana's situation, yet she was closer than anyone to uncovering their anonymity. The bag of chips wrinkled in his armpits.

"I'm sorry." He chuckled. "I wasn't expecting this. But, um, how do you know so much? You two never speak — Wait! I did catch you two in the bathroom." Then, a wild thought crossed his mind before she could speak. He gasped. "Are you a stalker? Is that why you snuck into the boy's dorm?"

She was disarmed by his speculation. "Ah, what? No. I was," she tried to devise an excuse, "visiting a friend."

Unfortunately, her reason wasn't very creative. Theo saw right through it. "Oh, please. All your friends are stuck-up girls with no hobbies."

"Well, you're my friend," she quickly fired back.

"Well, I. Um." Theo stumbled on his words.

Finally, she came clean. "Sasha told me."

"The Lioness?"

"Yeah. She's been my friend for years, but Theo, I need to understand his circumstances."

"Why?"

She paused. "Ah. I'm… drawn to him. There is something about him —"

"I understand," he interrupted, "but there is something you need to understand, you know, before you get too close." His playfulness extinguished. He had to prepare her for the pain that would ultimately result from their rebellion masquerading as loyalty.

She could see the gears spinning in his eyes, debating if he should tell her; if he could trust her.

Subtly, he leaned in and lowered his voice. "Ana's condition is strategic. He uses the dangerous state as a camouflage."

"What? Really?"

"Mutants rest to revitalize themselves, like a recalibration. Without a reset, you'll continue to drift away from ideal health. Naturally, predators avoid the sick and dying, thus Ana lingers on the borderline of death. If he regenerates, a specific someone can find him and kill him."

"You mean Sarolt?" Geda guessed. "And he cannot rest at all?"

"Well, the length of a mutant's slumber is undetermined. Considering Ana hasn't slept in so long, if he did, I'm afraid his slumber could take fifty years to complete or worse, I may die of old age before he wakes."

A cold chill washed over her. "But… Theo, isn't Ana resting right now?"

"Not really. He's just conserving his energy, but if he is not careful, I could lose him to R.E.M. sleep."

"And there is nothing we can do with Sarolt in the Oasis?"

"More like, there is nothing we can do with Sarolt alive," corrected Theo.

"Huh?"

"Not only is Sarolt hunting him, the True King wants her blood. Now, Bog is leveraging us to get it. Neither will stop until Ana is dead."

A stiffness stalled Geda's heart. "Until he is dead?"

"Geda." Their march stopped. "Regardless, Ana will have to die. Not today and not tomorrow but eventually. And until that day, it's our job to keep him alive."

Her brow narrowed. "And Ana knows this?"

"That's how it has always been. As punishment, the True King can call on him to lay down his life without warning. I fear Ana will be the bait for Sarolt's capture. They have already begun discussing his final rites."

Geda huffed.

"Don't feel discouraged. Ana has a plan. The Monarch can't survive the Malam army. Everyone is willing to sacrifice everything to suffocate the True King."

"And he must die," she repeated.

"He must die in the right way, at the right time."

Geda was offended. Death was the only future Ana had. "Is he nothing more than a sacrifice?"

Those words hurt Theo. It was a reality he neglected to face. Instead, he chose to ignore it until the final day. "Unfortunately," he whispered.

Geda grew defensive. "And you're with the church?"

"It is because of Ana that I am with the church," Theo whispered.

Geda stopped her interrogation. The exchange benefited no one; it only served as a realization factor. Theo assisted Ana on his journey to damnation. Yet, in his wrong, he was right. She experienced it in the auditorium, inciting affection for the martyr. Agitated, she picked a movie and he stuffed more snacks into his arms. He could barely maintain the mountain he collected.

"We should get Ana something, too," she offered.

Theo froze. He remembering he forgot to meet with Currant for supplies. "Shit."

"What is it?"

"I was supposed to meet Currant."

"Well, then. Let's go."

"I can't. He is in the Outlands for the next week." His gaze danced around the store. "I don't think they have anything here that would fit his appetite. We will have to make another stop," he replied, knowing that whatever they got to satisfy Ana's need would be dubious at best. It was too late to contact Currant, and finding a stocked supplier at this hour, no less outside reservation, was dangerous.

Theo dropped his load at the register. The cashier smiled when Geda gave him the film. "You'll have to forgive me for eavesdropping. Were you discussing Anastas?" he asked in a strained manner as if he was holding his breath.

At first, Geda was thrown off by the cashier's statement. *How did he know?* But then it struck her. This man was mutant. She overheard their conversation with human ears. So, of course, he overheard theirs. "Yes."

The man nodded. "He is a good man."

Cautious, she looked back at her friend. Theo pursed his lips. Then, he snapped his fingers, recognizing the man. "Yeah! You were in Professor Currant's Anthropology class with us."

The man's name tag read, "Ammon." Bald, septum pierced. Again, he nodded. "Yeah. If you are looking for quality supplies, a butcher shop is nearby. Just head right out of here, take the first corner, and the alley will lead you there."

Theo thanked the man as he bagged their supplies.

"Tell the owner Anastas sent you. The butcher will provide you with everything you need," assured Ammon.

Geda grabbed the receipt from him. "Thank you," she said suspiciously, still trying to distinguish if she had seen him before.

"Anytime." Ammon waved.

As the door closed behind them, Geda did not hesitate to ask, "Was he really in class with us? I feel like I would have remembered him." Ammon was a character not easily forgotten.

Theo laughed. "He was. You just didn't see him. He specializes in invisibility, seeing him took considerable effort on his part. Now, he said the shop was this way?" They headed right and followed the brick façade. The right-hand wall broke open to a narrow passageway. "This must be the alley Ammon mentioned. Tight."

The alley was barely wide enough for two people to walk side by side. They were forced to proceed one at a time.

"I don't trust this," Geda expelled.

Theo could see her nervousness. She was right to be cautious. Mutant business was risky business, especially if Ana's name was involved. Some mutants believe turning Ana into the queen would end the feuding and suffering. Others saw him as the tool he was.

"Stay behind me," said Theo, taking the first step.

She did. With a sharp inhale, her fingers interlaced with his, and Theo guided her into the mutant world.

The passage was poorly lit. Moisture spewed from steaming pipes. Residual water echoed their movement and everything in between. Metal tings and rustlings made for an unsettling approach, but that was just the sound of a working city.

Then, something huge ran across their path. Geda gasped and grabbed onto Theo as he stopped. With the creature gone, he released the breath he held, relieved. "Phew. It's just a shadow." A Saltus. There was no going back now.

The path ahead was seemingly endless. "It keeps going," Theo was amazed. Darkness inhabited the reaches of his human eyes, and his sight could not penetrate the surface for proper judgment. The same happened behind them.

Theo got the sinking feeling this might be a trap. *If it isn't, it's a damn good place for one*, he cantered. Just in case, he fortified his defenses, stiffened his shoulders, and pulled Geda closer. He pushed through the unseen until, finally, the light was found.

Like a breath of fresh air, a yellow light in the distance blessed them with an illuminating haze that quickly transformed into a storefront. The long alley emptied out into a dreary cul-de-sac. The only functioning streetlight highlighted the building's entrance, labeled by the butcher's sign, The Body Shop.

"We're here," Theo said, releasing her.

"This is it?" Geda speculated.

They froze at the sketchiness of the place. Exhaust exposure warped the building's façade. Broken pipes spilled waste into the streets. And bones cluttered the edges, human or animal, perhaps even mutant. Outside, walking corpses paced, waiting for free scraps like feral cats.

Again, Theo grabbed Geda's hand. "Come on," he said and took a step forward.

"Wait." She hesitated. Her hand slipped from his sweaty hold. "Aren't you afraid? I mean, they are hungry. We can't just…"

"What's wrong?" he asked, turning back to her.

"I don't think this is a good idea," she warned.

"Geda," he whispered gently, closing the distance between them. "If it were Ana's hunger, would you be so afraid?"

Her eyes widened. Realizing her discrimination, her tense shoulders dropped.

Seeing he got through to her, Theo's smile returned. He offered his hand for her to take. He offered his guidance into the world she wished to bathe her purity with, all for the curiosity of one man. "There is no difference between their hunger and his," he said.

He's right. Geda reached for him. Their fingertips curled, and she joined him in the light.

As they approached, her grip remained strong. Starving eyes judged their new competition. The large bag of snacks wrinkled as they walked, irritating the skeletons in the street. Snarls were thrown in their direction. "You have enough to eat," one growled, trying to scare them.

Geda held an expression, confident in the man escorting her, but it did not hide the nervousness within. Her breath was uneasy. She was bound to fumble. The only thought running through her mind questioned how Sasha endured these demons daily, for she knew not every mutant was as gentle as Ana.

Closing in, Geda felt a breath on the back of her neck. It wasn't until Theo's hand cupped the door handle that the strays backed off. As he pulled the door open, Geda caught sight of the dark mark on Theo's hand, a shield. "A guardian," one mutant hissed, repelled by the mark.

A small bell chimed their entrance. Unexpectedly, the interior was freshly renovated, welcoming and warm, with no linger of decay or chemical cleanliness to cover the foul business. Hardwoods contrasted with iron antiques, and an overhead chalkboard displayed packaged specials.

"What should we get?" Theo considered the bundle options: Emperor's delight - 20 ounces of the tenderest meat, Armada - 17 ounces of lean meat, Trilemma - 12 ounces of tendinous trimmings, and many more. Among the options were packages based on conditions. The Hazard package, for example, allows quid pro quo in exchange for equal dilemma; essentially, it was a customizable package to fit the customer's affordability - only for those in need.

"So many options," said Geda, doing the math in her head.

"We just need something for the night," Theo said.

"How may I help you?" asked a deep voice. Through the back curtain, a freakishly large man came to assist them.

Theo and Geda hesitated to answer. They were both stunned by the man's massive stature. He was easily seven feet tall and had a muscular body to match it.

"Um. We are here for a friend," Geda mumbled.

The butcher's brow rose. "Oh?" Was he expected to know?

"Anastas sent us." Theo bravely took the leap.

The butcher looked Theo up and down. He spotted the insignia of the guardian shield in the boy's purlicue. "I will see what I can do," he said, returning to the cutting room.

Geda and Theo shared a speechless stare. They understood the risk. They felt it in the air, but this was mutant business. The hair standing on the back of their necks was a normal transaction.

Suddenly, Theo grunted. His mark pulsed. *Ah! Ana. I know. I'm working on it.* Stretching his hand, he rubbed the mark away. Pinching and twisting the skin between his thumb and index finger, Geda witnessed the mark fade. It wasn't a typical mark. Human flesh couldn't darken upon command. Perhaps the creature that branded it could.

Ana. She looked at her watch. 9:18 PM. *We have been out for too long.* She started to get antsy.

As minutes passed, the crowd outside the door grew.

"Maybe this was a bad idea. We are going to have a hard time leaving," said Theo. Geda agreed. Looking out, lingering eyes glared back at them. Then, almost as if they were replicating, more eyes found the window. One became two and two became four and four became more.

They backed away from the increasing sensation.

"There's so many," she gasped

"Geda, how fast can you run?" Theo reached out for her hand.

Then, out of nowhere, an enormous hand met their shoulders. Theo released a screech as he jumped from his skin.

Meanwhile, the girl casually turned to the substantial man. "Oh! It's you," she greeted.

As the young man gathered himself, the butcher turned to her instead. "Your friend is right. It's 9:28 PM, feeding time. If you leave the way you came with this on hand," he lifted the package, "you will be mauled to death. Please, use the rear exit and don't linger." He handed her the package and glared at the boy. "This time, guardian, it's on the house." The emblem of Theo's loyalty, however, was an unintended solatium.

"Thank you," said Geda, unknowing.

"Tell your friend we should meet up sometime. It's been a while." The massive man returned the kindness with a smile; a crooked glimmer displayed nefarious intent. The mutant smile was the gateway beneath the fake façade. Within it, Theo recognized the man's true identity, triggering a trauma response.

Romulus! His guardian instincts exploded. Quickly, Theo threw himself at Geda, separating her from the man. All his weight slammed on the mutant's foot, crushing the intricate bones within, dismantling his steadiness should he chase after them. Theo grabbed her arm and rudely pulled her through the curtains and to the back. Across the wet tile, she ran to match his pace.

"What's going on?" she yelled.

Theo charged through the door harder than he would in game. The door burst open and slammed closed behind them. He barred it with a nearby board.

"We need to get home fast," gasped Theo. The expression on his face carried a betraying seriousness, almost as if he failed in his duty to protect his most precious. "I exposed us."

"What do you mean?" Geda asked, grabbing onto him and steadying him. His eyes, wide from the mistake, fell back to their normal strength when he discovered her touch. Then his gaze met hers. In her bunny color, he saw kindheartedness and sympathy toward his anguish.

"I know him," he whispered, trying to swallow

Geda nodded. "Okay. If we need to go, I can keep up. Take me home. Take me to him, Theo."

Take her somewhere safe. Theo fully understood the order So, with her consent, he did not hesitate to whisk her from the growls and cries of the feeding horde. And ultimately from his foolish misstep.

What seemed like seconds later had actually been hours. Ana was awakened by someone's touch, her touch. A quiver existed within her fluid elegance. But it was *her* touch. He watched as her fingertips brushed against his frugal exterior, delicately tracing the edge of his surface.

Then she huffed. Her inhale was far from smooth. She was still trying to catch her breath. Obviously, something had happened, but Ana was too weak to ask. Then, from his high position, he heard the door to the apartment closed. It got her attention.

"Is everything okay?" she asked.

Theo paused. "Um. No. So... I was right. That man was a C.O.V operative."

Her heartbeat dropped. "And we gave him Ana's name." The Order will soon know Ana's location.

"I contacted the church. Ana will be moved to a more secure location."

"When?" she asked. The VHS case popped open.

"Before morning," Theo answered, placing the tape in the device. "The night is alive. They will have to wait for the astrological shift, or the relocation will not be secret. The shadows speak," he explained.

A finger curled around one of hers. She noticed. *Ana!* When she looked down, the beast had fallen back into the sanctity of sleep. He was at peace. And so was she.

"Do you know where they will move him?" Geda asked.

"I'm sorry, Geda. I can't tell you because of your connection to the Order," Theo regretted.

She was quiet.

"But I'm sure it's not too far," he reassured. *She probably doesn't want to hear that she won't be able to see him for a while,* he thought. *I should save that detail for later.*

Movie on, Theo turned to see her petting the tiger. He watched, silently observing. *I'm going to have a problem keeping these two apart. She even broke into the dorm to see him. What's going to happen when he is at the safe house?*

He sighed, pondering their relationship. Despite being complete strangers, their familiarity with each other, the complete disregard of personal space, and unspoken respect contradicted normal behavior. He was sure to enforce the distance between them, but still, they knew each other. How? It amazed him.

I guess that is what it means to be familiar, he considered. Whatever their relationship, he knew enforcing their distance now was futile.

"Be careful, Geda. He can be grumpy," warned Theo.

"It's alright." Still, she took his advice and climbed down.

As they took a seat, Theo spotted Ana's eyes glistening in the darkness. "The movie's on."

Geda plopped down on the giant bean bag with a bag of popcorn. Separated by his endless supply of snacks, Theo joined her. As they got comfortable, she handed a plate to him. On it was a cooked portion of the meat. "Try it," she ushered. "After all that, I had to make sure it was alright."

Curious, Theo took the plate. "You cooked it while I was out?

"Hmm," she hummed, confirming.

"Did you have some?" He wasn't going to try it if she hadn't. She nodded.

Juices slid down his finger. Theo took a bite of the sirloin, tasting it to validate the encounter. Tender and moist, the meat melted as he chewed. "Mmm," he hummed. Tender and moist. It shredded in his teeth and tantalized his palate, leaving him wanting more. Surprised, he inspected the half-eaten piece. *So, this is what mutants fight for in the games.* "This is really good," he said.

She smiled. "I thought so too," and glanced up at Ana. She found him closer to the edge of his compact space, enjoying the movie. At times, she swore she saw him smile.

Although his vision was blurry, Ana knew every word of the iconic whip-wielding archaeologist and his glorious adventures. He knew the stories by heart, read the fakes, and once lived the real as a Templar of God. He reminisced through the medium and anchored his mind with the repeatable script.

Geda spent more time viewing him than the television. Ana often met her gaze. She was content to see his awareness had returned. She reached up to him. Touch was security, a sign of stability. In return, Ana dangled his hand to hers and their fingertips hooked.

"We got you a snack," Geda said. She grabbed a second bowl sitting to her left and gave it to him. Within, raw meat was sliced into edible pieces, perfect for a lazy consumer.

The beast accepted her offer and placed the bowl by his side. As the movie played, he slowly enjoyed her generosity.

All was nice and calm until Theo's overconsumption created hiccups. Soon, he would have to tell Ana about his encounter with Romulus. Soon, the movers will come, and soon things will change.

CHAPTER 13

Cradled by the Moon

Searing heat plagued the Oasis the following day. The wind whipped the freshly cut patches of green. The crickets song brought in the start of the summer. During this time, water became more valuable than blood. With frequent uncalculated rainfall, the need became all the more apparent.

On days like today, men practiced harder than ever to secure the win for their city. Amenities such as ice cream and SPF serums were vital for comfort during the summer but extremely limited to Decider champions. The high temperatures proved too much for mutant aprication, resulting in many unusual absences.

However, the action was too good for Ana to miss. The entire Gibbous community was invited to survey their city's team practice. People of all ages, including elders, children, and adults, gathered to watch the Falcons and discuss their strategies and chances of winning.

Some sat on the bleachers, while others enjoyed picnics by the fences, soaking up the sun. Lovelorn individuals pined for attention, hoping sweat from a player would meet their graces. It reminded Ana of the gladiator days.

Theo as a gladiator? he imagined. *And his juices were her aphro-disiac or good luck charm?* He chuckled as Theo intercepted yet another play.

To his left, children played with make-shift kites, jumping and running to catch a breeze. One kid got lucky. His kite hit a draft and effortlessly lifted a foot over his head before planting back onto the ground. Ana smiled at that too.

There wasn't a cough of wind to save them from this heat, unlike that day 30 years ago when the world ended. Watching the children reminded him how pleasant the weather used to be. It took him back and he could feel it now just as before. Surprisingly, water washed over his feet. The wind whipped his hair maniacally. His lungs filled with sea breeze and the rainbow kites took flight, lifting up to 200 feet over his head. So high, they nearly swept the children out of their shoes. Something ultimately did.

"Oh! You're here," a voice called to Ana's lower right, breaking him from the miserable trance. It was Geda, surprised to see him.

"Hi," he welcomed. They shared a smile. *She must be here to watch Theo play,* he considered and offered the seat next to him, patting the tailgate. "You can sit up here." The height of Theo's truck granted a better viewing advantage over the other spectators.

"Thank you. Did I miss anything?" she asked, setting down her bag.

"Not much," Ana replied. In all honesty, he wasn't paying much attention. After all, he came here to escape the noise of his new residence.

Geda climbed the rear wheel, threw her leg over the side of the truck, and sat next to him. As she did, Ana instinctively searched the field for her partner, Darin. He wasn't there. He glanced back at her, carefully examining every detail of her wonderfulness, searching for misplaced imperfections caused by the Raven boy's touch. There was none besides a hint of last night's escape. That made him very happy.

"I see you are doing better," Geda noted.

"Ha! Yeah. I think I just needed some sunlight." But, of course, Ana wasn't going to admit the time convergence was getting worse. "About yesterday, did Romulus say anything to make you feel threatened?" he asked.

Geda was displaced by his sudden concern. "Romulus?"

"The Butcher," he explained.

"Oh, no. It's just seeing that side of mutant life for the first time. That was uncomfortable. And Theo…" she recalled his spontaneous outburst, "I don't really understand what happened."

"I'm sure it was a shock. Most of us are accustomed to the lifestyle. We don't see the horrendousness of it anymore. We are all feeling the shortage following the last Decider. Even the church rations lasted me half the usual time due to… inhibitions. I didn't expect you to go to a Separatist establishment. I'm sorry it resulted in a dangerous encounter."

"I can get you rations," she offered.

"No. Don't use your resources on me. Someone will find out, and I won't have that on my part."

Someone, she considered. *Darin.*

"Geda," Ana said.

"Hmm?"

"Romulus is not a friend," he expressed. "He is a dog loyal to his restraints, a decent man unable to think for himself. That is his strength. His selflessness to command negates all emotional hindrances. Should it serve an order, he won't think twice about fulfilling it. He is a tank of a mutant and shouldn't be taken lightly. Don't be so friendly if you cross paths with him again."

She heeded his warning. "Is that the reason for Theo's reaction?"

Ana gathered the right words. "Theo and Romulus have a history. That is all I will say. But, if Theo deemed it unsafe, you should listen to him. I'm sure there was a good reason."

"How often does Theo scream?"

"He doesn't. Why?"

Geda replayed the scene in her head multiple times. She shook her head, asking him to forget why she asked. Honestly, she didn't see the reason for Theo's reaction. She didn't see the danger in the butcher but still trusted her friend's perception. Clearly, she had more to learn. At the time, she only feared the horde of stray cats. She did not think to fear the man feeding them.

From then on, they weren't much for conversation but enjoyed each other's company. They watched as the ball was pitched into a receiver's hand play after play. Runners twisted and twirled around defenders, dodging hits. And repeat. Each play created a new lineup, and the crew did what came naturally. With that said, the fun never captured Ana's interest. Geda did.

A small butterfly jumped around her shirt and fluttered from one spot to another. Much like the fieldmen, it twirled and flopped the ends of her hair, consuming every morsel of available goodness and sweat, as if there was a shortage of it in this weather.

She shouldn't be here, he thought. Geda's complexion was beyond fair. The sight of sunlight would blister her skin, yet here she was, next to him. Sweat beaded his brow. Concerned, he examined her. Her flesh was pink and coping with the Oasis's desert climate, yet she did not express any discomfort.

"Are you alright? The heat is not too much?" Ana asked.

She smiled and said, "I'm okay. It's not too bad right now."

The more concerned he was for her, the more mindful he became of his own limits. As he watched her receive a million butterfly kisses, he thirsted for a similar action. But, when he straightened, lightheadedness blinded his senses, and he drooped to one direction. The lacking hydration simply wilted him.

"Are *you* alright? How long have you been out here?" She supported him.

"For a while," he admitted.

"Well, here. Lie down." Unexpectedly and effortlessly, she pulled him over onto her lap.

He froze, but his muscles did not contract against the movement. *What am I supposed to do?* He was embarrassed. Head on her legs, he wasn't sure what would happen next. With her, it didn't matter.

Geda found a boxed water in her bag and broke it open for him, stabbing a straw precisely into the groove. "Here." She handed it to him.

He welcomed it, savoring the liquid as it filled his mouth. Warmed by the sun and delivered by the Grecian Goddess Astraea herself, it was everything he desired. He sipped, basking in her invasiveness.

"Better?" Geda asked.

Ana didn't speak. How could he admit to such treatment? Though it tarnished his pride, he relished this retreat. It was ticklish and strange, but alleviating. He never felt so free, mentally, since his claim. The shade, the water, the heat, and how he rested so comfortably.

It was her, the intersection of all senses; they traveled through her. Her shade, her water, and even her warmth negated atmospheric displeasure. She was the cooling breeze his mind desperately needed. With her, he could rest peacefully.

As her little finger outlined his curl, the wind gave birth and fanned their position. There, he caught a whiff of cocoa butter and jasmine in the brisk suddenness. *Sunscreen*, he recognized. She was covered heavily in it.

He smiled. *She's fine.* Worry-free, his eyes inadvertently closed. Exhausted and drained from the scorching heat, Ana drifted off into a R.E.M.-like state.

As a result of her affection, Geda witnessed a holy transaction. The marks on his face slowly subsided, receding and lingering in the grey line of his eyelids. *Did I put him to sleep?*

"Ana?"

"Hmm?" he hummed.

She sighed, relieved he was not that deep. That could have been bad. She was surprised. She didn't intend to have this effect on him. His vulnerability in her presence was noted. As humbling and frightening as it was, she cherished his trust. However, it was a trust displayed in public and though Theo was close by, she felt the need to protect it. Recalling the blade in her bag, she pulled it close just in case.

From then on, she paid more attention to him than the game. As he breathed easily, she tossed dark curls away from his face. The fine filaments soaked up the nectar the butterfly did not devour. Beads glided along his ruby necklace. *With everything at stake, how is he so calm? Devil.* A thought beckoned the back of her neck to be covered. She grasped it. *Does he know?*

Shortly after, the crowd expelled a loud cheer. Practice was over. People gathered their belongings. Over the commotion, the coach congratulated the team. "Good job today, boys! Let's take that energy to the Wildcats tomorrow and ruin their day."

Without hesitation, Theo came running their way. Jogging, he undressed, shedding his pads and equipment. Everything on him was drenched, including his hair. Sweat visibly flew from him. Somehow, he always managed to be filthier than the others. "Just a sign of his hard work," Ana would say.

"Hey, Geda." Theo tossed the equipment into the bed behind them. Panting, he fought to cool down. "My water." He pointed to the thermos behind her.

Geda grabbed it. "Oh! That's cold," she said, handing it to him.

"It's all ice," he explained. He left it in the blazing heat to melt.

"I wish I knew that. I could have used that to cool Ana." She checked the mutant again. He was still calm, carefully hibernating.

Ice clanked around as Theo drank what water remained. A tinge of brain freeze curdled his mind. *"Gher!* How is he?" Theo winced.

"He's okay," she answered.

Theo leaned over him to see. "He looks good, and… he's asleep? Wow. Good job, Geda. How deep is he?" Theo poked Ana's nose. It scrunched in return. "He is not that far. Ana has never been one for the heat. With the weather like this, I'm surprised you guys stayed to watch. Of course, you didn't have to. Speaking of which, Darin missed practice again."

"Ah, yeah." She lowered her voice. "He has been taking work very seriously."

Theo raised a brow. "Enough to stop being a team player?"

"He is the heir to the Order, so…" She shrugged.

He caught her. "Ah! So, now you'll talk about it? I should have used Ana against you a long time ago."

At this point, Geda had become a staple in their group. She surrendered. "Yes." All for Ana.

Theo wasn't angry. In fact, he was curious. It was impossible to get Darin to speak about his life in the Order and he still had a job to do as an informant of their rebellion. He used her voluntary capture to learn more.

The truck lowered under Theo's weight. "So now that you feel open to discussing it — which I appreciate; I know it can be hard to talk about some things — I have to ask, how did you become involved with the Order?"

Geda was halted by his level of sincerity. "That's what you want to know?" She scoffed. "You could ask me what Raymond's favorite pen is or something more confidential, like how many doors are in the Joytech lobby. If you are going to use me, you can do a better job at it."

Theo smirked. "Well, I was hoping to use *you*, not the information you possess. Besides, would you even tell me those things?" he tested, drinking more water.

"Waterman Expert ballpoint pen and there are thirty-six doors on the first floor of the Joytech building. I'm not really sure how many are in the hangar," she spilled, unhesitantly.

"How many of those are exits?"

"I don't remember."

Theo laughed. "You must be very close to Raymond to know his favorite pen."

"He was always there for me."

"What about your parents?" he asked.

"I don't know my parents," she whispered.

He didn't believe her. "You must have had someone?"

"Raymond, but..."

"Mr. Sambuca?" Theo couldn't believe it.

Geda talked over his excitement. "It was always him and Sasha. They are all I had until my caregivers were assigned. Parental confirmation has never touched my skin, or so I have been told."

Ana's eyes opened.

It was apparent Theo had stumbled upon a sensitive spot. "Hey. I don't want to believe that. Do you have any idea where they could be?"

Geda paused and thought. "Raymond told me my biological parents are on the oceanic front, securing the sand bar of shadows, and they left me in his care."

"Do you think they will come back?" Theo asked, knowing some soldiers volunteer to stay at the front lines indefinitely.

"I don't know if I want them to. That sounds bad, but I'm scared to know the truth," Geda was smiling, but her heart was drowning. "When I was young, researchers would tell me I was the one success they had, but they threw it away. They left me behind and I don't think I'm willing to face the truth any time soon."

"Well, I'm not going to make you." Theo withdrew his insistence. He understood what parental absence felt like.

She shrugged. "Um. Yeah, so I never knew my parents. I was raised in the halls of the Order, where I met Darin. Under Raymond's supervision, the labs welcomed me with open arms, and they became my playground. Evelyn, Branch, Jakobi."

Ana's face melanated, hearing those terrible names again. Theo noticed.

She continued, "The whole team became my family. Around the time Darin was named heir, Raymond decided it was not ideal for me to roam the halls. So he provided two highly regarded individuals to guide me through life. They were so good at their day job that they needed another project to manage," she antagonized.

"Maybe. You can be a hassle." Theo was telling the truth, and she was aware of how she could be at times.

"If it wasn't for Raymond, I don't know where I would be. I could have grown up on the streets or, worse, the outlands."

At that moment, realization flooded Ana. Hallowed by the sun and the embodiment of the moon, this woman was the bridge between worlds, a beacon of neutrality. Perhaps Raymond saw this too, thus why he protects her, why he is willing to sacrifice his son to save her; he cherishes her beyond corporate restrictions.

She doesn't need guidance. She had the heart to abolish darkness, the heart of Mother. She truly was in danger of a royal claim. If the wrong hands embraced her, it could lead to a cataclysmic event, and in reverse, without this creature's support, his efforts to secure a new nation would be hopeless.

The man in her lap shifted. Like a butterfly, a soft touch brushed her jaw, his touch. On his wrist were four dark numbers similar to hers, 1141, a melanated memory. Then her eyes met his dual shade.

"Please don't speak so highly of him," Ana whispered, sincerely. "You don't know what people have done for their beliefs." That was not the first time Geda has heard this.

"Okay!" jumped Theo. "We should get Ana out of this heat before he burns." He grabbed Ana's arm and pulled the beast up from Geda's sanctuary.

"Ah," groaned Ana. Comatose remained in his limbs. He didn't want to leave Geda's shelter. He would endure Ra's flames for a lifetime to stay at the maiden's waist, to sleep in her shade, and bathe in her refreshing breeze.

"How about a sundae?" Geda suggested.

Theo drooled, "Ah, that would be nice!" Ice cream was always satisfying on smoldering afternoons. It's conducive for blistered minds, of which there was plenty.

CHAPTER 14

Abrasive Alignings, Augmented Awakenings, and Auspicious Assignments

The Joytech Telecommunications building is the tallest skyscraper in the Oasis. Centered in the eye, Joytech serves as the crossroad of commerce, a hub of public affairs and manufacturer of synthetic mutants. However, it is primarily controlled by C.O.V., the world's most prominent military force responsible for enforcing mutant laws. Over half of the building supports military functions. Even the ground level served as a hanger.

Suits entered for capitalistic negotiations. White coats buzzed into various labs. Engineers arrived to ensure all citizens had an infrastructure connection. And upon closer inspection, military efforts could be seen in day-to-day operations.

Behind the over joyous receptionist and frosted glass panes were helicopters, armored vans, weaponry, and soldiers.

General staff maneuver vehicles into position, preparing for the subsequent guarded shipments. Grinders sprayed sparks as mechanics prepped machinery for the nightly hunts. Crates of artillery and technology were loaded for deployment. The remaining half of the building was divided per department demand. All in all, things were in order.

The divided entities reunited in the main halls, a highway-like system of people surging in two directions, branching throughout the conglomerate. Along the pathways, soldiers marched in formation waiting for the next order. Without the eye-shaped patch, the Venator insignia, service men and women were sentenced to L.O.S., life on standby. Their responsibility was internal service, guardsmen, but realistically their only purpose was to fill the void if a Venator fell in battle, or if ever, human numbers were outmatched in the war against the Malum Saltus, they would be there. They serve as the Oasis' final means of protection.

Until they are needed, the soldiers work quietly, anticipating a battle call some may never hear. Vigilant and attentive, they listen for any opportunity to fight as a hunter on the front lines. Each and every one hunger for the title hero, to become a Venator agent or greater, a Lion of the Order. However, none are qualified or tainted enough to be called such. Without a national emergency, the soldiers were left with ordinary tasks. Pinning for action, eager eyes stare at the elite as they pass.

"Doesn't that bother you? The way they look at you?" Geda asked Sasha.

"Sort of," the Lioness replied. "But their desire is justified." A glimpse to Geda met curious eyes. Sasha illustrated further, "They want to be out there, fighting the war on the coast. They want to breathe in the air stained by corruption and protect humanity as they were trained. They were told their entire lives fighting was their born purpose but population laws limit who gets sent to death. Until the time comes when everyone is summoned for the final battle, they will remain itching for action."

Hand gestures amplified her point as they walked. "Its ironic how they volunteered for service and I did not, yet I am the one fighting and not them. They feel robbed of their duty. This is not what they signed up for. I sympathize with that. They want to be me, and I often wonder who will try to kill me to take my place." Sasha watched the passing soldiers. Many forcefully averted their gaze from hers.

Geda frowned. "That's a really dark thing to say." Then, she witnessed sorrow hover over Sasha's mind. "Is everything alright?" she asked.

The agent rested her hand on Geda's arm, and their stride yielded. "Yeah. I'm just —" Suddenly, she jolted forward. "Uh!" Her thoughts were broken by a careless youngster going too fast in the crowded hall. Geda caught her. Sasha then whipped around, "Hey! Watch it."

The young man bowed and apologized for his misstep, "I'm very sorry, miss." He gathered the scattered pieces and rushed onwards.

"Good catch." Sasha patted Geda's arms, awkwardly removing them.

However, Geda's sight tracked the object he was carrying. "Um? Did you see that just now? What he had?"

Sasha quickly found it. "A case of Nostalgia?"

Suspected of thievery, the two women looked at each other and hurried after him. The boy's trail led them to the hangar. There, the package was placed in the bed of a truck, one of sixteen preparing to deploy. Each vehicle had a case among its surplus, enough to satisfy roughly five hundred mutants. Where would he be going with that?

"Woah. There's so many of them." Geda's expression glowed with excitement. "Is this your party?" she asked Sasha.

It wasn't. Looking over a sea of weapons, Sasha got a terrible feeling. "Geda, this… this is not something to get excited about." Breath left her chest. Deployment of this magnitude was never a good thing. Sasha checked the database on her watch.

There wasn't a Lion deployment scheduled for that afternoon and only a Lion could escort a convoy of this size. There was something odd going on. The Lioness grabbed the next person exiting the tunnel by his collar.

"Woah, now! Calm down!" he exclaimed.

"Who is in charge of this convoy?" she demanded to know.

"I don't know, ma'am. I'm just doing what I'm told."

"Wait." Geda attempted to extinguish her forwardness. "What is going on?"

Sasha shook her head. "Nothing that would require this much manpower." She jerked the man one more time. "Who authorized this transport? Who are you receiving orders from?"

Before the man could answer, someone called to them from below. "Geda!"

Darin! Sasha had almost forgotten about him. She watched his approaching silhouette through the diamond grate walkway, an inevitable look of irritation flooded Sasha's face, yet her look to Geda was apologetic.

"You're here?" he cheered, bouncing up the steps.

"So, you are leading this operation?" spat Sasha.

"Yes. Isn't it exciting?" Darin smiled. "Geda, you should join us." He moved to welcome her but was stopped by the agent.

Sasha placed her arm in front of Geda. "Darin, need I remind you? You do not have the authority to deploy convoys," she kindly forewarned as her eyes pierced into his soul.

However, Darin did not fear her. "Tell that to my father," he exhorted.

Geda sighed. Their tension was typical, a product of their protection over the white lamb. She brushed them apart and pulled his focus to her. "What is going on, Darin? Why are you mobilizing?" She gently asked, calming his aggression like always.

He stepped closer to touch her, to fall deeper into her down. Again, the Lioness pushed his hand away.

"You are starting to annoy me," hissed the prince.

Geda knew that tone. "Okay, now!" But no one was listening.

"I only came to speak to her. You shouldn't get in my way," he told the Lioness.

"Then do so. Your talk is the only thing I can't stop." Sasha squared her shoulders.

"Very well." Darin took the opening he was given and turned to the woman patiently waiting for him to speak. "I must go soon and won't return for a while. Father has given me an assignment."

"That's good." Geda's eyes squinted a heavenly glow.

Her support forced a smile upon his face. He continued, "We are making a stop at the Rose Garden then to T-Shan for recon."

"I hope all goes well."

"It won't," growled Sasha. After all, she was raised there, on the eastern mountains of the outlands. Even if he made it to T-Shaw alive, one foolish step and he would be a goner. They were completely under prepared.

She proceeded to tell them why, "Across the desert, it is safest to solo the shadows. Numbers draw Malum hunger. You would know this had you completed your Lion training. What are you doing with all that Nostalgia?"

He didn't answer. Instead, Darin's jaw tensed. Geda inched back further as a wrinkle formed on his brow. *Lioness, she knows everything, does she?* he simmered. He despised the way she always talked down to him. He couldn't beat the agent but knew someone who could. He smirked at the thought then threatened her with it. "I would stop if I were you or else I will send Romulus to tighten your muzzle."

Recognizing the name, Geda's eyes widened. *He is selfless to command,* she recalled Ana's warning and witnessed its truth on the fearless Lioness; how even she recoiled at the name. What was the man capable of to make someone like her cower?

The threat was prominent. There was nothing she could do to keep his hands off Geda. After all, her scars were still healing from his last puppetry. Obedient, Sasha lowered her arm and closed her eyes in submission.

Satisfied by her defeat, Darin proudly walked past her. However, the Lioness surrendered not to him but to the outlands she once called home. Scenery filled her reasoning, and the heat imagined parched her tongue nicely. *Home.* It was where she left her heart. She always reverted back to it for discipline.

Many have bravely crossed the outlands unharmed and saw nothing but dust in the furthest regions. Those that perceived more beyond burning eyes found themselves swallowed by concertinaed earth. She knew how to distinguish the difference. She prayed it too would swallow his army.

"Geda, I want you to join me." The Lioness's eyes shot open. "I want you to see the land beyond the Dunes, experience nature. It will be magical." His finger brushed her arm.

Geda didn't recoil. "Really?" She was intrigued.

Sasha's soul froze. *She's actually considering it?* Geda was overlooking the true danger of his mission. It wasn't the outlands that hindered her allowance but the publicity in the city. As dictated by history, going to the Rose Garden with guns always ended in blood.

Darin knew what he was doing. He saw an opportunity to bring her into his world. Sasha witnessed him implant a cogent seed into the young lady's reasoning, seeking to blind her with exploration to defile her purity with rich viscera. She had to do something. She had to protect Geda. But, when she reached to stop him, she summoned a feral response.

"Sasha!" barked a deep voice, reverberating from the hall behind them.

Raymond! Sasha's spirit left her body. Reminded of her discipline, she relaxed her senseless aggression as the Lord neared.

Geda's chest throbbed. The Lioness was prepared to cull evil away from the young. Was she afraid of her friend? No way. But she couldn't deny the indifference experienced after observing Sasha's anger for the first time. "Sasha?" She reached out to her like Theo would, offering her empathy.

Ashamed, the Lioness dodged it. Garage bay doors chuckled as they went up, almost mocking her temptation. Geda could not help but feel for her.

When the approaching footsteps ceased, a breath fell upon Darin's neck. "Move, boy," ordered his superior.

The Raven boy complied, giving Geda his farewells. "Until next time, my love." Acknowledging only her, Darin disembarked.

Geda went to greet Lord Raymond but was immediately stopped by a dreadful sight. By Raymond's side, a freakishly large man was confined to normal construction standards. His head missed the lights by centimeters. Even his shoulders were angled to contour to traffic. She recognized him without hesitation. It was him, the butcher Romulus.

Her heart raced. *This man is aware of my connection to Ana. What could come from this confrontation?*

Raymond's attention remained fierce on the other woman. "A Lion has other duties to attend to." His cryptic message was clear. The Lioness gave Geda a quick glance, and obediently walked away.

The leader turned to the one remaining. Geda gulped her breath. "As my son mentioned, this here," he motioned to the man, "is Romulus. Get formally acquainted."

"Hello," she greeted him nervously.

"He will be your guide today," addressed Raymond.

"Good evening," greeted Romulus as if they had never met before. However, his tone remained the same, cruel yet welcoming.

Silence preceded. Their gazes surveyed the other. The opportunity to confess his knowledge was there, but he did not take it. Instead, he stayed loyal to his self-confidentiality. He certainly was, as Ana said, a man strict to command, and Raymond trusted him with his most valuable. Somehow she knew she was safe, at least within the tower.

Raymond got to the point. "I am transferring you to the lower levels for an official project."

This was a surprise. Geda had always dreamt of being on assignment. "But my internship?" She wondered why the sudden change.

"Will continue in this new position. Traditionally, this request would have taken place after graduation, but a recent discovery requires extra brilliance. I feel you are best suited for the job. Here." He handed her a key card.

Her mouth fell open. "I don't know what to say." Knowing the key card granted her unlimited access, she felt she could return to her childhood, to the way things were before. This was the best gift Raymond had ever given her.

"You are the only one who can complete this," he assured. "This will be your forever project. I will not ask anything more from you." Raymond's hand rested on her shoulder. Emphasizing the point, it was a fatherly touch, one she rarely received from him.

"Sir, you need to look at this," interrupted Lion Tuwile, handing the Lord a tablet.

Observing the issue, Raymond nearly moved on before granting his dearest *daughter* best wishes. "I have faith in you, Geda. You will know what to do when the time comes. Romulus will show you the way through the complex levels. Be sure not to get lost. You wouldn't want to end up in the wrong place." Raymond then took his leave.

Geda waved.

"Shall we?" Romulus motioned to the elevator.

Down the mezzanine, straight across the garage, and at the leftmost corner was a personal lift to the lower levels. Standing on the designated square, the butcher hit the red button. The platform lowered into a metal sheath adorned with protective plexiglass windows. An automatic shutter closed at the top, encapsulating the system into a proper elevator, and down they went.

In the elevator, the two remained silent, considering how they met. Geda tried to change that. "So, you own a butcher shop."

"I am a mutant," he replied, bluntly.

"Oh, I couldn't tell."

"It's obvious," he fired back before considering who he was talking to. She had barely splashed the waters of the mutanity world. She did not know the depths it contained.

How else would she have known outside of my smile? he realized.

Romulus was not acquainted with typical citizen conversation. But, after some thought, his tone developed a gentler touch. "Synthetic," he explained. "I run a shop to feed those in need. With the increasing shortages, I use my connections to ensure a constant supply for mutants at risk so they do not become aggressors."

She was surprised by the sudden compassion. "That's… rather honorable." It was clear that their initial meeting carried some misconceptions. To the point, she almost inquired about his relationship with Ana, but she stopped before allowing false trust to pave the way to his damnation.

Minutes drug by. Numbers on the counter slowly ticked down. A7. A8. A9. B1… *B1?* she caught. *Wait.* The digital screen went beyond the limits of the buttons. Romulus saw her confusion as she double, triple, and even quadruple checked the keypad.

He explained, "Level A is the forefront of this company, housing manufacturing, research and development, and storage. Level B is the historical wing of the Order. You will work there, researching and maintaining the archives." He pointed to the keypad. "There are nine subfloors after each main floor zero. A0 being the exception, ground level."

"How do I get to level B?" Geda asked.

"Hit A twice, and it will take you to B. All of the floors are conjoined by this platform. Remember, after A, floor zero does not exist."

"What happens if I hit A five times?" she asked, curiously.

He paused, surprised she knew the system's limitations, and replied, "You don't want to do that." She wanted to ask why but his expression told her otherwise. He added, "Unless instructed or escorted, do not go past level B."

"That's kind of difficult," Geda remarked.

"The input for the floor selection is not obvious for a reason. It's to prevent people from going where they shouldn't." He didn't see the flaw.

"And once they know to hit it multiple times to descend further?" she challenged.

"By then, they have been forged to our discipline and proved their metal. They will not go beyond the standard to complete their work. There is no room for curiosity among our staff. I kept this in mind when I designed the lower levels."

"You are the architect?"

"No. Raymond is the architect, but, as he once said, an organization is a collective of its people. Those most trustworthy had an impact on the building's physiology. I was entrusted with cradling the Order's core functions. However, as you pointed out, my securities rely on the Order's enforcement of teachings. Typically ingrained, if those start to fail among our colleagues, the Oasis will be in great danger. Anyone can shut down manufacturing, destroy the reserves, and pillage the labs; we would lose so much."

It was clear his mind was littered with caution, constantly mulling over the probability of something happening and, if it did, actions to stop the assault was easy conversation. With that said, there was much Romulus kept hidden. Geda was wise enough to know if an intricate system existed for a simple transportation platform, there must be more security measures than what he described, especially for anyone attempting to disrupt any sustainable function of the Oasis. The possibilities made her shiver.

By B2. Geda changed the subject. "How do you know Theon?" she blurted out.

The name took a moment to register in his brain. When he finally answered, she wished he hadn't. "I killed his mother." Shocked, Geda turned to interrogate him but her words tumbled into nothingness.

Unexpectedly, the elevator dinged and stopped at B3. The doors slid open, and in walked a slender woman, distracted by an electronic device. The large man suddenly stiffened, sucking in his breath and straightening his posture. Cautious, Geda did the same. If this woman enforced his posture, she did not want to endure the same repercussions.

She inspected the woman. Lean, her muscles spoke for her

structure. Pearl-like hair was twisted up in a crown. The loose strands amplified the unique color and opaque translucence; of spider silk.

Flat against the metal walls, they gave the divine being all the room she needed. In a sense, they did not exist in the woman's presence. They stood there, motionless in the corners. Resisting, sweat blistered Romulus's brow. There was only so much breath he could live without. Mutant, he fought to keep it in, to keep the darkness down, but the fight was nothing he could not wrestle. Though the struggle was evident, not one strip blemished his exterior.

Seconds began to feel like minutes. *How much longer is this ride?* Geda thought, feeling her cheeks change color.

B5. The woman soon became aware of the silence and ignited the space with a hum. Vibrant tones curled imperfectly into a twisted melody, entrancing and gut-wrenching. It was ironically familiar to Geda. She was pulled into her rhythm, like a pup to a parent call. Ups and downs. Up, up and downs. Her score cascaded and rose, entangling Geda's subconscious. The echoes of her mysticism called to be discovered.

Geda leaned in. Peering over the woman's shoulder, she invaded the privacy of the electronic device. Though her hair whipped beautifully like spider silk on a warm spring day, it did not distract Geda from the silent conversation.

S: He is the culprit of Leo's capture, a selfish betrayer that is easily swayed. He could be very beneficial to us in the future.

D: Or detrimental. Mason has proven to have no loyalties aside from himself.

R: His morality was perfectly exemplified with Leo. They had been together for hundreds of years which he quickly abandoned for power. That level of integrity is not suited for our manipulation.

Sarolt is typing…

Before Geda's curiosity got the best of her, floor B7 arrived, and the woman took her leave. Consequently, she nearly followed her out the door. Romulus stopped her, blowing their cover. His sharp lunge broke the air. The woman caught her scent and paused after stepping from the elevator. Realizing she wasn't alone, she pivoted and her gaze met Geda's. Recognition influenced a grin. Somehow the woman's wickedness left a heartwarming sensation in Geda's belly. It was familiar, like Ana.

Ding! The elevator doors began to close.

"Wait!" Geda was not ready to leave her. She had many questions, but the doors met before she could confront her.

Romulus's breath exploded, "What are you doing? Are you mad?"

Geda did not understand. "Who was that?"

"That was the queen! Do not seek her, or she will destroy you." He spoke from experience, wiping the sweat from his forehead.

The queen! Her heart skipped a beat. *I was infatuated with Sarolt. Why?* She swallowed her excitement.

Surprisingly, Sarolt was as familiar as a mother's touch yet distant. This heartwarming apprehension was unknown to Geda, the orphan, but the cold was reminiscent of her lover. The emotion conflicted her.

Geda now understood the extremes of Ana's neglect. This woman was an abyss, a dark hole. Without an anchor, one would easily be consumed by her power.

Many thoughts swirled from their encounter, too many to distinguish flavors from words and signs from cautions. Then it came to her. Collectively, Geda was the curious one. She was the danger Romulus spoke of, the threat Raymond carefully curated. She held the choice.

The elevator dinged at B9. "We are here," said Romulus.

The doors opened. Geda's sight was embraced by modern elegance hybridized with ancient elements. Some of their most notable findings were displayed at the entrance and continued down the hall to the observation deck.

Vases, candelabras, jewelry, weapons, hieroglyphs, and textiles. Her eyes didn't know where to linger. Stone, metal, pottery, fabric, crystal, and iron. Ranging from all shapes, colors, and textures, her senses absorbed the flow of time, from the first record to the unintended end thirty years ago.

"The Order has dedicated itself to restoring human knowledge after the incident thirty years ago," Romulus introduced. "The collapse of Arnireth culled the minds of billions. Ancient artifacts had to be rediscovered, and modern technologies had to be relearned. The demand for stabilization was unbelievable. Thus we encapsulate knowledge so that it will never be lost. Come on, this way." He led her in a different direction.

She followed him through more security checkpoints until they reached the base of operations. The central observation deck, a circular room, flourished with archaeologists and researchers. Among the rough culmination of minds, gentle touches were applied, unveiling the hidden. Conservationists carefully restored and replicated the mysteries resting beneath. At the very center, a stone tablet stood erect on a pillar secured by a glass case.

Romulus was in the process of introducing her to the team when he found her missing from his side. He looked to his left, gone. He searched his right, gone. He soon found her surveying the ancient items around the room.

"Sir, do you want me to get her?" a lab technician asked.

Romulus refused and waited, studying the girl's approach. After all, ensuring she got well acquainted with one particular item was his job. As she bounced from one artifact to the next, he analyzed her behaviors, her carelessness, her proclivity to curiosity, and her natural attraction to stone pieces. *There she goes. Almost there,* he squinted at the gamble.

"Let fate reunite them," Raymond encouraged upon assigning the task to Romulus.

The technician persisted further, "Sir, you must stop her. She can't get too close or she will contaminate the surfaces."

"No. Let her do as she wishes."

Finally, Geda found her way to the stone tablet. By then, a group had gathered around him, begging that she stop. He silenced them and highlighted her discovery.

They gasped at her proximity. A few started crying.

Geda froze upon receiving its natural glamour. At first sight, she was enamored by the limestone. Something about it lured her in. Familiar, it resonated as something prematurely lost and forgotten. *I know this tablet,* she ruminated.

As she stepped forward, it spoke to her. The whispers of a bodiless army stifled her brain. She felt the pain in her wrists as if she painted the engravings, the raw damage of her nails dragging across the slate repeatedly. It felt as if the very fabric of her being originated from this stone. It felt like Ana.

Raymond was right. She found her direction, Romulus thought. "It would seem you are more knowledgeable than expected," he congratulated her as a wetness dropped onto her lip. "You must maintain your health for this endeavor," he added.

Geda nodded. "I know," she said, wiping the blood away from her nose

At the tower's pinnacle, Sasha waited patiently for Raymond to return. Code name: Raven's Nest, Raymond's office offered the best view of all the Oasis. From the tallest building, an individual could see the domed hills lining Crescent City and the mountains beyond Gibbous.

In the vast pace, the only obstruction of the mirroring floor was a massive mahogany desk and the throne of the Order. Its front panel was embellished with the Sambuca family crest, a raven towering over a crown framed by rays of swords.

It was not long until Raymond marched in. As he made his way to his desk, Sasha noticed his pocket was empty. "Your extra key card is missing."

Instincts beckoned him to check until he corrected himself. "Ah, yes. I gave it to Geda. She will now be working on the Gammal project," he informed.

"Is that wise?" asked Sasha. "Sir, I believe it is too early to introduce her to the tablet. The consequences of her health—"

"I understand, but we are running out of time," interrupted Raymond. "My hand has limited cards, whereas the True King has many options. If I am correct, this decision, be it early and potentially destructive, will lead to the monarch's downfall. The earlier she learns who she is, the quicker we succeed. Even if it goes haywire, she must know what she is up against."

"How can you be so certain? Geda is not a tool. She is a delicate being."

"You could not be more wrong, Agent Coumarin. This is what she was made for."

"And the wager?"

"Oh, I intend to keep it," promised Raymond. "Geda means too much to mutate."

"And if others try?" Sarolt's voice entered the conversation uninvited. "The True King will see your affection for the girl and use it against you, if he hasn't already."

"Then, I will finally unleash the Lions to behead him," said Raymond.

"You mean her?" The queen scoffed at Sasha. "She has tried before and failed."

"I was a child," Sasha fired back.

"This is a monarch we are dealing with. The True King!" reminded Sarolt.

"I have not forgotten," said Raymond.

"To kill a king, you must be a queen."

"Then you are ready? You have the dark army?"

The queen looked insulted. After all, she sheltered under the enemy to hide from the True King. "Even I am not powerful enough to end him. Thus we must collect all the pieces of Malum Saltus, why I need Geda to remember, why I need the vials of Zarin. Only the True Queen has the power to stop him. I need the queen's scroll."

Raymond's gaze met Sasha's. She knew the expression and offered, "What do you need me to do?"

"Miss Sasha Coumarin, I must congratulate you. Your diligent efforts as Lioness has delivered Geda to her rightful position. Your mission is successfully complete. After ten years, we can now focus on the True King. To begin, I need you to investigate a lead for me. Of all people, you are more acquainted with the subject than anyone."

"Who is it?" Sasha asked. On his desk, a classified folder flipped open, displaying the portrait of a basic man. *Chadwick*

Joans, she recognized. It had been years since she saw his face. "I thought he died."

"As did I but I suspect Marcy has been keeping a secret. Do everything you can to prove me wrong. I would hate to ruin our relationship with aggressive action. I gave her the neutral zone as condolences. I would hate to take it back."

"I understand." Sasha bowed and started to leave when Raymond spoke up again.

"Oh, and one last thing." With a wave of his hand, the double doors busted open. Two men entered, dragging a bloody mutant.

"Leo?" she recognized.

The Separatist leader was thrown to her feet. The beast groaned. Metal restraints lacerated his wrists as he struggled. The snare around his neck chafed raw flesh and enforced a kneeling posture. His condition twisted her stomach. After so many years of service, she had grown tired of the inhumane treatment imposed by the Order. Unfortunately, it seemed she was the only one who sympathized with mutants.

Sasha wanted to help him. She could easily dispatch the soldiers grasping his reins and free him, but she would not be able to escape the man hunt that would follow. As strong as she was, she couldn't stop the Order. Instead, her gaze returned to Lord Sambuca, searching for an explanation for this cruel display.

Did he place this injured moggy here to punish me? she suspected. *Or is this a test?* Undoubtedly, Raymond knew her philosophy and purposefully went against it. Leo was clearly at his breaking point, a perfect medium to send a message. This was his final judgment, and Sasha was being made to witness it.

"What is going on?" Leo's voice croaked, begging to know.

Raymond remained silent. A slight tap on the electronic device broadcasted live surveillance to screens around the room. To Sasha's surprise, Darin's team was already at the Rose

Garden and moving in. Guns loaded. Soldiers got into position. Tacticals ascended the building and blocked all roof escapes.

Her heart dropped. "Raymond, don't do this," she begged, taking a step forward. Suddenly, the light on the vampire's collar turned red and audibly charged, ready to discipline the innocent. She stopped. There was nothing she could do without harming Leo. In this matter, she was being reminded of her place.

Sasha held her breath. *I was right.*

Raymond addressed them, "Your message, Leo, has sent shock waves to my doorstep. Now, my enemy is snooping where he doesn't belong. So much so that the fabled flower of the Rose Garden has taken root among the church."

Leo's breath caught in his throat. "What do you mean?"

"It was Mason that turned you into C.O.V. We recruited him as an informant and, in exchange, crowned him as the new leader, only his faith is not with me. Along with him, several Separatists openly support the enemy, Leo. I cannot have that."

Riffles were raised as they surrounded a building.

"Wait. What are you doing?" Fear crackled from Leo's chest. "Sasha?" The snare around his neck tightened as he reached for her. But she had nothing comforting to say.

Her fists clenched. "They sent a team to occupy your establishment. Everyone inside will die."

"What?" He dropped to the floor, breathless and defeated. His Mason had betrayed him. His family forced their fate. He could save none of them.

Leo watched as the team entered the building and apprehended every soul. He recognized every face, once knew all their preferences, awaited their celebrations, and once comforted their downfalls. They were his most loyal, loved, and tolerated. Then, among the quick camera movements, the bartender was thrown at Darin's feet.

"Ah, Mason! Mason.? You. You are there."

However, Leo's sorrows had no impact on the one who ordered it. "Your absence has been evident among the Separatist population. Without your feverish nurturing, your flowers have turned to weeds. Your roses have been defiled with empty promises and treasonous congregations," embellished Raymond.

"Then, release me!"

"Mason was supposed to be enough."

"Lord, Mason is not a criminal," Leo corrected. "Please."

"No. It's quite clear."

Raymond touched the screen.

The order went through.

Sasha held her tongue.

Flashes blinded the cameras.

Gunfire fractured the audio.

Screams were overshadowed by Leo's cries for mercy. "No! Stop this! Sasha! Please. Only you can stop this. Please!"

His pleas ran through Sasha's consciousness, sickening her with nausea. She knew better than anyone; once an order was initiated, it didn't stop until it was complete.

To think Darin wanted Geda to see this, she recalled.

However, Leo was wrong. Murder was never meaningless. It had purpose. Sasha gave it purpose. She stood there and watched, obediently becoming a witness. More flashes and bloodshed, water outlined her vision.

Mutants or humans; whichever, she witnessed their slaughter unhesitantly. *Let it not be in vain,* she insisted.

In her vision, Raymond leaned forward, the carnage amplifying the golden pupils beyond his glasses, and he whispered, "You will do well not to go after my son again," yet his words intended a different meaning, "His kill is not meant to be yours."

The assault ended shortly after.

Sasha slowly released her breath, devouring the tears not shed.

"Mason!" Leo screeched. There wasn't much voice left after wailing at the floor. Marks muddied his beauty, and heartbreak bruised his face. Again, Sasha wanted to comfort him but couldn't.

Charade over, Raymond ordered, "Now, get back to work." As if programmed, Sasha pivoted on demand. Her body moved on its own but her soul was brittle. Her only hope now was going after the True King but first she had to see Marcy. As the door closed behind her, no one moved to collect the man curled on the floor.

CHAPTER 15

Sasha's new mission commenced the following day. Clouds plagued the sky, trapping in humidity. Combined with northern wind, it created a relief they needed from the heat. Still, many sheltered as it was evident a storm was brewing, a simple but unusual thing for this time of year, or in fact, the past ten.

Since Memorial Day, any irregularity became the highlight of the news. "The strain in unusual weather patterns continues as more clouds roll in from the north. Combined with the front coming up from the southwest coast, we can expect some more unusual activity," reported Wyatt. "Experts question how the newest weather formations will affect efforts on the Mare Nostrum front lines. If unaffected, they say the new front domination could lead to a season of wealth and Oasis productivity, replenishing the water reserves and crop growth along the Dunes."

Reporter John complimented him, saying, "Others have expressed fear, quoting: 'the sudden weather shift, specifically its concentration of the Oasis, is reason for alarm; an omen, some might say, that we should all listen to.' In related news,

Lord Raymond has lifted the state of emergency for mutant citizens, ruling weather conditions no longer life-threatening."

"Just in time for tonight's game."

Regardless of citizen activity, or state of emergency, Marcy Joans did what she loved best: cooking. She kept a strict routine and like clockwork, so did Ana. At 4 o'clock, he closed the door to the upstairs loft, twisting the lock back as Marcy preferred, and then hopped down the steep stairs.

Chewing on the last remnants of his meal, he was hit by the aroma of a witch's brew, a savory concoction of herbs and spices, amplified by citric acids and neutralized by sweet rice bathed in butter. It was Marcy's famous bowl, shrimp gumbo, popular for making full men hungry again. Ana's pallet welcomed the flavor, using it to fuel his motivation for the work.

Halfway down the steps, the heat from the burners warmed his core, and by the time he reached the bottom floor, sweat beaded his forehead.

It must have been busy at lunch for it to be this hot, he considered. He was surprised to find the dining room empty. "Oh, right. We have the afternoon off," he remembered.

"Big game today!" added Marcy, shelling more shrimp than normal. Every month, establishments close during the match to observe the Decider and selectively reopen upon finale. During the long quadrille, They worked to create enough replenishments for the evening rush. The abundant surplus developed an intoxicating aroma. Slow simmers impregnated meats with goodness. No matter the results, Marcy's restaurant was always packed afterwards. However, during the game came an absence of people, most notably Theo.

The restaurant was quiet. There was no laughter or crowded conversations. The only noise come from rumbling boils or banging utensils. The ambiance was even calmer without his presence, for without Theo, there was no music. Ana took the honor of playing his own tunes for now. As he connected the music player to the stereo system, the doorbell chimed with a new customer. *Oh, who could that be?* he perked up.

Expecting the friendly face of an untimely regular, he grabbed an apron from the hook, tied the strings over his belt loops, and danced his way down the hallway. As usual, the serving door was weightless and swiveled with barely a touch. But as he met it, he instantly froze.

The door was barely cracked open when Ana saw who the customer was. Blond with caramel strands, a scar lined the peak of the woman's cheek, just below her eye, an identifying mark he recognized anywhere. She was a C.O.V. agent, but not just any agent, an elite hunter. *Lioness!* he screamed internally, retreating back into the hall.

The virtuous Lioness was crowned the homemade title after successfully apprehending seventy aggressors by age ten; arresting and killing mutants with conditions similar to his, all on her own. There was once a time when he felt her gaze on him but that was ages ago. Did she have eyes for him again?

Quickly, Ana held his breath and pressed against the wall, praying he was not spotted. He was. Quick glances captured his retreat, but she did not chase after him.

Instead, the Lioness settled into the booth with such ease that one might assume she was a regular. It wasn't an unlikely prospect, given this was unified ground. After all, Marcy Joans seated all walks of life, including heinous Order supporters. That said, it was rarer for someone of her caliber to visit.

Though she tried to hide it, Sasha's disguise poorly concealed her identity. She reluctantly submitted to society's standards. With that said, the blouse she chose highlighted her discipline rather than extinguished it. Tight sleeves rounded with her muscles. Weaponry on her belt peaked from under the fabric's edge. Even the light pink color didn't suit her. It drew away attention her features. It was clear she was only comfortable in loosely fitted clothes.

Marcy quickly attended to the customer. "Good afternoon, Ms. Sasha. How may we serve you today?" she said with a large welcoming smile.

Peering up from the table's menu, Sasha's stiff exterior melted in Marcy's presence. Marcy's radiant green eyes, aura, and overall presence made her cheerful. "Hello," returned the Lioness.

As usual, Marcy stuck to business. "It's been ages since you last stopped by. Things have changed. Would you like to hear our specials?"

"Yes, please." Just listening to Marcy caused memories to flood her mind. It was euphoric until she noticed the wrinkles and lines on the black woman's face, a feature the Lioness did not share despite being around the same age. Though Marcy's face reflected their enduring relationship, the fact Sasha did not age due to C.O.V. poisons weighed heavily on her, among many things.

The host floated images of jambalaya, frog legs, splattered and fried fish eggs, and savory bone broths. As Marcy recited the menu, the agent's mouth watered over the delightful options unavailable in her jurisdiction. In all actuality, it was Marcy's cooking that enforced neutral law. Probation from her restaurant was the punishment for those foolish enough to cross her.

Sasha sympathized with those banished from her house. All the same, she enforced self-expulsion as repentance for past mistakes. In fact, addressing her guilt was the very reason she was here today.

After their fallout, Sasha would anonymously visit to hear her friend speak. But when Marcy recognized her, she would leave without ordering. As someone tainted by the Order's secrets and indirectly involved in the disappearance of Chadwick Joans, Sasha felt unworthy of consuming the heavenly meals offered by Mrs. Joans. However, today, Marcy wasn't going to let her escape.

As the women conversed, Ana slinked away in the opposite direction. Inching slowly, he did everything to not make a sound. His mind, however, was a symphony of debates for he did not understand the complexity of their relationship and still assumed the Lioness was there for him.

Why is a hunter here? Is she here for me? Is she actually going to eat? Wait, are they allowed to eat? Curious, he paused to think of an answer, remembered the danger, and returned to his sneak.

Focus, Ana. That's the Lioness! Do you remember what happened last time we met? I was imprisoned. Do not underestimate her! Regardless, all channels of thought ended with one conclusion. *For Marcy's safety, I shouldn't be here.* He had to hide. *But where?*

As the only attendants in the dining hall, their conversation echoed down the hallway. "Mrs. Joans," Sasha cut off the enticing offerings. "I am here on official business." Marcy clicked her pen closed. Sasha continued, "We need to speak to the individual residing in the living quarters above."

Ana froze. That's him!

Marcy's kind smile faded. She couldn't help but feel boundaries were being crossed.

Before any opposing statement could be said, the Lioness quickly outlined, "There is a reason for my appearance. The Order believes you are harboring C.O.V. property, specifically regarding the late Chadwick Joans. Please tell me that isn't true."

Marcy recognized Raymond's voice in her words and fully understood why it was Sasha that presented the accusations and not anyone else. "Sasha, it is unlike you to overstep," said Marcy.

"I know."

A moment passed between them before finally, Marcy made a declaration. "Especially since I am not harboring anything!" Her uncomfortably raised voice caused Ana to jump. After all, it was meant for him to hear. "I have nothing hidden in my closets or under my bed!"

Ah, the closet! Ana thought. It was a good hiding place. He could burrow in the cleaning supplies and pipelines. He headed there. Besides, the crimes she may confess were not for him to hear.

"C.O.V. property?" Marcy scoffed. "Seriously, Sasha?"

The agent insisted the host calm down. "Alright. That's enough." She whispered, embarrassed by the woman's charade.

Marcy slid into the booth and lowered her voice just enough for Sasha to hear. "Why would you ask me this? You of all people."

"Raymond is insistent," whispered Sasha.

Jade green eyes judged her. "And you volunteered as his messenger?"

The girl huffed. "I had no choice. The others would have made this far worse."

"Do you know what they did to him?" spat Marcy.

"No."

Silence proceeded. Marcy was hurt. Memories of a better time surfaced. It has been many years since she enjoyed her dear friend's company. The Order's priorities wedged them apart; how it too affected her husband, Mr. Joans. And she was expected to cooperate after all the organization had done? No.

"I cannot believe you. I don't believe after all this time you know nothing. Do you realize what they've done to him, what you've done to him? To my husband? He's dead. Because of you. Tsk! Did... did you come here for that reminder? To feel human?" Marcy shook her head. "He's dead," she emphasized through broken speech.

A surge of guilt water Sasha's eyes but still faked a smile. "That's all I needed. I will inform Raymond." She stood from the table but a hand caught her wrist.

"No! You will stay and enjoy my plate," ordered Marcy. Leaving to prepare a dish, she was still talking to herself. "After ten years, you would think she would have already eaten from my restaurant by now, but no." She threw her hands in the air, returning to the kitchen.

As she wiped tears from her eyes, Sasha couldn't help but suspect the truth of Marcy's words. Despite being bubbly, Sasha knew the fire her old friend possessed. If she really wanted to hurt her she would. *Marcy is protecting something and it has to do with Chad.* Was there a chance he did not die from her negligence? She would do anything to prove it, to get the guilt of destroying her best friend's life off her conscience. *Chad, what did they do to you? What are they hiding?* She was determined to dig deeper when she got back to Joytech. Then she remembered, *Wait. I didn't get to order anything.*

After Sasha left, the restaurant was officially closed until the match produced a winner. For now, they had time to relax. "Service will be available after a champion team has been decided," read the sign on the front door.

As the sun fell onto the horizon, Marcy worked the key into the lock of the upstairs apartment. It was a delicate process, one you had to get right or the locking mechanism wouldn't release. It showed its age, just as she liked and opening it required a hard push to unstick the structure from the floor

From the closet, Ana heard the effort and emerged. "Is she gone?" he asked without words. Marcy waved him into the apartment, confirming the coast was clear. He slinked from the dark and rushed to her. Despite having been there multiple times, with each reentry, he was doused in the warmth of her personal expressions.

The restaurant's vibrant, rich style continued upstairs. Oranges, reds, and violets splattered through textures and shapes of sculptures, drapes, paints, colored glass, and accents. Even the kitchen cabinets were a master collection of raw woods, exemplifying the creative need in absence of manufacture expense.

Reusability was a common lifestyle and could be seen throughout the place. Recycled pieces provided surfaces as tables. Personal plants purified the air. The babbling hydroponic system siphoned and reused water cyclically throughout the building, driving nutrients to a diverse vegetable garden across the hall. Organic fats anchored warmth when melted by fire, and when given a wick, flaming candlelight nullified the mind. All of which were tied together with engraved chthonic symbols. Like Ana, Marcy believed in the old gods, not the new.

Ana took off his shoes while Marcy stuck to her routine. As always, she skipped the comfort of cushions, banked right through the kitchen, and onward to the bedrooms.

Typically, she would return in her nightly attire and with a good book, and as she explored the novelist's adventure, Ana would recount his previous endeavors. Twisting the ring on his finger, he would inch open the barricades preventing the past from overwhelming his receptors.

Slowly, memories would flood his senses, washing away daily anguish. He would smell the rust of decaying metals, feel the clashing pains he endured for his religion, and embrace the soft texture of robes cascading over his mortal plains. His ears would eat the crunch of processing powders. His grip would feel the fatigue of the grinder twisting medicinal juices into a paste, and relish in the clergyman's hands working the healing substance. *Leo.*

He would savor the sight until it was extinguished by his indifference. Like clockwork, reminiscence always reverted back to Leo when he wasn't thinking about Geda. But tonight, he would channel Theo. During the game, his champion required his energy and concentration, not the ghosts he abandoned.

However, as Ana prepared, his nose detected an unusual scent coming from within the apartment. Its familiarity made his stomach growl. *It's coming from the kitchen. Is she cooking?* He turned to check.

Just as he did, Marcy returned from the back rooms and placed a blender in the sink to be washed. He noticed the remaining remnants. *Muree?* Ana speculated. It matched the smell. Strange, meat puree was something Marcy would never eat.

His eyes squinted. *Is there someone here? Someone not human?* He listened carefully but didn't don't hear anything. *Whoever was here is no longer.*

But when Marcy's eyes met his, she wasn't trying to hide anything. Her actions were open as if telling him, "Hey, sometimes I find a stray on my balcony. If you see him, do not be afraid." But again, she didn't say anything. She just hummed until the blender was spotless and sat it on a drying cloth. Letting it go, he laid back down.

Ana relaxed, releasing all the stress of the day. *Theo,* he summoned their bond. The stripes on his cheeks swell as he dropped all restraint, delicately opening the flood gates and testing how for it would take him. He was carefully not to get washed away.

Staring at the ceiling, a memory slipped into his vision.

"Will you take me with you?" he heard little Theo ask, only to be broken by a flash of light. And again. He did this repeatedly as each movement in the nearby mirror distracted him out of the trance.

Aggravated, Ana went to fix the mirror's angle and discovered a slip of paper wedged in the wooden trim under the emerald shall, a detail that had previously gone unnoticed. The layer of dust told its age. The small note read, "Gone hunting. Don't hold your breath waiting for me. Love, your only."

The letterhead of the stationary belonged to a man named Chadwick Joans, L.T.C. Ana's heart settled. For as long as he had known Marcy, there was never a man in her life. "Chadwick Joans?" he whispered. The name was almost familiar.

"Please don't touch that," Marcy requested.

"I'm sorry. I didn't know you were married," said Ana, placing the note in her hand.

"That was a long time ago," she mumbled, returning the letter back into the groove of the mirror, back where Mr. Joans had left it. "He was a Venator. Very particular, he kept his work and his life separate. He always expressed the possibility of not returning home from his job. One day he didn't, and this is all that remains of the man I love."

"I'm sorry, Marcy."

"Don't be. I do what I can to honor him, carry on his ways, and teach others his ideals; to keep him alive in some way." A crackle formed in her voice.

Ana smiled. "You mean to tell me all this neutrality was not you. I don't believe that."

She beamed at his tease. "We shared the philosophy, but Chad was bolder than me. He magnified my hope for peace and prosperity. As an elite, he fought for his beliefs, took pride in his efforts with the company, and strived to do what he thought was right. Ironically, the day he doubted was the day he disappeared." It was evident the pain hasn't healed.

Ana reached out to her with his hand and she took it as always. From there, he led her to the cushions, asking, "If you don't mind me asking, what happened?"

Marcy sat with him. It took her a second to consider what to tell him. It was, after all, an Order secret. She licked her lips, refused the liquid's request to escape her eyes, and then said, "There are several stories about what happened to the point I don't know what to believe. The official C.O.V. report says he died in the line of battle. Sasha discovered his team dispatched on a secret mission…" Her tongue clicked, held her breath resisting the tears, and then released the fatal words, "and never returned. If she had not taken hid gun, maybe he would have."

She took in a jagged breath, preparing herself. "Ana, I buried him — well I buried the remains I was given. I even got my revenge. I started a new life and built this wonderful place. My grieving had finally ended. Then, one afternoon, I came in and found the note had changed."

She retrieved a slip of paper from the place closest to her heart and divided the folds. On the stained page were the words, "I am alive and love you well," written in blue ink, the same jittery font. Ana's heart squeezed. He knew the pain she felt. It was prevalent when he recently saw Geda. He embraced it when he claimed Sarolt.

Marcy's voice lowered to a steady whisper in case of those listening, "Whatever happened, he is not the same as he used to be."

Ana's brow scrunched, trying to understand what she meant. "The muree. Is he a mutant?"

She shook her head. "I don't know. He won't let me see him but I can tell when he has been here. He moves things around like he used to. Just the other day, I found this." Marcy opened the drawer to the coffee table and pulled out a roll of paper towels mostly consumed. At the flap, there was a poor recreation of a scroll seal drawn quickly in candle soot. Opened, streaks of blood littered the absorbent paper in multiple directions.

Ana immediately recognized what this was meant to replicate, the queen's scroll, an item passed down the royal line. The makeshift scroll pushed him into the chair with new conspiracy, and from there, a new plan bloomed.

Unbelievable! An artifact written by divine beings, collectively violated by the True King, would indeed contain a secret he, a male royal, could not access, a secret that could grant Ana freedom. Ana knew precisely where it was hidden.

Marcy saw a smile surface on his face. "It seems crazy, but I believe it may be a sign," she said.

How did I not think of that? Ana nodded, nearly speechless. "I think you are right."

"Regardless of how haunting these little interactions can be, they give me comfort. He still exists, among what he takes and leaves behind," added Marcy.

"Still an answer to what happened and how to help him would be better," sympathized Ana.

"Now Raymond is looking for him."

"Why?" She shook her head. "Do you want me to find out?" he offered.

"No. Chad is at peace. He is living the way he knows how. I don't want to stir anything up. I don't want to scare him off. When he is ready, he will join us from the shadows. I am always open for his return whenever he is ready." Marcy took one last look at her sacred letter and returned it over her heart.

A moment of silence fell upon them. Ana couldn't help but feel responsible for her husband's absence, being mutant and all. He looked down at a scar on his hand. It wasn't until she got up to make tea that he said, "You know that Theo knows about me?"

"Of course," she chirped from the kitchen. "He is the one who told me." She cut around the corner, returning with a hot cup. "I vividly remember how we met. To think someone like you casually found me. The Devil had walked through my door and offered his help. How could I refuse?"

Ana let out a little laugh. "Theo said something similar once."

Her interests peaked. "Really?" She shared a sorrowful memory. Which one would he tell?

"Yeah. Did I ever tell you how I became Theo's caregiver?" asked Ana.

"It was a bus crash."

"Is that all you know?"

"It is what I was told."

"Hm."

"What is it?"

"There is a correlation between Chad and Theo's story."

"How so?"

"Roughly ten years ago, Father unified his sons. We were brothers three: the Devil, the Reaper and the Disease. We were tight until the Disease, Casimir, wanted to spread. His desire reached new heights around the time Chad disappeared. He affected Theo. He may have affected you too."

"I remember him. He caused the mass Hysteria. If I run into him, I'll kill him."

"You don't have to. He is already dead," Ana said confidently. "When the bus crashed, I saved Theo, but I also took him from Casimir."

She tensed. "What did he do to Theo?"

Ana would rather not say. "Theo never said," he answered,

which wasn't entirely a lie.

Ana recalled the time when Theo was barely a teenager, like it was yesterday. The public intercity bus they shared had missed the desirable exit on the freeway and decided to turn around for it. He recalled how the boy's nervous grip grew tighter, how ignorant the other passengers were to the impending danger, nonetheless the one on board with them.

Ana recollected the child's despair. He could taste it from rows away and chose to take advantage of it. Dagger in hand, the mutant king left his seat, luggage, and everything behind to fulfill his master's order, "kill the boy."

Suspected of contamination, the boy was all but 5 feet tall, with brown hair and a bruised complexion. The clothes he wore were not his. Aside from the metal column, Theo clutched tightly to his shoulder bag, and clung to the security of music. However, the rhythm did not subside his paranoia. Hyperawareness kept him tense.

As he got closer, Ana could see the emotions stir within Theo. When his eyes met Ana's dual gaze, he did not falter. He was enamored by their difference. Then he saw Ana's in-human difference. His eyes grew wide with fear, and breath left his chest. Dread captured him and he shivered under the impression of being captured.

However, Theo's trepidation was not brought on by the mutant before him but instead influenced by the semi barreling toward them with no desire to stop. When Ana's gaze returned to the boy, Theo's eyes did not beg for him to stop. In fact, he welcomed the beast and the blade in hand.

"You were there to kill him? Publicly?" Marcy interrupted.

Ana explained, saying, "Bog loved Theo. They played all the time. In revolt, Casimir took Theo captive. He became Casimir's obsession, the object of controlling the monarchy, but he underestimated the boy's capabilities. Eventually, Theo got away. The Cousin King hunted him down. In response, Bog tasked us with punishing Casimir, undoing all that he had done, including culling the boy out of fear of corruption. I believed it was the best thing to do until I met Theo. I quickly saw things in a new light and to this day, I suffer the repercussions of defying duty."

Marcy's gut twisted. She could only imagine the repercussion Ana endured for not harvesting a beautiful soul like Theo. "What happened next?" she pushed for more.

Theo was not afraid of the demon overshadowing him, the weapon in his hand, nor his intentions. What broke him was the proximity of the creature he deserted now barreling toward them.

"I still remember Casimir's desperate expression," Ana whispered.

Casimir, the Cousin King crowned by Sarolt, shared a similar heart to her. He knew the impact would cost him the life he wanted, but keeping the boy from Ana was worth it.

Casimir blew the horn, warning the boy to move, but Theo couldn't. He was paralyzed. He was sandwiched by death on all sides and was forced to make a choice between two evils.

Unexpectedly, the boy opened his core to the wielder of the blade. He gave himself to the Devil. "I'm ready." The innocent surrender disarmed the holy aggressor. As the dagger rolled from Ana's fingertips, he cradled the child from the collision.

The semi-truck slammed into the bus, lurching Theo and Ana forward. All around, people were jolted in unnatural ways. Twisted and crippled, they were shaken from their seats. Ana pivoted differently, missing Casimir's reach by inches. The impact flung the two from the bus while the Cousin King went down with the wreckage.

Their flesh hit the pavement with little sympathy. The road's teeth broke open Ana's hand trying to ease their tumble. Under him, he found the boy clinging to him. He was safe. Thankfully, only his shoulder suffered the impact.

Not far from them, the bus teetered on the edge of the freeway, full of broken people, and inevitably fell into the traffic below. Screams ignited the carnage that followed. Forty lives for the price of one.

The day was host to a multitude of sin. Instead of pulling wounded survivors from the wreckage, Ana watched for Casimir's survival and prepared for a fight that did not come. There was no sign of life. The assault vehicle remained lifeless on its side. There was no metal creaking with struggle nor blood to signal his position. Along with the blade, Casimir was lost, consumed by fire.

Ana looked upon death from the edge, which he had stolen a child. The heat of the flames scalded the eyes, a warmth he had endured numerous times, and each time the fire left an engraving in his heart. This time it was the boy.

Theo peeled himself off the pavement, wincing the shoulder burn. The contents of his bag cluttered the road. The strings connecting him to the aggressor king had been severed. The mp3 player beneath his hip had cracked and died, yet he was still alive, all thanks to the stripped man, the tiger.

Thankful, Theo looked at Ana. The flames of the passengers had reached the height of the overpass, embellishing the Devil's stature.

"'There, death stood before me, held me under the euphotic surface of life, and risked it all to keep the surface from breaking. In his stillness, I witnessed flickers of the flames in the frays of his fabric and sought to capture him, tether the ends of his rupture.' I remember Theo's words like it was yesterday.

Under his oath of guardianship, Theo confessed his heart to me. When I saved him, he knew I wasn't human, and ever since, he devoted his life to helping me keep mine." Ana clung to the words recited out of love, but it was apparent there was something else contaminating his reminiscence.

"What is it?" Marcy pressed.

Ana took a breath, hoping she hadn't seen his doubt. He couldn't hide anything from her. "Recently, he learned I was a royal."

"So."

"Casimir was royal. He doesn't talk about it but I know he harbors disdain against the royals. To him, I am no different from Casimir," Ana said. *I can't become Casimir.*

Marcy quickly corrected him. "That's not true!"

"Perhaps not, but I fear Theo has lost faith in me because I am a royal. He saw what I did when I saved him and witnessed the potential again recently. It scares him."

Marcy wiggled her finger. "Theo's loyalties are strong, and your faith in him should not waver." She was right. "I'll admit, this separation certainly has intensified your vulnerabilities and potentially his. Without you by his side, he cannot protect you so easily. You are suffering remote proximity, thus creating false doubts."

Ana was surprised. "You are familiar with guardianship?"

"Not completely but in the past, I have seen what it does to partners that distance themselves. Romantic or not, the yearning can be detrimental, and the mental instability can make your condition nuclear. You need to go see him," she advised.

"The game is tonight," he reminded.

"And you can't go because of the queen."

Ana fell back into his lounge. "Yep."

But it wasn't just that. He had raised that boy. The last thing he wanted was to see him get hurt.

As Marcy opened her book to the night's adventure, Ana recounted the stars of the night Theo proposed to be his guardian.

It was around this time of year, late May. Flowers had bloomed and the night carried the warmth of the day. The atmosphere rustled with a restless city. The twisting highways above them rhythmically hummed with speeding traffic but nothing was as serene as the patch of wild flowers they played in.

Lounging in the petals, Ana waited for Bog's order. As a nice breeze swept the underpass, the colorful weeds tickled his cheeks causing him to lose count of the stars twinkling through the gaps of the concrete freeways. Peace had fallen upon them like dew.

Unlike the tiger, the young boy could not sit still. A frequent crunch soothed Ana further as Theo snagged flowers from their stems and decorated the mutant's curls with decapitated flora heads and breaded necks.

When the child had finished flowering his savior's hair, he interrupted his stargaze. "Are you listening?"

"You asked me to take you with me." He was listening.

"Yeah.... I can do this. I can help you, if only you'd let me. Accept me." The boy was mature with his words. After his innocence was consumed by the Cousin King, he was a shell filled with sharp inspiration. What Theo didn't know was Ana had already accepted him, but was hesitant. To Ana, shackling the boy to him would not be any different from Casimir.

The sky was bright, along with his eyes, a perfect night for a claiming. Ana gave him a warning. "I am not the only tiger in this commitment you wish to establish. Yes, you would be bound to me but also to my service to others. You will be an extension of my power and, by that, a branch of our master. You are asking a lot you are unaware of."

Theo sat back into the grass beside the lounging beast. "If I am unaware, then will you show me?"

"I will. Know your request must be approved by our master. Even if it's not, I accept your devotion so long as you welcome mine." Theo gave him the biggest smile. Ana counted the stars in his eyes. *Theo.*

Spontaneously, the phone in Ana's left pocket chimed, bringing him out of his dream. Breathing life back into his lungs, Ana's sight was blinded by darkness. Marcy had gone back downstairs, shutting off the lights as she went.

He pulled the phone from his pocket. It was a message from Bog, "Meet me tomorrow in Crescent City. We need to speak." Ana sighed, falling back into the fabric. That's when he found an unusual item resting on his chest.

It was the makeshift paper towel scroll. *What's this doing here?* Ana thought, perhaps he grabbed it in the middle of the night. Skeptical, he placed it on the coffee table… next to the makeshift paper towel scroll?

There are two of them?

Instantly, movement caught Ana's eye. A shadow in the shape of a man moved from in front of the covered mirror and walked past the arm of the chair and into the kitchen. Ana was frozen.

The man was unlike anything Ana had ever seen, no creature of this reality. He was not human, not Malum, and certainly not a ghost, but his body was all the above, physical, consumed by darkness, and soulless. As quick as he appeared, he disappeared, leaving Ana to decipher what had happened.

Ana released the breath concreted in his chest. *That must have been Chadwick, just as Marcy warned,* he told himself. *He showed himself to me.* Ana couldn't believe it. He took another breath to settle himself. *The scroll, he wants me to find it, to use it.*

His brow narrowed with insult. *Only a queen can use the scroll.*

Is he suggesting I kneel before Sarolt, and sacrifice myself for an ally... an ally I could use. But will she listen when I call on her? Will she see beyond the rage she holds for me? he considered, rolling the small red charm of his necklace in his fingers. *Oh! If only Chad could speak, tell me what he knows.*

Ana looked again, but the shadow man was nowhere in sight. He sighed, exhausted. He would see what Bog wanted before making a decision. Fireworks thundered from the Arena. Soon, they would have to get back to work.

CHAPTER 16

The Deciding Match

On the night of the monthly Decider, thousands flock to Crescent City to witness a game between human Falcons and mutant Wildcats as they battle over the remaining monthly surplus. After last month's unexpected victory, the revenge of the mutants was heavily advertised days before, and no one was going to miss a slaughter of a good time.

The Arena stadium suffered to accommodate the demand for attendance. All who can scream were present for the event. People bottlenecked at the gates, making crowd control all the more difficult. Lines extended outwards in both directions, to Gibbous and Crescent, moving at a estimated staggering pace of one person per minute.

Management was forced to utilize unethical measures to ensure everyone's safety in the event of an attack, whether a Malum attraction to the mass congregation, a beacon igniting from an anxiety episode, or an aggressor birth incited by the results of tonight's game. To meet this, mutants were segregated from humans and placed in the topmost areas. In case of an emergency, humans, slower to escape, were limited to lower seating. The quickest exit routes were tailored to each group's physical capabilities and endurances. To help in the endeavor, C.O.V. agents patrolled the aisles, an unusual detail.

The exterior televisions aired the first announcements. "Welcome to this month's Decider, marking the 350th game since its congressional launch thirty years ago," cheered News Anchor Wyatt.

"Shit," hissed Breanna. "At this rate, we will never get in." She wasn't the only one that felt that way. So did Geda and the hundreds still waiting in line.

Geda watched the screens dispel the historical significance of the "fair" fight but quickly tuned it out, concerned by her friend's agitated state.

Breanna collected herself. "Geda, Thank you for coming with me. I know you don't like these things, but I really didn't want to stand in line alone. You see how bad it is. I don't know any of these people," expressed Breanna. Just an hour before, she asked Geda to escort her when Tiffany canceled to write her paper. For her safety, Geda felt compelled to join.

"Anytime," she replied.

The lines stopped moving again. Breanna huffed, "Oh! Come on, people. I want to see Theo."

Realistically, the reminder of Theo playing influenced Geda's attendance. She had to show him support after all. And not to mention her support for Darin.

Despite Breanna's affection for mutanity, this was her first attendance at the stadium. Like Geda, she had a strong opinion against the sport. However, last month demonstrated there was hope, a chance for humans to win. And, like many, she regretted not seeing the victory firsthand. This time she would not make the same mistake. If only she could get in.

The announcements continued, "As you can see, the seats are warming up as citizens flock to the stadium to witness tonight's players. Tensions are building as victory can be in any-one's favor," illustrated John. "Will the Crescent City Wildcats reclaim their reign as undisputed victors? Or will the Gibbous City Falcons protect their championship title? We are all itching to find out."

"Regardless, this will go down in history as the most leg-endary event of the century. You do not want to miss this," chimed Wyatt.

Geda and Breanna were going to if they didn't do anything. The potential of disappointment became a stiff protrusion on Geda's ego. She had hoped to cater the experience for the woman who recently became her friend.

Geda looked around, scanning the commotion for an easier way in, as did everyone else. Unfortunately, they saw everything she did, including the agents cutting in line to pass through the checkpoint, undisguised and loaded.

Then an idea popped into her brain. Scanners at the entrance enforced commissions. She looked at the mark on her thumb, 7541. *Technically I am an agent, but will I register as one?*

She lingered to act on it but suddenly chose to. *Oh, screw it! Life is too short not to find out.* Geda grabbed Breanna's hand. "Let's go," she said and stepped out of line. Just as she did, a dark figure cut her off. "Oh!" she recoiled.

"Pardon me," apologized the hooded man and he continued down the path she had planned. Apparently, she was not the only one who had this idea. Geda shook off the interaction and followed him to the stadium gates.

Geda swallowed. Her heart was in her throat.

How is this working? she thought. Her eyes never left the fo-cus point of their charge. Something about this man made her attentive to his every detail. How was he able to walk ahead of everyone?

Successfully at the gates, the hooded man was recognized by one of the synthetic guards. "Peacekeeper," bowed one guard. The hooded man nodded in return.

The man, and the girls unknowingly behind him, were expedited to the terminals for scanning. Under the register, his left hand tensed. Focusing, a dagger insignia emerged from a deep dermal layer, embellishing skin with imperfection and staining human color with malus.

Mutant, Geda identified.

The Peacekeeper swiped his hand under the reader. It scanned.

No way! She gasped.

Entry required chips. Everyone had to pay, embed themselves with the dagger symbol, but this man entered with nothing more than a mental image. The Peacekeeper sensed a defensive energy swirl behind him and turned to see what it was.

His eyes meet the girl he crossed, Geda. She spotted the heavy lines in his eyes, the crystal structure within them; tiger. He was genuine, a true mutant. Immediately, her resistance soothed. She was wrong. This was a warrior of the old gods, a being who fought for humanity. This man had already paid the price to enter.

"Next!" called a guard.

"Finally, let's go," ushered Breanna. She pounced forward, scanned, and entered. Geda was next.

She stepped up.

The same guard recognized her. "My lady," he bowed.

Geda nodded to him and placed her left hand under the light and scanned her unique digits. *Bling!* She was free to enter.

They were finally inside the Arena and right on time. The ceremonial announcements were coming to a close. It was almost time for the game to begin.

Competitors made their way onto the green. Slowly, both teams emerged from their secure locker rooms and circled their opponents. Touchless taunting was encouraged to fuel the fight. Mutants snarled, displaying their deadly teeth. Insidious smiles from the humans ejected their horror. Jeers all around, the two teams sized up each other.

Aside from the familiar faces, Theo detected something rather disturbing about the group.

"What is it, little Devil?" growled the creature circling him. Little Devil was the name Datura Thorne always used to tease Theo. "You seem distracted today." He tussled, flexing the rose thorn covered muscles.

"Your team is short two members," Theo explained. "There must be eleven." Teammates within earshot of Theo tuned into the detail.

"Ooooh!" voiced Datura. The mutant was impressed. "Is that so?" On either side of him, the two missing players materialized with exhales.

Theo's skin crawled.

"They recruited new members," shuddered Darin, stepping up to Theo's side.

"Specialized in Cloak, we will have to use their breath against them," informed Lion Sabre. "Watch your feet. They may be invisible but they are not silent."

As swiftly as they appeared, the two mutants disappeared.

Theo frowned. This fight will take every bit of his training and then some. He has never faced a cloaked mutant before, let alone two simultaneously. There was barely a blade of grass to indicate the phantom's position. His nose was blinded by arena commodities. Food stands, firecrackers, and flashing lights nullified his focus. It was a perfect setting for the Wildcat's new tactic and enough to make Theo feel pressured.

Almost instinctively, both teams lined up on the center line as the game's judge took the field. With the ball under his elbow, the referee took his time. Once there, Datura continued his annoying teases, this time aiming at the referee. "Come on, Roth. Wish us a good game."

Though mutant, Referee Roth cared less about formalities, a fine example of Separatist mentality and a perfect specimen to determine the game. He was unbiased, even to his own kind.

Finally, the announcements transitioned. "The teams are lined and ready," said spokesman Wyatt. "And here they are, tonight's representatives, both Queen Sarolt and Lord Raymond Sambuca." The announcer handed it off to those now joining them.

"Good evening, ladies and gentlemen, human and mutant," Sarolt welcomed. "Tonight is a special night, marking the anniversary of the Arena and the declaration of sport."

The microphone was then handed to Raymond. "Tonight will go down in history as one of the toughest battles this Arena has ever seen!" he cheered. "Humanity must prevail against a force analogous to the fall of Arnireth, a theatrical display of modern cliché. As a reminder, these games do not depict a superior race or genetics but a superior mindset and heart. Now…"

Sharing the mic, Raymond and Sarolt said in unison, "Let the game begin!" initiating the night's event. The crowd screamed.

At the signal, Roth lifted the pitch towards the sky, and the ball was smacked in the human's favor just as the representatives took their seats.

Raymond's brow raised. "Oh! A fortunate start. Does this foretell the outcome of the event?" He teased the queen.

Sarolt chuckled as someone handed her a drink. "You have forgotten the purpose of the Arena, my Lord. It is not about the game. It is about the players. Tsk. Victory often depends on the right player, and what better way to find that being than the Arena."

Raymond swallowed dry, *Right,* silently admitting his recruitment through the monthly games. However, Sarolt's reminder was more of a warning. They were not alone and to be on the lookout for the True King.

I'm sure that man child is nearby, observing, waiting. She scanned the crowds, but there was no sign of the inconspicuous creature. Sarolt sighed and returned to the man to her right for more conversation but found him distracted. She discerned where his attention resided, on a young albino lady, rows away.

The girl? His so-called daughter. He's concerned for her. So much so that his sight never leaves her.

Not far from the royal box, the Peacekeeper statued as the crowd swung themselves wild. People flailed their arms and banners, formed signs of representation with their extremities, banged their heads, and whipped their hair to the lively music orchestrating beneath the royal bench. The one thing they did not do was leave their precious seats, which made locating C.O.V. agents easier, just as he wanted.

Venators remained active. Evenly distributed, they marched the aisles indiscriminately. With belts only loaded with handheld weapons. Regardless of limited weaponry, each one was ready to act, be it human or mutant causing the disruption. He wondered, *Which would misbehave first?* Perhaps it would be him, the observant Peacekeeper.

Hunting a hunter, he analyzed each one, seeking the wielder of the so-called King's Blade, the Lioness. He exhaled in frustration. *She's here. I know it. But where?* He was convinced, but his eyes did him no service.

In such gatherings, there was bound to be one creature, like him, to harbor emotions for a particular Venator, an element

C.O.V. mitigated through design. Instead of the usual military fatigues, each Venator was dressed head to toe in specially designed armor. He diligently scanned each agent but it was impossible to distinguish them beyond their weapons. From balaclavas to boots, a thin Kevlar body suit protected the soldier from bites and fatal stabs, maximizing agility with minimal equipment required for crowd control.

Unfortunately, this meant agents lacked the typical poison and antidote pack they generally carried, the crutch that kept them intact during a mutant confrontation, a highly fatal exchange. He catered his approach accordingly, acknowledging their sacrifice for the occasion. Still, he would appreciate the ease of finding the notorious woman more.

Suddenly, the ball was spiked into Theo's grasp. Nestled perfectly against his forearm, he stampeded through a narrow gap. His knees tucked against his chest, hips loose, and muscles loaded. His speed barely outmatched his opponent's. He scored. The crowd cheered as he dropped the ball at the try.

"Theon Bastille has done it again, making that a 12 point lead for the Gibbous Falcons!" cried announcer John.

As Theo passed the goal line, Datura was hot on his heels. At a moment's breath, he congratulated him, "Ha! You've been working out but don't think I'll let that stop me." But his eyes weren't so nice.

Theo acknowledged the challenge, and rejoined the defensive line.

Datura pounded his chest. "Now, show me! Where do you keep such power?" he growled for show, intentionally fanning the flames of Theo's drive.

It came to him. *Ana.*

Theo exhaled.

Punt! The ball was hot for the taking.

Datura secured the grab with a sly sneer. Missing by inches, Theo stumbled but recovered.

He planted his feet and exploded with all his might.

Fifteen yards in, Datura was within grappling range.

But before Theo could make the lunge, his body suddenly stopped. His speed was yanked from him, halted by something. Unpadded, Theo hit the ground with the same intensity. "Eerrm!"

Then at last minute, he remembered the invisible land mines of the opposing team. Dread flooded him. How could he have forgotten?

Reeling on the ground, Theo registered the defender's grasp and looked at his foot. Exhaling, the man appeared. It was the video store clerk, Ammon. He thought he recognized him initially. Now, up close and personal, it was undeniable.

"It's you!" Theo exclaimed.

"Yes, but this time, I will not be so sympathetic." Ammon placed his other hand further up his shin.

A bolt of shock traveled through Theo's brain realizing what he was doing. *Don't break it!* his mind screamed.

As soon as the thought flared in his mind, Ammon pressed down on his shin and swiftly lifted Theo's ankle beyond the tension of bone, snapping the support, tearing muscle, and immobilizing the athlete.

The break was so violent that it could be heard from the stands, along with Theo's screams. The audience cringed with glee. A few, including Geda, stood in shock. A couple vomited their potluck. In all, people were outraged. They roared at the awesome gruesomeness planted by the mutant team. Even the queen was appalled and pleased.

"Yikes! That's gotta hurt!" commentated one of the spokesmen.

A sign was made on the field by one of the players, generously calling for medical help as the game continued.

"You know what that means, John?" added the other spokesman, Wyatt.

"Theo has been disqualified and will be pulled from the field," John bantered back.

Theo's inhale screamed agony, and his eyes surged with discipline resistance. His body, however, tingled with the endurance of vessel damage and muscle displacement. Aftershocks pulsated in his teeth and raging nerves stung his fingertips, as he suffered brain blow from his securities being taken so quickly. After all, he was human. He had no chance.

Curled, he defenselessly avoided the players charging the field until Darin and Sabre got to him. To Theo's amusement, the pain was paid back. Within seconds, Lion Sabre crashed into Ammon harder than any man could withstand, knocking the mutant inoperable, probably forever.

"Back at' cha!" Theo barked, cursing the following surge crippling him.

Darin rushed to Theo's side. "Theo!" He grabbed his hand and squeezed.

Theo squeezed back. "I'm alright." Then came another surge of pain. He winced.

"Here comes the stretcher," said Darin. "Don't worry. We can finish this. You've done enough," he assured but Theo was not so sure. In reality, along with Lion Sabre, he had done everything. Three-quarters of the points scored were his alone.

He was thankful to have such a good team, but he knew once he left the field, the Gibbous City Falcons would not be able to maintain the established lead. They would lose. And as such, he reflected this loss onto his guardianship capabilities.

His pride shriveled. *I can't help him,* he slowly cried as the paramedics took him away. He was ashamed and helpless, unable to support Ana in the storm he voluntarily stepped into. Just like the game, an unhappy ending was inevitable for his dearest mutant.

Sarolt witnessed the boy's expression and a terrible pain grew in her chest. She, too, knew the impotent root of failure. "It's rather unfortunate how a civilization must suffer the consequence of one person's actions. What kind of society have we preserved?"

Raymond was put off by her empathy. "That is the nature of mutanity."

"Such is the reason to serve nature."

"I do not disagree," the Lord acknowledged, "but the unnatural must fall for nature to rise. It will take more than us to shatter the system. It will take the children to insight insubordination and extinguish the institutional debauchery I placed to keep them naive. When that happens, I will no longer be able to protect them."

"Then they will not need protection. We will. We must prepare for their awakening," she defended.

"It's too late," Raymond shot back. "The awakening has already begun."

"Even Sasha?" asked Sarolt.

"She has always been awake. Even the kings are turning in their sleep." This caused Sarolt's eye to slide in his direction. Raymond quickly interjected, "I hope to harvest their resources should they display interest."

The Lord's suggestion left her considering what he meant for the remainder of the game. *So, Raymond hopes to ally with a king to take down the Holy Monarch? He might be onto something.*

Following Theo's accident, excitement in the crowd grew. Foul shots ignited a primal fury among the hungry. To live up to the hype of last month's game, citizens itched for the violence, demanded bloodshed. If they deemed it, the incapacitated, like Ammon, could become fodder for the crew or confetti for show.

As the chaos grew, Venators made their move to calm the masses. All except one. Unlike the others, this agent winced and recoiled at the athlete's injury. From the Peacekeeper's experience, there was only one elite hunter with a strong sense of humanity, Sasha.

He looked closer, filtering the agent's characteristics to confirm her identity. They possessed a similar build to the Lioness; same height, broad-shouldered, flat-chested, a physical representation of endurance.

The weapons holstered also reflected her preference: sub-machine gun pistol on the dorsal strap, standard backup pistol on the hip, but the signature blade and long range rifle was missing. Not exact, but the suspect matched the profile more than others.

That must be her, the Peacekeeper glared. he found his target.

It wasn't long before the agent felt the mutant's gaze and turned. Seeing it was him, she fled.

She's on the move! He jumped to chase.

He rushed to the first exit on his right. He knew the ins and outs of the Arena, knew exactly where she was headed, and planned a path to intercept her.

Speed uncloaked his identity. His shoes squeaked at every turn, unable to slow his run, leaving the wall to compensate. One step on the brick and he straightened to build more speed. Left around two corners, right through the service halls, and he crashed head-on with the escaping agent.

His hands filled with the Lioness's fabric, lifting her off the ground. Heavier than he remembered, he slammed her against the wall hard, knocking all thought from her mind. Something about her was different. He had done this numerous times, but it never went like this. Her instincts should have reacted but didn't.

It's not her, he realized. Disappointed, the Peacekeeper unveiled the agent and found the face of a man, her twin brother. "You?"

"Ariel!" winced the victim, begging to be released. "Er! You have returned."

Ariel scoffed. He couldn't believe he was fooled. "Yaromir Currant. What are you doing here?" The Peacekeeper growled, letting him go.

Falling to the floor, the priest replied, "Observing. For my master."

"You chose to take her place?" Vocalizing it, Ariel's dismay grew. He thought for sure he had her.

"I needed anonymity. We have the same training. Filling in was easy."

"Unless you deal with someone like me!" Ariel barked back. "That was incredibly dangerous. There are others who hold grudges against her. Unlike me, they wouldn't have stopped. Where is she? Sasha was meant to be here?"

Yara smiled at his persistence. "You have gotten rusty."

"Don't anger me, priest."

"I searched for you, you know, quite recently. I was sure if I found you, freed you, you would find her on your own. Instead, when I ventured into the outlands, all I found was your destroyed coffin. You woke on your own and still you haven't found her. The pale prince is blind."

"You were looking for me? Why?" asked Ariel.

"You are an omen. Your resurrection inevitably breeds destruction," answered Yara.

"Is that you want?"

The priest nodded. "Death surrounds the Devil. Life will wage war with the shadows. The time has come and the Reaper without his scythe is just a Peacekeeper. You were so confident I was her. How did you know I wasn't?"

"She is faster than you," defended the mutant.

Clearing his throat, Currant's voice returned to normal. "More like, you are more receptive to her expression than mine. With the slightest weakness she exposed, you wouldn't have pressed so hard," the priest added.

The mutant curled his nose. "You are wasting my time. Where is she?" he asked.

"Where she always is, at Geda's side. Sasha mentors her."

Geda? 7541. Ariel immediately translated the name into a code he's seen before. Those numbers were on the girl's hand following him into the stadium. *What are the odds?*

Spontaneously, Ariel left the priest and rushed back to the stadium seats.

Left out of the service halls, right around two corners, down the corridors, out the exit door, and into the revolting crowd. Albino, Ariel found the pale-complected girl bearing the institutional name 7541. As expected, she was not far from the royal box or Raymond's old gaze, but again, the Lioness was nowhere in sight.

Ariel sighed. *Sasha.*

Since his involuntary disappearance, there seemed to be a supernatural repulsion between them, most likely brought on by the queen now coordinating their collision. Despite his repeated efforts, reaching her seemed futile.

CHAPTER 17

Factional Strategy

Crescent City was still buzzing with energy the next morning. After the deciding outcome, citizens flocked to the west for parties. Comparable to Memorial Day celebrations, most newfound rations were consumed in hours. It will forever be known as "the night mutanity conquered humanity."

Journalists raved on about last night's turn of events. Broadcasts echoed from open doors. "My question is, why does Lord Sambuca allow mutants to participate in the game? Why do we accept such inequality of power on the field?" the interviewer questioned harshly.

It seemed like every human had the same question, and after a morning of hungry reporters, the gentle public figure Wyatt Brannon was not so politically polite. "You saw the game, didn't you? You watch every game and hyper-analyze it to your perspectives, albeit to ultimately incite critical thinking among the community but it is delivered to uneducated citizens, misinterpreted, and then used to fuel unnecessary fires."

Married to a mutant, Wyatt was not too keen on anti-mutant propaganda or the use of information within the Oasis. Thus why they became reporters, to maintain information accuracy.

"Okay, now. Okay." John Brannon patted Wyatt's arm, trying to calm him. It wasn't working.

Wyatt exerted more, saying, "Do you realize these are how games are played? The playing field will never be equal if you have a diverse group. Some will have strengths and weaknesses, and it is up to the opportunists to take advantage of such attributes. That is real life. Raymond has honored it by enforcing nondiscrimination among the players."

"That's right," John nodded in the back.

"You are upset because, for once, you got a glimpse of success and, with little effort, it was taken by a genetic advantage. Now, I know you haven't said this but based on previous interviews I know it's coming; are you directing me to the suggestion of limiting the Decider candidates?"

"I am," Tiffany admitted.

"Then consider this," Wyatt insisted, "if we — I'll just use the word — discriminate abilities among mutants and say, 'You can't fight 'cause of cloak,' then why don't we do the same thing with human athletes. 'You can't play because you are a Venator or you're strong or from the outlands.' You see what I'm saying?"

"That isn't what I mean," Tiffany refuted.

Tired, Wyatt provided a closing statement, "My point is, the Decider is open to anyone willing to sacrifice themselves for their city as representation of their sacrifice thirty years ago, which is what they did last night."

Silence fell on the interview, forcing Tiffany to end, "Thank you for taking the time to reflect on last night's events with us. Listeners at home can find John and Wyatt on the late-night Brannon show and throughout the day on Channel 15 News. You have been listening to 94.3 Radyo Oasis." Music proceeded, brightening the air.

Following the celebrations, the sidewalks of Crescent City were bustling. Shop owners prepared for a new wave of commerce. Street stands opened on every corner. It was barely noon, and people already filled the streets for tarot card readings and amateur plays. Even the alleyways were full of life, and the cats that typically coward in the shadows partook in the enjoyment.

Ana's face was the only one that showed any signed discontent. He had spent the morning in the hospital with Theo, casting his leg. Now, he had to face Bog. Walking among the liveliness, he ignored the offered escapes. Bog had summoned him. Why?

Perhaps he had news about Raymond's offer to surrender Geda's tag in exchange for his son's life. Or did Bog catch wind of the Lioness's visit? Maybe he heard the spreading gossip of insurrection? Either way, he couldn't help but feel unsettled, especially after Theo's incident.

Further down the strip, things were close to normal. Cafes offered alfresco dining complimented by descent weather and a morning breeze aromatized by the flower shop next door. On the other side of the street, book shops wheeled out clearance adventures, and antiquity dealers illuminated their wildest findings.

Ana's pocket vibrated with a call. "Hello," he answered.

"I see you are doing well on your own," Bog replied. The statement was ridiculous. Ana was falling to pieces, barely holding on.

"I see," he did say, which meant literally. *He can see me,* Ana realized. *From where?* He searched for him.

His eyes scanned all the buildings and found the child across the street, dangerously close to the roof's edge with a phone to his ear.

Bog smiled. "Very good," he praised.

Ana noted the bistro a few feet away. "Come down, and we'll talk," he said, ending the call. As Ana took a seat and ordered, the child made his way to the lower section of his kingdom. Swinging on pipes and bouncing off signs, he stuck the landed on a pile of books the shopkeep just stacked.

"Oh, my!" she yelped.

"Thank you, miss." He waved.

Unaided, the boy crossed the street illegally, but no one dared to stop him. Mutants saw his authority. Humans, though typically disturbed by the combination of his youthfulness and mutanity, cooed at him. The enigma of mutant offspring stirred the mind during this exciting time.

While not in his usual garbs, Bog looked like he originated in the concrete jungle. His clothes wrinkled from exuded alleyway steam. His hands and face were smudged with filth. Evidently, he had been running the rooftops for a while.

"Enjoy," wished the server, sliding two cups onto the table.

"Thank you," Ana returned as the child jogged up and pulled back the opposite chair.

Without warning, Bog welcomed with heavy news. "Raymond has tagged the whole city."

"Jesus Christ," Ana cursed into his mug.

"Yes, my son. Which is why time is of the essence. I'm surprised Theo isn't tagged already."

Ana froze. *Why hasn't Raymond gone after Theo?* The fact he hasn't tried meant a lot to him. "What is Raymond planning?" he asked.

"He is building an army," blurted Bog.

But, once again, Ana saw uncertainty in his master's judgment. "Why?"

"Against me, of course! That much is obvious, or he is at least toying with me, hoping I will make a premature move, trying to rile a reaction from me similar to how he taunted you." The sad thing was, it was working which terrified Ana. His master was known for being destructive while emotional.

"What needs to be done?"

"I need the queen, and I need her now. Only her blood will give me full control of the army," Bog demanded. He could see the rejection in Ana's eyes. "Did you forget why she was claimed? All the heartache you went through to accomplish the deed?"

Ana almost rolled his eyes. *Accomplish? Like Sarolt's dark birth was meant to be an achievement.* He submitted and answered simply, "She was to be used for your purpose."

"I used you to turn her, to be a harvest for power, and to this day, she continues to evade my grasp. It is almost amusing, the way she always manages to escape."

Ana's gaze narrowed in to a glare pondering the accusation.

Bog leaned forward. "I need her now more than ever. You've had your fun. It is time to fulfill your end of the bargain."

His sudden demand simmered within Ana, trying to make sense of it's origins. An emotional god was a deadly god. His next move depended on the cause of his determination. *Raymond hasn't made a move yet. Bog must be aware of my insubordination. The game has begun.* Ana took a breath concealing any scheme.

"Do you understand what you are asking? It's a death sentence for me."

Bog didn't care. "At this point, it's a death sentence for you either way, but you know that."

Ana did. He knew the outcome of his commitment to madness. He also suspected Bog would use him as bait one day. He was okay with it. Of course, at the time, he had nothing to lose. Now he had Marcy, Theo, and Geda. After his death, all the love he was given will be replaced with shadows commanded by Bog. Ana won't be able to save them, just as Bog wants.

His master continued, "To be honest, I'm surprised you lasted this long, but of course, you had my help. Continue to trust me and I will see that your death will not be endless. While you are away, Theo and Geda will be protected by the church."

"I don't want them with the church," admitted Ana rather foolishly.

The child glared at him. "What are you saying?"

Ana took a breath. How could he explain his reasoning and come out unscathed? There was an obvious fault in his loyalty, backtracking now, would make it more apparent.

"I now understand Ariel's indifference," Ana said, intentionally triggering the child. "I understand the importance of the church, but the game we play to stay superior isn't worth the life we lose."

A vein emerged on the child's brow. Perhaps his abandonment during Ana's desperate state was too harsh. Bog exhaled through his nose to calm his fury. He was too quick to aggression at the mention of his other son, Ariel, a tactic Ana commonly used against him.

"Ariel is not a part of this. I will soon call you and there should be no hesitation when I do. We are finalizing the construction of your sanctuary. Currant will contact you for the final details." The child gulped the last of his coffee. "*Gah!* Help me capture her, and I will heal your suffering."

"And save Geda from her tag?"

The child's stare bounced back and forth, focusing on Ana's eyes before answering, "Ultimately."

"Alright then," Ana agreed thoughtlessly.

If Bog succeeds, Ana will sleep forever as the Malum commander. Bog's new control over the queen's army will blanket the Oasis. If it was time, he had to focus beyond surviving more than the day.

"Any ideas on the trap?" Ana fished.

"I cannot give you details. You will know when the time comes," Bog replied. "It will be marked with the shield symbol." He pushed a slip of paper across the table. On it were nine numbers. "Father Currant's new number."

Ana took it.

"You will bring the queen to me." The child's brow lifted, emphasizing his the seriousness, then spun his departure.

Looking at the paper, Ana tried to remain resolute. This was all happening too fast. He still had questions, all of which revolved around Geda. To die without knowing would be more damning.

The server appeared out of nowhere. "Are you ready for the check, sir?"

His dual eyes meet hers. A light blinked from her earpiece, similar to Leo's collar. Knowing Raymond may be listening, Ana replied, "Yes. Thank you, Olivia."

The mutant server set the ticket on the table and leaned in close. "May the king rest in peace," she wished, knowing what it would bring.

Ana smiled. The end was coming and the people were ready. "Until then, my lady. Spread the word," said Ana.

Flattered, she assured, "They hear you, your majesty." Olivia returned the dishes to the cafe.

Devouring apricity, Ana mulled over his next steps. Considering Bog's behavior, he was unsure whether to attend church alone. After all, he never fully trusted him. And Geda. She needs to be prepared if Bog tries anything.

CHAPTER 18

Recruitment of the Faithless

That afternoon, on Morana Street, the double doors of Heavenly Springs Community Church of God creaked open, encompassing Geda and Theo with the welcoming interior of the religious establishment.

Red carpet and ascents clashed with the white walls and ceiling. Mahogany wood and walnut trim amplified the contrast. Aside from the warm color of the pews, their sight was pulled to the massive crucifixion mortared against the tallest wall.

Geda was amazed. It was unlike any church she had been to before. The ambience stifled all evil from her heart. And silhouetted by the shadow of Christ was the man they came to see.

"Ana. I thought you were joking when you said you wanted us to attend church with you," Theo said, hobbling on one crutch.

Ana stood to greet them. "Surprising, I know. I usually meet Father Currant outside of holy ground. This is the first time in ages I've stepped into one of God's temples."

Immediately, Geda's mind referenced Ana's condition to religious stories, how, traditionally, the Devil and his kind were not allowed in the sanctity of the Christian Lord. *Ana was not evil but the darkness that plagued him was,* she painted internally. Geda wanted to ask Ana how he was feeling but was interrupted.

"We are meeting with Currant to go over Ana's last wishes," Theo informed her.

Though heavy hearted, she was surprised, honored even, that they would include her in such a private matter. "I don't know what to say."

Ana cut her off. "Don't be so formal. There are not many people left I can trust."

Theo could tell something was off. "What is it?" he asked.

Ana released the breath he held and admitted, "I am going to make a deal with the queen."

"Are you crazy?" Theo screamed silently, nearly attacking the mutant. All his hard work to keep Ana alive and safe from Sarolt, and now this? Theo was distraught.

Ana threw up his hands in defense. "Perhaps, but it is the only option beyond Raymond's offer," he said as if Geda wasn't there. "After the meeting, go to the bureau's vaults. See what you can find on shadow possession. Knowledge is key and may be the only thing that can save me when the time comes."

"Did something happen?"

Ana explained, "Bog wants the queen now."

"And you must expose yourself?" speculated Theo.

"I need her allegiance, albeit temporary. As queen, only she can wield the powers of mutanity. In the vault, there is a weapon, a scroll. If we can get it to her," he paused, lingering his gaze on Geda, "we can end this."

Before Theo could speak, Ana lifted a finger to his lips to hush the conversation. Someone he did not wish to overhear was now within earshot; someone at the back of the church.

Changing the subject, Ana pointed to the cast on Theo's right leg. "How's your leg?" he asked.

Theo groaned, replying, "Hurts worse than Casimir."

Geda watched the biggest smile form on Ana's face. Amused, he sat before God. Any jab at the Cousin King represented good spirits. In the pew, he leaned forward and began to whisper.

As Ana said his usual prayers, Theo squeezed Geda's arm. "I will go inform the priest we are here."

"Okay," she said and Theo scampered to the back.

Meanwhile, her gaze returned to the man kneeling before the Christian influence. Loose curls fell from behind his ears. At first glance, he was charming and delicate like a beautiful ivory statue.

Feeling out of place, she sat beside him, careful not to interrupt his concentration. Her ears picked up minor words in his conversation, but couldn't translate his concerns due to poor Latin skills. Geda wasn't one for prayer, but she respected his moral choice.

Conveniently, the massive chapel was sparsely populated, apart from one devout follower who entered shortly after. To be closer to God, the elder lady sat in the first row on the opposite side.

As they mumbled quietly, Geda's eyes wandered, devouring the aesthetics. Soft hums trickled down from the lofty ceilings like a healing mist. Under the crucifix, rows of candles lined the room's width, flickering and popping from hours of burn. Sunlight filtered through the stained glass windows, and fluttered the white walls with a sparkling rainbow glow. Her fingers danced in their projection.

On the second story, an ornate mural expanding the width of the balconies. Every inch depicted the rise and fall of human history and the Christian religion until the collapse of Arnireth. She leaned to see more but it was blocked by renovation scaffolding.

The church offered so much, her eyes had nowhere to rest. In her opinion, the location was grand and fit to serve someone like Ana. In fact, the more she did look around, the dizzier she got. Shapes started to appear where there were none previously and disappeared from where she was certain. She felt lost in her stationary position. It was sickening, breath seizing.

Across the aisle, harsh whisps from the older lady fell on Ana's ears. "Please," she begged, "let this harvest be bountiful." He peered over at her. Her quivering words were intentional, almost like an attack. His suspicions were correct.

The room's color melted away, the candle flames flickered out, and the once warm atmosphere turned cold. When Geda's strict posture began to slouch, Ana realized what the woman was doing. She targeted her. Through whispers, the woman had spun a spell, siphoning the air from Geda's lips and causing her to lean further into him.

Quickly, Ana grabbed Geda's wrist and merged his energy with hers. "Don't move," he advised through her confusion. No longer subjected to the woman's curse, his voice flowed through her senses and woke her consciousness. Feeling dizzy, she followed his instructions. As she regained composure, she discovered her lean on his shoulder and decided to stay until she noticed the defensive look on his face.

"What is it?" she whispered, following his deadly glare to the woman across the aisle.

"I am not the only one here," bellowed Ana.

Accepting defeat, the lady recollected her breath, finished her prayers, and departed. Unsatisfied, her gaze met Ana's as she walked by. Glaring, she swore in Greek, threatening, "I will end you."

"Amora," he returned under his breath. The lines on his face displayed a defensive front, but the woman remained unfazed.

Geda saw the woman's true nature as she passed. The woman exhibited impressive speed and responsiveness for someone who appeared to be over a century. Geda recalled the mutant discipline of consumption; how by rejecting consumption mutants will age, and the wrinkles on Amora's face spoke of rigid practice.

With the lady gone, Ana released the hold on her hand. "I didn't notice you were being followed. People like her, masters of drain, I can't sense them."

"What do you mean?" Geda asked, straightening from his shoulder.

He stumbled, "Did… you not notice what was happening to you?"

She shook her head.

"That woman was draining your energy."

Geda was baffled. There was a difference in her energy than before. "I had no idea," she whispered.

"Some mutants have adapted a dependency of alternative sustenance, devouring the energy of others, water, and even fire. We call the ability drain. Thus the candles," he explained. "It's perilous and practically untraceable, but more humane compared to other methods. It's clean but it takes a lot to satiate the need."

She looked down at her hand. Red marks gradually faded from his rough hold, his protection. "And Theo? Does he know?"

"Yes. Theo is trained to handle anything a mutant is capable of."

After last night's game, she was doubtful. Ana saw it on her face. "He will heal," he promised.

"You weren't there. You did not see. The mutant appeared out of thin air and effortlessly broke him. His screams, Ana."

He grabbed her hand again. This time gently. "I can imagine but Theo did his best. Be glad that is all Ammon did. Invisibility is very rare and sometimes things can only be learned from experience. For you, Ammon was one of them. There are many mutant abilities and powers. One day, I'll show them to you."

"What do you do against drain?" she wondered.

"Against drain? Hold your breath."

Theo hobbled onwards, slowly making his way to Currant's office until a confessional curtain exploded open.

Unexpected, Theo leapt with fright and dropped his crutch. the child, however, could not contain his laughter.

"Oh, my god! It's you." Theo cursed, gripping his knees. He should have expected the child from Ana's reaction earlier. They had to be careful around him. "What are you doing here?" he asked. They stood at a precipice of change, good or bad, and until things fell into place, a loyalty had to be maintained.

Bog smiled. "I was testing your reflexes. I heard what happened. So, it's true. Someone broke you," the child said disappointedly.

"Nobody broke me," Theo bravely corrected. "I'm as potent as ever."

"We will see. Well, come on then," the child ushered the young man into a secret meeting. Checking his surroundings, Theo suspiciously entered the confessional with the small boy and Bog handed him a slip of paper.

"What is this?" Curious, Theo opened it. Nine numbers were written in black ink.

"You will need it when the time comes. Alright. Now, undress me," Bog ordered.

"What?"

The child raised his arms, waiting for his shirt to be pulled off. "I need help changing."

"Umm." Theo hesitated. He wasn't comfortable with this exchange. A church member undressing a small boy, not his own, in a stereotypical setting? The thought was molesting.

However, this *was* Bog. He constantly pushed the boundaries of his subordinates. This is not the first time he has done such things to him. Even worse, Theo couldn't refuse or he would be punished. Bog was superior in every way.

Ana would understand, Theo told himself. He took a breath and did as he was told. "What are you changing into? You can't just run around the church naked."

Bog was offended. "I've done it before, and I'll do it again." He then pointed to the wooden bench. "The dress is in there."

The seat lifted, and Theo retrieved a bag of ecclesiastical robes. "What are these doing in here?" he murmured. Bog didn't answer. He simply held a prideful expression, closed his eyes, and waited to be undressed.

As he pulled the dress from the protective bag, Theo speculated Bog's comfort at requesting such service in a church. Perhaps that's how he fed, by luring unsuspecting victims into a false scenario. After all, being in a child's body had it's advantages. Theo stopped himself. If he dwelled on the topic any longer, he might be tempted to ask something he didn't want to know the answer to.

The dingy casual wear was stripped from Bog's body. Disgusted, Theo couldn't help but ask, "What have you been doing? Your clothes are filthy. You are usually very clean."

"Doing some dirty work."

Dressing for church affairs was a delicate process. It required multiple layers and each had to sit right. During it, Bog's gaze never left Theo's injury. "Does it hurt?" he asked.

"Yes."

"I hope you can withstand it."

Theo paused for clarification. "What do you mean?"

"I am concerned about Anastas."

"As you should be," yet another bold statement slipped from Theo's lips, but this time, it was called for. In fact, Bog reserved some tolerance for the young man for this very reason. Without it, he wouldn't think twice about dispatching the sharp tongue. "I, uh."

"No. Your right. Anastas is unwell. I have never seen him this bad." A red alb fell gracefully over Bog's skin, and the buttons at the neck were fastened. "I should have intervened ages ago and put Anastas to sleep myself."

For a moment, Theo thought he detected hate in the child's voice but brushed it off like all the foolish thoughts rattling in his head.

The boy continued, "He is dangerous, unstable. I'm afraid he will hurt someone. If he attacks the wrong person, it could send shock waves through the Oasis. He is, after all, a king."

Theo understood what he was trying to say. "Well, that is why I am here. So long as I am with Ana, I won't let that happen," he reassured, fluttering a lace surplice over Bog's red dress.

"Yes, you are a good guardian," Bog noted.

Theo kneeled to tie the laces of his shoes.

As Bog looked down at him, memories of Theo's youth came back to him. He recalled how they first met, how Theo never questioned how he never grew like the rest of the children and how deep his love for Ana became; how terrible it would be for his heart to break as a result of Ana's mistake.

"Should you ever feel betrayed or hurt by Ana, do not hesitate to call me. That slip was my number. You are his dearest friend, and I wouldn't want anything to happen to you. Look at me, Theo," Bog lifted Theo's chin tenderly. "It's okay to do the right thing."

Theo silently nodded, completing Bog's change of wardrobe.

"Okay!" the boy chirped and rushed into the hallway, colliding with the priest. "*Mmph*!" He fell backwards onto the floor.

"Oh, Bog!" exclaimed Currant. "I didn't see you there. Look at your dress! It's quite nice."

Theo split the curtain to see what was going on, revealing the child wasn't alone in the confessional.

Father Currant's gaze met Theo. "And did Theo help you?"

Bog didn't answer. He recognized the condescending tone of Currant's speech. Rage boiled on his face. In this puny form, he was powerless against physical obstacles, a side effect of his true power. If only it didn't take so much energy to use his abilities, he would vaporize all those who made a mockery of him.

They were all aware. However, before reaching to help him up, the priest savored his fall. Milliseconds of gratification and Father Currant reach out his hand. "Here, sir. Let me help you." Any more, and the royal child would have severed someone's head.

The wait for the clergymen was taking longer than expected. To pass the time, Geda analyzed the books cradled on the back of the pews. Pages of hymns and verses colorized the void. The notes capered a melody in her mind. Nodding her head to the rhythm, parchment flipped dangerously in her fingertips, carelessly gliding her natural texture across a razor's edge.

Realizing the duration of his stare, Ana swallowed and detached his focus from her. Entertained by her behavior, he savored their saturation, not in the subject but her red. Her albinism devoured the vibrant reds, lusciously bloomed in its spray and rippled its fabric. Hunger must have hit his system, or perhaps symptomatic delusions. Either way, he wanted to taste it.

Something about her captivated him. On the night they first met, both recently and millennia ago, she was in a sea of red. *It is silly,* he knew, *how cynical it is to be fond of your demons, to be entranced by someone who wears carnage like armor.*

On the contrary, he was at peace in her gentle chaos. So much so that he wished to explore this feeling, to embrace and to hold. He was forced to resist. He was forced to endure. *I must not get too close,* he told himself. *I. I…*

His teeth clenched.

"I hate it."

His regrettable admission thankfully pulled her away from the pages. "I hate it here," he continued. "I'd rather bury myself." Yawning, he stretched his arms and pulled at his face. He even let out a groan.

Geda found his pandiculation amusing. "Why?" she wondered.

"Churches are so quiet and cramped with emptiness. They are so secure and serene. I could easily fall asleep," he said, staring at the ceiling.

Geda swam with misery. There was nothing she could do to comfort him. She couldn't protect him from his enemies or stand against the queen. Comparing power, she was nothing but a whiff of air to these beasts.

"It's frustrating, especially when I don't want to sleep now."

The phrase plucked her heartstrings. Whether intentional or not, her devotion neared the edge of revolution when finally, the priest arrived.

"Sorry for being late," Currant welcomed.

She stood to greet him. "Father Currant."

Ana did the same and spotted the boy at the priest's side in proper garb. A disgusted expression of surprise flashed across his face, just the reaction Bog had hoped for. He couldn't help but smile, a smile which, to Ana's detection, made Geda's charm fade.

"Geda, it's good to see you," Currant acknowledged.

As the priest debriefed everyone, Ana could help but feel uneasy with Bog in the same room as her. There was uncertainty around the child's potential reaction toward her. Ana searched her expression to measure her awareness of the danger. From her rigidity, she clearly knew the boy wasn't human from his smile, and felt apprehensive by his unusual aura. Instinctively, he closed the distance between them and her tension settled, witnessing the impact of the security he brought her.

Ana's gaze then moved to Theo, who had observed the same. The mutant's gaze sharpened, glancing to Bog and back. Theo bowed with his eyes, understanding his new order.

Bog cannot be trusted, especially not in the presence of Geda. He was unpredictable, and a second thought must not be taken to protect her, essentially telling Theo to give up on him and swear commitment to her instead.

Then Currant turned to Ana. "It took me forever to find this," he said, handing him a linen wrapped object.

Surprised, a childish smile lifted Ana's face. "You found it!" He carefully handled the relic. Old, the wrappings frayed under his delicate touch.

"Yes. Although, it needs some repair. After all, you haven't written in this since 1014 AD"

"What is it?" wondered Theo.

"An old memoir. Accounts of Christian history," answered Currant.

"It's just a book… that I write in. There is something I need to remember," Ana admitted.

"1014 AD? That's six years after the coronation of Queen Sarolt," the child pointed out.

"Yes," Ana reluctantly recalled. "There is a tactic in here we can utilize against her."

"Speaking of, we should discuss your arrangements. Let's begin." The priest ushered them to a separate room and laid out designs of a crypt. Blueprints of a circular hall rolled onto the table. Just as Currant described the structure was, "fit for a king." Marble and ornate to highlight his youthful victories. The designs were Grecian with Turkish flair, reminiscent of Constantinople. Once emperor, the Great City had shaped him. From his mutant conception to the city's rebirth as the Oasis, he played a pivotal part in the city's success.

Everything was already in print and ready to be finalized. Currant required confirmation before setting it in stone, literally. "I used the sketches in your book to design the structure and commissioned specific texts into fresco pieces to celebrate your historical achievements," he orchestrated.

"May I ask which events were included in the mural?" Bog inquired.

Currant listed off his ideas, "The baptism of Constantine 337 AD, the prosperity of Constantinople 510 AD, he religious unification of Alexandria and Antioch in 7th century, .the capture of the True Cross under Khosrow II 614 AD, Antipope 855 AD, and Coronation of Stephen I of Hungary 1001 AD."

"No modern achievements?"

"I prefer the early years," explained Ana, agreeing with the selection.

Currant pointed to hemispherical cuts in the floor. "Royal wells will flow here. Functionally, the sanctuary will match Ariel's resting place."

"How deep will it go?" Ana asked.

"It will be fifty feet beneath the necropolis."

Impressed, Ana had nothing to add. This was taking shape, and soon, he will sleep peacefully. It felt unreal, foreboding in a way.

Geda had numerous questions, but the conversation was too intense to allow for detailed explanations, leaving her thoughts to wander. While they spoke, she couldn't help but linger on the knowledge lurking in the leather-bound pages caressed by Ana's touch. Her eyes struggled to leave it alone.

She desperately wanted to grab it and bask in the wild adventures of Emperor Anastas. She could imagine reading it, flipping the pages, and destroying it to soothe her curiosity. The satisfaction would be suffocating. The dust in the crevasses would asphyxiate her wonderfully.

Geda took a deep breath to tighten her resolve, questioning her reasoning. *It's just Ana,* she brushed off, but it was him. It was filled with Ana's firsthand account, his experiences. How could she not peek behind the cover?

"Alright." Currant clapped his hands, ending the meeting. "Well, I will let everyone know your preferences, and the team will make the final adjustments." The small child helped roll up the designs.

Ana hesitated his departure. "What is the projected completion date?" he asked.

"33 days from now."

"Thank you, Currant," said Ana endearingly, knowing this may be the last time they meet. *For all you have done for me.*

Meeting resolved, Theo led them out of the small conference room. "You guys go on ahead. I have some things I need to do here."

Ana flipped open the dusty old journal. "While you are down there, look for this," he requested, tearing a page from the ancient manuscript. Exasperated, Geda grabbed her chest. Her scream lodged in her throat as he carelessly handed the leaf to Theo. Before he could question the illustration, Ana told him to, "Keep it to yourself. You will know it when you see it. If you happen to find it, bring it to me. Until then, please be safe, Theo."

"You do the same," said Theo before returning to the priest.

"Is that all you needed? We didn't stay long," she asked, wrapping her arm around his.

"Yes." Ana lowered his head so only she could hear him. "You should know I requested your company for a reason. In any unforeseen circumstance, I would like you to ensure my final wishes are honored and carried out accordingly."

Surprised, she looked at him. His expression was shamefully serious. "What are you saying? What about Theo?" she asked.

Ana shook his head. "He knows, but I can't ask him to do this. The burden…" His dual eyes told everything his heart couldn't. Ana was all Theo had. To ask him to manage his final days would dissolve his innocent smile.

"I understand," she accepted.

"Besides, if you ever find yourself in a position beyond your control, you'll know where to find me," he added.

The large doors of the church closed behind them. As the sun settled in their rendezvous, Ana felt it was only right to take Geda home seeing as though she originally rode with Theo. However, as they made their way to his car a block away, a figure emerged from an alley, interested in the dim beacon and targeted him. Ana put his arm around the woman accompanying him.

"What is it? The shadow?"

He nodded. "Keep walking. An aggressor is most likely nearby."

Geda's expression changed, realizing he was talking about himself. "Are you okay?"

"I am further than I care to admit," he said.

Regardless, her hug remained. Ana still had some fight left. It was hard to believe he would one day cease to exist.

"Are you sure you will become an aggressor?" she asked.

"It's undeniable. The shadows have been following me for months, and soon I'll be a beacon for their colonization."

"I won't let that happen."

He almost laughed. She got a glimpse of his clipped teeth.

"You don't believe me?" she asked.

"No, I do." He blushed.

"Glad I could help," she whispered.

"Theo is looking into it. Don't worry. I will be okay," he reassured but as he looked over his shoulder, he could not deny the frequency of Malum encounters.

The shadow figure followed them. Slowly, it would take a giant step, exhaust itself with the effort, take a breath, and then reignite the chase. Its stride easily cleared six feet with one leg swing. She gasped as it got close.

"And so will you," he said, pulling her in. Closer, their sides were now touching. "We were blessed." Ana looked over his shoulder again. "He is dying, decaying. Had he been youthful, this conversation would not be so relaxed. Let's see him off, shall we?" Geda gave him a gentle nod, trusting him. "I'll take you home, and the shadows will track me back to my place."

"Track you?"

"Malum are unable to distinguish mutant from human and frankly, don't care to. Blood is blood. To the desperate, a human's life is a cheap exchange to escape possession," a choice Ana was willing to take, just not with Geda. "In this position, you have the same targeting signals as me."

"Oh." In thought, her fingers played with his side.

"Do you mind walking? We can watch the sunset this way."

Considering his question, Geda looked back at the shadow. Her heart skipped a beat as it got close again and collapsed with exhaustion. Ana leaned in close. She didn't know what took her breath away more, the shadow or him.

"If it's too much, I will redirect him now," he offered.

She wanted to stay. "No. This is fine."

"I won't let it get too close," he promised.

For miles, their posture did not change. With her shoulder cupped comfortably in his grasp, their sides were destined to never part. Eventually, their walking pattern matched. Outer then inner, the three-legged march made it back to the sorority house with death swinging in the outskirts.

Night had fallen, blanketing their rhythm with a chill neither of them could satisfy, a chill amplified by the absence of their follower. It had been a mile or two since Ana remembered to check. Now that they had reached their destination, the need was more prevalent. In the corner of his blue eye, Ana detected they were alone. The shadow did not follow.

Where did he go? He scanned the surroundings, but there was no sign of the thing. *Odd,* simmered Ana, thankful nothing happened as he again got lost in her presence.

Just before his foot hit the front steps, Ana's dark eye caught Darin in the kitchen window, and here his woman was, alone in the beast's arms. Ana sighed and quickly drew breath from Geda's lips with a soft leap up to the second story. Landing on the roof, he swiftly put her where she belonged, in her nest.

Bewilderment accentuated her complexion.

"Darin is here," he explained. "I've caused enough trouble for one night," he added, still looking out for the shadow that followed them.

Geda grabbed him before he closed the window. "Wait," she whispered but her mind could not keep up with his proximity. After all, he was here, in her window, inches from her bed, with those opposing eyes, bearing an inhuman strength beyond illness and pigmented with stripes highlighted by moonlight.

Breathless, she wished he would stay but socially her hold required a reason. "Ana. Do… do you fear death?" she asked.

His departure vanished, and his weight settled back on the wooden frame. "Why are you asking that?" he asked, staring into her bunny shades.

For the first time, she had no explanation for her curiosity. So, she conjured an analytical response. "As someone who has lived a long life, what are your thoughts on the afterlife? How has history altered your perception of the end?"

If only my fears were as simple as death.

Internal debate was evident from his grip on the window, which was used to support his lean. He let out a breath, and stripes briefly darkened as he replied, "No. Death seduces me."

Her eyes widened.

The doorknob rattled. By the time the door creaked open, the window was empty. However, the mutant's statement was everlasting.

"Curse this old house — Oh! You're here? I was trying to surprise you." Darin expressed, holding a large bouquet of flowers.

She turned to him as if nothing happened. "I am surprised," she said, studying him as fresh flowers replaced the decaying beauties on the vanity. Compared to a mutant, his movements were poorly disciplined. His immature sway was inefficient and his step was uneven. It was nothing like the creature she danced with. Still, he was a man.

She went to him.

"Oh!" he yelped, not expecting the sudden affection.

The dried flowers made their way to the trash. "Leave them," she suggested. Death would stay in their presence. She pulled him in. Their lips met with another man on her mind. And again. And again.

"What's gotten into you?" Darin smiled. He found her assertiveness appealing.

"I've missed you," she whispered.

With that, he took dominance. Submitting to his routine, her gaze went back to the window, hopeful of the mutant's linger. However, Ana was no longer there. They were alone, but the Devil remained on her mind.

Beneath the chapel, Theo followed Currant down a twisting corridor. On the way to Guardian Hall, they descended further, hopping over pipes, through service corridors until they found the shield symbol. There, an immediate handle was pulled, and a secret entrance cracked open.

"It has been years since I've been this way." Theo ducked his head under the door. To his surprise, Currant did the same. If he recalled correctly, church officials were not allowed in the guardian facilities, unless....

"Father, are you also a guardian?" he asked.

Yara Currant lowered his head and grumbled, "Yes. I am." A pride worthy title, yet disdain clouded his reply.

Did he not want to be a guardian? Did he have a choice? Theo considered. He knew his experience with guardianship was not universal. Many have had a more difficult introduction to service. He couldn't help but wonder, *Who does he protect?*

A stone path directed them down a long hallway that cut through more of the city's infrastructure and led them to a wooden door which opened to a basilica-style hall, Guardian Hall. Columns and martyr paintings flowed along the cathedral ceilings to a hole like the Pantheon.

From the streets, this was nothing more than a water hole. And at the center of the main room was the vessel of their holy water. Those seeking reassurance would lower a cup on the pulley system and scoop from the endless wells of guardians to bathe away their sorrows.

Moonlight poured in from the heavenly oculus. The corners untouched were illuminated by traditional candle sconces.

Theo was home. It was here he signed the Book of Guardians, vowing his allegiance to Ana. During his youth, he found shelter amongst the ambiance. His senses were honed by the echoes of the rock, the training dummies hardened his shell, and his fingertips callused under the paper's edge. Theo spent his youth in the archives, learning the philosophies of saviors. He was confident they held the secret to helping Ana.

Walking through the hall, a sermon could be overheard. At the well, a petite elder led a congregation of children with assistance. "To the mothers who have thrown ye children down the well, may ye be forgiven," he prayed.

Unwanted and abandoned, the Bureau of Guards took in everyone willing to serve God through worship, dedication, sacrifice, hard work, or simply living.

Hearing the old man deliver oral stories rekindled Theo's memories. He wanted to sit with them, but he was no longer a child. He had grown into a servant of mankind, a keeper of the savors, a guardian.

A child gasped, "Brother Green, we have guests!" They were surprised to see adults return, a rare occurrence.

"They must be guardians," cried another child. Though they aspired to be guardians, it was uncommon to meet one.

"Brother?" A young girl got off the ground and tugged the robes of the assistant. "Can we speak to them?" she asked.

The hooded assistant silently turned to them with a foreboding gentleness and stature very similar to the Butcher.

Theo stopped and waited for his answer. After a second, the assistant answered her without making a sound. Orchestrating through sign language, he said, "No. Those men are here for an important reason. Leave them be."

"Aww, but brother!" the child whined.

"Nadia, you can speak to the guardians after you become one," said the elder Green. He regathered the youngsters. "Now pay attention."

Theo turned back to Currant. "I guess we can go now."

The priest had to pull himself away from the assistant, who met his gaze again. "Right," he acknowledged and opened the door.

"Do you know him?" Theo asked, lighting a candle with nearby matches. Grabbing for them was instinctive, another behavior ingrained in Theo.

Currant did the same, striking a match against the wall. "Kind of," he replied. "We ran into each other once." It was clear Currant still had a lot he didn't want to say. Descending another set of steps, he cleared his throat and said, "His name is Victor. He is a force of nature."

"I can tell." Theo laughed. That was an understatement.

"He is the Arena champion. If you ever cross paths with him, do not take him lightly," warned the priest.

Theo stopped. There was something different about Currant now, like his wounds were exposed. The established clergyman had pitfalls oozing with violence and experience. Theo's confusion could be felt in the air as if he was questioning whether he could trust the priest. *This man has been serving Ana for nearly ten years, and I am just now seeing him for who he is?*

The middle-aged man softened and opened up. "Ten years ago, I worked for the Order as a low-rank Venator, but eventually, saw the errors of my ways. Guardians were once my enemy, and I had the misfortune of getting in Victor's way."

"What made you change sides?" Theo asked.

"That's a tale for another day," said Currant. "Before I converted, I devoted my soul to protecting my family. I took on the ecclesiastical so they could live a better life. I had unknowingly become a guardian and found myself here."

A couple steps more, and they were in the heart of their teachings. The narrow stone pathway led them to a dungeon-like chamber. The darkness made it hard to see, but the pressure of the cluttered space told them to be careful.

They took a moment to light the sconces. Loose pages and rolled scrolls came into view, nicely tucked away into cubbies. Leather-bound books formed the walls of the space, towering upwards over ten feet. Apart from mildew, the air was smudged with cedar and sweet grass.

Witnessing it again reignited a spark in the young man's eyes. "Wow. Geda would love this place," Theo remarked. He read the title of the first book he laid his eyes on, a descriptive outline composed by a connoisseur of human flesh. "Oh. Perhaps not," he corrected himself. "Hey, where are you going?"

"I have my own business to attend to," said Currant, going the opposite direction.

"Alright," Theo accepted. He contemplated where to begin. His eyes went back to the aide-memoire and found there were more books on the dark topic: "Dreams of the Unawakened"- records of verbal tribulations from sleeping beasts and "Bureaucracies of the Damned"- a study into the unwritten natural laws governing mutant society.

I guess I'm in the correct location, he thought. Even after years of studying in the Bureau's library, he had no indication of the vault's organization. He looked at the pile menacingly. There was so much to sieve through. He nearly forgot what he came here for. Theo clapped his hands and focused. *Okay. We need any knowledge on shadow possession and the process. As well as a weapon? A scroll,* he remembered. And then he saw a wall of scrolls and froze. *I'm gonna be here all night.*

Pushing the workload aside, he started on the right, in a section that seemingly detailed and debated the motives of the Malum Saltus. Conference transcriptions outlined scientific conversations and bibliographical research notes. Unfortunately, there was nothing there that would help Ana.

The lower left pile expressed the conflict of the mutant's insatiable destruction. He randomly selected a book and read the passage,

> "It's a hunger that gnaws the deepest
> pits of your bones and pulsates through
> veins to tips of the nerves. It drives anyone
> to an indescribable madness, a scathing
> desire followed by throat-screeching yells
> of desperation not your own that echo from
> the inescapable canals of my brain and is the
> source of my primal functions. The anxiety
> is crippling and drains everything from the
> adrenal complex."

Theo quickly closed the book, saving his eyes. "The hell," he exclaimed. With that said, the condition described was comparable to Ana's. He opened the book again and flipped through the pages, but it did not entail anything beyond the horrors of an aggressor's mind. It was the last thing he wanted to read.

Theo rummaged for hours, looking for specific words: pharus, umbra, emorior, and exedo; any Latin synonym for beacon, shadow, fall, and devour.

Fatigue ached his muscles, and the pain from the game returned him to tears. Along with frustration and exhaustion, the continuous reminder that time was almost up for his in-human savior resided in every piece of literature. However, it kept him going.

Theo pushed harder to find a solution. He skimmed books and parchments, unrolled pages of scripture, and dashed thro-ugh the hallways trying to find hidden secrets in the murals. No matter what, he did not stop. There had to be a solution in here somewhere.

Theo dug deeper, rudely disheveling the library. Then, as he haphazardly unhinged a journal barricading hundreds of loose papers, a scroll dropped to the floor with an unusual sound.

Blink!

"Huh?" Theo's eyes went straight to percussed instrument escaping him. *What's this?* He went after it, abandoning the paper avalanche, and stopped the object from rolling further. It was heavier than expected and it was clear why.

The scroll rod was made of the purists metal and carved with ornate symbols and unreadable text. One emblem, however, was recognizable; the eye, the Venator insignia.

"Wait. This looks like —" Theo unfolded the page Ana gave him. The scroll was identical to his drawing, with emphasis on the eye. "The eye is a mark of Zarin?" he read.

The scroll was too beautiful for the rugged archive. It be-longed in a castle. It belonged to a queen. Then it hit him. *This is the queen's scroll! This is the weapon Ana was looking for.*

Then he considered what that meant, a weapon only the queen could wield it. Reason beckoned him to peak under the seal. Theo held his breath as he untied the binding thread, carefully not to destroy the artifact. *It fell open.* He slowly un-rolled the parchment on the nearest antique desk. His eyes were immediately overwhelmed.

Metallic phrases shot across the page in many directions. Precious gems were woven in the papyrus. Upon closer inspection, some looked to be written by hand. Gold leaf with fingerprints. The tips of minerals oxidized like blood. Jade quill scratches resembled string embroidery. Impressions of ancient writing tools shimmered amethysts. And the blood-stained corner turned the paper to copper at the point of highest saturation. The scroll reflected light he had not seen collectively.

Theo was speechless. He knew queens had a shimmer in their lifeblood that mutates when spilled. But this! If this was truly the queen's scroll, then he was looking at a backlog of royals and the signatures in blood.

Queens! he registered. There were hundreds of them. *After the True Queen, Sarolt was the only surviving queen,* he thought. This defies his teachings, against what everyone knew about the Royal War.

Was the weapon evidence against the True King? Was Ana's plan to release this to the public? Or was there something hidden within the lines of shimmering foulness that invoked the wrath of gods?

Theo pondered and speculated a million things as he stared into the reflective phrases. Texts of emerald swirled with gold, diamonds jutted childishly, and encircled were trimmers of opal. He could distinguish the mindset of the individual the day they signed it. It was marvelous.

Among the passages, Sarolt's signature was there in spinel fashion. "Saroldu?" *That must be her real name,* he considered.

In hopes of discovering something, Theo attempted to decipher the passages. However, the ancient texts had seen better days. They were damaged, aged, or the language had been lost to time. Plus, he didn't speak Persian, so Sarolt's record was not beneficial. He soon gave up and closed the scroll. In doing so, he found something.

Indentation? he felt. Curious, he angled the scroll's surface to his eyes and made out faint marks and slashes like a hurried translator. The pressure of a being's hand bled through onto the original. Latin or French? He could nearly read it

Theo grabbed a piece of coal and spare parchment from the drawer and delicately colored the mark, revealing what was hidden. *Please be something,* he begged, desperate to find a solution for Ana.

The rubbing found where the writing had ceased. He lifted the paper to reveal its secrets and read, "The blood of a queen is most precious to mutant life. It embodies health for all life drinks and wealth all envy to obtain."

Health! Theo jumped up. The answer to Ana's condition lives within the queen.

He quickly rolled the scroll, and stuffed it in his pocket. "Yara! I'm leaving!" he yelled, cleaning up his mess.

Now that they have a direction, accomplishing it, however, will be a difficult task. As Theo navigated through the vault and back to the church, he pondered how he was going to acquire royal's blood. It's not like he could simply ask Sarolt for the cure, not without heavy compensation.

Did it matter? Either way, Ana's life was on the line. The duty of guardianship called to him. It was time for him to lay down his life to save his beloved mutant. The chapel door busted open. Theo was on a mission, until he wasn't.

Wham! Something struck him in the head. Strength vanished from his feet. Before he could grunt, he collapsed onto the ground. Did he not see the beings on the other side of the street? Or how they had crossed to confront him? He was so focused on one thing, and for his failure, he will pay.

On the ground, Theo struggled to maintain consciousness. *What? Who?* His mind could not muster the words, and his muscles would not stiffen for conflict. As a warm substance trickled down his neck, the last thing on his brain was how he seized the day. He whipped it away, hand red with blood, and suddenly, a brick wall encircled him.

Shadowed figures hovered over him like smiling crows but one man was prominent over the others.

"Ow! That looked like it hurt," he said, teasing and twirling the blunt object. "Are you alright?"

The man's face was too familiar. *Ana?* Theo guessed but he knew better. *No. Those aren't his eyes.* The name soon came to his tongue. "Darin. Darin? What? What are you…" Confusion weakened him more. He caught another breath and awed at the other faces. He knew them all, his teammates. "You're all here?" Recognition disarmed him more.

Darin grabbed hold of Theo's arm, steadying him. "Don't worry about them. They are just here to carry you but me on the other hand…" He held up a long syringe in front of Theo's swaggering gaze, making him partially aware of his intent. "Just know I had to do this." The object's function registered and before he could reject it, the needle pierced Theo's skin and injected something into his blood-stream, erasing the rising sun from his sight.

CHAPTER 19

Candelabra at the Ready

Everything continued as if nothing happened, as if the world's greatest mission had not been ignited. Hours later, Marcy opened the restaurant at 8 o'clock. Around the same time, Ana visited the dormitory and found Theo had not returned. It was even later when Geda discovered the incident and solidified her decision to join the cause.

Until then, her day started like usual. An alarm woke her at 7:50. She consumed a breakfast bagel with coconut water on the public transport to Gibbous station, and walked two blocks to Joytech. There, she welcomed the friendly receptionist, stopped by the marketing department to visit her adopted parents, and by 9:30 a.m., conducted a routine meeting with Raymond.

Every morning was the same. Dr. Jakobi took her measurements, weight, vitals, and recorded last night's dreams, which she often lied about. "The Dunes bloomed flowers," Geda simply said, expressing only a fragment of the whole picture.

In her dream, the Dunes did bloom. The dying fields were revitalized. As she walked among the flowers, the sand compressed and spilled over her feet, revealing the roots and the bodies fertilizing the new beginnings.

Armageddon littered the surroundings. Death became the living, the art of rebirth. She became a part of the cycle of life. As recognition became inevitable acceptance, dancing flames whisked her away with breathless whispers of an ancient name. The dream was so captivating. How could she describe something so imaginative to logical people? They wouldn't understand.

With no reported abnormalities, the doctor cleared her. "Just as always, everything is good," said Jakobi.

However, Raymond was not satisfied. "That doesn't answer for the nose bleeds," he argued for a cause of her frequent flare ups.

"Epistaxis is common. I don't believe it is linked to her condition," said Jakobi. "It is most likely stress. So long as the bleeding is not acute, I would not be concerned about them."

Although Raymond respected the doctor's opinion, he had no margin for error with Geda.

Before more tests were ordered, Geda interrupted with, "Have you seen Darin?"

"No, I haven't," Raymond replied, straightening his papers and intentionally avoiding eye contact. "He should be in the conference room with the board of directors, as should I, but this paperwork demands my attention. Why?"

"There are some final arrangements we need to discuss before tomorrow," she explained.

The Lord paused, recalling the importance of tomorrow. "Right, the ceremony. I'll be sure to send him your way if I see him. Try to have a good day, Geda," he said softly. His care was heartwarming.

"Thank you. You too," she wished. Then, with a slight bow, she departed to the next item on her agenda: the Historical department internship at 10 o'clock.

Mindlessly, Geda descended the spiraling core of the tower. Her mind swirled with many things. Overall, she was bent on the sins committed hours before. The treasonous act of fantasizing about someone else carried over into her dreams. Hungover, she was guilty, voluntarily plagued by a beast. It shivered her skin, much like the gruesome beauty of the scenery.

As the name C.O.V. suggests, the epicenter of the iconic building was a holding facility for captured mutants, a shifting chandelier of encapsulated inmates, rehabilitating their vicious crimes or poor circumstances.

The conflicting morals of the construction complemented her internal state. Her actions were loyal but her desires were satisfied by unconventional methods. Strangely, it was soothing how the two aspects harmonized.

Despite being crowded by large tanks, the space was remarkably quaint and airy. Sunlight beamed through the high windows, casting rays though the green specimens and shiny pipes. The stairway was illuminated like the stained-glass windows of the church they visited the night before.

The breathtaking view was exclusive to the Order's corporate elite: managers, officers, mercenaries, business owners; the ruling class. So, it was surprising to find the significant chamber secured by a regular maintenance door. Cut off from average society, it was the only way to reach the Raven's Nest, to see Raymond physically. All of which made her appreciate the beauty of their horror more.

Bubbles gurgled from movement.

With each step, she couldn't help but look at the collection. Every tank was populated. Hundreds of mutants laid in wait, enduring the acid. Some beings retained their shape while others soaked for ages, unable to ever be free, now sediment in the concentration.

Then, Geda's eyes glimpsed a familiar face and stopped. *The messenger,* she recognized him now as she did when he whispered in Ana's ear. He was the one who made Ana angry.

She inched closer. Deep in meditation, the mutant did not sense her, allowing her to analyze his features uninhibited by emotion. At first, he reminded her of Ana, but they differed in many ways.

Unlike Ana's smooth skin and unkempt style, this mutant's face pitted with time, a sign of self-reliance. Thin like Theo's mane, his dark brown hair rested straight. Instead of an inmate number, at the top of his cell she found a name. "Leo?"

Immediately, the mutant's eyes shot open, causing the girl to jump. She had called his name, unintentionally summoning the beast. "Sorry!" she apologized.

Reminded of his position, the man ground his teeth, and his brow scrunched with anger. "Move on, girl," growled Leo.

However, Geda was unfazed by his display. "No. I want answers," she said selfishly.

But Leo knew the law. "You are not an agent," he returned. "Nor do you have the authority to interrogate me."

She did so anyway. "You were sent to Gibbous University as a messenger. What was the message?" she asked.

Too exhausted, Leo brushed her away. "Why don't you ask your father?" he teased, aware of her orphan situation and her sensitivity to it. He hoped it would deter her.

It didn't.

"Just tell me, what did it have to do with me?" she insisted.

This got his attention. "So, you noticed?"

"It was obvious."

The mutant hesitated, contemplating if he should tell. "You know the secrets you seek are not mine to tell?"

"Yes."

"And having this knowledge can create enemies of allies," Leo warned again. His generosity had ulterior motives. Filling the mind of Raymond's most precious with demoralizing but true secrets would harm the Lord significantly. Anything done beyond the Lord's control hits him in the sweet spot. *I shouldn't.* He knew he would pay for this later, but the resulting heartbreak between father and daughter was worth the death sentence.

"I am prepared," Geda consented.

Pleased, Leo expelled the water from his lungs. "Raymond sent me to barter a trade."

"What does he want? If it pertains to me, he would have told me." She insisted.

"Unless he just can't bring himself to involve you." Leo pointed to her neck. "You have been tagged by his miserable offspring."

So, that's what this is about? Her hand brushed along the tag's surface, but her expression did not possess surprise, only anger. Raymond was bartering her life when they already had a wager.

"You knew?"

"Yes. Raymond has always been honest with me. What was the bargain? My tag for what?"

"The prince's life," he openly stated.

"That's the message you delivered?"

Leo tilted his head, watching the blood drain from her face. "Yes, but like before this is not news to you. You knew this was going to happen. Why the sudden change in heart rate?"

Geda tightened her jaw. *Because it was supposed to be my choice,* she wanted to say.

Since Darin pulled her from the rubble of the Joytech collapse ten years ago, they were chosen to do a fateful dance. However, their closeness was divided by the whispers of conspiracy and shattered any hope of success. The conversation that turned Darin away resurfaced in her brain. It was fresh despite occurring nearly eight years ago.

"Father!" Darin rushed to the Raven's desk dragging Geda by his side. "You lied to me! You told me we were on the verge of discovery, of queening a royal of our own. The solution is right in front of us. Why are you giving up if we are this close?"

"The quickest route is often the most dangerous. We are not prepared to face what lies in wait. Besides, there are other priorities that require our attention. A good leader knows how to balance progression and stabilization," Raymond tried to counsel the boy, but he wasn't open to education.

Darin grunted, "So once again, we diverge from our goal."

"We will return to it," his father insisted.

"When?" he continued to challenge. "By then, it will be too late. Our technology will be useless if we let Armageddon ensue, which inevitably will if we let the royals do what they want in this human playground." As he preached, Geda agreed but unlike the Raven boy she knew everything Raymond said had an unspoken truth behind it.

"Have you considered how your choice affects the world? Your pursuit of royal claim may have far greater consequences than Armageddon."

"I have. That is why I have taken matters into my own hand," Darin said menacingly. "I have replaced your tag in Geda with my own."

"You did what?" Both Raymond and Geda were outraged.

"I will not allow this potential to die, father."

Hearing the violation of trust, Geda's soul nearly left her body. He had strapped an untested bomb to her chest while she wasn't looking. *How could he? And when?* Her eyes denied any consent and Raymond knew the crime his son had committed.

"I did not agree to this," she uttered breathlessly.

"Come here." Raymond motioned her forward. His chair pivoted, and as requested, she took a seat on his lap. He parted her hair and saw the injection point upon her neck, a small pimple.

Raymond gave Darin a most authoritative expression. "Do you understand the seriousness of your actions? In case you have forgotten, allow me to remind you. Geda's life support is no longer operational," he expressed. "She may be more fragile than any human but it would be cruel of me to deny her a normal life. The tag I provided her with was a safeguard in case of emergency. Your tag is unqualified, barely in trials. You have taken her security away."

"She will not need the security," answered Darin. "I intend to synthesize her shortly. She will be unstoppable, the weapon we have been fighting for. I will show you."

"I know of her potential!" shouted Raymond. How could his son do this? *He is so blinded by this, he has become insensitive to life.* Raymond was distraught.

Darin extended his hand. "Then allow me to train her to be the queen you have always wanted, just as you taught me. What do you think?" he asked.

Raymond nearly laughed. "You ask for my opinion after the fact? You have never trained a queen. Despite what you think, they cannot be controlled."

"You speak as if I am a thing," mumbled Geda.

Darin noticed. "If you don't like it, you can always kill me," he offered. Raymond wouldn't kill his own son, or so he thought. His father was tempted.

The Lord turned to Geda. "My dear, it seems you have been claimed and I do not have the power to save you. If you ever disapprove of your king," his eyes shot to the boy, "bring me a new one, and I will make you a proper queen."

Ana must be a king! Raymond wants to take advantage of him, Geda conspired. And from Ana's comment last night, "It is the only option outside of Raymond's offer," it was as if he considered taking it.

"I'm afraid," she admitted.

"Of?" asked Leo.

"It's a trap," she explained. "That message was meant to ensnare Ana, to capture the king and make a queen. I was bait!"

Leo was suspicious of her accusation. "What makes you so sure?"

A heavy weight compressed her chest, admitting, "He was just a mutant. I purposely sought him out for a personal vendetta. Then I met his heart — but now it's too late! They know."

Her schemes were careless of the repercussions but his misfortune started to make sense. Until now, Leo assumed Ana was to blame for his downfall when it was this girl all along. "You? You *were* there! You must have been the one that led a Lion into my garden! Your efforts incited carnage in my roses! Do you not realize what you have done?"

She shook her head. "I do but I don't know what to do."

Leo was outraged. "You? You have done too much already. Above all, you brought Ana into the light. Now everyone sees him. You are the cause of his anguish and will be the fall of his reign. You are the reason for all of this, Geda. You have caused so much pain. You are the bringer of destruction. You are death! What will you do when my king fulfills the bargain, when he kills what you love most?"

Air solidified in her chest. "He can't. He's too weak. He…" *If he tries, he will die.* She couldn't bear to hear the words she was thinking, for they were undeniably true.

Leo chuckled, satisfied by her dismay. "You have no idea what Anastas is capable of. He will most definitely kill Darin. I would know. He once did the same for me."

"I have failed him," she whispered to herself.

His smile melted. Her concern made him sick. Clearly, she cared for Ana. Despite his hurtful intentions, Leo pitied her. To be in her place, begging for a way to save the paramour, it was maliciously nostalgic. It hurt.

"Failure," said Leo, "is when you change, mutate, and become the boy's puppet. Is that what you want?"

"No. But —"

"You are not complete. The veracity of your conception still plagues the mind. I understand you seek the evidence of your birth within the gears of this machine, but until you feel the touch of fiery pain and retrace the steps last taken, the mystery will remain. You will never be able to save him from his cruel fate as long as the two of you are entangled."

The wisdom of his speech was incomprehensible yet somehow ignited a path others kept secret.

He continued, "Geda, when the time comes, run. It is the only way to save you from a synthetic life. Drop Ana. Your association will only get him killed."

Processing the suggestion, a twitch surfaced under her right eye, a significant twinge Leo associated with a dead man, Casimir, the very man who coerced the Devil back to holy ground. A haunting sense of repetition came over him.

"Listen," he beckoned. "Ana will not act on his own. He is too delicate to be careless. He follows the ordinance of the church. There is a child —"

"There you are," an unexpected voice called to her right, causing her to jump.

"Romulus!" she gasped. His approach was silent.

"It's past time for your lessons," he returned, then noticed who kept her from her appointment. "You shouldn't converse with prisoners. They will fill your head with conspiracies. Let's go."

Geda did as she was told and followed Romulus.

However, Leo wasn't done. He called out to her. "Ana will fulfill the bargain! He would do it out of love, not for you but for the face you possess!"

Geda stopped. "What do you mean?" she turned and asked before he was out of view.

"This war is centered on a revolution of events," he rushed. "The opportunity for domination repeats with a bloodline. The same happened to Sarolt, and the same is happening to you. Do not let them use that to their advantage!"

"I think that's enough," growled Romulus, coaxing her to move.

"Remember the boy!" Leo called out one last time as they vanished around the bend.

Boy? She wanted to know more but her mind focused on meeting each step. It wasn't until the next landing that she remembered the young boy in Currant's shadow at the church, present yet unnoticeable.

Was that the child he spoke of? she wondered, half tempted to go back for more information. If only it wasn't Romulus who led her.

As the excitement settled, guilt blemished Leo's tongue. He allowed his emotions to get the best of him, jealous of her relationship with Anastas and his anger towards her creator. He called out hoping she could still hear him, "You don't have much time left, Geda! You are still a child! You must become more than that!" The maintenance door slammed, and he remained an ornament on the chandelier, unable to escape.

Romulus was not the only soul to intercept their ruckus. Reverting back to a tolerable position, Leo felt eyes watching him. He traced it back to the queen. She had been watching the whole time, peering down from a conference room above. Under the reflection of specimens, her face contorted with schemes and subtle fulfillment.

Thankfully, her uneven dimples were quickly cauterized by the discussion in the room behind her. Her attention was redirected by a businessman groaning, "As always, Raymond is absent."

The board of directors often gathered to debate the future of Joytech, a routine venture and the Lord was generally late. His attendance was red tape the room grew tired of.

Regardless, there was still those that supported Lord Sambuca's policies. One man rebutted, "And like usual, matters discussed here will be brought to him for a final approval."

A dark-complected male sympathized with him. He pulled his sleeve back and read an analog watch. "It's past ten o'clock. Shall we begin?"

His eyes met an older aristocrat across the table, to which she replied, "I'm sure the Lord won't be much longer. He's most likely wrapping up a stack of paperwork. That's usually his reason for delay."

A bag of bones slammed the table. "That's easy for you to say. That man's a mutant. He dilly-dallies and wastes our time doing things on his own accord. Waiting for him isn't making me any younger. Let's get on with it."

The woman scoffed. "Now, we know who the anxious one is. Afraid to die? Then synthesize. After all, you were the project's angel investor and majority stakeholder. Or perhaps the project doesn't live up to its expectations?"

A debate exploded in the room. Pale, wrinkled faces flourished red and shook intensely to solidify their point. They spat upon each other with each breath but not one word was heard.

Among the screaming, the queen sat peacefully, picking dirt

and gunk from under her nails. So long as they did not target Raymond all was well.

Things started to fly across the room. Papers shuffled with each expression. Sarolt didn't care. In fact, she found it very amusing. Each representative despised the rest and utilized each other as a foothold to become the legendary associate responsible for vanquishing the True King. Realistically, none of them have influenced the company enough to deserve credit.

The spectacle conjured a sense of nostalgia. As a Persian queen, her time in court was often filled with screaming, an annoyance when she was a human is now the only call back to before she became bitter and cold. It was music to her ears. Sarolt smirked, *Humans.*

A boulder voice cut through the yells, "We wouldn't need the Lord's approval if Darin sat on the throne!" The music stopped. The room lowered to a hush. No one objected. Silently, they were all in agreement. This got Sarolt's attention.

"Even if there was a way to remove Raymond from power, we would have done it already," noted one businessman.

The queen's eyes darted around the room, analyzing the sudden political shift.

Bones cracked leaning forward. "The man has been in power long enough. It is time for a new face of the company," added another old man motioning to the opposite side of the table.

There, Joytech's prince humbly rose. "That wouldn't be difficult to achieve," Darin proposed.

Sarolt's head tilted, catching on to what he was doing. *Is he really planning a mutiny? Now?* The prince was eager to replace his father, a position she could not afford to lose.

As she readied her claws to defend the Order, a rap on the window broke the tension. *Tap! Tap! Tab!*

They all looked in the direction of the low noise.

"What is that?" squinted a board member.

"A bird?" questioned another.

Tap! Tab! Tap!

They looked closer. It was black with shimmers of scarlet against the sunlight, jittering viscously like a hummingbird but was the size of a pigeon. Something dripped it, and Sarolt recognized what it was. "It's a messenger pigeon," she said.

"From who?"

"Sarolt, I advise against that."

The window cracked open enough for the bird to squeeze in. Her finger brushed the bird. Its dark contamination rubbed off onto her touch. *Blood,* she recognized. *Ariel's but… he wouldn't send a bird like this.*

"Who is it from, Sarolt?" they asked again.

"The king," she replied somberly. *That pathetic priest, Anastas.* His personality was etched into the creature's behavior. *You used a blood reserve? For me?* She was undoubtedly flattered considering he needed it more than her.

As the room returned to Darin, she pondered her enemy's consideration. She lingered with him in her palm. *Anastas,* she sighed. After all, this was their first encounter since the collapse of Arnireth. Oh, how their romance has changed; how he slowly kills himself to avoid her. So why was he reaching out now? Her heart twisted. *Are you at your end, dear prince?* After all this time, she was not prepared for their dangerous game to be over.

She flipped the bird over to expose its dainty little legs. Wrapped around one limb was a discolored slip that read, "The scroll for a crown."

The King no longer defends the God? She was intrigued by his offer. It warmed her heart so much she laughed. Was he serious? The queen's scroll was the very weapon she needed to drive the royal monarch to his grave. Even if it was temporary, his absence would be astronomically beneficial. Needless to say, Ana's proposition was enticing but first she had to save Raymond.

"It's high time the Order found a suitable fixture on the throne. Darin," the eldest gentleman at the table grabbed the young man's arm, "has been a staple in synthetic research, an outland pathfinder for human expansion and economic growth."

"You might be on to something. Let's conduct a performance evaluation to formalize the decision. Raymond holds great power. It will take some convincing for the public to accept the change," another councilman agreed and more followed.

Like usual, Sarolt was in a sea of indifference. *Are they seriously going through with this?*

As much as she hated Raymond, she needed him – everyone needed him. Beyond her ambition, Raymond reestablished life when all seemed hopeless. Without him, who would maintain it? An arrogant child? She would do anything to keep him power, including allying with the Devil.

Let's see how serious Anastas really is, she conspired. The messenger pigeon exploded in her grip and her gaze shifted to the boy.

Sarolt slithered her way into the conversation, twirling her finger until it landed on the wood conference table, a touch that silenced everyone. "You are being too ambitious. Are you not? The gods are not in favor of this," she warned.

"What suggestions do you recommend we take?" asked the business woman. But it was only Darin who she spoke to.

Looking the boy dead in the eye, she continued, "You have a desire with no support. The Lions will not take kindly to the transition. Some may even try to decapitate you. How do you expect to conquer without weapons in your arsenal?"

Darin realized her words were valid but remained fearless. Aware of her tactics, he wasn't going to let her into his head. "I have Geda," he replied and recited the company motto, "As long as we persevere, we can succeed at anything."

The council cheered him on, "That's right!" Not one of the board members opposed it.

We will see how you act when you lose her, simmered Sarolt.

The colors and expressions of her face changed, melanating the unique pattern her species, for a millisecond, just enough to implant fear into her observers. Her spinel eyes pierced deep into the boy, grasped his soul, and whispered a curse onto his name, "You have a death warrant bound to be satisfied by a very advantageous beast."

The room behind them grew unsteady. "What makes you think that?" Darin challenged.

The wicked woman got closer, intensifying her hold on him. "I read it on Leo's lips. Geda has chosen her king. Could it be the same mutant who graced your flower in the bathroom?" she insinuated.

The fear seed in his gut bloomed. "How... how do you know about that?" Doubt consumed the young man's pride. He was no longer the brave leader the investors thought him to be.

Sarolt smirked. *Too easy.*

Darin's mind shattered with accusations. Ideas swirled in his brain and all reasoning was engulfed with the mutant's foul touch. And Geda, she was there privately in the beast's company. Together, they were entwined like snakes, wrapped in the mystery of something unmistakably ancient and entranced by violating an undisclosed prohibition. How could he forget it?

There's no telling how long they were together, Darin considered. *Did she have time to propose to him? Did she really choose her champion, a king, to dismantle me? Or was she just wooed by him?*

He then recalled her different texture, how direct she was just the night before. Her seduction was fueled by inspiration. And her hair, deprived of all flavor, radiated frankincense, a signature scent used in the house of God, a *mutant* devotion! Her betrayal is unmistakable.

Hurt, Darin glared at Sarolt, almost thankful for the warning, turned away and left.

Satisfied, Sarolt turned to the board. "You see! Explain how a man, intimidated by a lesser king, shall lead the Order to a greater future." They couldn't.

She continued, "After all these years, Raymond stands absolute against the highest monarch, the True King. He will remain on the throne of the Order without question."

Afraid of her power, the investors cowered in their chairs. Not a peep was made. Anxious eyes scanned the table to see who would dare. The woman glanced at the old man. The dark-complected man rechecked his wrist. To Sarolt's fortune, no one showed any resistance.

"Good. Continue discussions. Raymond will be here soon," she ordered, and, as if waiting for a command, the room reignited with fiery once more.

Ding! The elevator doors opened to the underground level B9, carrying the very determined young prince. Disturbed by the queen, Darin entered the historical wing looking for answers and the being to grant them, Geda.

His mind raced with questions and his heart churned with emotions on the many possible responses she could provide. He could hear her justifying his death with little argument. Undoubtedly, her admission to guilt will be clear and concise, absent of the emotional cloudiness he drowned in. That's just who she was.

Geda was logical. She didn't cling to the erosion of feeling.

The barreling force hardly affected her expression. She always chose the right words, without stumbling over their meanings. The magic of language was lifeless to her registry, yet she mastered the spell unconditionally. To this day, he has never seen her trip over her mind. Perhaps that will change today. He would reveal the honesty hidden beneath. Today, he would see if she truly valued him.

Unfortunately, today was monumental for the history department. For the first time since its procurement, the Gammal tablet was displayed beyond the glass security for analysis. Everyone joined in the action. Even researchers from other floors oohed as Geda and her team sampled the stone and measured the engravings.

Darin soon found her mingling among the interns. "It looks like your name," one said to her. In the excitement, Geda never saw the prince coming.

Abrasively, Darin pulled her away.

Geda jumped, "Darin!" His grip was uncomfortably tight on her arm. "What is this? What do you want?" she asked. Roughness was his signature but the total disregard for the public display had her worried. There was something on his mind that made him insecure. Fear pulsed in his touch. The heartbeat of his tight fingers gave away the distress he tried to hide.

What could be causing this? she wondered.

His voice started as a whisper. "You like them, don't you?" he insisted, pulling her into the hall.

Looking at the faces passing by, everyone knew what was about to happen, but no one did anything, including the doctor; dictated by the standards of their complicated relationship, no matter what don't touch, don't get in the way, and don't come between them, for they were the Raven's children.

Regardless of the reason, even she couldn't make out what

he was saying. "What?" she asked.

Neither could he. The minutes spent churning nihilistic thoughts ruined his approach. Instead, he shook her. "Mutants! You assimilate with them, don't you?" he yelled and released, throwing her into the wall and busting the skin on her elbow, and as always, he kept coming back for more.

"The vampire in the bathroom, who is he?" he interrogated. "Is he the one who wants to kill me? Hmm?" His fear. His pain. His seriousness. It was all too real, and he refused to lighten up. "Have you been seduced by his kiss?"

His questions were nonstop, giving her little time to respond, and each time she didn't, the pressure increased.

"Stop this!" Geda ululated, fighting his hold.

He didn't.

Nothing she did answered nor denied him. To him, she wasn't taking him seriously. To tame her struggle, his body pressed against hers and forcefully grabbed her chin, directing her attention to him. There, she saw it. He had processed the questions repeatedly to the point he believed in a reality that never existed.

She tried to deny it. "No! It's not what you think. Eh, let me go! He is Theo's mutant," she insisted, but no matter how many tears she shed, he resisted them.

"I'm going to kill him."

"You don't understand!"

Darin just shook his head. How could he trust her?

Her words were poison.

His father wanted him dead.

She was all he had, but now, he was alone. Or so he thought.

"I will kill him before he gets to me," he assured. His mind was made, and nothing was going to change it. When she tried, he smothered it. Her breath formed a plea, but his hands caught the breath in her neck, preventing it from exiting.

"I'm going to kill him," he repeated, though his determination meant nothing compared to a mutant's strength, which she tried to warn.

"You… can't," she wanted to speak but couldn't. Cornered, she was helpless and soon wouldn't exist, which scared her more than Darin's emotional threats. Her air ceased. Blood pressurized her face.

"After all I've done for you!" he grunted.

The buildup on her mind became blinding. He said he would kill Ana, yet his hands squeezed her neck. He was killing her.

How did we get here? rung the last thought on her brain before it went silent. Sensation left her body and her fight softened.

"Don't worry. I've already begun," he extinguished her further. Darin took measures before confronting her. To her dismay, she was left for last. At this point, there was nothing she could do. Her eyesight faded.

It's too late… Ana…

"Implant complete," called a radio.

"10-4. Bring Theo in," Darin replied, mistakenly moving his hand. Air flowed back into her lungs.

Her brain sparked. *Theo?*

Instinctively, Geda's eyes shot open. She was confident Ana was his target.

Darin sensed a change in the being beneath him and reinforced his domination. His angry eyes met hers. Veins of albino irises had dilated and flooded red with hot tears, dislodging his gale.

Swiftly, her knee rammed into his groan, separating them.

Her training screamed, "To immobilize an attacker, aim for the diaphragm!"

She punched him, just as Sasha instructed. One hit was

enough to stun him.

"Ugh!" Darin staggered backward, gasping and choking on the spasm.

A part of her felt terrible for hurting him. Never did she think she would have to go this far, but here they were. He panted for oxygen and she coughed on its bounty. Her brain pulsed on its surplus.

One more hit should incapacitate him, she suspected, granting him one last swing, landing a left hook onto his temple.

"Grrmm!" he expelled, collapsing to the ground.

"Ah!" she winced, not prepared for the impact echoing back into her bones. As another wave came over her, her brain jolted. There was no time for self-pity, not with Theo in danger.

Theo! she remembered. With fearsome deep breaths, she ushered movement back into her body. *I have to stop whatever he has started.*

Quickly, before he woke, she dug through his pockets.

She found his phone, and his hand found her wrist.

She froze.

His fist collided with her cheek. *BAM!*

Splitting pain cracked through her skull, nullifying her fight. As she slumped to the ground, fighting the inevitable numbness, her blurry vision registered him coming back for more. "No," she moaned. But, rather, Darin left her with a final grievance.

"I wanted to make you my queen!" Unproud of what he had to do, he snatched his phone back and marched off, leaving Geda to scramble alone.

The skirmish, however, was overheard.

Darin's bark reverberated to the closest security room causing the agent to turn from her workstation. Without a word, her eyes went to the superior in command, Sarolt.

The queen chose to ignore the ruckus. "Focus on your work,

Sasha," she ordered.

"Yes, ma'am." Reluctantly, she did as she was told.

Knowing Geda was most likely at the brunt of Darin's scream, her instincts were triggered to chase after him. She was forced to restrain herself. If she got out of line anymore, there would surely be severe consequences. *Geda is no longer my concern,* she reminded herself though it felt wrong. Nose wrinkled, she went back to monitoring the deployed teams. It wasn't long before Darin barged in.

"I want all eyes on convoy G!" he ordered.

The keyboard clicked, tracing the coordinates to the transport's location. Waiting, Sarolt noted his new damage and concealed her pleasure. *Geda certainly put up a fight. The girl has bite. Good,* she mused.

The wall of monitors flashed each street corner until convoy G could be seen. "There," Sasha found.

"Who is on this team?" asked Darin. With a couple more inputs, the screen listed the names detected by trackers. "Thank god." He sighed with relief. "Romulus made it in time."

Sarolt was impressed. "You found someone that actually knows what they are doing. Heavily armed, sealed, and fortified. Even I would have a difficult time intercepting what's inside," she begrudgingly admitted.

"Given the importance of the subject, only the strongest Lion in our arsenal can complete this transport," said Darin. Sasha silently shook her head.

Strongest, huh? Just then, Sarolt got a beautiful idea.

"Hmm. We'll see about that," she mumbled. Secretly, her thumb captured the coordinates of the convoy with the message, "Guardian inbound to Joytech," and sent the location to a hunter capable of testing Darin's strategy.

Down the hall, Geda found the leverage to fight her forced

sleep. "Erh." Grunting and moaning, she wiped the blood from her lips and pushed herself onto her feet. *Darin.* She had to stop him. Using the wall as support, her breath coursed heavily with each step until control returned to her body.

Unfortunately, she had no clue how to find him, what his plans were, or how long she had been out. He could be miles away by now. All seemed hopeless until she heard his voice emanating from a room she passed.

She stopped. *Oh, that was easy but what now?* She had no plan on how to confront him. What would she say? What was his plan with Theo? Would he even tell her? Regardless, she doubted she would be welcome.

Pressured, her eye began to twitch uncontrollably. Defenseless, she came to terms with their separation. *I doubt my revolt will be forgiven.* At this point, she fully expected to be murdered if she faced him again. Just in case, she armed herself with the nearest object, an ornate candelabra on display.

Geda inched her way to the door, candelabra at the ready. She exhaled and mentally prepared, hoping to catch Darin off guard.

Darin. She adored him but the look in his eyes as he tried to kill her now fanned the flames of her violence. His caress on her neck singed with bloodlust, filling her with a desire to crash open his skull and squish rubbery intelligence between her toes. *Today, this ends.* She held the candelabra firm, grabbed the door's handle, turned the latch, but stopped. Darin wasn't alone.

"E.T.A. forty minutes for convoy G."

Sasha? Geda recognized. *What's going on? If she is overseeing this?* she questioned. The Lioness was only called to handle the most important and delicate missions.

Confusion settled her fury, feeling the weight of the ornament she carried. With Sasha present, her plan to take him out herself was thrown out the window. She had to find another way to save Theo, but how? Curious, Geda peered through the door's gap. A wall of screens illuminated the dark room, flicking back and forth as it followed a line of armored vehicles, followed by rows of computers and control panels. Darin stood, watching the wall intently while Sasha worked the keys to satisfy his demands. Standing feet from her was the silver-haired queen.

"Your plan to use Ana's human against him was smart. Theo will lead us to him." The queen praised Darin's cleverness until a familiar scent surprisingly met her nose. "However, you made a mistake."

"How so?" questioned Darin.

She turned to the young man, catching sight of the girl through the cracked door. "You harmed his woman."

Spotted, Geda froze.

"My woman!" Darin bravely corrected her. "And I barely touched her. She is fine."

Sarolt glared, unconvinced. "I can smell the blood from here." *To be harmed by the person you love*, she knew the feeling. In a way, she sympathized with the girl. Despite her jealousy, she wasn't going to highlight the spy. If anything, she would have left so that the child could bludgeon him with the weapon in her hands. Instead, the queen turned her back to the girl.

Geda released the breath she held, relieved to remain anonymous. But as she exhaled, something dripped from her nose. She cleaned it off. *Blood.* Careless of her condition, she was hell bent on saving Theo and focused on the monitors. *Ana, do you know?* she worried.

"E.T.A. twenty minutes," Sasha called out.

Soon, there won't be time to act. Geda was pressed for time, but there was nothing she could do, not here. The best she could do was wait for the convoy to arrive and deal with Darin then.

Miles away in Gibbous, sirens blared, signaling civilians to yield. The convoy escorting Theo formed a line through traffic headed to the center of the Oasis at alarming speeds. Outfitted with two and a half inches of protection, the brutal grey masses were weaponized for any assault, the perfect machine for any type of urgency.

Inside, Theo woke with a searing pain in his head and leg throbbing. "Ah," he groaned. His senses were scrambled and violated by sharp noises. People spoke coded phrases. Metal clinked, weapons were loaded, and the interior rattled from broken roads.

Where am I? What's going on? his mind raced. Before he could get his bearings, the truck rocked, throwing him from the seat. He landed on his shoulder. "Ummf!" Bound, gagged, and blindfolded by bag, readjusting himself was difficult. He worked to get loose but froze when new footsteps marched around him.

I'm not alone, his mind jolted, then remembered how he got here. *Darin,* he cursed. His head still ached from the blow he suffered at the hand of his so-called friend. *Friends,* he corrected himself. They were all there. "Just know that I had to," Darin had said. He was certain it was him stomping around but grew unnerved by his unpredictability.

What the hell does he want? Ah! The scroll! Theo remembered. He had placed it inside his jacket. Wiggling, he felt it there. *Thank God,* he was relieved.

However, the scroll was the least of his concerns. Upon closer inspection, the stomping did not match Darin's body structure. They were from something larger, broader, and stronger.

The unit bounced again, pounding his bruised shoulder.

"Grr," Theo groaned.

The heavy stomps now approached. Theo curled in defense.

Swiftly, the bag was ripped off his head and Theo instantly recognized his captor, the Butcher.

"Fuck, it's you!" yelled Theo, muffled by his gag. "What's going on? What are you doing with me?" He had so many questions. After all, the man was a dealer of flesh.

"Relax," ordered Romulus, balling up his fist. "Or do you want me to hit you again?"

Theo shook his head and complied as a gun fired outside.

"What's going on?" yelled their driver.

"Look alive!" commanded Romulus.

"Where are we?" asked Theo.

"Shh!" snapped the big man. "Gibbous."

"And we're under attack?" Theo squealed behind the cloth in his mouth. In city full of humans; it didn't make sense.

Romulus gave Theo a look that silenced him. "There is only one creature that would dare. The Peacekeeper," he answered.

Dread radiated from the Butcher. Theo could almost recite the internal prayer Romulus crafted, begging it not to be the suspected beast. A part of him wallowed in the man's unsettlement, but then reality set in; if the Butcher feared this creature, so should Theo.

A mutant with that power must be on the same level of the queen. *The Peacekeeper?* Theo could not place the name. He couldn't recall seeing it in books or hearing it in tales. It was not referenced by Bog or Currant but it was mentioned by the rebellious Anastas.

"Perhaps I should recruit the Peacekeeper's help," Ana once said, and Theo will never forget the disgust on their master's face from just hearing the name.

So that's how it is? Theo perceived. *I am right to be afraid.*

Outside, weapons readied and pointed, anticipating a fight but when it came, nothing gave the soldiers warning or time to react. All was silent except where the aggressive entity searched.

A man saw it pass by. He pulled the trigger. "There!"

But as he warned the others, the soldier's voice was cut off by the sharpness of the beast's aggression. Bleeding, the man fought to the last second of life. Still, the effort was pointless.

Others joined the gunfight. Bullets sprayed the prowling beast. Searching, he pounced from one vehicle to the next, leaving a wake of devastation in his path.

"Peacekeep'ah!" another soldier screamed as their body severed in two. Before the soldier took his last breath, the beast completed a sweep of the truck and left before it blew into pieces. The explosion shook the remaining vehicles and blood became the color of the convoy. More gunfire ensued among by acrobatic melee forces in attempt to halt the beast's approach for a few seconds before also becoming fodder for street cats.

"You stay here," ordered Romulus, as he twisted open the security hatch. Stripes melanated around his eyes but it was nothing compared to the face that broke through their confinement. The Butcher crashed to the ground and on top of him was a ferociously savage man with equally horrifying strength at half the size, the Peacekeeper.

As the beast stood, Romulus did not. Unconscious or dead, Theo didn't care. He was more concerned with this demon's gaze on him.

Their eyes met. With a glow similar to Ana's, piercing greys refracted like diamonds and froze him like winter rain. Strips covered his face, over his forehead, around his eyes, down his cheekbones, and under his chin. Theo had not seen a mutant's true face as vivid as his until now.

This is not just any mutant. This is a tiger! Theo identified. *This is how Ana is supposed to be.* The man was the most terrifying thing he had ever seen. Tall, broad, slender, muscular, and ruthless. This man was capable of dismantling masters of horrendous deeds.

Target found, the tiger stepped forward. Motionless, fear crippled Theo, resonating from the low humming bellows of the approaching tiger. All control was gone. There was no fight, no drive to survive; he was paralyzed. Theo felt so small. The beast could consume him in one swallow. Only Romulus could save him now but he too remained motionless.

That man is dead. He must be. Theo convinced himself, and in his mind, he was next.

"Hey!" yelled the beastly mutant now kneeling to him. This got the young man's attention. Theo blinked and found the aggressive state of the tiger had subsided. Remnants of darkness clung to the mutant's eyes but vanished everywhere else. While the mutant untied his hands, Theo couldn't look away from him.

Unbelievable, he was amazed. The man was utterly ordinary, completely human. Without the camouflage of his kind, the blood covering him was more evident, along with his prominent teeth, yet somehow, now Theo felt safe. Perhaps his disarming strength provided a sense of security, similar to how he hoped for the Butcher's wellbeing. The sign of desperation did not set well with him.

I should have handled this better, Theo told himself. *Pathetic.* Still, the man's gentleness melted his frozen nerves away, or perhaps it was the friendly way he spoke, acknowledging the young man's shock.

"Come on," the Peacekeeper said, assisting him up. "Let's get you back to Ana."

He knows Ana! Theo immediately labeled him as an ally and

willingly obliged. "Okay," he accepted, and the beast lifted him away.

"This can't be happening! Where is Romulus?" cried Darin. Everything was fine a second ago until the screens exploded with gunfire and silent destruction. Now the convoy was immobilized.

"Squad! Come in, squad!" Sasha called out, but the radio was silent. "Sir! We lost communications with convoy G."

"No shit!" Darin barked back. The metal table took the brunt of his fists.

Sarolt, however, couldn't hide her smile.

As he coped with failure, she soaked in the commotion. "My! This was certainly unexpected," she faked. Pleased by what she had set in motion, a laugh tumbled out on its own. "Muh ah ah ha!"

Theo was in there, he realized. "Did I just kill my friend?" Unable to bear it, Darin fell into a seat on the first row. *Theo. Please be safe,* he prayed.

"I'm looking," Sasha assured, flipping through the footage.

Without the silhouette disturbance, Geda saw the carnage at its full intensity. Her jaw dropped. The convoy carrying Theo was now in flaming ruins. Plastic and metal wreckage scattered the intersection. Pieces of agents littered the street. Blood, guts, and limbs sprinkled the scene, staining the asphalt. Theo, however, was nowhere to be seen.

As tears clung to his eye line, Darin stood. "Go slower. I need to know who did this." They watched frame by frame as a dark entity crashed into the convoy. The slaughter of men was captured in slow motion but the creature remained a mystery.

"Is it him?" Darin asked, suspecting it was Ana.

"No," answered Sarolt but she also wasn't going to give

away her hunter.

Geda, on the other hand, agreed. *It had to be him*, she thought, inching away from the door. *Who else would do this to save Theo besides Ana?*

Leo's words came back to her like a curse. "You have no idea what Anastas is capable of."

Was this what he meant? Intense destruction. So many lives were lost.

Her heart pounded faster. *Theo.*

She had to find him and make sure he was safe.

And Ana.

He would be accused of this massacre. She had to get to him, to warn him. But then she paused. *Wait, they moved him*, she remembered. *I don't know how to find him.*

The brass in her hands now felt heavier than ever. Astounded by her white-knuckled grip, her reflection morphed with the brass surface, rippling along the roses were inscribed at the bulb of its base.

Roses, she considered. *Leo.*

"He once did the same for me."

The realization of that statement weighed her heart. They once cared for each other. The man knew everything about Ana. He would surely know of his safekeeping. Putting the candelabra back, she ran to see him.

At the control panel, a frame finally captured the aggressor. Sasha's eyes widened. "Ariel," she whispered, recognizing the ghost leaping between transits. *He's back.*

Darin whipped around to Sarolt. "The Peacekeeper? I thought you got rid of him?"

"I did, but it is hard to contain the strong," she replied.

"So the Peacekeeper took Theo. Hmm?" he vocalized, headed to the door.

"Where are you going now?" inquired Sarolt.

He dared not tell her after all the meddling he endured from her today. He simply smirked and replied, "To get Theo back." The door closed behind him.

With the childish distraction gone, it became apparent the Lioness was stuck on the Peacekeeper's return. She cycled the images repeatedly, mulling over his absence.

More schemes flourished from watching her. *The scroll is in progress. Now, for my blade,* conjured Sarolt. "A warrant still exists for Ariel's arrest," she said, encouraging confrontation.

"There's two," corrected Sasha.

"So why not go after him? After this, I'm sure there will be another one. It may even make Raymond happy. How long has it been since your blade met his?"

The images stopped. "I cannot act without Raymond's approval," said Sasha.

"What is he going to do? Hand you over to the True King?" teased Sarolt. "You are above Raymond. Take matters into your own hands."

Sasha denied. "No... but uh, should we stop Darin?"

"No. Darin is determined to survive against an enemy he has yet to make. I want to see what happens."

"I understand." Sasha stood from the controls. "I hope Geda is okay."

"Hmm." Sarolt was intrigued. *After all these years, the Peacekeeper has returned and this was her reaction?* The queen gave her the warmest smile. "As do I."

Above ground, Geda's breath hastened. Rapid steps climbed the central spiral looking for the messenger she spoke with earlier. *I need to find Ana before they do! Only Leo will know where he is!* "Ah!" She nearly tripped. Readjusting, she counted the numbers on the tanks.

486. 487. 488.

Her gasps became hoarse.

663. 664. 665.

Then she came to the tank with a name.

"Leo!" Geda shouted.

The Separatist's eyes opened. "What is it?" he asked, surprised to see her in such a state.

"If the church moves Ana, where would he be?" she asked. Huffing over her words, she spoke too fast for him to understand.

"What?"

"Where would they move him?" she yelled.

"Ah, to the church or whatever safe zone there is in the Oasis. Why?" *Did something happen to him?* He wanted to ask but if something did happen, she certainly had no time to answer.

"Safe zone? What safe zone?" she rebutted, then remembered the neutral zone. "The restaurant! Thank you." And she left.

"Wait! Geda!" he called to her, deeply troubled.

She stopped.

"If they have moved him, *he* is doing a dangerous thing." Intentionally, 'he' was made a mystery. "Be careful," Leo warned. "*He* is the one you should watch out for."

"I don't understand. Who is *he*?" she asked.

"*He* is…"

CHAPTER 20

Children of Bargaining and Masters of Grief

T heo!" Concern escaped Ana's lips early in the morning, and ever since, he was determined to get his guardian back. When he found Theo had not returned home, his mind weaved various scenarios and considered endless possibilities to the cause. By the time he got the call confirming his worst fears, Ana had already crossed the Oasis twice, searching to claim the boy before anyone else did.

"I have him," read the message. "Meet me below the Gibbous Crossroads." Ironically, where Theo proposed to Ana.

The Crossroads were once a beautiful place. Beneath the weaving layers of highway systems was a field of wildflowers, a natural park curated by neighborhood communities to honor native species and the unification of beings. Shortly after, the park's water sources were redirected. All that remains now is a patch of brittle dirt, dry plant material, and broken memories, a perfect representation of the outlands in the heart of Gibbous. Only those of mutant orientation remember how it once was. Because of this, he was comfortable meeting the proposition, even going as far as suspecting the messenger's identity.

Ana was there within minutes.

Tires locked up, and rubber skidded to a stop, kicking up gravel. When the dust settled, the nose of his Challenger faced a civilian SUV.

His heart jumped, but he knew better than to foolishly reveal himself first. *Something isn't right,* he detected. The vehicle across from him did not belong to who he had hoped and caution blared in his mind. Making matters worse, he couldn't tell who was inside the car or if they genuinely had Theo with them.

This would be a good trap, Ana thought. *Dangling Theo so closely.* His grip twisted the leather steering wheel. *Come on, show me!*

Standing off, they contemplated the other's actions. Finally, the passenger door opened. It was Theo.

Ana's restrictions relaxed. "There he is," and he went after him. Disregarding the driver's door, Ana collided with Theo, wrapping him in a storgic embrace.

Crutchless but in his mutant's arms, Theo's shock subsided and the emotional build up was released. "Ana," he quivered. Air surged through his nostrils, trying to hold back his troubled waters. However, the more he fought it, the more trauma resurfaced.

"I've got you," Ana promised. However, it was not enough to subside the branding in Theo's eyes. The features of his demonic savior shackled the boy. That beastly mutant, the true face of the tiger, and the ferocity of the creature's determination; it all came back to him upon safely returning.

Ana recognized his condition. *He must have seen something outrageous.* "Theo. Hey! Did they do anything to you?" he asked, but his words would not materialize.

"I…. I…." After several attempts, he gave up and just shook his head. Honestly, he did not know. After Darin hit him, he had no recollection aside from the transit carnage.

"Lay into me."

Theo did, falling deeper into the arm of the Devil. His breathing soon matched Ana's. With the arms wrapped around him, he felt more secure than he had been in a long time, recalibrating him to the proper wavelength. The shock seemingly evaporated, as if Ana absorbed it all. Theo was free, saved like the bus crash ten years ago.

Yet, in all actuality, the danger still loomed behind them. The driver's door to the other vehicle shut, and Ana's attention went to Theo's savior. Again, his heart thumped. Approaching was the man he anticipated. He couldn't believe it. "Ariel? It is you."

Untrusting, Theo's hold tightened on Ana.

"Brother, its been a long time," answered the beast.

Ana's head bobbed. "Thank you," he said softly.

Theo felt a slight tinge of Ana's voice in his ear. He was genuinely grateful to have his guardian back, forming a warmth he didn't know he needed.

Brother? Theo picked up. *Is this animal related to Ana?* He turned and caught the eye of the tiger bearing a human face.

The man squeezed Ana's shoulder. "We have much to discuss," said Ariel.

"Not here," Ana replied, taking the disturbed boy away.

"Then I will follow," said Ariel, returning to the other vehicle.

Encapsulated by the Challenger, Ana hesitated to turn the ignition, allowing Theo to settle. Silence pressurized them. "Are you alright?" he asked. Though there was no response, he witnessed Theo's shoulders melt into the leather.

The devilish engine roared to life, shaking the interior and idled. Tones changed and stabilized with Ana's breath. Theo read it all. The fight to find him was evident at startup, and the guardian's return soothed the machine's purr, bathing his conscience even more.

Theo inhaled and finally unleashed, "What the fuck? What is he?" He always found a way to make Ana smile.

"What do you mean?" asked Ana.

"Oh, don't give me that! Do you know what he did?"

"I can imagine. You have a bit of blood on you." Ana went to rub it off when Theo smacked away his parenting and proceeded to paint him a picture.

"He just tore through an armored unit like I tear through single-ply toilet paper."

"I see you've calmed," Ana said under his breath.

Theo continued to exaggerate, "Then, when he is all bloody and scary, he gently treats me like a child."

Ana waited for him to be done before responding. "Ariel, he's my… younger brother." The drone of the engine changed as he put it in gear.

Theo had many questions. Retracing its tracks on a dusty path, the Challenger met sturdy pavement and howled to the falling sun. In the side mirror, he watched the accompanying vehicle follow close behind. "Brother? You two are so different," said Theo.

"We serve the same master," Ana simply explained.

"Bog?"

Ana nodded. "One day, Father returned with him, and he's been a part of our family ever since."

"Just like me," mumbled Theo. He watched the black S.U.V. flow with the curving highway and considered the man in the driver seat; how the two mutants shared comradery for generations. How close must they be? Then it hit him. "Wait. Why have I not heard about him until now?" Theo asked. "You did the same with Geda. What else are you not telling me?"

"It's not like that. Those things did not matter at the time — *She* wasn't supposed to, not in your lifetime." Ana sighed.

Their brotherly relationship was bound only by the fact they were in the same boat and could not survive without the other. The delicate threads tethering them were enforced by a brutal man. It wasn't an easy explanation.

"There are stipulations surrounding Ariel's line of duty to the monarchy," Ana eluded.

"The Peacekeeper is not royal, is that it?" guessed Theo.

"That's right. Ariel is not a royal under Bog's reign." Ana left it at that.

There was more to the story than what he was willing to say, at least for now, leaving Theo to speculate. "Bog removed his crown without killing him. His strength is incredible."

"Strength is his power. Just as I am known for cleverness, Ariel is the strongest."

"So what did he do?"

"He loved the wrong woman."

Theo was dumbfounded. It was the same story as Ana; right woman, wrong time. "What is it with you men and your women?" he teased, but all the same, he was seriously concerned that their desires would send the world to great destruction.

Thankfully, Ana found it amusing.

"If he is your brother, where is his engine?" Theo asked.

Ana looked in the rear-view mirror, back at the sizable S.U.V. "That's a great question."

Inside Marcy Joan's, Theo nearly fainted from Marcy's squeeze. "Oh! Thank goodness, you are alive! Oh, I was so concerned. To think, you were kidnapped by that awful organization. Poor little Theo," she pampered.

She stroked his hair, pulling fine fibers from his scalp. Ana grimaced. Turns out, there was such a thing called over-loving. Then, he realized, "Wait. How did you know?"

Remembering others were in the room, Marcy's attention went to them. "Oh, Ana! Your friend, she arrived earlier looking for you."

Theo perked up. "Geda?"

Marcy nodded. "Uh-huh. She told me what happened. The poor thing was in such distress looking for you, so I let her rest upstairs. I hope you don't mind, Ana. She seemed knowledgeable. I assumed you two were on good terms."

"We are," he confirmed.

Loose, Theo saw an escape. "I will go check on her," he assured and shot to the stairs.

"Oh! Okay, I guess," laughed Marcy.

Ana motioned to the man behind him. "Marcy, this is Ariel," he introduced.

"Ma'am," nodded Ariel.

Fulfilling a mannerism, her hand met his. For a moment, she lingered on the obvious: the mutant liner on the eyes, the stark, bland hair, and the jewels of his irises. He possessed distinctive characteristics of a particular gentleman her colleague, the Lioness, once described. Linking the identifying details in her mind, she felt her heart stop. "I know you," she would have said if Ana had not interrupted her.

"I'm sorry, but we really should check on Geda," he ushered.

She understood. "Please. I will be up shortly." And they left her presence.

The loft door nearly left its hinges when the young man barged in. "Geda!" called Theo.

Surprised, she jumped to her feet. "Theo?" She fully expected him to be in Darin's possession, yet here he was. He went to her and wrapped his arms around her. Physical, she embraced him. "Are you okay?" she whispered.

"My head hurts terribly, but I'm alright."

She would be glad but something haunted her. "Implant complete," rung Darin's radio.

Geda feared the worst. *Theo, did they…?*

With him in her arms, she investigated his neck. Her fingers ran through his hair, pulled him down, and there she found it, a small injection mark at the base of his skull, barely the size of a pimple. Her embrace weakened.

Again, the door opened, and their eyes met.

When Ana's eyes laid on her, his heart tightened. The sight of the young man draped in her warmth was not what disturbed him. It was something much more profound. As he approached, a different filter shaded his contrasting gaze.

She knew he saw it, the touch of love upon her face. Deep down, the repercussion of his emotions frightened her, but still, she presented the damage to his judgment without hesitation.

Ignoring the grown man cowering in her arms, Ana's hands cradled her face. His piercing eyes analyzed her structure and narrowed at the obstructions.

"Geda, what did you do?" he asked. His usually warm voice strung a bitter cord for a newfound enemy. Tears filled the edges of her eyes, ashamed to admit what had transpired.

Theo, however, did not understand what he meant. His head lifted from her shoulder and, too, spotted claw marks on her jaw and neck accentuated by faint bruising. Dried blood clung to the edges of her nose and her cheek puffed from Darin's hit.

Recognizing the signs, his chest shuddered. "Did Darin do this?" Theo asked, threateningly.

Unwelcomed, Ariel remained by the door. He absorbed the warm environment, the lush use of red and turmeric, and the behavior of others; how his brother maneuvered around fragile things, specifically the girl at his fingertips. *That girl.* There was something about her. He couldn't quite put his finger on it.

"That's not the worst he's done." Her voice groveled, high-lighting, "You've been tagged."

"What?" Ana grabbed Theo to take it out.

Thankfully, Marcy entered at the right time "No! Don't! You'll kill him. Ah, Ariel! Why didn't you stop them?"

Ariel was dumbfounded. "How am I supposed to know?"

"I am not comfortable with a C.O.V. device in his head."

Marcy understood his frustration. "The tags are notorious for being impossible to remove without inflicting death."

"Then what are we supposed to do?" asked Ana.

"A key," answered Geda.

Ana looked at her. "A key?"

She then realized what she was about to say was top secret. From their expressions, even the tigers were unaware of this detail. "You don't know?" she whispered to him.

"Know what?" encouraged Ariel.

"All the tags have a key. Two pieces linked. The key to a tag is another tag," she informed.

"And removing a tag without a key always results in death," added Marcy.

"So, between two tagged individuals, there is only one key and only one will survive."

Geda nodded. "Synthesis was made to be realistic. The tags represent the mutualism of guardianship and the fundamental stabilization of the claim."

This made Ana indifferent. All the pain of experimentation, scientific dissection, and inhuman medicament, and that was the Order's enormous success? The chemical signals bonding master and servant?

What else do they know? he worried, looking at his hand. An ominous thought popped into his brain. *If they know about the chemical bond, is the tag really all they did to him?*

Ana grabbed Theo's hand and lifted it to his lips. Darkness flooded the edges of Ana's features, summoning the remnants within his guardian's body.

"What are you — *Ahrow!*" Theo gritted his teeth as the dark sign of guardian commitment emerged from deep dermal layers.

"It's still there," sighed Ana with relief.

Ariel peeked over Ana's shoulder. "Such a terrible place to put it."

"It needed to be visible," said Ana.

As they bickered, Geda watched the dark spot twist and turn, as if the Malum essence was trying to escape the boundaries of human flesh before setting in it's original position. *An implant of darkness, a vow of unconditional acceptance and assistance,* she considered. It was beautiful.

Ana's eyes met hers once again. "You said there was a key. If I bring one back, can you set him free?"

Her eyes widened. To kill in return for his life. Was he really going to do that? Of course, he was. "You have no idea what Anastas is capable of," again Leo's words haunted her, and he was right. Ana was willing to murder to save the one he loved.

"Hey now! Wait," Theo fought back. "We are not taking a life to save mine."

Geda agreed, "He's right. We don't know the scope of the tag. It could be a normal one but knowing Darin, his key could be unique. After all, he enjoyed Theo."

The thought made Ana sick. His face twisted as he stepped away.

"What about your key?" Ariel asked her directly. "Would you willingly sacrifice yourself to save the boy?"

Ana gave Ariel a look. "Excuse you?"

"Have you been listening? That would kill her," Marcy objected.

However, the question was not meant to be taken literally. Ignoring them, Geda braved the oddly superior being. "Am I being asked?"

Ariel's eyes softened. "Unfortunately, the question will never be vocalized. It is a thought you must already own." His words resonated with Sasha's teachings.

"I couldn't even if I wanted to," she answered. "My tag is unique. I am Darin's key, and he is mine."

"The Raven's children," commented Marcy.

"The deal," highlighted Ana. It all made sense now and held more weight.

Theo went to him "Ana? What are you thinking?"

"Tell me more," Ariel demanded the girl.

She did. "Aside from the Raven's children, the Lions are linked together and the entire population is linked to a master key."

Ariel pressed on, "Who is the master key?"

That she could not say outright. Doing so would endanger the identity of her family. So, she whispered a simple hint, "Who is the master of all the Oasis?"

The answer was subjective, but they all came to the same conclusion, "Raymond."

Geda emphasized further, saying, "Until death, no one has escaped their tag without a key."

Ana lifted Geda's chin to look at her once more.

"That's not entirely true," chimed Marcy. "I do know of one person who has."

"Who?" asked Theo.

"Sasha," realized Geda.

Marcy nodded. "The Lioness is the survivor of everything.

I will give her a call to see what she can do."

"Thank you, Marcy."

Though it had been years since the two faced off, Ariel did recall a little scar within the tiny hairs on the back of her neck. *Was that the price of your freedom, Sasha?* Thinking of her, he caught himself fiddling with his jacket.

He scanned the room, concerned someone saw his nervousness. Thankfully, the remaining occupants were focused on the well-being of each other.

"Are you feeling alright?" Ana asked Theo.

"Me? Is Geda feeling alright?" Theo turned to her. "Geda, what happened?"

"I'm okay," she assured. "Darin and I just had an altercation, but you must know, it was Darin who did this."

"I know. Him and the whole team attacked me when I left the church."

"What?"

In preparation for Sasha, Ariel gathered himself for departure. He placed his hand on Ana's shoulder, and they exchanged a silent appreciation for each other. But as he turned away to leave, Theo pulled him back into the conversation.

"It really wasn't that bad. Honestly, Ariel was the worst of it." Theo motioned to him. "Romulus was there and everything. He was nothing compared to this beast."

Geda's eyes met his jeweled gaze. "Ariel? I feel like we've met before."

"We did briefly, at the game. 7541," he replied, pointing to the tattoo on her hand.

Theo nudged his arm. "Hey! How did you learn to fight like that?" he asked. He was clearly distracting himself with conversation, but Ariel could tell the tag was devouring his confidence.

I know the feeling. So, he obliged.

Ariel's brow raised, pondering a response. "Hmm. Well, we've all battled in war and fainted death at the losing sign. Taking a blade to the chest for the sake of your anonymity is detrimental in every regard" — he thought for a second — "but, I can't pinpoint a specific event that influenced my fighting pattern. When the time came, the movements and strength were already there."

Theo's eyes glistened. "Wow."

"Do you want to talk about it?"

"Yes, please," he replied and together, they sat around the coffee table to discuss experiences like childhood friends.

All they could do now was wait. As Theo surrendered, so did Ana. Depleted, he looked Geda in the eyes, then passed her for fresh air. The day was most definitely trying. It was understandable for silence to do most of the talking but his last gaze carried a defeat she could not withstand.

Although he intended to bathe his stress away under the night's sun alone, he allowed her to invade his solidarity.

"She was there," she said.

Geda, Ana resonated and faced her. His exposure wore a new shade of darkness.

"Sarolt," she clarified.

"Do not say her name," he scoffed. Retreating, she chased after him.

"She was there, Ana." She grabbed him, refusing to speak to his back. "And she is capable of anything. I saw the manipulation she spun to get what she wanted. She sewed Darin's mind, corrupting him to use Theo against you like she did with Mason and Leo." This got his attention. "What else will she do to get to you?" she questioned, fearful.

He was surprised by how steeped she had become in their

culture. "She will do everything she can to find me and hasn't. *That* is what scares me," he admitted.

"Are you sure you should be making a deal with her?"

"I already have. Sending Theo back to me was her response."

"What? Why would you —"

"I had no choice, Geda! They took him and I couldn't do anything. I couldn't see him on the Malum network."

"You used the shadows?"

"I used everything and still couldn't find him. So, I let a bird fly regardless of any consequences that may befall me. Now, Theo is safe. Tagged and soon to be synthetic, but safe. You don't know what that means to me."

"I do."

"Darin ambushed him with nine other men. Why do you defend him?" Ana challenged. "There was no influence needed. He acted on his own accord" — his touch brushed her damage — "did that on his own accord. Why do you protect him?"

She shook her head. "You misunderstand." As her eyes watered, the brittle cord in her voice broke. "He's my family."

"But you want him dead. Was that before or after he touched you?"

Her eyes widened, realizing he was right. *I have. Since when have I wanted this?* From a young age, Darin and Geda were inseparable. They were in love but eventually his childish touch grew firm. Even when he assumed the role as heir to the Order, it was not the pain he influenced that caused her tension to flourish. It was her jealousy.

Darin had a life, a fruitful purpose, and a constitution that required minimal effort to survive. His tag was a security measure against accidents, while hers was a necessity.

She was a shadow of her former self, longing to be more than what she was, so much so that she was willing to kill for it. She consulted death for change, married it, and became it to subside her hunger. The extent of her actions was previously unknown and the awareness of her desires fearfully clarified her character.

As Geda filled with shame, a part of her bloomed, beckoning Ana in. A finger caressed her, and another inevitably fell into place. Then another and another. Soon his gentle hold replaced her lover's imprint and the two settled into this magnetism.

"It is not uncommon for a woman to witness a man's rage, but never should it touch the one he loves," he said, glimpsing at her lips, wanting to meet them. *No*, he refused and instead pulled her into his chest, burying her in his safety.

Her scent engrossed him. Citrus and vanilla overwhelmed his pomegranates. "You, of all people, know what sacrifices we must make to protect the ones we love."

Words clogged her throat, evident by the grip on his clothes. *It's him! It can't be but it is.* Since her inception, there existed a summoning, a call to reunite with the wandering soul aimlessly lead by the unforgiven.

Ana and Darin, two were very similar. What was thought to be found in Darin turned out to be overglorified imperfections. Meanwhile, this man, this mutant, imperfect from expensive sacrifice, carried the heart of cherished enemies and frightful lovers. He was generous in his speechless descriptions, caressing in his every action, and welcoming despite any indifference.

Anastas. He was the wanderer who carelessly halted her power. The memory went beyond their flesh contact. It sparked her D.N.A. upon olfactory registry. She smelt it on him, staghorn, validating the feeling.

"I'm not going to kill him," Ana said bluntly.

She looked up from his clothes.

"That is what concerns you?" he asked, peering down into

her bunny eyes. But it wasn't. It was clear she clung onto a part of Darin that was not him. It was not *him* that she loved, but Ana.

She shook her head and nuzzled deeper into the man she had always wanted, catching him off guard. Her chest ached, confident not to let go even though it would take nothing to blow him away. Her grip held onto him tighter as if he could disappear any second.

"Geda, are you crying?"

She nodded.

"Why?"

She refused to say. Instead, she caught her breath and changed the subject. "You moved," she replied, muffled by his shirt.

"Hmm." He released his breath, cradling her deeper in his shawl. "I'm sorry."

CHAPTER 21

Revolution of the Scroll

Moments later, the balcony door slid open. Rejoining the others, Ana and Geda intercepted a vibrant conversation between the needy guardian and the beastly savior.

"Doing so would release a force of magnitude proportions society has not felt in over thirty years," Ariel warned as they made their way to the sofa.

"What are you guys talking about?" Geda asked.

"Beacons," replied Marcy as Ana planted himself in the armchair close to his brother.

Meanwhile, Geda hovered behind Marcy, pondering her heavy response. *Beacons or beaconing, the eclosion of a dark chrysalis formed from prolonged Malum exposure,* she once read. Her gaze instinctively went to Ana.

The physical body can only endure so much before breaking, spewing oppressed energy, and ultimately summoning Malum Saltus to feast on the infested body. It has been on Ana's mind for a long time and undoubtedly, he would soon meet the same conclusion.

Theo could see the weight form on his mutant and offered a reassuring detail. "I found the scroll," he said.

As expected, Ana's expression brightened. "Do you still have it?" he asked, interrupting a sip of tea.

Reaching into his inner coat pocket, Theo pulled out a rod of marvelous quality, collecting everyone's attention. Contrasting the shimmer of purity, the discolored antique parchment was further amplified by the warm décor.

Interested, Marcy leaned forward. 'What do you have there?"

However, not everyone was thrilled by the object. When Theo handed the artifact to Ana, Ariel's breath lodged in his throat. "Ana, why do you have that?" he questioned rather aggressively. If the scroll has reemerged, it could only mean Ana intended to use it.

Ana held the scroll tightly and begrudgingly admitted, "It's time. Father is distracted, and I aim to use it against him."

Ariel was outraged. "Have you lost your mind?"

"Yes actually," Ana laughed. "That's why its now or never."

"It will be your death in return," Ariel persisted.

"It will be my death regardless," refuted Ana. "Have you forgotten? Even I am just a knight in his game. At least, this way, I will not go down alone."

"And the queen?"

"At this rate, I may not have a tomorrow. If I am to succeed, I need all the power I can get."

"So I arrived at the right time," said Ariel.

"No," corrected Ana. "I am not asking you to join the cause. In fact, I'm encouraging you to stay away. I can't bear to see you endure another repentance."

Ariel wasn't going anywhere. He reclined further into the sofa. "Why does that matter? You'll be dead, remember. You won't have to witness it."

Ana smirked. Technically, he was right. "Still, that's not something you should ever experience again."

Ariel could not disagree with the idea of the True King's absence. Though he dreamt of his father's death numerous times, he was still bound to the workings of the higher power. "What makes you think he won't kill me when you're gone?" asked Ariel. "You are the only thing that stopped him in the past."

"That's not true. Your lineage guarantees your life, and when this is done, only you will be left standing. Your duty as Peacekeeper will be gone and we will never feel his wrath again," Ana expressed.

Ariel was taken back by his sentiments. *He endured all this pain to force Father into a precarious position,* he considered. *I hope he was the strength to follow through with it.* "Did you miss me that much, prince?" he asked.

Ana took a sharp inhale. "I'll admit it's been hard."

"I can tell. You put too much on your guardian," stated Ariel, requesting to examine the artifact. "So you are giving her the weapon to deal the final blow."

Ana handed it to him. "That was the plan, but after receiving her charity, I'm afraid my bargain holds less weight."

Geda's eyes followed the scroll.

Ariel pulled the threads and loosened the tension of the parchment. "I disagree. She sent me the S.O.S. to terrorize the Raven boy," he informed.

The flap fell open, shining with rainbow scripture. Behind him, Geda gasped. Flashes of color impolitely stamped and scrapped ignited her fascination. The sheer quantity weighed on her understanding.

Theo laughed. "I had the same reaction when I first saw it. We are taught there are only two queens but according to this, there were tens of thousands."

Ana nodded. "It was a rude discovery for me as well. When Ariel learned the True King had ordered Sarolt's claim, he showed me the scroll. Names of women I previously coerced carved bitterly beside Mother's before becoming fodder. Father crowned them to consume their power. Only two queens, the True Queen and Sarolt, grasped their power and took back control. They became known for their defiance and thus why most people think there are only two."

"What happened to the True Queen?" inquired Geda. Though physically absent, the majesty remained on everyone's lips.

"That's the mystery and root of this war," answered Ariel. "No one knows."

"Supposedly, Raymond knows her location and holds it over the monarch's head," added Marcy.

"Do you believe him?"

Ariel snickered as Ana gently explained, "If Raymond truly had her in his pocket, the game would not have lasted this long."

Considering the meaning, Theo's gaze found Geda admiring the surface Ariel entertained.

"Like gemstones," she whispered, amazed.

Looking around the room, they sat as a family. Different streams of conversation bonded where they were weak. For the first time since the kidnapping, Theo was finally able to let down his guard. That is until he heard what Ana said next.

"So, how is the scroll a weapon?"

Everyone froze.

How did Ana not know how his weapon worked? Cleverness was his specialty. So for him to not know something was an outrage. The fact that Ariel did made his smile even brighter.

"Watch," Ariel demanded. He twirled the scroll closed and tied the threads, protecting the history within from further damage. His left hand encircled the center, stretching the forefinger to meet the thumb. His right hand cupped a pommel of the scroll rod, placing his thumb perfectly over the carved eye, and twisted.

With a fraction of his might, the metal torqued loose.

All in attendance gasped. The rod was now open.

"A hidden chamber?" suspected Geda.

The scroll tipped, and an object fell into Ariel's hand.

"What is it?" Theo moved to get a better look.

Ariel fondled it into a better position and lifted a maroon vial for all to see. Sealed in wax, it, too, possessed the eye insignia.

There it is again, the guardian noted.

"Blood?" Marcy judged.

"Of the highest octane," emphasized Ariel.

Not convinced, Marcy smacked the cushion. "Queen's blood! Ana, that's the weapon? You cannot approach that woman with this."

Theo, however, was convinced. He recited the scroll's scripture, "Queen's blood is the embodiment of health for all life drinks and the source of wealth all envies to obtain."

A terrible idea then surfaced Ana's brain, *Health.* It took everything to restrain himself from snatching the vial from his brother and consuming it.

"I'm sorry," chimed Geda. "Why would the queen need queen's blood?"

Ariel filled her in. "It's a common practice. Higher beings retain samples of themselves to remember who they were or what they were made of. The blood's potential depends on the power of the being, and nothing is stronger than the True Queen. This is a retainer of her most holy. Consuming this would turn a beacon into a baby."

He looked to Ana, who was quietly scheming. "Consuming this would grant a mortal the power of the gods, raise the dead, and forge weapons from thin air. Imagine the power Sarolt will gain with this." He gave the vial one last look then slid it back in the scroll's core.

"Do you have vials like this?" Theo asked Ana.

"No," he admitted. "The risk of someone abusing your reserve is high. A royal's blood is sacred."

"What about you, Ariel?"

"I do," he said. "I made Ana a necklace with one."

Ana frowned. "I used it on a pigeon."

Ariel's shoulders dropped. "Such a waste."

"I can't transfigure my blood."

"I'll get you another one."

As comforting as he was, there was something he said that disturbed Geda. "Ariel, are we in danger?" she asked. "With this power, can we trust the queen to honor the deal?" For Ana's sake, she did not feel confident in the risk.

Ariel thought long for an answer that would not come. Instead, he warned, "If this plan doesn't work and Father survives, then I would fear. Now, as far as *if* we can trust her? Sarolt is probably the most faithful mutant of all."

Ariel looked at the scroll and back to Ana. "You understand Father has been searching for this blood since before your mutant birth?"

The air surrounding the Peacekeeper swiftly became stagnant as if his suggestion conflicted with his submissiveness to the Devil King. Human support spiked with defensive quills.

Finally, Ana broke the tension. "You knew of the blood's existence. Why did you not present it to him?"

"I —"

"You would have been greatly praised," added Ana.

"I know where my devotion resides."

"Do you?"

Ariel swallowed. *He knows I have been helping the queen.*

"Unlike you, I am not trapped by obligation. Since you crawled to me weeping and bleeding, I have wedged myself into power as a buffer between beings. I am the one who has been in control."

Ariel's brow dropped.

"Don't feel betrayed. You wouldn't have known. You do not see what spawns from my fragile suggestions. Subtly, I have been influencing Father to confront the inquisition, and weakening him with false securities. It all started with the scroll. I stole it and birthed the perfect warrior capable of destroying him."

Ariel was aghast. "Intentionally? You loved her."

"I still do," confessed Ana. "And one day, I will pay beyond life for my sins, but that day must wait until the board is set. The warrior must wait for the perfect moment to strike down God. Until then, I sip from Erebus's cup, gradually enveloping his nutrients for more than survival against the maiden I betrayed but also to persuade the holy monarch I am weak so he may use me as bait."

Ariel cut him off. "Have you forgotten Arnireth? What happens when you lose control, and the hive comes for you? Will you sacrifice the few million remaining? Will you tear the world apart to destroy him?"

Ana could not convey his reasoning. Intelligence was his power but careless consideration was always his downfall. Little details were often overlooked to secure the goal, yet as he looked around the room, he saw expressions of determination, trust, and unwavering cooperation.

Sacrifice was inevitable in his position. A choice between evils, and he did what was necessary to break it. They understood how the Oasis's current struggles were minuscule compared to the war. They knew their efforts supported only a fragment of the solution expanding lifetimes but were devoted nonetheless.

"I will not stand against you, brother, but allow me to stand beside you," requested Ariel. Ana straightened with surprise. Before he could refuse, Ariel illustrated further, "Death will undoubtedly be your success, Anastas. I can ensure life prevails in your wake. My act will be viewed as antagonistic. Lives will be saved while clearing the way for you to dethrone God."

"Ariel, know death was never my intention," disclosed Ana.

"Then, do we have a deal?" Ariel offered along with the scroll.

Ana hesitated for a split second. Sarolt's coalition and Ariel's involvement was an uncalculated risk, but he needed all the strength he could recruit. Ana accepted, "Very well," and took back the weapon.

The morning pulled at the fabric of night, and those unacquainted with its excellence inevitably drooped. It wasn't long before Marcy went to bed.

"Sasha can't make it," she checked her phone. "There was an aggressor in Crescent." Ariel's heart thumped but before he could ask for more info, she reminded them to, "Clean the dishes when you get done."

"Yes, ma'am," Ana and Ariel said in unison.

Silence then fell on the men and the two brothers locked eyes. The tense staredown registered in Theo as a sizing game, a common tactic among mutants. Avoiding the crossfire, he gathered the porcelain, and carried the serving tray to the kitchen. Geda followed after him. Now alone, they were able to display their wide menacing smiles, flexing their features, and establishing limits to the age-old game of teasing. Held breath cleared the board and they began.

The clock ticked past one. As the guest, Ariel took the first shot with his words. "The boy is oddly familiar, almost resembling an old love of yours. Ironic."

"Is it morning already?" stretched Ana, easily brushing off Ariel's poor attempt to get under his skin.

The Peacekeeper was just getting started. "Last I saw you, you were not bound by a *guardian*," implying Theo was more of a burden than a helper.

Ana twitched, feeling the dagger of his brother's tease but it was not enough for a Malum reaction. His turn. "Last time you were around, I'd just met little Theo."

"Oh, the time you had to kill him?"

"Though you claim to have a guardian, I don't think I have ever seen you with yours." Ariel's expression twisted. It was definitely a touchy subject but Malum did not stir. Ana pressed harder, "Why is that, Ari? Don't have one anymore?"

Instinctively, darkness flashed across his face at the thought. "*Hiss!* You got me," Ariel accepted defeat. Walking it off, he combed the loft's finer details, looking everywhere except his brother.

As the winner, Ana savored his reward with the right to questioning. "You think I wouldn't notice? You've been fidgety all night. You disappeared. Why?"

Ariel laughed, "Ha! Your beloved witch tricked me into slumber and sealed my sanctuary. It took me years to break through it."

"Ariel!" barked Ana. "You know the consequences of breaking your slumber before its time."

"It's nothing I can't handle," he argued.

"Is that arrogance?" Ana detected.

"Not entirely." Ariel turned to face Ana. "There is an anxiety, a ticking sensation echoing to the end of my being. The Malum are stirring, preparing for something."

"A beacon?"

"I don't know. I thought it was you, but you've evidently

kept yourself together."

Ana smirked. "It's worse than it looks."

"They say you haven't slept."

"It's been a while."

Ariel was on the verge of lecturing him but resisted. Anything he had to say his brother already knew. Besides, bickering wouldn't help the time convergence. Plus, it was not like Ariel was one to talk. He would soon pay the consequences for interrupting his sleep. "Please make other arrangements," he said instead, insinuating not to use the Order's resources.

"Bog is building a new sanctuary."

Ariel's brow lifted. "Does Geda know?"

Ana swallowed a breath. "Yes," he simplified, but his brother noticed the authentic details he tried to hide.

Jeweled eyes squinted with speculation and whispered, "Is she a familiar? I have seen how you restrain yourself with her."

"It's different," said Ana, "and I catch myself getting involved. I try so hard not to." Leaning closer to speak more privately, his eyes meet Ariel's glistening gems with complete sincerity. "I long to be with her, but I don't want her to want me. Does that make sense?"

"It does." In his own way, Ariel understood.

The tangled disaster called infatuation he held for another was not worth the desiccation it would bring. His endearment would deface the statute of morals, singe judgment with bloodlust, and erode the values harvested by his beloved. All because of who he was to the god he served. And for that, he kept his most adored at a distance. Cherished and unseen, his love became his greatest enemy.

As the morning sun rose over Marcy's home, the mutant brothers reminisced old memories. Accompanying Theo's faint snores, louver blinds diced the rays flowing into the open. Snuggled in his arms, Geda curled deeper to avoid the light. As they slumbered on the couch, the mutants summoned scars to the surface and chuckled quietly about the past.

Whispering, Ariel pointed to a mark on Ana's knee before it disappeared. "Oh! Do you remember that one?"

"Ah," Ana recalled. "I got that the last time I went home."

"Sanliurfa, what a beautiful city. Well, it was beautiful," corrected Ariel. The city, like most, was now ruins. "You should take Geda to see it someday. Douse her in your history."

The idea excited Ana, more specifically, his brother's consideration of meaningful things to do with a significant other. "Yeah. Can you imagine what it looks like now?"

"Like everything else, ruined skeletons, but she would see its charm."

"Good morning, Marcy." Ana welcomed as she meandered through with a coffee cup. Still asleep, she waved and silently headed downstairs. "Do you remember this one?" asked Ana, pointing to the new scar on his forearm.

Ariel smiled with excited whisper. "Oh, yeah! 1032. You got that from stealing a pear. It took weeks to heal."

"Who knew General Maniakes would get so angry about distributing rations to starving men," laughed Ana.

Ariel smirked. "They didn't hunger much after that, and no one said anything about the reappearance of your hand."

Downstairs, chairs unturned from tabletops, stoves ignited, and tableware chimed with a napkin roll. All could be heard from above.

Listening, Ariel couldn't help but praise her. "She certainly is spry."

"Isn't she?" Ana said proudly. "It's already 7:50? The restaurant should open soon."

In his proximity, Ariel felt Ana's admiration for Marcy. The tiger looked upon his brother. In his final days, despite his condition, Ana was genuinely happy, his smile glowed, and his animation came from the heart, not from the demanding respect carved by their father. Thinking about it, this was the first time Ariel saw Ana for who he truly was. It warmed him. He never thought he needed this and it was all thanks to the people supporting him.

"You have a beautiful family, Ana." The words seemingly fluttered out on their own. Ariel did not hide the jealousy contained within.

They are my family, realized Ana. *Marcy, Currant, Theo, and Geda. They are all beside me*. Pride filled his eyes and a smile lifted his antiquity. "They could be your family too if you decided to stay," said Ana. "Will you?"

"I will," Ariel softly replied. "Just tell me what you need and you shall receive it, brother."

And so, Ana did. "When the time comes, I need you to ensure their safety. The battle between the royals will be great, and I will inevitably be the epicenter. Don't come back for me. Get them far away. When it happens, I expect the explosion will be great."

Ariel heard many things in his request, but nothing spoke of survival. *This will be Ana's last stand. This was his dying wish*. "Very well," he accepted, living not only up to the title of Peacekeeper but also the name of Reaper.

At 7:59 am, on a Sunday morning, June 1st, the breaker switch flipped, illuminating the open sign of Marcy Joans. At the entrance, Marcy was surprised to see the street was so packed. *Busy?* she questioned. *This early?*

At 8:00 am, the deadbolt twisted, disrupting a connection somewhere within the mechanism, unleashing an unearthly force throughout the whole building. Everything shifted with the magnitude of a miniature atomic bomb; light pulse.

The loft was hurled into a blender. The furniture flipped. Decor took flight. Mutants were thrown around. All from the quake. It was as if a missile had landed at the front of the building.

Choking on the dust, Ariel found himself in a new position. "What the fuck was that?" he yowled.

Ana threw the bookshelf off his back. He too stumbled on what had transpired. He took a breath but found that security was hard to achieve. "Theo?" called Ana. "Geda?"

Ariel found the guardian in the rubble next to him. "He's unconscious… and breathing," he answered.

"Good," coughed Ana. Not far from him, Geda groaned, crawling out from under a pile of books. Ana found her outstretched hand and pulled her free. "I've got you." Thankfully her damage, if she suffered any, was indistinguishable from the rest of her marks.

"What was that?" she whimpered.

Ana didn't have an answer. As air filled in from below, it got harder to breathe by the second. Debris kissed his lungs, and a sanguinary aroma salivated his tongue. *Blood,* he identified.

A tipped clock chimed a dying tune reminding him what time it was. 8:00 am, opening time.

Marcy?

She was downstairs.

His heart ceased. "Marcy!"

CHAPTER 22

Malum Baptism

F ootsteps tumbled down the stairs as Ariel struggled to keep up. Cloth, dirt, and dust cluttered the air with a charred yellow haze. At this point, the smell of bloodshed was everywhere, but the concoction made it difficult to navigate. They feared what they might find. With a flip of a switch, the haven had become hell, and the beloved caretaker was on the frontlines.

"Marcy," Ana shuddered. Cutting around the corner, he slipped on thrown plastics. Catching himself, the scope of ruin came over him. "Oh my god," he gasped.

Kitchen utensils crawled into the hallway. Cutlery and silverware perforate the remaining obstructions. Pots and pans were tossed from hooks. And boiling stews flooded the floor.

The main dining room, however, was not as lucky as the kitchen; only the building's steel frame endured the blast. Splinters and shattered fragments dangled the entryway. Ceiling tiles and lights were torn from their places. Cushioning stuffed the air. Wire harnesses were ripped from their tethers. Drywall fractured into billions of pieces. Tables panic, toppling over others for safety. Electricity rained sparks on the powdered glass.

They breathed it all in. There was nothing left to identify the once welcoming Marcy Joan's. The same could be said for the woman with the same name, yet to be located.

Beyond the destruction, vehicles screeched to a halt. Intruders arrived without hesitation. Doors slammed with determination, one to every three men. Though the brothers could not see, their mutant ears picked up the sound of men shouting, "Secure the area!"

"The Order," coughed Ariel. "Get down," he advised, diving into thicker dust clouds. Ana did not follow. "Where did you go?"

Ana risked it. He crawled through the rubble, searching for his employer. "Where is she?" Ariel heard him mutter, patting the ground and feeling for her.

Ariel didn't stop him. Finding Marcy was crucial. To think, she took the brunt of the explosion. If she was alive, she would need medical attention fast. But there was a dilemma making her rescue all the more complicated.

I can handle these guys on my own, Ariel thought. *How many are there? 10? 15?* More vehicles arrived, doubling the body count and weaponry. As guns clicked and readied, the steady mutant became uneasy.

Are they here to occupy the neutral zone? What is Raymond doing?

There was no explanation for the surrounding soldiers until one called out to the rest, "Subject 1141 has been sighted! Stay alert!"

A cold chill ran through Ariel's veins. *Ana! They are here for you.* "What did you do?" he hissed.

Geda heard the vehicle doors slam from the loft. Recognizing the sound, her stomach tightened but she had to be sure. She place Theo down gently and ran to the window but not before her phone chimed with a haunting message, "I'm here."

Ana heard the order. Danger infiltrated their broken paradise, which made time against him even more noticeable.

Marcy. He searched harder.

He combed through the rubble, touching every wood piece and broken scrap but his sight was fading. Anxiety curdled clarity. The shaken air dried his eyes, yet a boiling heat watered them. *How could I let this happen?* he blamed himself.

Tears released with silent cries.

The weight he unknowingly displaced onto others suddenly became apparent. In this case, the being dearest to him suffered the burden of his mere presence; his greatest fear came true.

Ana's breath began to tremble as he rushed. Instability grew for he knew what would soon follow. The march of his harrowed queen would come, effortlessly flow over the destruction, grab hold of his collar, and pull the beating heart from his chest, ending the pitiful existence of Anastas, the first archbishop of Hungary and defiler of her majesty. Fear created fantasy but who else would ravage such hostility?

Regardless, death was on his doorstep, and he could do nothing to reject it. The act was inevitable, like the wind blowing in a storm, which is what Sarolt was: thunder, lightning, and hellfire. Bound to his relations, he could no longer run. If it meant saving Marcy from further annihilation, he would face her valiantly.

Finally, his touch met a fleshy surface. *Marcy!* He saw her color through waves of disruption. He had found her. Soaked in blood, grime caked the shell of her unresponsiveness.

"Marcy," he cried out to her, almost calling her mother. As he unearthed her shredded body from under a table, thankfully she was still breathing, but barely.

Cradling her, his heart shattered with repercussion. She could have been dead. She still could die. They had to get her to a hospital fast. If only there wasn't an army blocking their way.

"Clear!" announced a soldier.

They are here for me, conspired Ana.

"Eastbound. Clear!" secured another.

It's all my fault.

He has been here before. History swept over him as a sting of convergence tied the two incidents together. Day became night and steel became granite. Holding onto the dead, gore-splattered pavers and collapsed columns crinkled his mind. Rufescent waters stained nearby aqueducts and flames consumed the great city he once nurtured, taken by the vengeful queen. Now, his valiant metropolis rested in the flesh of a black woman.

Lasers scanned the fog searching for any sign of the target. Ariel ducked from view and strategized. *If I concentrate the dust, it should be enough to get everyone out of here.*

His muscles contracted to move when suddenly an impulse anchored him. Darkness touched his skin and traveled up his body. Corruption, a sensation he was all too familiar with, swallowed him out of nowhere. *What is this?* his insides screamed until he realized it wasn't coming from within. It came from Ana.

Primal energy emanated from his brother, struggling to contain his seal. Amplified by his emotions, Ana's exposure began to shift.

Ariel grabbed him. "Anastas. Hey." Ana met his gaze. The grey jewels rounded with kindness, establishing a foundation for him to stand on. For the moment, Ana was safe from the chaotic waters consuming him. Finally, he was able to breathe.

"Come out and face me!" a youthful voice screamed from the streets.

Darin!

Ariel watched reason vanish from Ana's eyes.

"It's him." Ana dropped all effort in disbelief.

He was prepared to feel the burn of his queen or the slice of Raymond's chains, but the boy? He was the one who did this? Darin. He blemished Geda. Now, he has destroyed his home. What reservation Ana had for killing the boy was gone.

Upon hearing the boy's cry, the bucket under his feet no longer existed. Ana crashed into the sea of chaos. The previously repressed influence flooded his system, quenching every follicle and muscle for a fight.

Malum possession overcame him, fueled by nature's residual aggression, and increased his endurance to the firepower Darin wielded. But Ana still had to be careful. The primitive source of power was dangerous. Prolonged exposure would make him an aggressor, unable to normalize. In this true form, he was one step closer to the name sake, Devil, and soon the boy would learn it.

Gently, Ana placed Marcy down and turned to the wide-eyed Peacekeeper. "Do not let me go too far," he requested.

Knowing he couldn't stop him, Ariel bowed. "Very well." It had been ages since he'd experience this side of Ana. How could he refuse? He, too, stood and prepared his body. He fluffed his muscles, distributed the Malum to his limbs, and radiated the energy beyond flesh to vibrate the air. "Additional protection."

From the street, the morning sun rippled through the airborne impurities, curtaining the offensive in heavenly rays. However, it did not embrace the tragic rubble as the dust grew thicker.

"Go get him," ordered Darin.

Safely surrounded by his marksmen, he waited patiently for the demons to come to him. And they did. One by one, lasers found the mutants in the cloud of dust, but their weapons were no match for their fury. With a glance at each other, Ana and Ariel sprang to action.

Face-striped and hair lined, the tigers took advantage of the decreased visibility and morphed the dust pattern for complete discretion. "I've lost sight of 'em!" cried a soldier before his throat was slit. Together, Ana and Ariel apprehended the outer lying scouts, encircling the target at the center.

"Here they come," tensed Lion Sabre, unsheathing his blade to protect Darin.

As the dust cloud migrated to the street, the wailing got closer but it did not deter soldiers from their line of duty. More bravely entered and soon the dust was inescapable. Red spray petrified the air in broad daylight and colored the ambiance with scarlet fog. Audible crunches and visceral contortion reached the boy. A severed arm even hit the windshield behind them.

"Take aim," Darin commanded. He knew they would come for him, purposefully baiting them into the gunman's line of sight.

No mutant can survive excessive shredder penetration. The blood loss would be too detrimental and recovery too expensive, Darin thought, smiling at the potential. *You pathetic mutants may reach me but will lose more muscle than I have worth devouring.*

In his mind, it was the perfect plan. But Sabre did not agree. "What?" The unorthodox protocol caught him off guard, but his men executed it thoughtlessly. "Wait!" he ordered but it was too late. Before Sabre could stop them, weapons fired at shadows prowling in the haze. Bullets ricocheted off nearby properties, sliced through windows, and splintered into nearby pedestrians, but the projectiles never landed a fatal hit.

Their defenses quickly became a puppet show written by martyred saints. Chunks of flesh and distasteful parts were thrown as a warning to cease the assault. A few hesitated.

"Fire!" Darin ushered again, reigniting their command but it was too late as murder surrounded them. Their eyes crossed, trying to keep up with the mutant aggression. Slaughter lived at every angle. Too late did the young man realize they were sitting ducks.

"Fire! Fire! Fire!" Darin desperately called. Bullets crashed through vehicles, busted bricks, and chiseled pavements. His soldiers could not shoot fast enough. It was not long before they joined the shower.

The growls of the tigers got closer and, too, echoed in the boy's mind, silencing rationality.

This is their final attack, recognized Sabre. As a last resort, he pushed the boy back. "Get behind me," he ordered, determined not to pay for the boy's mistakes. He wasn't fast enough. Effortlessly, the Lion's throat dislodged, satisfying the revenge of a different demon. Pale hair and robust features.

It's him! Darin froze. *Its the beast that tore through my convoy, the Reaper.*

Remnants of his protector gurgled at his feet. Sabre pointed. "Be... behind you."

Darin mistakenly turned. Before him stood the real mutant he wished to end. His eyes widened, and reason clogged his throat. "You?" croaked the young man.

Face to face, he got a good look at his enemy. Bold stripes displayed his retention of darkness. The same was not present when Geda was in his arms. "Ha! To think she chose you!" the young man scoffed. "How weak? Pathetic!"

Clearly the boy did not know who he spoke to.

Ana exhaled and his stripes grew bigger. Darkness flowed, filling the vacuoles of his skin. Four scars melanated across his forehead, 1141, displaying Raymond's signature.

The Devil! Darin recognized.

The beast with those numbers was forever known as the fallen angel to the Venator society. The Devil's lore was legendary. From the young man's expression, he knew it well. But to think someone of his ruthlessness was casually present in day-to-day living; how he sat with them in class like nothing, and Geda, how she chose him of all people.

Stunned, the Raven boy fell in the face of judgment. Palms busted under his weight. "You're… you're him. You're the Devil. Unbelievable…"

Mutants have many names. He fully expected the other demon – the strong, resilient one ripping meat with his teeth, to be the divergent king. But no, it was the mutant he caught bewitching his woman. It was Theo's roommate. It was Marcy's kitchen hand. It was the scrawny beast on his radar the whole time.

Bones snapped ominously in the background as nutrients were shucked by the other demon. *He's going to do the same to me!* cried Darin.

Fearful, he retreated, scooting as far as possible. Ana easily kept up. Darin's back eventually met the convoy's front bumper. With nowhere to run, he outstretched his hand and begged, "Devil! You misunderstand. It was a deal, and I wanted to live." He prayed, but this fallen angel was unforgiving.

Not wanting to sully his hands, Ana pulled a shotgun from a nearby corpse.

Darin's voice broke, pleading harder. "Wait! Please!"

Empty shells spat from the barrel, and new ones inserted.

The Devil didn't slow as the boy had hoped.

"Wait!" Darin insisted. "No! It was Sarolt!" he claimed, attempting to redirect the aggressor.

An effective tactic but not today, not with Marcy like this, and not after what he did to Geda.

Darin's eyesight twisted down the black barrel.

Ariel just watched.

With one last breath, a light flashed before the young man's eyes. Weight evaporated from his body and his soulless shell slumped to the ground, dead by the hands of the Devil he tested.

An unprecedented worry lifted from Ana's chest. In its absence, he realized what he had done. The contract he had no ambition to satisfy was ultimately fulfilled. Geda's tag will be removed and Bog will be out to get him.

Shit. The weapon slipped from his fingers.

For the moment, he lingered in the chaotic aftermath, the fragments and splatter emphasized by heavenly rays. Bliss, he breathed with uncomfortable ease as the water's edge encroached upon his peak, tingling along the way.

Without reason for possession, Ana started to choke, suffocating on Malum essence. "Fall into me," urged Ariel, wrapping his arms around him and ending the bloody dance. Ana did. Together, they sank to the ground.

"Here." Ariel handed him a femur. Cracked straight from the source, red bone marrow contained regeneration properties crucial for Ana's stability as his mind was too focused on centering and not healing.

The weight of his brother returned as he drank. *I wonder if this is what Sarolt had in mind when she encouraged his bloodlust,* Ariel pondered. *Marrow is the most potent source of vitality. A consistent feeding would strengthen his resolve.* He then considered all the carnage and the little amount he collected. *It's going to take a lot of death.*

Sirens blared in their direction. "They're coming," said Ariel, pushing Ana to attention. "We need to leave."

Ana shook his head. "I'm staying with Marcy."

Ariel understood. "What do you want me to do?"

"Get Theo and Geda out of here." Ana threw his keys to Ariel. "Make sure they are okay. I don't want them to see this."

"I will. Be safe, Ana." Ariel agreed and leapt to collect the others.

Burying his identity with a deep breathes, Ana returned to Marcy's side until the paramedics and C.O.V. arrived. Drained, his thoughts conflicted with trivial details, one of which persisted. After confronting the boy, he saw they were not so different.

At the hospital, Ana waited for Marcy's results. Thankfully, she got to there just in time to stabilize her condition, but the wait to see her was killing him. In the meantime, he patiently remained in a hallway chair, untroubled by the carnage he outfitted, abiding the many gasps of those passing by.

His fingers tapped away the seconds. His ears were quenched by the muddled intercom, the swinging door song, and nearby concerned conversations. He listened for any notion of Marcy. There was none.

For once, he felt time drag on, time he filled with endless sighs, an expression of dark overdose. His mind crinkled from Malum linger. Vacuoles thirsted for a response, and his fibers ached from the limits recently stretched. In all, he was still recovering from the aftermath.

Ana sighed again. *I hope Theo calls soon*, he wished, unaware that his phone was missing.

"Breaking news out of Gibbous," the television overhead caught his attention. "The beloved establishment Marcy Joan's was attacked this morning, suffering a catastrophic explosion, leveling the restaurant's infrastructure. The source of the damage is still unknown and currently under investigation. However, at this time, sources claim two aggressor mutants may have been involved. We now go live to the scene of the incident," reported News Anchor Wyatt, transitioning to Reporter John for eyewitness accounts.

"I heard yelling and gunshots rippling. *Blahpp!*" expressed one neighboring shop owner. "Then they pointed in our direction, and bullets rained on our place. Do you see that? Look how big that hole is. And this" — the man picked metal fragments off the ground — "This is a shredder. I could have been hit by this! They are everywhere! My question is: since when did C.O.V. become so absent-minded of people?"

"That's an excellent question, sir. One we expect Raymond to answer," said John. He thanked the gentleman and turned to the camera. "Wyatt, people are shaken after this morning, saying the business day started with an earth-shattering quake that nearly cost them their lives."

"My thoughts go out to everyone affected. Thank you, John," returned Wyatt. "In light of today's event, some locals theorize this was an attempt to capture the notorious Cousin King Casimir. Others suspect a terrorist attack, or retaliation for the Rose Garden — Oh?"

Wyatt was then interrupted with a new document. He paused momentarily to read it, during which his expression changed. He cleared his throat and continued, "I have just been informed, the Central Organization of Venators has officially released a statement claiming the attack was organized and committed by none other than Prince Darin Sambuca."

Aghast, he resorted to reading the official report directly. "Investigation into the motive is underway. In the meantime, C.O.V. and Joytech assure the public actions are being implemented to prevent this from happening again. Official agents responded to the scene after receiving an anonymous call from a concerned citizen. Though those in the vicinity were unharmed, the attack resulted in the death of the offenders, including Joytech royalty Darin Sambuca, the famous son of Lord Raymond Sambuca, canceling the highly anticipated wedding scheduled for this evening."

Ana's heart dropped. "Wedding?"

Wyatt continued, "Lord Raymond Sambuca is scheduled to speak shortly on today's tragedy. In the meantime, local authorities and C.O.V. are working to resolve this case. Now," he sat the page aside and moved on. "In other news, the pits of Arnireth have been inactive for thirty years. What could this mean for the future of the Oasis?"

"Wedding?" Ana repeated, questioning the news source. Then, it hit him. Darin and Geda, they were meant to be married. *Marriage,* he had taken that away from her. After all, the boy choose the mutant's march over her's. *Today?* Her lover died by his hands. All that remained was a broken promise. *Geda,* he imagined the hatred she held for him.

"Why the long face?" asked the gentleman sliding into the seat next to him, interrupting the sudden awareness of chunks littering his skin.

"Leo."

"You certainly made a mess, my friend," Leo commented, curling his nose at the brain matter plastered to Ana. "Be grateful you are still alive."

"Ariel helped," Ana simply stated.

There it was, the reminder of their opposition. Leo grimaced, "Ah. Tsk. To the point then. I am here to honor Raymond's deal." He cleared his throat and read from the Order's letter, "The organization is livid at Darin's selfish actions. Acting independently, the prince violated several regulations, including the Common Boundary Law, causing the death and injury of several valued personnel. The Order appreciates your selfless actions."

Leo nudged him with a clenched hand.

Ana looked over and Leo's hand opened, revealing a small metal dowel, Darin's synthetic tag. 5 mm of engraved surgical steel bore the Raven's insignia, highlighted in blood. Such significance was held in such a tiny object, enough to create segregation among species, districts, governments, and religions. This charm, in particular, shackled him with despair. It resembled a death he would never be cleansed of. It was the key to the end, but more importantly, the key to Geda's freedom.

Leo continued, "In response, you have been granted the good Samaritan status as a reward."

"Hypocrisy," voiced Ana.

Leo rushed through the rest of the letter. "With Darin's tag in possession, Geda's tag will be removed this evening. Lord Raymond has agreed to fund the rebuild of Marcy's restaurant, and repair any nearby property damage."

Ana didn't respond. His eyes glazed over, heartless towards the words of a soulless man. The same could not be said for Leo. When he leaned in, he regained his attention. "Whispers have circulated of your impending slumber," eluded Leo. "If you seek organizational protection of your assets, the Order aims to honor the deal."

Whispers? The shadows? Ana was interested. "What else do they say?"

Disarmed, Leo faltered. "Well, the church is digging, building —"

"My sanctuary."

Leo's collar blinked but was allowed to speak freely. "The dead speak on the prospects of a new commander. Ana, please tell me it isn't true," he begged.

Ana shook his head. He refused to reveal anything with Raymond listening. Even so, how could he tell Leo of his deadly plans? He did, however, admit to one thing, "I… have made a deal with the queen." His dual eyes told Leo everything.

Before his emotions could surface, Leo quickly retreated back behind the corporate mask. "Theo and Geda will be safe in their hands!" he demanded.

"Will they grant me freedom from experimentation?" tested Ana. He knew how much the Order valued their research. If they honored his request, his friends would indeed be safe. Agreement also meant efforts to reproduce the royal claim had dissolved.

A light blinked in Leo's ear. He nodded with Raymond's answer, "For the time being."

Ana was beyond relieved.

Knowing this might be their last goodbye, Leo gave Ana the documentation, stood, and bowed with tear-lined eyes. "It has been an honor," he said. With the message delivered, Leo was forced to leave.

Shamefully, Ana watched him walk away. After decades, he finally made peace with the Order but still could not save the man under their control.

"Sir," a nurse called for Ana.

"Ma'am?" He stood, hopeful for news.

She skipped over and said, "I appreciate you waiting. Mrs. Joans has a very supportive family —"

"Can I see her?" Ana interrupted.

The nurse refused, "She is stable, but… she is currently being questioned by a Venator. They are here for a report on the accident. I suggest waiting. Plus, given the circumstance," she referred to the filth he was covered in, "I'm required by law to submit you for questioning, but it would seem the Venator has already signed off on it. Can you think of why?" The nurse had cause to be suspicious. He, too, was curious.

"Who is the agent?" he asked.

She hesitated. "Hmm. Lioness Sasha."

Sasha! He stiffened. *She was at the restaurant a couple days ago. Did she have something to do with the explosion?* He suspected she did. "I need to speak with the agent," Ana insisted, brushing past the healthcare worker to confront her.

"Ah, sir!" The nurse chased after him. "Sir, I wouldn't recommend that," she respectfully urged, but the mutant's hand had already pulled the door open.

Hysterical threats bombarded him, expelled by the shop owner, intended only for the agent to hear. Distracted and unwelcome, Sasha nearly ran into him on the way out.

"May God curse you, Lioness! If I ever see you again, I will not restrain my blade. I will kill you," promised Marcy.

Their conversation was over the second it started. Marcy's words sliced Sasha's security away. Once friends, the Lioness forcefully endured all that Marcy had to inflict. Pain lingered on her face, an expression Ana sympathized with. Sasha took all the blame. Why?

When the Lioness met his gaze, he had his answer. Marcy needed a target, someone to hate in order to heal. For some personal resolution, Sasha volunteered, a selfless act among her kind. Hurt, she counted her wounds and quickly left.

"Anastas!" Marcy gasped. "Please tell me that is not your blood."

"No," he said, rushing to her bedside to grab her hand.

It belongs to the men responsible, that felt wrong for him to say.

Darin. How could he admit to killing him? At that moment, Ana considered the Raven boy's final moments, how the human bent under his mutant pressure. If he were human, he too would grovel, just as the boy did. Then Ana remembered he did, time and time again.

As Marcy spoke, his mind drifted to Geda and how his actions must have grafted a disdain similar to what Marcy held for Sasha. After all, he did break his promise hours after making it.

The sensation of her crying suddenly felt real. It washed over him as if she needed him. She was summoning him. Releasing a deep sigh, he swallowed her call to be with Marcy. Guilt curdled him more.

"Honey, are you alright?" asked Marcy, breaking his trance.

"Ah!" Ana found himself staring at his hands. Stripes covered his face. He rushed to hide them.

"Are you okay?" she repeated.

"Yeah. Sorry," he said, reverting to normal, but she knew better.

She knew the matter he wore was the result of revenge. "Is it the blood?" she asked. Ana shook his head. "Why don't you go shower, and then we'll talk?" she suggested.

"I'm alright," he insisted.

"Go," she demanded, pointing to the bathroom. He went.

Regardless of his stability, a wash was definitely needed. Human rust painted every inch of him. Confined space amplified the smell, toppling his senses. It was so strong his eyes started to water, among many things. With that said, a simple wash would not suffice. He required a total drench.

Warm water flowed over him, body and clothes. The red vanished from his flesh and dark clothing, but still color circled the drain. *Where is it coming from?* He grew frustrated, scrubbing the fabric hard, uncorking his bottled stress and tearing the seam of his shirttail. Lifting it, he discovered an opening between his lower left ribs, a puncture to the spleen.

His legs nearly gave out. Even after consuming the mortal elixir of vitality, he wasn't healing. There was no hope for him now. Loss of regeneration was one of the last things left to go before total possession, before beaconing. He was on Death's doorstep. Would he have the courage to knock?

Confidence cascaded with the sacred nutrients. *I have to stay strong,* he told himself. Falling into doubt would forever lose himself. Another slow but fierce breath refortified his resolve.

Geda, I need to see her before I can't.

As night fell on Gibbous, Ana stayed at Marcy's side until she fell asleep. Damp, he savored their last moments together. He smiled recalling their first introduction.

He vividly remembered how the strange woman had plucked him from the sunshine and shoved him in a seat. "Eat," she insisted, sliding a plate in his direction.

Dumbfounded, Ana judged the dish. Crawfish and jambalaya, an unusual delicacy among the colony, one he always skipped over in the past. Now with the world gone, he thought he would never see it again. He was glad he did. Ana took a bite. "Hmm!" He chewed. "This is good," he complimented with a mouthful of chunky soup.

"Wonderful!" cheered Marcy.

During this time, the restaurant was nothing more than a dingy baroque husk but she saw its full potential. "I aim to build an empire here," she embellished as he swallowed more. "I will rule with my flavors for what is a man without good food and rest? Nothing but emptiness." The unknown woman spoke with such veracity, it resonated in his soul and eventually she became the home he had searched endlessly for.

Since then, he was conscripted into her clan. She later learned who she had invited into her company. "The Devil, of all people," she would mumble under her breath. Gaining his loyalty with the power of her craft was validating enough. She welcomed him regardless of his past, which ultimately led to her brush with death today.

Marcy, he resonated, watching over her slumber. His fingers danced around hers, debating waking her.

No, he chose. *I won't wake you. I won't say goodbye, not to you. Please forgive me.* His touch then left hers, walking away forever.

After some time, Theo awoke with an unusual feeling. His head pounded, his lungs were smothered with debris, and his body was bruised by collision, yet one sensation infuriated him. His guardian symbol singed without remorse.

Ana, he murmured.

The guardian was being summoned, but when his eyes opened, his mutant was nowhere to be found, nor was he at Marcy's. Even stranger, he found the beast Ariel climbing out the dorm window.

"Where's Ana?" Theo quickly asked.

Ariel stopped and pulled himself back in. "At the hospital."

"I need to get to him," Theo grunted, getting up.

"He's only there for Marcy," Ariel assured.

"My hand," Theo winced under the Peacekeeper's explanation.

"The restaurant is gone," Ariel continued. "The Raven boy planted an explosion that nearly took the neutral zone off the map. The blast knocked you further into sleep."

Theo's face contorted. "Ana?" he breathed.

"He was very upset to say the least."

"No, Ariel. My hand!"

"What about it?"

"Where is Ana?"

Ariel then recalled the boy's guardian mark. Ana had implanted him with darkness. If Malum surged in Ana, it would appear in Theo too. Generally a bewildering notification, the pain had him screaming.

Theo gripped his hand intensely with the other. "Ah! My hand!" he squealed, afraid of why it felt this strong. He was on the verge of tears, nearing panic. It had never felt like this before. It felt like... like he was losing Ana. *It can't be,* he refused but a six sense told him otherwise. "Ariel?" his voice broke.

The mutant rushed over, snatched away Theo's other hand, saw the mark and froze. Malum essence commanded the surface, boiling flesh and tearing muscle to return to the original source.

Ana ignited hours ago, pondered Ariel. *For it to still be like this could only mean...*

Theo witnessed his expression drop and instantly knew what it meant. "Where is he?" he whimpered. "I have to go to him!"

However, the tiger was three steps ahead of him. He was prepared to defuse an aggressor, anything to save his brother but lacked his location. Ariel summoned his true face and lifted Theo's hand to his lips as if to bite him.

"No!" he resisted, refusing to lose his mark, his connection to Ana. Unbeknownst to him, Ariel's massive fangs were the least of his concern.

The proximity of darkness collided with his, engulfing Theo's hand with black flames that tickled Ariel's face. Connecting to the network, Ariel found Malum centralizing, converging to one location. Leaning a little further, he saw Ana at the heart of the attraction.

"Stay here," he ordered, leaving before Theo could insist otherwise.

CHAPTER 23

The Tangential Effects of Spiritual Tethering

In the latest hour of night, Geda's window opened for a ghostly shadow to appear, a welcoming Ana debated on meeting. After the day, yet another pact of vengeance was fostered against him. Hesitant to confront her, Ana watched from a distance, but simultaneously, longed to confess his reasoning, his transgressions against God; his god, her.

Even though the man was harsh, Ana did murder her lover. He could imagine the pain and rage brewing inside her. He could hear the chatter conflicting her mind. It pained him. He would gladly accept the smite of her blade to return life back to normal for her.

No, his intellect refused. *I must stay away.* In his debate, he came to terms with his internal self, agreeing only to make note of her well-being, satisfying his yearning for repentance.

I need to see that she is okay.

Thankfully, the house of ladies was comforting in his place. They came and went, handling the courtesies of others calling on the event.

"Hello," Breanna answered the endless phone calls. "I'm sorry. The wedding has been canceled. Please understand this was unexpected. Haven't you seen the news? Yes. Yes, sir. Thank you. I'll be sure to tell her. Right. Bah, bye."

Her friends assured her tomorrow would be better, but nothing seemed to get through to her. Past the curtain slit, he saw her tear-stained face. Sorrow mixed with sensible freedom. She was still processing her emotions.

Getting closer, Ana noticed the cut on the back of her neck, created by surgically removing her tag, just as Leo said.

The women came and went, offering gifts of comfort. Their muffled concerns danced around the wedding, careful not to harm her. Then Ana saw it. Next to her on the bed laid a beautiful white gown and the many ornaments Geda was meant to wear today. A weight emerged in his chest, envisioning how it would feel to lose the opportunity. After all, he had a sense of it.

He imagined her wedding; beautiful, white, and flowing. Were things uninterrupted, she would have approached Darin with a bouquet of flowers. They would have had a small ceremony on a rooftop in the city, surrounded by geraniums. Instead, her groom waited for a vampire to come to him, and Ana ruthlessly painted the occasion red.

Two feet away, Ana took her sorrow in. He observed her silence, her contemplation of what surpassed. She would touch her hands, beckoning them to be clean as she did nothing to hinder Darin's transgressions. Gazing upon the dress, she could still hear his childish pleas, feel the immobilizing anticipation of his impending death halt her call to authorities. *Ana.* How could she question if he would do it if she asked? The gunshot ricocheted in her mind but a part of her was secretly satisfied. She looked back at her hands. *What is wrong with me?*

Ana had seen enough. *She's alright. The pain will heal in time,* he told himself and leapt from her roof line before the wind gave him away. As the house consoled her, he sought to be with his own kind, to be among the bag of bones begging for scraps in the streets. He was no different. There was one job left, and then… death.

"I am ready."

Everything was in position. When the eclosion happens, everyone will be notified. All that was missing was Bog's spontaneous summon of death. There was no telling when it would happen only that it would; just how dying should be.

I hope Sarolt is ready, Ana prayed. The success of his plan relied heavily on her. It would be devastatingly ironic if she didn't participate.

Uncertainty blistered his gut. This was not how he wanted his relationship with Geda to end but knowing she was no longer endangered by the boy made walking away easier. *It was necessary,* he convinced himself. *It had to be done.* One day, Geda will understand and forgive him.

Then an even worse thought stopped him. *How will I say goodbye to Theo?* he considered as a physical sensation equally as terrifying came over him.

Caution pumped in his muscles. Something wasn't right. He saw it without seeing it. He missed it in his angst, but the evidence of conspiracy remained. There was no breeze among the woods but the trees told him of it anyway.

"Eeerrrmmmnn. T. T. T," they spoke. Sounds of ancient beings reached out to him. As always, Ana listened to nature's warning.

"Eerrrggm. T. T. T" They swayed in the opposite direction.

The tension of time washed over his feet like a cold current. He shivered.

Above, the falling moon pulled the horizon sideways, and below, the shadows cried as they elongated. They too had something to say. Again, he listened.

Nothing, but like the trees, they said everything. Their defiance resonated on the inside, shackling him with a warning, "do not walk away."

The further he got from Geda, the more wrong it felt. Even nature disagreed with his decision. He couldn't do this. How could he leave her like this?

Geda deserved more than this, he admitted. She earned more than a visual checkup. He owed her an explanation, a confrontation of the most unforgiving. *I should speak with her.* Ana sighed, preparing to endure the most onerous confession.

As he turned, he caught a figure staring at him through the trees. A tall, old, scruffy-looking man circled him from afar, analyzing the choices he would make.

The True King? Ana's heart skipped. It had been ages since he saw the real identity of his master. *What is he doing here? And why is he coming from the sorority house? From Geda?* Before he could ask, the entity vanished.

Windward, distaste then came to him from her direction. *Blood?* The corruption salivated his pallet. It could only mean one thing. His heart dropped. "Geda!"

Ana ran to her. Twigs snapped under his careless approach.

The ironized scent grew stronger.

He feared the worst. Human grief often had a sharp edge, and on her bedside table was a sheathed dagger, the king's blade.

Why didn't I notice it before? He pushed himself to go faster.

The house quickly came into view. From the corner, he saw the lace curtains dancing from her room.

With a leap, the entrance was right at his fingertips. He pulled back the fabric and found in the dark, a disfigured mutant of high authority cradling Geda close. Caressed by a corpse, the creature defiled her humanity with the touch of rotting flesh. His fatal grasp supported her deep slumber and feed from her exposure.

He poisoned her blood, intrusively digging his claws under her flesh. Exposed, the decaying beast savored all she offered, and leaned in closer with vial intent.

"Casimir!" Ana growled, halting his sinister kiss.

Casimir stopped. He had been caught. Or was he?

"Anahstassiuss," he sang, displaying his new toy with a broad smile.

Ignored him, Ana focused on waking the being within his grasp. "Geda!" he called out to her. Aside from the facial cues produced by the demon's twiddling digits. Her only response was a head tilt. From there, he saw it, a shimmer upon her lips, the nectar of a mutant's kiss, caught the moonlight. The transformative venom spilled from the royal's tongue and drooled onto her body. Though her neck remained unharmed, the sight disgusted Ana. The Cousin King, however, found it thrilling.

Heaving chuckles unrobbed Casimir's disguise. His true face was somehow more grotesque than his mask. Surrounded by decomposition, his wicked smile did not curl naturally, but split his features in two. He could easily devour Geda's soul in one fell swoop. And his twitching eye, that dreadful eye; convulsive reflexes kept the eyeball from falling out.

"How miserable it must be to witness this!" teased the Cousin King. The shadow's possessive grip pierced her flesh again, causing Ana to jump and the girl to groan. "To be her guardian and fail every time," added Casimir.

Ana's heart stopped. *Guardian? Geda?* He was lost for words. "She's —"

"A forbidden being? Yes, exactly as you left her. Same name. Same fate." As the wicked mutant spoke, her brow scrunched with more pain, waking the sleeping fro her trance. "Reborn to die again at the behest of your empty promises. Multiple lifetimes of failure. Anastas, I'm starting to see a pattern."

That's not Ana! The strange voice registered in Geda's mind. Her eyes shot open and she then found the man in the window. Now aware, fangs quickly fell to her position.

Geda grabbed the blade from under her pillow. As her mind screamed, her body moved on its own. The sheath flew across the room as the dagger's tip plunged into the cavity of the rotting corpse, penetrating the diaphragm. It did nothing but draw the mutant's attention.

She twisted it deeper, but Casimir simply looked down at it in amazement. The protrusion in his stomach was oddly recognizable. Geda gasped as the beast reared back for another strike.

Ana grappled him from her, ripping the claws from her flesh. However, despite being a walking corpse, even Ana was no match for the royal. Casimir quickly regained his strength and effortlessly escaped.

"King versus king! Oh, fight me for a queen! Ha Ha!" he sang, jumping out the window. Ana followed close behind.

As their voices got further, Geda was left in a state of delirium. Fangs, dripping venom, and crashing bodies. It all happened so fast. To her it was a terrible nightmare, a reflection of her unsettled conscience.

Alone, denial shivered her. *What was that? That creature! Why was the knife ineffective?* She mulled over the physical apparitions. That mutant, he was real, corporeal like the sheets underneath her, like the man in the window. *Man in the window?* she stumbled.

Ana. He was here. Remembering, her mind relaxed and she instantly felt safer. Grunts and crashes echoed outside, but shock continued to muffle her reality.

"Auw!" She grimaced, discovering the three lacerations the uninvited guest used to count her muscle threads. Dark blood seeped through her grasp. She searched for something to stop it but the nearest first aid kit was in the kitchen.

Mustering motivation to leave the safety of her bed, she grabbed a gown to cover her nakedness. As the silk slip cascaded over her flesh, the feeling of decay could not leave her mind. Though no longer there, she could still feel breath upon her ear, slobber on her neck, and pecks on her chest. And on her lips, there was a strange substance she detested. But the feeling of receiving it… she thought it was him… her guardian?

She shook the thought out of her head and viciously rubbed the sensation from her mouth. Her feet then hit the ground, and nearly slipped on the leather sheath and blood splatter. Reaching for the guard, her eyes scanned for the object that lived within it.

"Where is it? Oh, that's right. I never pulled it out." It was still stuck in the intruder's gut. Realizing what she said, a scream suddenly came from outside; his cry. She jumped out of her skin. *It was real!*

"Ana!" she yelled. Urgency filled her limbs. The sound of his agony brought her back to life. Ana was fighting the monster, and by the sound of the commotion, he was losing. She had to go to him. She had to save him!

Geda ran down the stairs. She would do the same for him. *I have to at least try.* She ran to reclaim what was hers, her Ana. Her mind raced faster. *Hurry! Hurry! I have to hurry!*

Careless of her loudness, all she wanted was Ana. There was no time for first aid. Skipping the kitchen, she just pressed the sheath into her wound to stop the bleeding. The wizened leather devoured all she spilled.

Deafened by internal screams, it took multiple minutes to notice the chaos had turned into silence. Geda slid to a halt and listened, studying the atmosphere before charging into a mutant scramble. Everything was dissonantly still. No commotion echoed through the interior, and no tussle rippled the exterior. From inside, the conflict no longer discernible which meant there was a winner.

She took a sturdy breath and cautiously approached the door. Though she was stable, her mind tripped over the meaning of the Casimir's words *Guardian?* she questioned. *How can he be my guardian?* Ana was much older than her. Plus, they had only known each other for a couple months.

As the front door opened, so did her mind; time convergence. Visions of the past seeped through, correcting what she surmised. Flashes of an old-time splintered from her frontal lobe, to her eye sockets, and through her pupils; a mental bloom. Images of a wilder time captivated her reasoning.

"You stand accused of being in league with Satan, the harbinger of darkness," barked a man behind the judiciary podium.

As she resisted the ruling, she felt the tether binding them together. Invisible, the link was strong as the day they made it. *Because that was the day we made it,* Geda remembered. A heat suddenly climbed up her legs.

"Ah!" Imaginary flames swallowed her whole. Among the visual chains, she glimpsed a man diving in to save her, the same man who jumped to her aid tonight. *It was him! Ana!* Nocturne drips followed her rapid breath, along with a desire to return the favor. *Ana.*

In the streets, only one being could be seen and from his curly hair and limping unsteadiness, only the hurt party remained. "Ana?" Concerned, Geda called to him as she approached. He didn't acknowledge her. Perhaps he didn't hear her. "Ana!" she called again but his march seemingly increased in speed.

Oh, no you don't. You're not going to get away that easily, she was determined to learn the truth. With the resurgence of their link, the demand for knowledge grew intense. Only a fragment of time bound them, but the power behind it lasted eternally in the souls of her reincarnation, and here she was, against the natural process, reborn from the fourth century as if she had never left. The evidence of their past accumulated and only he had the answers.

"Light of my queen, may death guide you to darkness," Raymond often prayed. She only now realized it's meaning; it's intention was to reignite a forgotten memory.

I thought it was just a saying, she huffed, *like how your favorite things deter you from fear. But, no. I remember now. Those were her Majesty's words before sending me to war and the Gammal tablet housed the very thing I needed to get the job done, the king's blade.*

She could feel the weapon in her grip like it was yesterday, but now it was no longer in her possession. Instead, she carelessly left it in the gut of a madman and was potentially used to harm her guardian, Ana.

It didn't take much for her to catch up to him. "Ana?" she requested, but again he disobeyed.

Ana didn't look back, rejecting the silent invitation that would become bittersweet entrapment. Though he wanted her, to be with her, his Geda, he now understood the reason for her frequent appearance. The curse of claimed guardians, his devotion chained them together upon his transformation and she was forced to relive the same consequences.

Ana refused to defile her spirit further, yet yearned to be devoured by their corrupted bond, to inevitably embrace death, anything to end the miserable repetition they created.

Find her, hurt her, love her, kill her.

Find her, hurt her, love her, kill her.

Early infatuation grafted endless misfortune. He did not want that for her. He wished to die without seeing it at least once.

Geda grabbed and tugged on his reins. "Ana, you're hurt."

"Ahrm!" Ana groaned, still struggling to get away. Straightening took labor, doing so made more vitality spill from his vessel. "Get away from me," he warned. The darkness, his sanity, everything, was slipping beyond his control. She could see it in his face. He gasped, "I shouldn't have come back. Ern! I was foolish… to think I, alone, could save you." Resisting, blood dripped to the pavement.

"What are you talking about? Ana, stop! You can hardly walk," she tried to reason with him.

Ana did not answer. Huffing, his face melanized. Shadows trickled down his brow, branched over his hauntingly beautiful eyes, and flowed across his cheeks; tiger stripes.

"Hah! I won't let it repeat," he said, doing all he could to elude her. His resistance increased, no longer affected by physical restrictions. Under the dark possession, he felt no pain. He felt nothing as the Malum waters filled his lungs.

"Stop trying to run away!" Geda begged. Blood weakened her grip. *I'm slipping!* "No! Stop! Please!" she cried, helplessly watching his humanity vanish. *Don't leave!* But all attempts she made to keep him were futile.

("Ariel, my hand.")

She then got the sense he did not want to be saved and her heart broke more. "You are going to do this, aren't you? You're going to do this to me?" She had lost him on his own volition. A pity, he had given up. And so did she.

"Fine." Geda released him and he collapsed to the ground. "Our fight hasn't even begun, and you are withdrawing like this?" Bitterness bloomed. A part of her felt ashamed for ever believing in him, betrayed even.

This cannot be how it ends, she disapproved.

With that said, she was only human. What could she do for an inverting being? How could she halt the eclosion of an event horizon? Ana curled the current. Unbearable to witness, Geda crumbled under the pressure. *The magnetism between us,* she resonated. *It vibrated from the tablet, and radiated from him. It all stemmed from him, Ana, my guardian.*

If he was going to die, let it not be lengthy.

His demise then trickled from her lips, "You were supposed to be my guardian, the one who guides and shelters me… Clearly not."

Wide eyes peered from his unfortunate bow, disemboweled by the sudden shift in her power. Towering over him, her hair whipped with a silver tinge similar to the queen who sought to damn him. This was the woman of his devotion; this was Geda. Breathless, she was everything he wanted. Now, she will deliver him to a desirable end.

"I did not leave you like this," she added.

Honest breath pushed him overboard. Toppled by a whisper, his brittle essence shattered, his wounds opened, and his mind converted. The threads of time snapped, and memories coursed freely.

("Ah! My hand!")

All around, history scattered like puzzle pieces. Thousands of lives saturated with emotion collided in a nuclear reaction. Old names, new faces, and death yet to come. Explosions imploded. Suffocating on reality, his heart was cradled within the wicked safety of possession, vomiting endless expression.

The strain twisted her insides. This power she unknowingly held over him; she was unaware it existed or the potential damage it could cause. *What have I done?* she despaired

Breathless, the beast ruptured.

As his soul inverted, the strips slide further across his body, down his forearms to his claws. Deep veins became superficial and gut-wrenching cries bellowed from an unknown origin.

"Ahlaeeeeh!" The reverb echoed in her limbs as he morphed into a shape fit for Malum consumption.

Her aggressions became the catalyst of his fragile chrysalis. The profound rawness unveiled the crystals hidden beneath. Remnants of his human soul, encapsulated in a blue like his eye, fragmented from the heart he exuded. Ana was dying. Her heart, however, wasn't ready to let go.

"Can I save him?" Staring at the blue jewel, it felt like the answer was right in front of her. Regardless of how they were bound, he was a part of her destiny, back then and now. In the past, it was not his weakness nor deception that led to her downfall. It was his selfless protection, and she would undoubtedly need it again.

Inevitably irreversible, she reached out to stabilize him but was stopped by the shadow's bloom. A dark essence emanated from his pores. Whipping with the wind, it cloaked him with black flames, protecting the transition.

Malum, she recognized its violence. Ana beaconed. He was becoming one of them. And those nearby started to gather.

"No. No. Stop!" she yelled, fearlessly latching onto him. "Ana, I'm sorry!" Hoping she got through to him, she cushioned his madness but the darkness was not made for human contact.

The fumes of corruption sucked the air from her lips, heat blistered her pale skin, and whips lacerated the inescapable. Still, she restrained the beast.

Fighting for his attention, she pulled his face to hers. She dove into his contrasting gaze, one black and one blue, and gave the demons her love instead. "Ana, come back to me," she begged. "Don't leave me again! Don't go!"

Head to head, he felt her in the sea of rage. "Geda." Grabbing on, his vision slowly returned. "Geda, I'm so scared," he whispered.

Surprised, her hold tightened. "I'm here! I'm here. I'm never letting go. Here, drink take this," he heard before a liquid cascaded over his withered tongue.

"Stay with me," her welcoming security kissed his ear as Nostalgia nullified all reasoning. Darkness flowed with little restriction. In their embrace, the smell of citrus and vanilla normalized his mind and the flaming beacon vanished from the Malum network.

CHAPTER 24

337 AD

We have to find it!" yelled a man armed with a pitchfork. "If we don't destroy the demon, more will join."

The whole village was in an uproar after a devilish creature swept their safety with leaping shadows. There was no answer for the reason, from where it came, or what it was. And to make matters worse, the young man Anastas suspected the demon was still among them. Distraught, the colony gathered at the main house, seeking guidance from their chief.

"The shadow will consume us all if we do not rid ourselves if it." said a fellow villager.

"The wretched thing must be here somewhere," rallied the healer.

"Let's search the outskirts," suggested a guard.

"No," the chief finally addressed. "Anastasius may be correct. The beast may be among us, but I will not warrant you to risk your lives in search of something that has done no harm. The raid was fruitless. The invaders took nothing, and no one was injured. The creature is but a shadow. When it does not find what it is looking for, it will move on."

"Chief?" a lady yelled from the back. "What in God's name was that thing?"

"Just another one of his creations," he replied.

"Sir!" a village guard approached. "Sir, they did take one thing."

This was news to the chief. "Go on," he commanded.

"The temple plaque is gone."

A faint expression washed over the leader's face.

This was a serious matter. He swallowed his emotion so as to not rally the villagers further. "The plaque holds great meaning but it is minuscule in value. It can be replaced. The souls of our people cannot," he declared.

The city plaque symbolized the peace forged by warring ethnicities. Unified, the coalition allowed the movement of people and ideas, fueling commerce in the unlikeliest of places. However, some tribes retain the old traditions.

God's land is God's land, the chief perceived. *They took away the very thing that signifies our placement, erasing the name of the city meant erasing our ideals. Removing it is a sign of war for within the stone rested God's weapon. I hope Anastas retrieved it in time.*

During his lengthy consideration, the village roared with conspiracy. "It's a threat," cried a farmer.

Again, their leader held up his hand, calming his unsettled brood. "I am unsure of what is to come. If you feel threatened, then prepare. In the meantime, you are welcome to wait out the night in the long house."

With the chieftain's closing remarks, the young Anastas slipped away from the masses with the very protrusion the Lord was concerned with, not the stone plague but the item held within, a ceremonial dagger. As the herald of the blade, it was his duty to guard and protect the artifact at all costs. Therefore, when he witnessed the creature's destructive search, he retrieved it immediately. It was then that the young man caught sight of the beast. Beautiful, the creature citizens feared most was vibrant and superior to their fragile structure; a force of nature they claim to be one with.

It won't be long before the demon discovers the dagger was not where it belonged and emerges to seek it out once more. Among its divinity, Anastas noticed predator features, specifically her sharp teeth; how easily it would hurt others. He warned them of the beast's capabilities but the leader advised otherwise.

A snake was in the chicken coop and they were expected to do nothing? He wasn't alone in this thought, but unlike others, he could actually do something about it. To save the village, Anastas had no choice but to confront the creature and hand over the artifact. Sounds easy, but he had never faced anything like this. He sighed, trying to quiet the surge of outcomes consuming his mind.

In the cold air, breath left heavy trails. Steam bellowed and quivered from his pit, enduring the inconsiderate weather. Winter in the region was brutal. The collar of his jacket stood against the wind slicing through the market. Lungs were susceptible to frostbite. Still, shallow breathing could not fulfill the oxygen requirement at such an altitude.

Walking through the peddlers and traveling merchants, Anastas reflected on the attack. The sun crept below the trees, extending their projected reach. A breeze rustled their fingertips. Whispers conjured spirits from the roots and their shadows morphed into human form. They danced, leapt, tumbled, and crashed, dispelling and reemerging in other shadows along the way. An army of many, the wisps marched with a fair-haired warrior cloaked in their essence.

The summoner of evil kicked the feet from under houses, searching diligently until a shadow placed the table in her hands.

With the knife's displacement, he shuddered at the impending repercussions. Now forced to face the being alone, he prayed for divine protection. "Please be with me."

Cutting across the courtyard, mention of the assault shivered from people huddled around a fire. "Did they take anything from your place?" one man asked.

"I have to completely rebuild but nothing was missing," grunted another man.

A woman leaned in. "They were here for something. The Getae don't attack for nothing."

"All they took was the town hall plaque," a nearby guard informed.

An elder cut in, "I think it was a message." They squinted at his madness. He explained, "This town was built with new religion. Now that it's flourishing, the old gods are angry. They sent a ghoul from the sea to curse us."

"From the sea?" They scoffed. "What are you talking about, old man?"

"There is only one God."

Hinges groaned as Anastas entered the stable. Now inside, relief came over him, thankful to get out of the weather. The sheer absence of wind was enough to warm him. Though his blood flowed, his muscles seized, detecting the evil entity nearby. He swallowed hard. *It's here.*

Anastas's eyes quickly scanned the place. The long barn housed many horses. Stalls after stalls lined the barn on either side, all occupied by livestock apart from the last on the left, the haymow.

Everything seemed untouched, but he knew better. The beast was here. He could feel it. Ears opened for a sound. Hooves stomped, mouths chewed, and nostrils blew. At moments, a reverb would nicker from one of the stalls, but nothing unusual stirred, making Anastas wonder if the demon truly stayed. He barred the exit just in case.

Spontaneously, in the furthest corner, hay shuffled from the empty pen. Anastas pivoted in its direction and carefully inched forward. Hot breath seeped through his lips in a fit of concentration. He tip-toed closer, avoiding any obstruction on his path capable of revealing his sneak. Stealth was nearly impossible. The route had deliberately been littered with the driest straw. Stepped on, it created the perfect alarm to warn of an intruder.

Shwift! A careless step halted him. His throat stiffened as the stirring sound grew louder. The beast was coming after him. This is the end of it all, or so he thought.

Instead, the hay rustled and settled as before. *Hoo! I can barely breathe.* He silently released his clogged breath. The shorter the distance got, the heavier his breath became. He was close now, so close he could see movement in the slits of wood. Sweat beaded his brow.

The stable's edge was now a hair's width away. At the precipice of confrontation, and most certainly death, the young man considered his next steps carefully.

Whatever this creature is, it hasn't attacked me yet. I'm sure it is aware of my presence, given my foolish misstep and frail balance. I should be vigilant.

Anastas peered over the wooden ledge and found the bringer of darkness, a woman. She appeared human. *Perhaps it was just a Dacian,* he considered. Pale and remorseless, she left him breathless.

In that moment, he realized they were wrong. It was not a demon that attacked them but a fallen angel. Without the armor of her dark army, the being appeared heavenly. A quartz woman, her hair reflected the sorrowful call of the moon, and her body possessed the strength of the same mineral. From the creases, she radiated a golden power from likes he had never seen. She carried the army of darkness with her, yet he was darkness compared to her, a fitting description of human trespassing on empyrean business.

In her lap was the stone plaque, accompanied by scraping noises. With the jerk of her arm and subtle grunts, Anastas suspected she was defacing the stone, which surely meant she wielded a tool. *She has a weapon.* He tightened his leather in case of a fight, when she suddenly revealed he was wrong yet again.

The deity raised her hands to the sky and whispered an incantation. Folding the air with a twirl of her wrist, her nails were not as graceful. Long, jagged, bent, and some broken, they visibly hurt. Her hands were empty. *She must have used them to carve the carve the stone.* He looked at her work. "G. E. D. A," a name of sorts covered "GAMMAL." To think her claws were strong enough to do that. Her hands… there was an unnatural strength to them. He wanted to feel them.

Her skyward reach fell, twisting with the magic of her words. Her touch collided with the other palm. Sharp nails drug down her arm, divided the fabric of her flesh, and released the liquid beneath.

Blood! It spilled across the stone etching.

Anastas observed the ritual in tense silence until she clawed deeper and deeper. Regardless of the demand for soak, no practice was worth the damage she inflicted, nor could he withstand the brutal self-mutilation.

"No! Stop!" he called out, tripping over the short stall door.

Surprised, she turned in defense and attacked, lunging at him.

Careless of her spell, she grabbed onto his cloth and drove him back over the railing. He crashed to the ground with the raging beast on top of him.

Threateningly, the woman jerked his collar tight, bearing her fangs, yet she was not frightening, not to him. On the contrary, the tranquility of her face scrunched into a new type of gorgeousness. Dark armor cloaked her skin. As she counted the off-tune rhythm of his system, he fell into a hypnotism, mesmerized by the inhuman pattern pulsating her shell. And her eyes! Her gaze bloomed like pale Passiflora, *Rota fortunate.*

Towered by the beast, he surrendered. If this woman was going to kill him, she would have done it the moment she latched onto him, and even now, if she were to end him, he would gladly accept this personal guide to the afterlife. Still, there was a calling. Before his end came, he had to fulfill his duty as the herald of the blade, its protector, by offering it to the divine in exchange for the village's well-being.

Her eyes followed Anastas's every movement as he carefully unsheathed the artifact from his belt. He jerked the blade free and from his waistline, the hilt of the ceremonial dagger slid into view. Instantly, her expression changed. She recognized the obsidian pommel and lazuli handle. It was the very thing she had been searching for. Little did he know, the blade was designed to harvest the cores of celestial virgins, and here he was giving it to one.

Her face was a mixture of elation, and curiosity. Without mouthing a word, she asked many questions, including the obvious, "Where did you get that," and "Why do *you* have it?"

For his mortal hands to wield the blade, she was clearly dealing with an entirely different being. Underestimating him, she retracted her aggression to reevaluate her approach. Anastas had other plans.

Swiftly, he grabbed her leaking wrist. Blood lubricated his fingers as he placed the blade into her grip. "Take it and leave," he demanded. "Do not harm this village any further."

The edge now hers, she did as he commanded, wrapping her damaged claws around the precious minerals. However, he could tell his request would not be satisfied by this alone. From the look in her eyes, her mission was just beginning. Now that she had the dagger, she had to use it.

"In the barn!" distant speech indicated their position, following the trail of the one who warned them. Villagers gathered with great suspicion. She could taste the distrust above the dried grass, but when her eyes turned to the young man, he was unaware of the impending danger.

Instead of running, Anastas bandaged her wounds. His compassion compared to those marching towards them surprised her. This man possessed no filament of betrayal, despite delivering onto her the king's blade, the chieftain's sacred dagger. He broke his promise to his lord, and yet none of his actions were an act of evil. On the contrary, they were honorable, justified and honest. He truly was God's man.

She noted the barricade's integrity. The young man may have used it to keep her in, but it will barely keep the villagers out. Soon they will enter, and when they do, they will find him pawning with power they do not understand. They will kill him. They will be merciless despite his kindness and without any recognition of his sacrifice. She saw it all before it happened.

Anastas noted her lingering stare. Inhibited by a language barrier, he tried to explain his actions in a way she could understand. "You are bleeding too much. We need to stop it," he attempted to communicate. It registered with the pressure he applied.

"(misplaced memory)," she spoke.

To his surprise, the wild woman replied in the same tongue. In disbelief, his soul's defenses dropped. "What?" he questioned.

She understood me?

Vulnerable, the pale princess pulled him in and their mouths met, gifting pleasurable textures and tastes. They entered him, and he relished in flavors previously unknown. Vanilla and citrus filled his pallet and incited the beginning of a transition.

Boom! Clink. A loud thud and iron clank sounded throughout the stable. And again. *Thume! Tink.*

The village rammed the stable door.

"We need help over here!" Anastas heard their call for more manpower, but the hold between them remained. In fact, it strengthened. He was aware of the incoming danger but feared losing knowledge if he pulled away.

Their lips twisted and he savored her more.

Soon guards will break in to seize them.

Will they understand what I did? Anastas pondered. *Most likely not. When they discover the demon with me…* He kissed her harder. *The demon, this beastly beauty, she's human,* he defended.

The door started to splinter. *Kracht!*

One more hit and they will enter.

The kiss pulled him off the ground and straightened him for the confrontation. She retracted. A trail lingered between them, along with his drunken desire to continue. An unnatural understanding grafted an improvised commitment, and on his lips, he felt them dry, retained the stickiness of her substance. Saturated in his flavor, she stepped to capture the final require-ment, slid cloth from skin, and extended her finger to meet him. Pupils swollen, he welcomed it.

Blargha! With one final hit, the villagers broke through the barred door. "Find them!" ordered the chieftain. "Anastas has the blade. If she gets her hands on him, if we lose him, all is lost." Many people poured into the stable, eager to satisfy their leader's wishes; mob mentality.

The ground crunched beneath their feet. Upon closer inspection, straw was thoughtfully distributed throughout the place. "Be mindful of your torches," warned the guard. "This is a trap. One wrong move and the whole barn could go up in flames."

"She's still here. I can taste it," gargled a second individual.

A third man turned and found them. "Anastas?" he called to be sure. The group followed the third man's sight to the left and found two figures in the shadows. The demon's grip was tight on the young man's collar.

"It's him," the guardsman confirmed. "I will go first. Retrieve my blade." Someone did. But before his hand met the hilt, another snatched it and charged blindly into the dark, towards Anastas.

"You brought this upon yourself, boy! You and your wretched bloodline!" The man cursed his mother and her replication of useless diseased children. Many believed Anastas should have been culled at birth. His support of pagan entities, and now this, only amplified his reputation.

As the man charged in, Anastas stepped forward, hoping to be the barrier between mindsets. However, the emotional did not hesitate. Fueled by nikhedonia, the neutral eyes of his people bent with murderous intent. As word spread, more citizens piled in to witness their death. They hungered for justice. The blade swung, and only Anastas's hand shielded him, only he guarded her. It was a waste of a good heart.

The fair woman grabbed the belt of her protector, grip pinched the skin, and slung him sideways. Off-kilter, Anastas fell into a the bed of dried grass. Exposed, the blade met the lady's midsection.

The attacker sneered at the ease of revenge. "I did it!" he told himself. "I slayed the demon." When in all actuality, he unshackled it.

The blade retracted. Their cheerful pleas died as her human color faded from her face. Laughs lodged in their throats as they witnessed an inhuman reaction. Her brow twisted, trying to hold the darkness in but it was too late. Like waves, it spilled into her expression, cuffed her chin, and draped over her chest. From her silent scream, they froze at the sight of her teeth.

Anastas caught her fall. His hands found her bleeding, Mortal, the red was endless. He tried to stop it but waves surged with every pump. Hissing the pain, the being curled into him, trying to hold on to whatever kept her human and he did everything to hide her susceptibility from their satisfaction.

"That's all it took?"

"Are you crazy? Did you see that thing? ."

"Let's end it. Quickly! Before it gains the strength to retaliate." Rallied, they approached.

"Don't touch her!" Anastas yelled desperately but they kept coming. They were cornered. *What to do?*

Trapped between two worlds, Anastasius looked among his people with disgust and hate. Hypocrites, they sought death for what they did not understand. How were these God's people? He denounced them.

Her purpose, whatever it was, even he did not understand. Still, he recognized its magnificence. This ethereal being went beyond their comprehension. She belonged to the hierarchy of nature, and his people blindly sought to destroy it.

Again, they came closer, pointing their torches for a better look, drooling over the lively corpse. "Give her here, boy," a man demanded.

Anastas refused. He was just a mouse to these hounds but there had to be something he could do. His eyes darted, searching for a diversion. Then, he remembered his pocket; spores of stag's horn, a magician's deception. He always kept it with him.

Anastas shoved his hand into his right pocket as they narrowed in. *It's still there!* Grateful, he pulled the being in more, enticing their torches closer. Swiftly, he jerked, slinging the yellow powder at them. They retracted, coughing. The flying particles clung to the flames, diffused and ignited into an unbelievable fireball.

"AHH!" they screamed, releasing their handles.

Torches plummeted to the ground, grasping the delicate hay stems. Flames traveled across pathways and engulfed every stall along the way.

"The horses!" called a guard, trying to save them.

Miraculously, shudders to the haymow opened, flooding the space with rich northern wind, uplifting the fire's uncontrollable state.

A way out! identified Anastasius, swooping an arm under the being's legs. "Hold onto me," he whispered and she did.

Standing, the Gammal guard witnessed an unsuspecting lamb become a wolf, a shepherd of evil, as both entities vanished from the hellfire they kindled.

Leaping from the high loft, the striped lady secured their landing, grunting under weight and injury, Anastas took none of the force previously calculated. "Let's go," he ushered her back into his arms, offering to carry her the rest of the way, and again, she accepted. With the blade in hand, she allowed him anything. For Anastas, her safety was top priority. She had what she came for. He was determined to put her back where she belonged.

Running into the forest, the outcome of his newfound allegiance clouded him with uncertainty, only that his actions guaranteed vanquish. He hoped the minute part he played was enough to save both her and the village.

Her, this inhuman beauty, majesty, and improbability who

captured his fancy to the point of suicide, she displaced him from his adaptation, showed him the reality of the world and heresy he was blind to; such ability was true magic. The moment he confronted it, he fell for the allure.

With the sacred weapon tethered to her waist, they dove deeper into the woods. Shadows morphed from the lumber, waiting for their commander to return. Despite the initial impression, her army was more helpful than argumentative. Ethereally, the warriors kindly followed, led, even spoke to him. They congratulated him with an imposition of hands. Unearthing from her nestle, the lady mumbled words to quiet them. One shadow went as far as putting the blade in her hand, reminding her of the mission before it vanished.

Anastasius studied the being. Was this the direction she wanted to take? Staring at the dagger, she was momentarily hindered by contemplation. Her gaze then met his, a choice was made, but returned to her nuzzle. In the shift, he found the bleeding had stopped, her grip still expressed a pain. With a lack of correction, Anastas continued along the path from whence she came, away from all desiring eyes. All except one.

Little did he know, another being marched amongst the shadows. Familiar with the dark kind, a child — a lion cub dressed in a fox's disguise, fearlessly followed their trail. Geda, however, did know. She witnessed the leaves shifting in the blade's moonlit reflection. The child never got close, settling beyond her striking distance. Aware of what the child would bring if Geda didn't stop her, it left her with only one option.

Suddenly, a stabbing pain pierced Anastas's bicep and shot to his fingertips, nearly dropping the lady. "Ahn!" he winced. *What is she doing?* He tried to see, but she wouldn't let him. "Hey."

In their bicker, he caught a glimpse. Nutrient-rich, the beauty devoured vitality through a torn section in his shirt, an unnoticed wound on his left arm. Blood pumped. Then it hit his heart. Removing his strength, Anastas collapsed to his knees, disconnecting her from him.

"Agh!" she groaned, retracting her teeth.

He gasped. "Are you alright?"

Anastas inspected her. Her wound was gone but a dark mark replaced the opening. Lifting the fabric further, he saw the mark was the source of her unholy pattern. To his surprise, the marks were fading. She was becoming human, exceptionally so with the tears.

Why do the marks hurt her so? he wondered.

Her divine transition was the reversal of birth, the bringing forth of an entity while subsiding another. Both collided at the intersection of her mortal tethers. Anastas now understood her reaction. The wound allowed darkness to slip through. The marks surfaced like nothing, but forcing them away took everything.

Until now, he had seen everything that displayed their differences, yet he remained curious and considerate. Initially, his fascination of her kept him alive. Then, when she lost control, he held her steady. And in opposition of his society, the young man wielded the power of earthly knowledge to save her. To her, he was a worthy wielder of the blade, but most importantly, she allowed him to ruin everything.

"Geda." Her name upon his lips, his sacrificial gift of nutrients, his ruthless guardianship, swift departure of contraband, and undeniable acceptance of her inhuman existence warranted him another kiss. They met, bloody and bewitched but short lived. The enthralling entanglement ceased with new yappings on the horizon.

Hounds howled forth a hunt. *The Chief!* Anastas knew he would be angry. "We need to leave," he rushed.

Together, they ran, deeper and deeper into the ancient forest.

The moon was high, but not one shroud of its magnificence reached the forest floor. Shadows blanketed their escape. At one point, only nocturnal sight could guide them.

Miles from the village, foliage became unfamiliar to Anastas and sounds grew new. Hounds evaporated in the distance, allowing the lapse of water to quench his ears. "The sea?" he guessed, curiously.

After an additional mile, they crashed into an opening, Ana's eyes widened. *This is the sea?* This was the first time he had ever seen it. His soul devoured it all: the breeze, the water, her.

As Geda stepped into the water, it wrapped her comfortably with a forgiving hug. Admiring his wonder, she invited him into the tide as they still had a way to go. He accepted and grabbed her outstretched invitation. Ice cold waves sloshed against his skin and warmed it all the same. It coaxed him in, welcoming him as he was. But before it reached his waist, a screech called their attention.

Caw! Looking up, a soaked black bird soared to them. *A message from the queen,* he knew but how?

Geda reached for it, but before the messenger landed in her hand, an obstruction shot the bird from midair. Their eyes immediately traced the shot to its origin. There, in the foliage, a golden-eyed child emerged.

"Sarja, stop!" yelled Anastas.

He knew the little girl. Just as he had always been at the chieftain's side, the pelt-born child lived in his shadow. In this instance, the opposite was true. A shadow stood, unfolding from her projection and materialized into a face he knew.

"Chieftain?" Anastas could not believe what he saw. *Lord chieftain! He just morphed like the demons Geda led. How is this possible?* he questioned, internally debating whether his time with Geda had granted him an awakening. The chief, he, too, had irregular teeth. How could Anastas not have known?

"Bogu!" yowled Geda. Her blade posed and ready to kill. This whole time her target was the progenitor of the village, his idol. She charged the devout leader.

"No!" Anastas lunged, but before he could apprehend her, Sarja let another pebble fly. Fired from a sling, the stone crashed into his temple, disconnecting his life from hers. The young man fell into the waves without a say in the outcome of the dark day.

Consciousness returned hard. The sting of his bicep grew, awakening God's servant. Darkness shrouded his sight but Anastas knew where he was, at the village cathedral. He had been here a million times. Eyes were not necessary to recognize it. Sighing the cold away, he rested on the hard pew inhaled the damp and stone air. He was no longer in the woodlands, no longer in the divine's company, no longer at sea. As he registered the wet cling of his clothes, he recalled his lady's aggression.

Geda! Adrenaline filled his lungs. He shot up to find her, but the blow to the head weighed him down. "Ah," he winced and discovered he wasn't alone.

Candlelight bloomed at the altar, highlighting the cross of God, which to Anastas was silhouetted by the village chieftain. "I once recall warning you not to play with snakes," he said, lighting more candles.

Conflicted, Anastas's heart felt heavy. The Lord had practically raised him. To think the honest man was a deceiver. *It's not true.* He refused to believe it but also wished for Geda to exist. For one to be real, so must the other.

"Little Anastas," the chieftain continued. "When your mother died, I promised to keep my eye on you, and that's what I have done."

As he spoke, Anastas saw his inhuman teeth. If he existed, so did she. He was relieved. "Where is she?" interrupted Anastas.

The scent of blood lingered in the air and wrinkled the chief's upper lip. Disgusted, he could not deny how the witch affected his most cherished student but refused to desecrate the sanctuary with talk of such demon.

"Spores of stag's horn." The chieftain returned the bag. "It was your mother's trick. She blinded me with it once. It is good to see you have kept her tricks alive, even though your actions lost us a vital resource, all for that pathetic creature —"

"Bog." The chief visibly stiffened. "That is what she called you."

The older man sighed. He couldn't lie to him. "That is my name, or at least, what they call me," answered Bog.

"They?"

"They, them, the demons, the savages, the uncivilized; call them what you want. They are all the same, unholy beings who wish to dissolve all that God has created," Bog illustrated. "They plague every city and political faction. Thus why the village is so secluded."

"But you are one of them?" Anastas felt betrayed. How could something so wonderful be hidden? The evidence was right in front of him for sixteen years and he never saw it. "How could you?"

It was a simple question, but for the chief, the answer had the potential to ruin everything. "Yes," he responded. "I am but a wolf among the herd to protect the sheep from shadows patrolling the night."

"Why didn't you tell me?" asked Anastas.

"If I had, your fascination would have ran wild."

"Or I would have been more devoted."

"Yes, your actions today clearly speak of your discipline," Bog harshly pointed out. "My leadership alone should have been enough for your heart to follow. Have you forgotten our purpose? We built this place to preserve his God's righteousness, rekindle societal morals, and strengthen our numbers."

"I remember," Ana reassured.

"Good," said Bog. Silence proceeded as both men controlled their frustrations. Anastas calmed his heart as the chief glanced over the forest surrounding their abode. He sighed. "You were coaxed by a nymph and bitten. My cautionary tales exist for a reason, Anastasius. Tell me why you assisted the devil with her assassination attempt."

Anastas lowered his head. "My Lord, the blade. I —"

"I got it back," growled Bog.

"What? How?" asked Anastas, dumbfounded. His lady had a monstrous grip on the ancient weapon. She wouldn't have given it up so effortlessly. *If he got it back, then…* The pain in his arm increased. He gritted his teeth, "Err."

Considering his value, Bog silently returned to the young man. "The creature obviously contaminated your mind, but that is not all she has done to you." He grabbed the young man's chin. "You have the remnants of a serpent's kiss, a venom transfer. Unnoticeable, you have been scolded with revering fantasy."

A bewitchment? Anastas touched his lips and found the oil residue from their deadly kiss. Fiction or truth, he could not deny the texture of their smooch, the twist of their lips, and the magnitude of their mesmerism. Drowning in her breath, he forged a new mind. Their sin was the devil's song, and he was entranced by its tune.

"You now realize the capacity of your mistake, and soon it will kill you. Your father will arrive shortly to take you from this village," ordered Bog.

"Sir!" Anastas stood, outraged. He never knew his father. How could he possibly expect him to leave?

"As punishment for abetting a demon —"

"You misunderstand."

"Perhaps, but your actions said otherwise."

With a pinch his candle's flame, all light within the cathedral extinguished, including the chieftain's earthly existence. Dark, the only sound permeating the air originated from Anastas's ragged breathing.

Distrust quickly surfaced. "Chief?" he called out, but there was no response. The man had vanished.

His candle plopped to the floor, and the horizon suddenly engulfed in flames. From right to left, a bright wave washed over the distant hill, illuminating the cathedral's ornate openings. The intensity was blinding. He recoiled. "Ah!"

Suddenly, the affliction in his arm traveled and singed, reverberating with the horizon screams. Looking closer, at the brightest point, a pyre restrained his lady, Geda, to be devoured by flames. The air in his lungs solidified, watching fire bite her soul. With each second, it grew higher, clawing at the sky. The cheers of his neighbors jarring at her pain disemboweled him. The spectacle raged with hate. Sadistically, they rejoiced the destruction of his religion, at the behest of a man not so different.

How can they do this? Anastas shuddered.

Determined to interfere, there was no escape from his prison aside from the small openings that were windows to her demise, barely large enough for his arm to fit through. The chapel was sealed; iron door locked. The stone walls did not budge. His strength could not topple them. There was no secret latch, no hidden entrance, nothing. Still, that didn't stop him from trying. For Geda, he would do anything.

Anastas fought and screamed like an animal in a cage. His spirit refused to break. In his fight, he spotted the chief crest over the hill. *He got out but how? It had to be magic*, his heart told him. Anastas stopped despite the blistering convolutions in his arm. Was he simply made to watch?

Bog's gaze fell upon him. His speechless command told him everything, *Disobey me and die.*

Holy! Anastas realized. *This is a church*. He turned to the cross. *God will listen*. Only God could free him. Anastas bowed with prayer. However, God knew better.

Anastas's God was internal. His God resided in symbolism. But most importantly, his God burned on the pyre. The cross he worshiped belonged to the old religions just as she did. *Help me save her*, his spirit called but could no longer hear the shadow's whisper, meaning the cross before him belonged to the deceiver, the God that stoked the pyre.

Kneeling, Anastas took a deep breath, recalling the teachings. *These walls are his holiness's moral boundaries, a prison of reflection. To be free, I must release myself from 'unholy' burdens. To be free, I must be to his liking. To be free, I must rid her of my existence.*

He was reluctant. For Geda, his beauty and nightly deity, he would do everything except let her go. But to save her, he had no choice.

I have to.

He closed his eyes and allowed the sensation of her well-being to fade; the presence of her spirit seeped from him, the color of her pale existence gone, her hair in moonlight vanished from his eyes, and the warmth of her bite now bruised him with anguish. Lingering, he removed the romance, ending any thoughtful expression he clung onto. There was nothing left but the everlasting smear upon his lips.

"Geda, even your name will be gone from me," he whispered.

With one last exhale, she was no longer in his consciousness. He became, as Bog intended, pure.

Clartch! The door behind him unlatched.

I was right! His spell worked. Now free, she became his number one priority; his deity, her. Reignited the urgency, he ran to her, to the flaming tower in the center of the village.

Bound to the pole, she was subjected to the cruelty of human justice. The villagers wasted no time crafting the exquisite chariot of fire. More fuel was tossed on to speed up the process.

How long was I out? rushed Anastas. Then he smelt it, the singe of his ammunition, spores of stag's horn. It sickened him. The blaze shot to the sky, swallowing the demon. It's brilliance then crashed and fanned, pushing the ogling spectators back. The crowd gasped. Some fell retreating. Whisps lacerated those too slow.

The raging fire became it's own being howling with each attack. At the heart of the heat, the heavenly beast growled for vengeance. In her native tongue, she cursed all who witnessed her destruction emotionlessly. After all, her calls only moved one man. However, the hill he climbed seemingly never ended.

When he finally made it, the time that transpired was evident in her destruction. Her flesh blistered, boiled, and ashened. Her beauty evaporated, but her spirit remained untampered in spite of those beckoning her metal to warp.

Geda wiggled and jerked. Somehow, the binds did not budge. Conjured shadows attempted to remove her, but the emanating heat dispelled them. To Anastas, however, they demonstrated how to get to her.

Without hesitation, he leapt onto the pyre. His human hands fought the flames, shoveling through hot coals to free her. His flesh tightened, enduring the scald, but the more he labored, the larger the pyre grew. It was of no use.

His feeble human hands could not reach set the celestial being. It was decided. The young man's strength was not the key to her freedom but someday, it would be. Though she loved the effort, a shadow demon tossed him from the stack. Confused, he blindly returned for her security, but her expression stopped him. The goddess displayed many lessons of letting go.

"If my suffering inspired negligence of your self-preservation, then I will give in," she said silently. She gave up to save him.

Anastas shattered. Helpless, he collapsed. The strength of his desire could destroy many, but it was not written in the universe's plan. Thus, he remained, honoring her last moments as a witness to her death.

The tears between them could smother the flames if only they did not evaporate. With irrevocable acceptance, the lovely being embraced God's fury and disintegrated into fine ash over the hours of the day. Obediently, Anastas stayed by her side. As her corpse crumbled, he mulled over his efforts. If he never interfered, would she still be here?

When only dust remained, it felt as if they had never met. All that was left of her was the kiss upon his lips and the tablet she defaced with her bloody name. In the end, the mindless populace was victorious.

"We could not have done this without you," Bog congratulated his student, adding to Anastasius's grievance. Ultimately, he was responsible for her demise. The chief continued, "You faltered her plans, which is the only reason you live, and she does not. With that said, you must repent."

Have I got a choice? Speechless, the young man looked up at him.

"If she had been successful, I would be without life. I am thankful you intervened, regardless of your betrayal."

Bog tore Anastas's left sleeve, revealing a bleeding dark mark.

Raven-like, the mark once twisted, trying to break through his skin. Now that the source had died, it settled. "She branded you. Upon your lips, I can see the refraction of a Judas kiss, the shimmering venom of her kind. You have been claimed." Reiterating it got through to the young man.

"Venom? I have been poisoned?" questioned Anastas, almost hopeful. Unsure of what that meant, he was glad a part of her resided within him. Soon, he, too, would accept death.

"It's more of an infection," Bog informed. "Without her here to comfort you, the darkness will slowly spread and consume you. Your human body will not be able to withstand it for long. Because I am partial to you, I will give you an opportunity to survive. If you live to its completion, prove the strength of your devotion, I will give you the cure. This task will be your repentance and you will be forgiven."

Bog waited for a response, but the young man quietly digesting everything. He took his silence as acceptance and continued, "You will join your father on a journey to Nova Roma. There you will convert a ruling man to our religion. I will meet you there for the ceremony."

Anastas wasn't granted time to consider. Before he knew it, he was bandaged in time for visitors to arrive from the far east. Upon arrival, the man laid gifts at Bog's feet. Pleased, the chieftain blessed him with the specific task and presented the boy to his father whom he had never met.

"Anastasius," he welcomed.

After 20 years, Anastas shook hands with his father and followed him to lands cultivated for humans hundreds of miles away. Walking and riding, days passed like weeks. Eventually uneven ground transformed into roads, which all lead to Nova Roma, a Byzantium city between two seas.

There, they were greeted at the gates with a message.

"Change of plans," his father read the slip. "The emperor now resides in Nicomedia, on his deathbed. We must hurry before he expires." And they did. The convoy twisted and turned through the municipality, ignoring all offered pleasantries.

Arriving at Nicomedia just in time, they were ushered into the royal villa. "Eusebius!" his father greeted another.

"Everyone has gathered," stated the politician.

"Let us commence."

"But the minister?"

"God will forgive us. Life waits for no man. His servant here will suffice," answered Anastas's father.

At their behest, Anastas assisted with the baptism of the Eastern Roman emperor. He held the clothes, prepped the oils and herbs, and blessed the waters. He was the hand of God in the ceremony. Unidentified, the formality ensured a successful ritual, but no feeling was greater than the faint taste of vanilla on his lips.

The ceremony came and went. Baptized, the emperor could now rest in peace, satisfying Bog's request and unknowingly catapulted the spread of their religion. Waiting for their leader, the crew took their celebration into the city, giving Anastas enough time to process his loneliness with fragrant wines. To his misfortune, he had survived. What next? What did Bog have in store for him? How would the man cleanse the venom running through him? Did he want to be cured? Of course not.

Geda. He wanted her.

Geda. Only he helped her.

My Geda. Not once did the demonic princess leave his mind. His sorrow for her amplified in the pale moonlight.

"Geda," he called for her, mourning.

"You know her?" a female voice replied.

Ana stopped. *She answered?* Shocked, he turned and found himself in the inescapable embrace of another being. Eloquent and delicate, she cradled him gently.

Geda? He was mistaken but the two were very similar. In fact, it was from this creature that Geda received her mentality. The authority resonated within him.

My queen! Mother, the origin of revolution nurtured warriors like Geda. Golden, the sensation of the woman's chaos was enticingly familiar. This creature, who held him so tenderly, was the source of everything Geda stood for and everything he wanted to become.

The mother queen inhaled him. "Yes. I see. She chose you." Her voice pleasantly alien. She caressed him; his face tear stained. His drunken heart quivered as black strips filtered through her beauty. "So valiant," she complimented him. "The claim is still there."

You have done well to preserve it, simultaneously said a voice not his own.

"Then, if you'll let me?" she asked, pulling him in. Closing the distance, her mouth swiftly fell onto his neck, curing him of the venom's curse, draining him of all strength, and blanketing him with sleep.

Before his last breath, the woman granted him some solace. "Her death will not be in vain. As a gift, you are now bound. Bring this back to your master as vengeance for what he did so ruthlessly. Little man, may this be your chance to live for what you did so generously." She then laid him tenderly on the pavement and vanished.

Moments became hours before Ana was shaken back to life by a familiar face. "Chief?" crackled Anastas.

"What did I say about playing with snakes?" Bog scooped him up from the street and inspected the damage. "Tsk. You've acquired the cure before I could administer it myself."

Ana's eyes widened. *He was going to claim me himself!*

Just then, he realized the state of the hold he rested in. Evidence of an attack remained on his master's clothes. The fabric was wet and lingered red on his skin.

"Whose blood is this?" Ana asked, disturbed.

Bog simply smirked and said, "Under my mentorship, you will come to understand the answer and the world you so desperately want to be a part of —"

"And the village?"

"Behind us."

With no way of refusing him, Ana surrendered.

CHAPTER 25

Cliffside

Ignorant to yesterday's dark conclusion, the birds whistled and tweeted as usual. A lovely breeze swayed the trees, rustled the grass, and crossed thresholds of a forgotten, unclosed window. Metal chimes dinged in the corner of Geda's room, and untapped papers scrapped against the decrepit lilac walls.

The room had been tousled by the forces of nature and the aftermath remained intact for observation the following morning. Ransacked and broken, bloody prints stained the window seal, and the sense of disturbance shackled the air, all of which woke the one resting.

The wind picked up with the scent of rust and breathed in new life into Ana. Sunrise singed his eyes. As his sight adjusted, he found her by his side. *Geda*, he reflected. *Ah! That time! It feels like I died.* Overcome with intense anamnesis, his head was still spinning and crashed back into the pillow. He blinked again, coming to terms with his survival but the only thing he could focus on was her.

After such a harrowing night, Geda blanketed him loosely, protecting him from unseen forces. Her presence had settled his turbulent waters. He no longer felt a nagging sensation in his mind, the churning of his insides, or any foulness pumping through his veins. He did, however, acquire a numbing vibration on his arm, a resurgence of a past long forgotten.

Pulling back the fabric revealed the raven mark, a guardian sign. *I am her guardian,* he recollected. He was unaware of it at the time but now with more experienced, the transaction was undeniable. All this time they had been linked. His chest bloomed and emotions rose. *That is why she always came back to me. And now...* He took the sight of her in. Now, she was by his side. Ana was finally at peace, not considering what had to happen to regain composure. In the calm rush of morning, it inevitably came back to him.

Casimir, he remembered the cataclysm. His breath inches from hers. *Geda?* Bandages wrapped her arm. Whelps and bruises covered her body.

His expression twisted. *This was Darin all over again,* he thought, looking at her wounds again. *She did pull me from possession. She disarmed a beacon and calmed the aggressor. With just a vial of Nostalgia? Where did she get that?* She still gripped it tightly. *Her pain saved me.* Grateful, he brushed the edges of her neck, carefully caressing the discoloration made by her deceased lover and counting the rhythm of her system.

"You're awake," she murmured, half asleep. Her receptiveness surprised him.

"Did you sleep at all?" he asked. She shook her head. "Get some rest," he insisted, but she refused.

"Not after what happened." She feared the potential nightmares.

"I'm sorry," was all he could say. Ana could not conjure the words he so desperately needed. He could smell without the twisting nerve of distaste and listen without a rattling brain. He could do many things previously unknown but versing his guilt was not a possibility at the moment. His only expression was himself.

His touch moved to her cheek. To his surprise, she opened her eyes, and saw him, seemingly human for the first time.

"Your face is better," she welcomed.

"You anchored me."

She thought otherwise. "I took my anger out on you. I pushed you further than you needed to go. I feel terrible… but you were prepared to leave without saying anything, without an explanation. Ana, how could you?" She clearly had more to say but felt enough damage had been done already. Still, what she did say was true.

"I didn't want to face you."

"That man…How are you my guardian?"

"You heard that?"

"I heard everything," she admitted. "I heard you on the roof, but you never entered. I thought he was you." She huffed. "If only I knew, I would have stabbed him sooner."

"Was that blade meant for me?" he challenged.

Geda showed her shame. Could he blame her?

Ana pulled her closer. "You are not the one who should be apologizing, Geda. I would have done the same if something valuable had been taken from me. I'm sorry. I can't take back what I did, nor do I intend to."

There was nothing but honesty in his words, yet the way he spoke unveiled a mature side to his childish exterior. To think, Darin's blood once saturated the hands that held her so tenderly. His soft brutality claimed her freedom voluntarily.

"Is it true?" she asked.

Still, honesty isn't always easy. Ana buried her further into him. Close, the smell of asphalt and despair permeated her nose, along with something bitter, something not citrus or vanilla.

"Yes."

"How?"

"Ages ago, I made a promise that bound us. You embedded me with darkness after inlaying a stone tablet with your essence."

"The tablet," she caught.

"A mutated guardian is a curse. Tethered, the souls will replicate for an eternity until the mark is satisfied. Since my transition, I have been lost, following the demands of the True King. I buried the signs behind the rest of the Malum sensation. It wasn't until recently that I felt the symptoms of the bind."

"Ana," she reached for his attention. Her touch rested on his abdomen.

He grunted, instinctively catching her wrist. "I'm unaware of the circumstances of your birth, but you are the same. You possess my binder."

A wetness slipped between her fingers. Sanguine, the source of bitterness, spread along the threads of his shirt and discolored her touch. She gasped, "You're wound! It's not healing."

"No." He already knew.

"Ana, what do we do?" She panicked, searching for more bandages. She grabbed a handful.

"Ariel. I need to see him. Erhh!" he groaned as she pulled him up right. "He needs to know about Casimir. There," he pointed to her phone on the table. "Ah! We can fix this while I'm with him."

She handed it to him. "How?"

Ana dialed nine numbers from memory. "Consumption. Ariel is the strongest of all of us. He has the energy to spare." The call went through. "Hey, I need your help."

"Ana! Are you alright?" Ariel frantically asked.

"Not really."

"Where are you? I have been looking for you all night. The

guardian sign crippled the boy."

Ana's stomach dropped. *Theo! The darkness has the same effect on him as it does on me.* "Is he okay?"

"He's fine. He fainted from the pain. But Ana, last night, I lost the signal. I couldn't find you. Where are you?"

"I'm with Geda."

That made his brother even more concerned. "Is *she* okay?"

"No."

"Dammit, Ana. Are you at least stable?'

Ana turned away as Geda put more clothes on. "For now. Where are you? I need to see you."

Ariel stopped running and scanned his surroundings. "Meet me at Caladium café. And don't push yourself! I can come to you," insisted Ariel.

The café he spoke of was not far from the university. "No, no. That's okay. I'll be there soon," said Ana.

Ariel got there before they did. Recognizing the mutant, the owner gifted him a timeline scrapbook constructed in light of his disappearance. It caught him up to speed.

Flipping through the pages, Ariel immersed himself in what he missed during his decade-long slumber. From the fall of the Joytech tower 10 years ago to the capture of Separatist leader Leo during the recent Memorial holiday, newspaper clippings filled every page for him to analyze.

"Engineers at Joytech find a cure for humanity," one headline read, disclosing synthesization to the public. Ariel wrinkled his nose. "Rations at an all-time low with harvest decline," detailed another. The next page read, "Heir to Joytech named."

"Ariel," called a familiar voice.

He looked up from the book and found his brother leaning on the albino lady with a wound prominent against his black shirt. "Ah, Ana!" He shot up and quickly took Geda's place.

"We will take care of this," he told her and took Ana away.

Geda understood. While they went to the back, she ordered three coffees for the table as a cover. Though her hands quivered, she greeted the barista as if everything was alright. They welcomed her with a steamed hand cloth.

Ana groaned as they moved.

"What on earth happened?" asked Ariel, trying to make moving as painless as possible. "You spiked and just vanished. Even now, I cannot feel you."

"Casimir. Agh! Kazimierz is still alive," Ana informed.

Ariel nearly dropped him in disbelief. "Alive? He died, charged with treason — Father destroyed him. Ana, I was a witness."

"As did Geda, yet here she is," added Ana. Strength faded from his legs as the Nostalgia wore off.

"Hold on. We are almost there." The door to the bathroom was in sight. "You beaconed, didn't you?"

Again, shame flourished within. Ana didn't give him a proper answer. He just whispered, "She saved me."

"Well you look great, brother. That's a problem; it's always the calmest before the storm," said Ariel. "You can no longer heal, and you reek of darkness. Soon, you will not be able to escape the call." Busting through the privacy of the small restroom, he transferred Ana's weight to the counter and took off his shirt. "We should have done this ages ago."

Ariel was right, but Ana wasn't listening. Once his flesh was bare, Ana ruthlessly took what he needed without hesitation. Dull teeth penetrated Ariel's sacred canvas, a forgivable maliciousness. The cannibal took the healing nectar derived from the gods; yet, another trait his dirty blood did not contain.

At the table, Geda sipped on her latte, patiently waiting when the open scrapbook caught her attention. "Heir to Joytech named," the headline advertised. *Darin,* she exhaled. He died exactly 24 hours ago. She no longer grieved his absence. In fact, she never did.

The caption under the article's photo read, "Pictured from right to left: Sasha Coumarin, Raymond Sambuca, Darin Sambuca, Sabre Strafe; the Order's greatest." Geda remembered that day vividly. She remembered the ceremony. She remembered everything about that day, for it changed everything. On that day, she chained herself to another's futile belief system.

Never again, she assured.

The scrapbook was extensive, containing everything from Joytech production reports to C.O.V. movement. If she desired, she could track Sasha's involvement within the city and on the coastlines. Upon closer inspection, it looks as though someone was.

Her fingers trailed to a section bookmarked by a previous reader. The most recent addition, June 1st, yesterday, read, "Among those being deployed, Lioness Sasha Coumarin is scheduled to return to Arnireth after a seven-year hiatus."

Geda was surprised. *She is leaving? She never told me.*

"Oh, good. Coffee," chimed Ana, casually sliding into the seat next to her. She was even more surprised to see him back so soon. Before she could speak, he answered her expression. "It's better now," he promised.

Across from them, Ariel scooted his chair closer. Looking at the book in her hands, he sighed. "I've missed so much."

"That's what happens when you overwork yourself," Ana commented.

"Well, it's better than not sleeping," Ariel shot back.

"So, Casimir?" she interrupted the brotherly bicker.

"Of course, my lady. Do you know who the weasel is?" asked Ariel. Clearly, he despised the man.

She shrugged. "I know he is a royal like Ana, but that's all."

Ana choked on his coffee. *How did she know?*

Ariel's brow raised as she patted Ana on the back. "Did you ask Sasha about Casimir?" he questioned.

Geda shook her head.

"Hmm. If anyone knows anything about him, it's her." A frown soured his face, reminiscing. "She had the misfortune of encountering the Cousin King, and he left his mark on her. Come to think of it, we all did in some way." Ariel shook thoughts of her from his mind and continued, "Casimir is a distant relative under the hierarchy of claim. Despite his poor character, he still possesses the qualities of his title."

"Why is he so hated?" she asked.

Silence fell between the men as if they weren't allowed to say. The foul stench around Casimir's name deterred all who told his story.

Finally, Ariel uncurled his nose and extinguished the taste with a refreshing sip of coffee. "Tsk. Let's just say he is a being with no honor or ethical integrity. The only time he holds any consideration for others is for his own benefit."

Sounds like someone I used to know, she joked.

She also mulled over how contrastingly different Ana was.

"To put it into perspective, if it wasn't for Ana's kind-heartedness —"

"And Ariel's chivalry," diverted Ana.

"We would be just like him," illustrated Ariel.

"Are humans any different?" challenged Geda.

"The rat was euthanized for forging a new kingdom outside Father's governance," explained Ariel, with each beat of the story growing more intense, unfolding his animosity toward the man. "He stopped at nothing to plant his seed once he found a structure strong enough for his roots to cling onto, he conditioned the person with fallacies, outsourcing their strength for total disruption. He is a fungal disease. There was not an inch of the Oasis unaffected by his corruption 10 years ago."

It's been ages since Ana had seen his brother so full of emotion. "Still passionate about it, are we?" he teased.

Closing the scrapbook, Ariel contained himself. "He died shortly after the Joytech collapse, so you understand the seriousness of your accusations. If the Cousin King is back, someone is undeniably nurturing him. Ana, I'm sure you've thought this through."

Ana nodded. "Its a little ironic. Raymond's deal had been satisfied. Geda's tag was removed, so why was Casimir there to crown a new queen?"

Ariel's mouth dropped. "Ms. Geda, you're lucky the act was intervened but I do see a tiny remnant of his effort, right there," he pointed to a small area of his lip. Mirroring him, she rubbed her lip vigorously. "Being a royal, no less a mutant, is an apathetic continuance. If Casimir is back and has chosen a woman worthy of being his queen, he will return to fulfill his goal if he is not stopped."

A chill ran down her spine. "But how? I stabbed him in the seal but it didn't faze him one bit," said Geda.

"Was he whole?"

"A rotting corpse," Ana replied before resuming his mental rumination.

So, whatever the support is, it's minimal, Ariel considered. "Show me where the blade went." He stood and Geda demonstrated, driving an imaginary knife into his mid torso, the same place the Lioness had once stabbed.

"And that did nothing?"

She shook her head.

"She also used the king's blade," mentioned Ana.

"The king's… How… how did you get the king's blade?" asked Ariel, dumbfounded.

"Sasha gave it to me."

"Do you still have it?"

"No. I lost it," she whimpered. "It was stuck in the… in Casimir."

"Fons et origo mali," Ana spontaneously redirecting them.

"You think the queen is behind this?" questioned Ariel. Ana couldn't say but his subtle facial cues led down a different path.

"Origo mali, the origin of evil?" Geda guessed. Her Latin was rusty.

Ana nodded. "That's correct. It's a term for the nutrients offered by the maternal claim. When mutants are in a predicament that requires superior intervention, they can return to the origin of mutation to heal. I was claimed by the True Queen, but she vanished ages ago. So if I need to access the maternal nutrients like today, Ariel is the closest contact, given his descendence." Geda saw Ariel in a new light.

"We shan't speak about that," Ariel mumbled, waving away the topic.

"And Casimir would return to Sarolt for his repair," Ana finished.

Before they got too far, Ariel stepped in. "But to my knowledge, Sarolt no longer supports the Cousin King. What about Raymond? Perhaps he went back on his promise as retribution for his son."

"No," Geda disagreed. "Raymond reflects the queen's decision. If she has abandoned him, so has he." The two went back and forth with conspiracies with alternating prospects. Out of the question, Ana tripped over the only remaining possibility, repeating it endlessly in his mind until finally it overflowed into his words.

"It's Father," he murmured. The table silenced. "He was there, among the trees, before I found Casimir."

Stunned, Ariel tripped over the insinuation. "Recruitment?"

The assumption is insulting. "I would not allow it," growled Ana.

"Have you done anything to anger him recently? You know how he gets when his pride is injured or his plans deviate. His maliciousness enjoys ironic punishment. You remember the time he cut off my wings."

Ariel was right. He had disobeyed his master. Darin's untimely massacre and Marcy's injury would be enough to overthrow any favor he had with the mutant God. As punishment, was Bog after Geda?

"Wings?" asked Geda. "On a mutant?" She had never heard of such a thing.

"A metaphor taken literally," answered Ariel. "As punishment, Father filleted my back, ripping every muscle apart to search for my wings. He always said, 'Only a divine being could dethrone him,'" Ariel jutted his chest out with authoritative emphasis. "And when I displayed what he perceived to be retaliation, he made sure I wasn't one of them. Ana, our Lord harbors the blood of queens. He could have easily revived Casimir and ordered the rat to procure him another subject. You bartered with Raymond, so he bartered with the dead. I never saw what happened to his body."

Defeated, Ana fell back into his chair. He didn't want to believe it, but it made perfect sense. Now that the end is near, he feared even more for her security after his death. *After I'm gone, will Raymond be enough to keep him from her?* he conspired.

"If, for whatever reason, Father is guilty, both of you are in danger," Ariel heightened.

Ana agreed.

Frightened, Geda grabbed Ana and whispered, "I thought you were king."

"I am a king of a nation under the command of God," he replied rather regretfully.

"And God wants me dead."

"No, no. God wants everyone dead," the Peacekeeper corrected. "Be more optimistic. God wants you to join the army of immortal suffrage, to be a loyal sister against the resistance."

"And to think, I just got you back," mumbled Ana.

Ariel flipped open the scrap book. "There might be something—" Double taking, strips suddenly flared across his face.

"What is it?" asked Ana, following his gaze to the windows.

Ariel stood. "I just saw him," he said dishearteningly, and rushed to the door.

"Who?" wondered Geda, as they followed him out of the shop. Spilling into the streets, they did not see what he did.

"Ariel, what is it? Who did you see?"

"Casimir. He has the blade," he answered. *Her blade.*

Just then, the quality of the air caught Ana's nose; a burning, sulfur smell singed his olfactory. The wind carried it from the college, from Theo. After faulting his father's plans, after last night, who is to say his guardian wasn't next?

Ana got a sinking feeling and before he could say anything, he took off running towards the university.

Without warning, sirens came blaring by, then the wails of firetrucks and ambulances. All headed in the same direction.

Geda grabbed the nearest person for information. "Excuse me! What's going on?" she kindly asked.

"Oh, a fire broke out at the campus," one replied.

Another added, "Seperatist Leo was giving a speech at the school when suddenly all hell broke out at the male dormitory."

Geda and Ariel shared a look.

Thanking them, Geda tried contacting Theo while Ariel chased after Ana. Her fingers couldn't dial his number fast enough. Emotion swelled as the phone pressed to her ear. It was ringing.

Theo, she prayed for his well being. When her sight leveled, she was encompassed by a crowd of fleeing students. Each person bumped, stepped, jabbed, knocked, and pulled her in the opposite direction. A force told her to stay behind but her determination was resolute.

No! I will go to him. Theo! Geda insisted. She rammed her feet into the ground and pushed upstream. Past the horde, she cut around the corner towards the smoke.

There, an expansive courtyard divided commerce from education. She saw the danger many ignored. A magnificent rumbling flame engorged the men's dorm.

The crackling pitch of the imploding building and the screams of those still inside magnified the radiant disaster. With that said, everything between the building and her was deceptively normal.

The call in her ear had no connection, "The person you are trying to reach is not available at this moment."

She dropped it in disbelief.

"Theo, are you still in there?"

CHAPTER 26

Time Converges

Furious flames ravaged the men's dormitory. Pressure accumulated, and heat shattered the windows. The blaze clawed at the building's facade and bellowed like a beast, climbing higher, hungrily devouring, swallowing man's creation in rippling gulps. As she got closer, Geda merged into the crowd of onlookers.

"Oh, my God!" People watched in horror.

"The fire is getting bigger!"

Those trapped inside leaned out of the upper windows and flagged for help, screaming for the Peacekeeper to save them.

"Don't wait for them. Just jump!" someone yelled from below. Many listened.

The crowd gasped as men flung themselves to the ground. A couple missed the safety nets of the emergency responders. Firefighters struggled to fight the conflagration, the audience, and the impatient victims. Chaos brewed further at the mention of terrorism only days after the attack on Marcy's. Mayhem became the crowd's mentality.

However, Geda was not one with the horde. She scanned the spectators for her friend. "Theo!" she called but received no answer.

Was he one of the few to jump? No, he was not among them, she found. He was nowhere in sight. *Ah! Where is he?* Her emotions rose, further pushing through the crowd.

"Theo!" she yelled again. Nothing.

She spun around, looking at every face in the crowd.

Suddenly, her sight caught a familiar gleam. Silver threads traveled among the people. She gulped, knowing it did not belong to the human masses. Respectfully, she brushed through the group to get a better look.

There it was again but the reflective strands swiftly vanished.

Geda chased after it. *Is that the queen?* She suspected her meddling, but she had to know. She had to protect Ana. She had to find Theo. *What if she took Theo?* Two steps to the left, one to the right, she slid between two folks, and her curiosity was satiated by terror.

Silver hair, slanted eyes, and geriatric flesh. Geda's heart shot out of her chest and her name spilled from her breath.

The older lady heard her call, and their eyes met. Only feet apart, Geda felt trapped in her gaze.

"The person you are trying to reach is not available at this moment." Yet again, the call did not go through.

An unpleasant smirk lifted the side of Amora's face.

"Where is he?" Geda demanded. Where was her friend?

But the only reply was the woman's breathless incantations.

Why won't you say anything? Frustration was seething, maddening. Geda inhaled and screamed, "What have you done with Theo?" Still, Amora did not speak. She only hummed her tunes and weaved a windward support for the fire. Working her magic, the flames folded in a different direction

Windows above exploded. Two mutants dropped to the ground with arms full of survivors.

Ana! Intent flooded Amora's eyes. Her muscles tensed.

Thoughtlessly, Geda reacted, grappling the old lady to the concrete. Amora was dismantled. She couldn't believe what had transpired and before she could do anything, the young lady fled back into the crowd. "Did she really?" she scoffed.

"Are you okay, ma'am?" a man asked, reaching down to help her. As did another. And the next.

Many more followed. She was surrounded by the generosity of humanity. Hands grabbed, pulled and lifted her up, but shifted, causing her to stumble back to the ground. The cycle repeated. Kindness quickly became infuriating.

"Get off of me!" Amora screamed, but the crowd was driven to assist. She was stuck in an endless sea of worker bees, induced by a lowly human.

"There's still more inside," Ariel told a fireman, handing off a the set of survivors. "Ana, go find Theo. I'll handle this."

Jumping back in, Ana felt the spell of his master bleed onto the property. Like a thin coating, it possessed an eerie presence and beckoned a hauntingly familiar demand for purity. Permeating from the structure, he had felt it before, millennia ago, in the prison of his religion. Feeling it now unnerved him.

So, this is it. This is Bog's trap, recognized Ana. His breath quivered. *To think, he used Theo against me.* The wooden stair rail fractured under his pressure. *Sarolt, are you here?*

"Theo!" He called out. *He cannot be here when the True King comes.*

"Everyone, clear out!" responders dispersed the congregation. As the crowd thinned, only select mutants remained: the Butcher Romulus circled along the outskirts; Amora kicked the last man and jumped to her feet; the Separatist Leo fought his collar; the breathless video store clerk, Ammon, was beyond visible; the thorn-tattooed player Datura cracked his knuckles for the incoming fight; and on the sidelines Reporter John joined barista Olivia while referee Roth ran to help his wife off the ground.

Among the many recognizable faces, other cloaked individuals appeared, lingering for what Geda assumed was the final showdown. Above, the sky grew dark. Humans gasped at the sun's eclipse. However, the mutants knew the sight of their master.

"The True King," shuddered Leo.

"He's coming," another mutant whisper.

Then she remembered the deal. The queen was surely there but the scroll was not. She gasped. *Ana! What do we do?* Without the scroll, there was no deal.

Inside the building, the flames were gnarly. The heat increased at an alarming rate insufferable to humans. Even the glorious mutants found the atmosphere tormenting. Poisonous vapors coated their lungs. Layers of flesh sloughed from extreme exposure. Torrid whips of heat inhibited their sight. They suffered hell for others to die another day.

Ariel endured the worst, clearing the lower levels as Ana reached the top. The flames had yet reached the upper levels. If Theo was anywhere, it was there.

"Theo!" Ana called out a second time, but received no response. The spell washed over him again, like waves combing the sand. It knocked him over and again, trauma squeezed the oxygen from his chest.

Ha! Can Ariel feel it? Does he know what this is? The moment he tries to leave, he won't be able to. Theo, where are you?

Cutting around the corner, Ana slowed to the beat of nostalgia. At the end of the hall, the last door on the left, their dorm had remained untouched by the raging beast. The embossed number 666 summoned so many memories. After all, it was a place he shared with his guardian.

Theo, are you here?

Instinctively, Ana grabbed the metal knob. He hissed, foolishly burning his hand. His palm blistered in seconds, but the singe remained endless.

He rammed the door with his shoulder, but it didn't budge. As usual, it was locked.

"Theo!" he called. No reply. *What if he's unconscious?* With a swift kick, Ana threw all his force at the handle, breaking it. The door flew open, and the room's heat emanated, searing his face. He recoiled.

"Theo?" he yelled. Again, no answer.

The room did not contain him. However, in the darkness, it was as if he had never left. Quiet and peaceful, the space was strangely secluded, absentminded of the fury culling to bequeath it.

As if in an alternate universe, everything lingered unimbued by toxic fumes. The posters and pictures had yet warped, illuminated with violet hues rotating from the sensory lamp. The beds were separated, the television hung in the corner, and the fridge that once chilled his meals stood in its original position. It was the same as the day he left. Theo must have maintained it for his return.

Entranced by the nest, the Devil stepped over the threshold. Everything beyond the four walls vanished; no vibrating flames, no horrifying screams, no splitting urgency to do anything.

Here, he found his guardian. Though not physical, the room possessed his heart and soul, blindly satisfying his search.

Here, Ana was home.

With that said, there was something that did not belong. To his left, on Theo's pillow rested a foreign object.

The queen's scroll? It's here? The paper was nearly fabric and deteriorating from energy his sanctuary did not display.

The flap fell open. Written in the blood of his majesties, phrases of every language told him many things. At the center was a warning, "Credence to the king is deceit."

"Ana!" she howled, shattering the illusion.

His environment suddenly changed, melting away into reality. His home disintegrated. A hellish scenery replaced the calming blues, the ground beneath his feet creaked, and the air he breathed became virulent. The tranquility he devoured was a manufactured lie.

Bog, Ana simmered. *He nearly had me.*

He secured the scroll in an inner coat pocket when his ears perked up at the sound of footsteps echoing from the hall. "Theo?" But when he turned, she appeared in the doorway. "Geda?"

"Ana, where is he?" she asked, raspy. Panting for freshness, she clung to the door frame for support. Tears battled the drying smoke.

"What are you doing here?" he snapped at her carelessness. *She cannot be here.* Impulsively, Ana flew to her and scooped her out of the doorway.

"Where is he?" she pressed into him. "The scroll."

"I have the scroll." He showed her. But as for his guardian, unfortunately, he couldn't say.

Theo. Why can't I find him? I can't summon him. I can't feel him. Death before him, he felt like a fish out of water. Geda was his last breath. Now, she, too, was where she belonged.

Emphysematic, he cradled her safely in the doorway. He scanned for an escape, but his eye witnessed the approach of the ghostly queen. *She's here,* he remarked, ironically pleased to see her.

"Sa—" Geda gasped for air."The queen is here," she warned, "They've gathered," until impurities choked her more.

Around them, the floor crumbled along the exterior edges. The cherished dorm caved in and flames shot up to the roof. The heat wave eradicated everything, including her strength.

"Haaa!" She melted in his grasp, tugging his clothes. Ana captured her descent and pulled her into his core. Though his bicep pained, his mind was not only on her.

Time was ticking. The bait has been set. The queen had entered the trap and inevitably the True King marched. There existed a heavy minute before the final judgment killed them all. If she wished, Sarolt still had time to deliver her vengeance.

This was the pinnacle of indifference, the true deciding match of who lives and who dies. Stratagems collided at the vertex that was the dormitory. As the True King crept in, warring factions crossed blades on the front lawn and when it is all said and done, tomorrow, humans will question who was the bait, the victim, and the mastermind behind misdirection. Regardless of the outcome, one thing was certain, Sarolt will finally get what she wanted.

"Anastas!" Ana heard Ariel's call but he couldn't move. They were entangled in the only safe portion of the building and it was quickly deteriorating. More of the building crumbled and the woman curled further into him. Close, her scent filled his vessel.

My most cherished, he imbibed. *She will die if I do nothing.*

Remnants of the past swirled in his mind, this moment indistinguishable from the last. Tossed to the pyre, flames bit her skin. Winces and whines twisted her deeper into him. The call back to her helpless ancient screams penetrated his bones, amplified by the deathly howls exuded from Ariel.

Sarolt found him.

Rusty substance surged through Ariel's teeth, drowning his vocalizations. Grip fierce against her wrist, he resisted the dagger nails penetrating his chest.

"What are you doing?" he growled. "I thought we had a deal?"

"And I thought you would have the blade by now," hissed Sarolt.

"Casimir has it."

"Oh?" She licked her teeth. "Was the Lioness manipulated by him again? How else would her blade leave her belt?" she teased to weaken his resolve. Instead, her advances fanned an aggression.

Carpal bones fractured under his grip; a jab for a jab. "Did you resurrect him?" Ariel spat. The refractions in his eyes shimmered with undisclosed hate.

"No. I no longer have that power," she openly admitted, pressing against his strength to go deeper. "Now, live up to your birthright. I cannot leave without your blood."

He scoffed. "You mean the spell? Without the blade — Err!"

"True blood has been spilt," acknowledged Sarolt.

Ariel slipped on her perspiration. He grimaced the penetration. "Ah! Escape is simple. Calm your heart to his peace... Ernn... you will be free."

"So he can kill me?" she expressed. "You misunderstand my intentions, brother. Your blood is not my key to this prison. I shall override the True King's power with your precious nutrients. Without the blade, your blood will be my weapon!" Sarolt lunged, releasing air from his lungs and ripping apart his meat to get to the crystal seed beneath.

Geda looked up at Ana. The distant ungodly screams produced a teary-eyed beast. Sarolt was coming and the groan of God's march settled into him. As death stepped forward, he was not as ready as he thought he was. Watching him process everything, her heart quivered with uncertainty.

If this was the end, she chose to be with him, to not give up and protect him. *Finally*, she was satisfied.

Yet, here she was, endangered by his redemption.

How could he let it go this far? He was the guardian, but it was she who held on so tightly.

Ana wheezed heartbreak. Tied to him, he was to be the pyre of her demise. For her survival, he would have to sever their bonds. Once again, he had to let her go.

Below the closest window, he decided would become her escape, awaited sufficient cushion for her landing. But before releasing her, he chose to make one final mistake.

Ana took a deep breath. "Geda, forgive me."

Before she could speak, his hands bore her face, and his breath met hers. A single touch clung to the other. His face brushed hers as they kissed.

Pulling away, her gaze met his magnificent eyes, one black, one blue, and for the first time spoke his name, "Anastasius."

Time folded onto itself. Blissfully, his mind converged onto one moment. The whisper of his name. The taste of her lips. Centuries of memories in a single collision. *Geda*.

Irresistible, he met her again, and this time, she was ready. Lips firm and unwilling to let go. However, it was a must.

Thrown, Geda flew through the glass; her descent aimed at a watery bed. Ana stayed, embracing the flame, accepting the queen, and ending the religious havoc in one dark day.

The building caved.

The fire swallowed him.

"Ana!" Geda screamed and landed.

CHAPTER 27

Altar of Insurrection

Sloshing waves and falling embers rocked the senses back into a fallen being. Swift inhalation reignited Geda's blood. As consciousness returned, she felt weightless in the narrow space, mindlessly paralyzed by collision.

Thoughtless, she stared at the starlight sky. Exhaling with terrible relief, she found it hard to breath. Her lungs were smothered, plastered with smoke, coughing rekindled the environment she was in.

A fire? Flames, her mind recognized the warning signs, heard the coals crackling to her left, but was disarmed by the ticklish sting of the water's outline against her blistered flesh. Burnt by the absence of sun, the encircling coldness ignited every nerve, washing open flesh and soothed an inescapable heat.

The pain was releasing, molting. She felt anew; her shell degloved most viciously from uncontrollable growth. Then, she tasted it, pomegranates. Remnants of her chains remained. Her lips were stained with his venom, him. *Anastasius*, she resonated.

The absence of his touch amplified their last embrace. The kiss, how she wished it was endless. But there was a spark and a scream, and how he remained in a dangerous position.

"Ana!" She shot up to save him but a heaviness shackled her. Blood discolored the water. It seeped from her blanched hair and down her face, a result of imperfection. Pressed, his calculation wasn't exact and a portion of her fall collided with the granite decoration.

The prominent six-story building was now leveled to the ground. It was barely recognizable. Smoke clouded the surrounding night and what little light came from dying embers illuminated a shattered cage. Ash fell like rain on a battlefield of spears and misshapen arrows that were the building's scrap.

Headboards were now tombstones and electronics became brittle pottery. All that remained of the dormitory was a skeletal cage surrounding the unfortunate souls unable to escape.

How long was I out? she wondered.

Among the choir of the dead, a dark silhouette kneeled in submission to a woman of opal reflections. Slowly, the queen confronted the charred statue. Her majesty denied the aesthetic of weakness but the state of her heart was undeniable in her expression.

A fever dream, she knew he was bait, a cheap request to crumble her empowerment. The effort was meaningless to the God requesting such sacrifice, but the king's careless acceptance shambled her.

"Ana? Ana, please move. She's coming for you!" Geda warned. Her voice cracked as she reached out for him.

To her dismay, the shadow did not move.

It did not shudder. It did not scream. It just was, a statue. There, he was, him and his unholy capture, a soulless entity beckoning.

"It can't be," Geda tensed. The king was no longer among them. Heart drop broke the meniscus and tears spilled over her face.

Inevitably, Sarolt's slender fingers stretched to claim her long awaited prize. Her paleness was vibrant against his ashes. Upon her touch, his surface caved, shredded and flaked into the wind. Sorrow warped her elegance. "It took you this long to stand before me, priest. Was it worth it, this buffet of pain you used as an escape? You fool," her voice rattled. "Do you realize what this dedication will allow Bog to accomplish?"

Bowing to him, she glimpsed a familiar object.

In the safest portion of his carcass, an ornate rod protruded from the folds of his midsection. *The queen's scroll?* she brightened. It fell into her hands with the slightest effort. Its fibers, embedded with the blood of matriarchs, had survived the harshest conditions, even time itself. Despite being subjected to insane heat, the delicate item was intact, uncomfortably insulated in the guts of the guardian king. With his sacrifice, Ana fainted loyalty to deliver her the power of the scroll as agreed.

Sarolt held it tight, conflicted by unrequited resentment. *How could you be so considerate?* she simmered. "Anastas, there is honor in your bravery."

A crash landed in the composite behind her. The shadow unfolded to be Romulus. "Ariel has escaped," he informed.

"Leave him be. I have what I need," she replied.

"My lady?" he questioned, then noticed the scroll delivered by the faithless son of the True King. "He understood who the enemy is. Does Ariel?" he remarked.

"Ariel lives in fear of his master," said Sarolt. "It will take a human heart to open his mind." A sensation crept up her back and nibbled her neck, the True King. *He's here.* After centuries, Sarolt finally turned away from Ana and set her sights on the real enemy.

"What happens now?" asked Amora, materializing from the shadows, bladeless.

"Ana," a voice whimpered behind them.

Sarolt's cold eyes met the albino girl bleeding in the fountain, and addressed, "Should you see the child, give him my anger and my thanks."

"Sarolt, this is it! He's coming!" warned the older lady.

"We cannot leave until the barrier is destroyed," tensed Romulus.

"Not while the True King is in his malicious form," Sarolt reminded, unscrewing one side of the scroll's rod. A vial slid out from the secret compartment.

Romulus gasped, "What are you doing? We don't have the blade. Without it blade, we cannot stab the monarch's heart."

"And until we have the blade, our survival is precedent." She uncorked the ancient tube. "This is not the only vial. We will have other opportunities and injury will grant us more flexibility. For now, this will do some damage." Flexing her right fist, they saw the reflective flicker of a diamond gauntlet.

She took a sip of the royal blood. "Here. Drink," she commanded, handing it to the old woman. "Without it, your survival will not be guaranteed."

Amora hesitated. After years of blood abstinence, devouring such a divine substance could be deadly. Regardless, she partook and handed the vial to Romulus. He finished it. Vial empty, the essence of the Mother flowed through their veins, granting them power of a thousand beings. Together they turned and faced God.

In the form of a man, the shade towered over them, eclipsing the stars. His ethereal parade stopped to materialize. The form stilled the wind, and hushed all in sight. His hand then raised to crush them.

Sarolt returned the movement. Fueled by queen's blood and amplified with the diamond gauntlet, her power shielded them and resisted his. Pressure between them accumulated, whipping out of any opening. Geda braced each shockwave. She ducked, missing other mutant conflict by centimeters. She was in a precarious position but even if she could move, how could she veer from her king?

Ana, she believed.

Malum rose from the bed of ashes. They stretched and stood from a long slumber. Sarolt smiled as darkness stripped her skin. A new Malum commander has risen and all who possessed it's essence knew of his presence. "There you go, priest. Get a feel for what you now command," she said under her breath. However, the shadows did not move in support. Instead, they were pulled into the shade, making the monarch more difficult to contain.

Sarolt winced.

The gauntlet cracked.

"No!" she screamed.

The shade bent down to them.

"Geda!" someone called her name. "Geda!" yelled the familiar voice, growing closer. Sandy hair then broke her view, and her eyes met the Lioness's auburn gaze.

"Sasha?"

Dumbfounded by her injuries, the Lioness held Geda's face as Ana once did. "What happened?" she asked tenderly, despite of her own state. She too had been fighting.

Hot tears welcomed her friend's cradle. "Sasha! I... I lost the blade," Geda admitted. "I've lost everything. Ana. He's —"

"I know. It's okay. But you're not done yet. Come on. Let's get you out of here. Can you move?" Sasha jumped in the fountain to pull her out.

No, Geda wanted to answer, but the shadow's impending bow finalizing her decision. *Ana.*

"Geda, we have to go!" Sasha hurried, but Geda's motionless body was too heavy to move on her own.

The True King crashed onto them, sending shock waves in every direction. Light exploded all around them. At the center, Romulus, Amora, and Sarolt held him back. With a hand adorned with the diamond blood flame of his son, the queen was determined.

"You will not keep me!" Sarolt screamed. Now to her level, she gave in and pierced upward. The True King's hand effortlessly caved, dispelling more force outward.

"Geda!" Sasha screamed as her sight faded. As she slipped into unconsciousness, the sensation of drowning was utterly comforting.

Instinctively, another stern swift of air filled her lungs and brushed the singed cavities within. Geda's eyes opened to the room's bright pale aesthetics and vinyl fabrics. *A hospital?* she recognized. Adjusting to the new environment took a hard minute. The profound change in aesthetics, transitioning from the zenith of mutinous insurrection, to a stale sanctuary was disheartening. The room felt like a lobby for a simulation.

Am I dead? she wondered.

Nearby fresh geraniums were potted in a water vase. Morning sun rays glistened through the louver blinds. It was unbearably pleasing and hauntingly different from what her subconscious had prepared for.

"Oh!" someone peeped in the doorway. Her attention turned to the white coat man now calling down the hall, "Good news, everyone! She's awake," he informed and returned to her with the sweetest smile.

"Jakobi?" she asked, rubbing the haze from her sight. Seemingly with new eyes, everything appeared more defined, including the fine lines of his face.

He bowed. "It's good to have you back, my lady."

Breanna, Tiffany, and the other housemates ran in, pushing the doctor out of the way. "Hey, she is awake!" Leann noted. "Are you feeling alright?" she asked.

Before Geda could answer, Breanna butted in, "You should be dead! Do you know how much head trauma you had?"

"What happened?" inquired Tiffany hastily. "The doctor said you were in that fire. Why were you at the men's dorm anyway?" As usual, the girls were invasive.

"I don't really know what happened," Geda answered. Although her memory was fuzzy, she couldn't deny that it did happen. The fire. The queen. The shadow giant. The kiss. Ana's death. Oh, how she felt she could have done more to prevent it.

"You are lucky to be alive, to say the least."

Three knocks on the door grabbed everyone's attention. They all turned. "Lord Raymond?" gasped the girls, surprised by their new guests. At Raymond's side was another hospital resident, the famous Marcy Joans.

However, before pleasantries could be distributed, Raymond threw up his hand and kindly requested, "May we have the room, ladies?" Everyone obliged and left the room without a second thought.

"Raymond," Geda cautiously greeted. As he approached, she searched for affirmation in his strong expression. Thankfully, Marcy locked the door behind them.

"How are you feeling?" he asked, pulling up a nearby chair

"My head —"

"You fell from the highest window and landed wrong. Your noggin hit the fountain's edge, a rather poor decision I might add," he said, brushing the fly away strains away from her forehead wound.

"It wasn't my choice," uttered Geda. In truth, she would have rather stayed in the fire, in Ana's embrace. The guilt surfaced in her eyes.

"What were you doing there?" he raised.

She gathered the proper words, explaining, "I escorted King Ana to the Peacekeeper to soothe his condition when suddenly the fires broke out. We thought the king's guardian was trapped inside and rushed to assist. We still don't know if Theo is okay."

"So, you entered?" Raymond quickly paused, calming his voice; this was not the time to lecture her. "The boy is okay," he informed. "He left the building shortly after the fires broke out."

Finally disclosed, a weight melted from her chest, leaving only the agony of abandonment behind.

The Lord continued, "The spectacle was meant to trap the royal sons."

"What!" she exclaimed.

Marcy gasped, "Raymond, Geda is a child. She is not versed enough to understand —"

"She knows enough."

"You made a deal!" barked Geda. "Ana was free, no longer to be hunted. You gave up your only son for that deal. How could you not honor it?"

"I did not agree to Ariel's protection," Raymond snipped back. "I do not expect you to understand the delicacies of this war. The children are key to our success, Geda. Without the loyalty of his sons, the True King is powerless. Ana had my full support. Understand that because of my promise, I could not save Anastas from the fate he was forced to accept. I could not ensure his safety with the methods available."

She was thrown back. "And what fate has befallen him?" she

asked. To her understanding, Ana died, but Raymond implied something more than death.

The Lord struggled to reveal the truth, until the glisten of her lips caught his eye; he reluctantly accepted. Sighing, he spilled, "In death, Anastas has been conscripted to the dark army. As a king, he has power over the Malum Saltus, acting as their dark general, and his loyalties to his master give the True King full control over the shadows."

Geda could not imagine Ana residing comfortably among the darkness. Flashes of his beacon impregnated her mind violently. She quickly shook them away.

"There was a shadow giant at the dorm," she recalled.

Raymond nodded. "The Monarch's malicious form. Geda, I don't think you understand the severity of Anastas's position. At any second, the True King can order an attack, summon Malum to wash over the land, and we do not have enough resources to stop him."

Her heart dropped. "Any second?"

"Any second," he reiterated. "It's up to us to stop him."

She considered what he said. Beneath her window, citizens walked by, laughing and sipping their coffees unaware. "You haven't told them," she noticed.

"No. The news would imply another genocide. Chaos would tip the fragile balance, and we would inadvertently destroy ourselves before the True King gets the chance."

"And Sarolt?" inquired Geda. "What happened to her?"

Marcy spoke up, "My sources caught her fleeing shortly after, with the scroll in hand."

"I see." Raymond paused, pondering. *Anastas accepted his fate only to hand off the artifact discreetly. He planned on becoming the dark general. Was that truly the best option for you, sagacious king?*

The Lord continued, "Life hangs by a thread, and every decision I make is to protect it. This is the way of the Order."

She nodded with complete understanding.

"I have been nothing but honest with you. You've seen your file. You know those five numbers mean something unholy. You chose your king properly and now, you have the venomous shimmer upon your lips, his venom. You now have a connection to the monarch's most powerful weapon —"

"Did you know Ana was my guardian?"

Disheartened, stripes flashed across Raymond's face and subsided. "I don't want to know how you found out."

"He beaconed in my arms."

"It was only speculation… A guardian is made when a being takes on a piece of mutant burden; a yin and yang transaction. The guardian keeps the mutant's human side alive at the risk of their own. Darkness binds the two and only death may divide them as it is the guardian's sole purpose to die for their mutant. Cursed guardianship occurs when a mutant's guardian is claimed, linking the two beings eternally until the binds are satisfied. Your guardian has never died. Over and over, he rejoined your side and watched you die."

"Forgive me," Ana's last request resonated in her heart. Sealed with a kiss, it was his last wish.

"The shimmer," highlighted Geda. "Is that the reason why I survived?"

"Perhaps," shrugged Raymond. "There is much even I do not understand about mutanity. Regardless, you and Ana, the two of you have ties that transcend natural boundaries. Ties even the monarch cannot obliterate. Revitalized, you may be able to pull him from servitude and away from his master's control."

Geda's eyes widened. "Is it possible?"

"In theory."

"Don't get her hopes up," said Marcy. "Geda, you realize to get him back your loyalty must be genuine. Your devotion must transcend death. It is an eternity of despair," she tried to convince but the Lord did not oppose. "You're serious? Giving him Geda will fulfill his desire for a new queen. He will have everything he needs to barricade the Vorota. If we falter in the slightest, we will lose everything."

"Relax, my dear friend. You forget I'm full of strategies. Geda will be fine," he assured Marcy. "Geda."

"Yes?"

"If this is what you want, this will have to be your mission alone. Understand that you will be secluded from my protection. Your morals will be tested. Your securities will be taken from you. Your happiness, your youth, and even life may escape you, all to unshackle the Devil from Hell."

"I understand," Geda agreed. There was nothing he could say to convince her otherwise. So long as there was a chance to save Ana, she was willing to take it.

Raymond was beyond proud of her but also afraid. "I'm not ready to let you go," he whispered.

Geda gave him a childish smile. "You don't have to, Father."

Raymond smiled, teary-eyed. *She called me father!*

"Alright," Marcy stepped in before he got too emotional. "I think that's enough for one day. Miss Geda needs her rest. It's not like she is going anywhere yet. You can visit anytime." Geda waved as Marcy pushed him from the room. The door closed behind them.

Now alone, Geda's mind spiraled. In just a few short hours, her understanding of the world changed. And Ana, he could be saved. But how? She was indomitably fixated but forced to wait. Injuries took time to heal, and losing him was the hardest one of all.

Helpless, she fell back onto her pillow. "Ha, Ana. Is this how it felt waiting for me?" *Ana*, she ruminated, filling the seconds they were apart. As the sun rose, he remained on her mind, and at night, they reunited in her dreams.

The following days were filled with more company. Geda's caregivers visited for appearances and gifted delicious offerings, chocolate-covered cranberries, her favorite. She shared them with all who came. To her surprise, there were many. Fellow researchers, sorority girls, and even Romulus stopped by with flowers. They all mentioned her miraculous survival.

In their absence, the atmosphere was not as joyful. Mind entangled, Geda experienced an unbearable depression and coughed the ash from her lungs. Even though time carried on, she replayed the same events over and over to see where she went wrong.

She was slowly losing her mind. She had grown so attached to a ghost that to find him missing caused intense separation anxiety. She was withdrawing from him. To think this is what he wanted, a distance maintained.

Ana had flooded her normality with sin and darkness, amplifying the pale colors of her heart. His tide retreated, unearthing fragments of the past, of the truth, and in the static state of the world, she started to see herself, to feel her true being.

Haunted by the Devil, she pined for his return, not for love but his existence. She required him to feel whole again. Everything had changed so fast. Unsympathetic to acclimation, time did not allow them to address his chaos nor the bloom of their relationship, just that it was and now is the fire of her fight.

At first, she feared Casimir's reappearance, until she recognized the shadows eclipsing the walls of her room at night, hugging the corners, and sleeping soundly in the crevasses of the equipment. Geda welcomed them upon remembrance of their new dark master; she searched the darkness for a sign, but no one was there to answer. Like her, he too was adjusting, or so she figured.

Thankfully, Marcy was there to help with the healing process. Her room was just down the hall. Lord Raymond had a kitchenette installed in her room until the restaurant rebuild was complete. To keep herself busy, Marcy experimented with new recipes and distributed them to others for approval. Naturally, Geda was her most honest and favorable judge. Along with savory creations, Marcy distracted her with grand tales of her youth, which often involved Lioness Sasha.

Eventually, Geda's longing was replaced with careful consideration. Thoughts like: where is Ana being held and how can she get close to the True King?

After a couple of weeks, she was cleared for release. Marcy helped her dress and pack. The entire morning was filled with nervous sighing. Unsure of where to begin, Geda kept her head high. *Ana, I'm coming,* she thought, zipping up a bag.

Suddenly, three knocks on the door attracted their attention. A fair-headed man leaned on the entrance instead of the expected dark-complected Lord.

"Ariel? You made it out alive!" Astonished, Geda ran to him and threw her arms around his neck.

"Oh!" Ariel grimaced. "Barely. And so did you."

Standing down, she noticed the damage he sustained. Scar tissue from second and third-degree burns covered his body. The event came back to her, along with his screams. She brushed them off. Happy he made it out alive… unlike his brother.

"I thought it would be best if someone escorted you home," said Ariel. He knew how hard returning to the routine could be after a horrific event. However, it became clear she did not need his protection.

A new fire burn in her alien eyes, a hatred, a desire for vengeance, but unlike Sarolt, the bloodlust did not dominate her power. Instead, her vendetta was spun with elegant threads, sharp enough to cut, which resided in minute refractions of her iris. He tasted the blood she would eventually shed.

"I would appreciate that," she welcomed and went back to packing her things.

Ariel's eyes then meet Marcy's. "Hey, Marcy," he greeted, inconspicuously inquiring about Geda's emotional state.

Marcy tilted her head and said his name in the softest, endearing, yet sad way, "Ariel." It told him everything. After all, he saw the shimmer upon the girl's lips. He too was still coming to terms with the new general. He knew what she had to do, but could not offer his support. To remain alive, he could not get involved.

"Ready?" Descending to the lobby. Ariel graciously carried her bags so she could focus her energy on movement, which required more than he anticipated. Her walk was unsteady and slow. At moments, he would catch her off-balance and put her back on track.

"Take it easy," he advised.

The lobby doors slid open and Geda's eyes met the last person she wanted to see.

Standing with anticipation, Theo went to hug her. "Geda! You're fully recovered!" She did not reciprocate his welcome. In fact, her soul crippled to find him okay.

She approached him harshly. Her grip filled with his shirt and jerked him to his podium, causing him to drop his crutch. "Why didn't you answer your phone? Huh? Where were you?"

Guilt emerged on the Theo's face as Ariel pulled her from him. Her heart dropped. "So it was you! You made the call. You killed him! Let me go!" She kicked and screamed, unable to break the arms around her waist. She had Sasha investigate the fire and uncovered the truth, a phone call summoned the queen into the trap and she set it on fire. Geda didn't believe it at first but his expression answered her doubt.

Ariel searched his expression but nothing denied her words. Astonished, his grip on her loosened. "Theo? You are his guardian."

Rightfully, Theo was ashamed. Convinced he had done the right thing, he did not realize his mistake until it was too late.

"He did not betray Anastas," defended Professor Yara "He followed command. Thus is the way of our Lord. You know this better than anyone, Peacekeeper," he added, reminding the mutant of his place.

Ariel curled his nose. "You're here to justify the change?"

"We all have our sacrifices to make. I am helping Theo cope with his." Currant's hand landed on Theo's shoulder, but he spoke to both youngsters. "I came to collect you, Geda, but it would seem someone else has done the honors for me."

Ariel's hold on her tightened. "What do you want?" he asked.

The priest lifted Ana's leather-bound journal. "Her name is in this book."

"It is numerous times," admitted Ariel.

"Yes, but this time it concerns King Ana's final wishes." Currant looked past the beast and to the girl. "We have much to discuss, my lady. So, if you will, please follow me."

CHAPTER 28

The Final Rite

On the western edge of the Oasis's eye was a rundown bar by the name Amora Roth. Boarded by steel, additional girders and trellises supported buildings against the wilder elements. The same could be seen in the surrounding structures, especially in the rear façades where Currant escorted them.

"Good afternoon, Roth," he greeted the man waiting for them. Expecting them, the referee spent the day preparing the place for visitors and now wore a sour expression.

"Roth," Theo acknowledged.

"Boy," noted Roth. Still coming to terms with their reason for being there, his expression smudged further and excused himself.

Currant divided Ana's book perfectly to the page he needed. As he gathered the final rite, Ariel noticed Geda stretching his threads. He turned and found the grunge ambiance had enamored her. She spotted the man she loved in the battered arrangements and scattered debris. His signature was everywhere amongst the survivalists. Thrilled to find him so easily, her other hand connected with the last place she felt his breath.

Ariel wondered if he was ever needed like this, not by Geda but by another.

"Do you know this place?" she whispered, only trusting him.

He nodded. "Ana spent a lot of time here. The owners are Separatists with differentiating preferences but Roth got along with Ana pretty well," he assured her. "As a metallurgist, he brought Ana's ideas to life."

Conscious of their mumbling, Theo glanced in their direction. Geda was practically hiding behind the beast, shadowed by his security, while he stood confronting, vulnerable to the future. He was alone, a feeling Currant knew too well. The priest supported Theo from a distance. Loneliness is a reoccurring expression of sacrifice, and he sympathized speechlessly with those who suffered its cold cradle.

Currant cleared the dust from his throat and began, "Upon his last wish, King Anastasius, Beacon of the Holy Monarch, Devil to the Lord, and Purveyor of God, deems his earthly possessions profitable to the survival of his successors."

"Successors?"

Currant reiterated, reading the king's scripture, "'Those who remain, impacted by my existence.' By that, he meant the two of you. Come forth," he ordered. "Here." He held up two identical keys. Geda chose the left and Theo the right.

The priest returned to the page and read the final passage, written hectically. His brow scrunched, trying to decipher, "Quid est Diabolus sine morte? Quid est Deus sine vita?" *What is the Devil without death? What is God without life?*

From Ariel's morphing expression, the phrase was a warning. Currant kept the detail of how the girl's name followed to himself.

With his key, Theo approached the shutter door. Having been here multiple times, to him the gift was obvious. Geda, however, hesitated. After all, this was the only physical remnant of the man she was never able to love. It offered minimal comfort and answered none of her qualms.

Currant closed her palm around the key. "I do not know the depth of the relationship you shared with Ana but I see he sparked your lifeblood. I also see the grudge you hold on to. Hatred will only grant you a dark birth," he warned. "Release it. Accept that Theo's actions served a higher purpose. Knew the command was ordained by the True King." A hint of detest curled in his throat, insinuating who to blame.

He continued, "Ana's bodily death was inevitable, planned since the eleventh century. We were prepared, but the act — oh god, the act had to be spontaneous After all, spontaneity makes death easy. Yes, Theo made the call and Anastas embraced it for what it was, not betrayal. You must do the same."

Seconds past as the priest's words settled into her resolve. She then looked at Theo. His stiff demeanor resisted the urge to return her gaze. No, he trudged onward, facing the future without hesitation. He had a mission. And so did she. Why let differences stop each other's tracks?

He's right, considered Geda. She stepped up beside him .

The garage shutters lifted, and the lights flickered on. Inside, two vehicles waited patiently: One sleek, streamlined Challenger, blacker than night, possessed the emblem of a demon on the side; the other was angled, edged perfectly to the highest wing, vitamin C Plymouth Superbird with a modified medallion resembling a raven rather than the classic roadrunner. Here, they slumbered peacefully. Unshackled like the edges of his mind, Ana left these pieces for the next generation to use in his stead.

The two successors were speechless. Ariel, however, applauded with excitement. "So, these are the final pieces." He went to them.

"Ana created these," Theo told Geda, following the tiger.

The Peacekeeper thoroughly demonstrated his respect for Ana's work; observing him was mesmerizing. He tested the paint's integrity with the slightest rub of his backhand. He bent at angles to see the light's reflection, appreciating the metal craftsmanship. In tune with them, he surfed with the light reflected off their skin, an electron whispering to its purpose. The most sensitive eye could detect the vehicle's excitement at the touch of his kind. But the actual value rested under aesthetics.

"You are going to have to educate them. All they see is ordinary metal," stated Currant, interrupting the electric bolt grasping on to the mutant's offered connection.

"Right." Ariel reluctantly pushed himself away. "Machines such as these are what branded mutants as tigers."

"I thought it was the stripes."

Curling his fist, Ariel contracted his muscles and stripes melanated. "It is, just as our eyes, claws, and teeth," he demonstrated each, "but these became our battle cry, solidifying the name. A mutant is nothing without his beasty." His thumb caressed the car again, clearly reminiscing about his machine before it was taken from him. "We may be strong but we are not fast. Distance became a weakness. Overtime, Ana fixed that."

"How are these different from other vehicles?"

"Nowadays, vehicles are fueled by plasma orbs or graphene generators. Tigerous engines are designed to consume the energy generated by the user. With that said, each one is different, specialized based on function or handler. My engine, for example, could be fueled by seawater. The salt build-up amplified the light exhibited by plasma orbs, extending the endurance of my patrol. The same concept would not work for a city dweller. Whether amplified by light shells, water, or solar, the engine's basic design and performance depends on the user's heart."

"And every tiger has one of these?" Geda asked.

Looking to Ariel for confirmation, Currant answered, "I don't think he shared the knowledge with anyone else."

The mutant shook his head. "If they have one, Ana built it. Only he knew how to construct these. He wanted a medium to outsource the Malum overload. Ana found a way to convert his pain into mechanical energy. He invented a furnace to burn his anguish."

"Even so, it wasn't enough for him," Geda whispered. Her fingertips traced the trim.

"He could drive for centuries and it wouldn't be enough," Ariel accentuated.

Theo put the key into the Plymouth's ignition and turned. It growled alive. Rumbling, the low tones hummed the chest. The metallic twang left Geda breathless with remembrance of the Devil's confrontational approach. Through the exhaust, the creator was distinguishable in its spirit.

Ariel bent to the cabin and gave Theo a final warning. "I'm sure you have ridden with Ana before. You know these do not handle like normal vehicles. These are built specifically for beasts to be handled by beasts. Keep that in mind."

Theo nodded.

"Operating the engine may take everything out of you. Drive them while you can, while their tanks are full, and before you have to pay to operate them. I doubt they will last long with the hearts of man controlling them."

Placing it in gear, Theo got accustomed to Ana's design.

Currant also bent to his window. "Where are you going to go?" he asked in case the trip required a tow.

Theo thought for a second. He didn't exactly have an answer. "Wherever my heart takes me."

Currant understood. "Do what you have to. Just give me a

call if something happens." As the Superbird pulled away, they watched him drive off into the distance.

"Where is yours, your beasty?" Geda asked Ariel sincerely. It was clear he loved his dearly. She wasn't wrong.

"With my guardian," he replied simply. "I have been trying to get her back."

"What's stopping you?" Currant interjected.

Ariel's brow raised, surprised by his support.

Geda reached for the handle of the demon. Meeting the interior, Ariel came over to help. "Geda, before you go, you should know, these creations are unearthly; some say a result of forbidden paganism. They are not entirely wrong. Each engine is named after the hearts pulled from our foes, Ana's more than mine. After all, he was wicked, shrewd, and very creative. It was his style."

Ariel pointed to the hellish emblem. "The demon is named after himself. He put his heart and soul into this. That also means this engine is specifically designed to be fueled by the heart of the Devil. There are no suppressants for the engine's thirst. You will feel the drain faster than Theo."

"I understand."

"Please take care of it," he requested. For all Ariel knew, this was all that remained of his brother.

"And the Superbird? Who is that named after?" she asked.

Ariel thought for a second. "I think you already know that answer," he said. "The little Raven."

Darin. Geda's heart quivered until she swallowed it. She put the car in gear.

"Where will you go?" asked Ariel.

"Beyond the Dunes," she said. "I want to see the world for what it really is, outside this manufactured haven. I need to know what I'm dealing with."

He agreed. "Be safe. The world isn't what it used to be."

As the mutant and the priest watched the last child leave, a concerning thought morphed Currant's face. "I hope they can handle it," he voiced.

Ariel patted his back as if they were friends when in reality they were not. "Relax Father," he said and started to leave.

"Have you met with my sister?" asked Yara.

Ariel stopped in his tracks and faced the man who once wounded him. *Why is this such a concern?* he wondered. "No," he said.

"You should."

Ariel's shoulders dropped. *What did he mean by that?* Usually, Currant disapproved of their contact. What changed?

"I know it is hard, but you will need to keep your eyes open. This is no time for slumber."

"That was not intentional."

"I know." Currant pushed the defensiveness down with his hands. He had a lot to say with little time to do it. "While you were gone, machinations were set and I fear they will soon be played. The results will be life-threatening. Stay strong, Reaper," he wished, speaking like the agent he used to be, and walked away.

"What does that have to do with Sasha? Hey! Where are you going?" Ariel wasn't done.

The priest lowered his head. "Back to my master." His chains were heavier than usual.

Ariel remained, stewing in the meaning of his words.

That day, the streets of Crescent and Gibbous City echoed with raging metal. Concrete reflected the sorrows of a fallen king. In their separate ways, Geda and Theo drove until the sun stained the sky.

The Plymouth leaned with the curves, and dove into the

darkest hiding places and dingiest alleyways, going everywhere a shadow would. The angled edges of the Plymouth glided along the street-lights and rippled the surface of darkness, to dip his toes in the water of his beloved royal, hoping to face the reflection of guilt and atone for his mistakes.

In the depths of Gibbous State, Theo found the Malum loitering, slow-moving in pain. Amassed, the group was visible without light.

Surrounded by creatures tethered to the king, will they consume me? he prayed, slowing to a stop. The jarring cam tousled the atmosphere of the underworld. Their heads turned. The look on the creature's face was quite exhausting.

There. Now, see that it is me, confronted Theo.

The shadow faced him, but did not move to kill him like he wanted. Unamused, the driver's window dropped. "Come on, Ana. Recognize me!" he yelled, pressing the throttle for more attention. The exhaust popped and gurgled. To his dismay, the disturbance only pushed the shadow away. However, Theo could have sworn he saw one smile as it turned.

Ana. Theo sighed and fell back in the seat. Grief crept into his mind, along with exhaustion. The engine started to demand more from him. He felt it in the muscles gripping the shifter; the fuel level halfway. He touched the throttle again. More energy drained. Each touch pulled more from his arm, and the increasing fatigue amplified his emotional state.

"So be it," he accepted. Should anything graciously kill him, may this be a form of punishment. He stared at his left hand on the shift, haunted by the guardian mark now nothing more than a blistered scar. As he put the car in gear, the events leading to Ana's death replayed in his mind. His heart still pounded with the desperation of when Ariel leapt from his window. Ana beaconed and he was left there to do nothing, a useless guardian.

No, Theo refused. He jumped up and chased after the mutant. He would lead him to Ana and he would save him, but as a human, the stairs held him back. "Wait!" By the time he was outside, Ariel was nowhere in sight. Fear struck him hard as he ran blind for miles, clinging to whatever trace of Ariel he could find. Not one thought of searching for Geda crossed his mind, a mistake he now wished he considered.

And when the sun broke the horizon, Theo gave up. Reality settled in. There was truly nothing he could do. His faith had to remain with Ariel and with hours of silence, no notifications to calm his concern, he sauntered back to the dorm, defeated, but hopeful that Ana would come find him. As he returned, he encountered the news reporting the restaurant's destruction and Darin's death on the dorm lobby television.

"Should you ever feel betrayed or hurt by Ana, do not hesitate to call," Bog once said, handing him a slip.

For Ana's sake, he instinctively dialed those nine numbers, unaware of whom it would summon. He turned and found Sarolt before him as the receiver of his call. *Sarolt?* Face to face, his body experienced many things; safe was no one of them.

"Shit!" Theo expressed.

"Indeed." The queen smiled, stepping from the shadows, devouring the fear swelling in his eyes.

Theo felt foolish. Shock twisted him. Then he felt it, the wave of imprisonment sloshed against his fallen body. *No! This can't be.* This was the end and Theo called it in. *Ana!* He cried.

Sarolt saw his erosion and sympathized with him. *How tragic! It was his guardian, the sheath that will shatter the blade*, she breathed.

"You love him. He was more than a father to you," she proclaimed. "Committed, you gave him your soul in service and protection. You were a proper guardian and for that, I will spare you, though nothing will heal your confliction."

She lifted his chin. "Guilt permeates for eternity. Do you believe Anastasius's death will satisfy what he feels in his heart? No. To be forgiven, you must repent."

"Repent?" he questioned.

"It is the only way to cleanse the soul of regret," she assured., licking the hot tears from his cheeks.

"How?" Disgusted, he was reluctant to know.

"Well, for starters, you can kill me. Stop me from fulfilling what you have set in motion. Do you think you can?" she teased, knowing full well he couldn't.

Theo shook his head.

"Then consider this, your master would have you betray those you hold dear, all for control," she said, taking the note from his hand. "What does that say about the quality of the man you serve? Imagine what he would do to Geda given a chance."

Geda! He was so focused on Ana, he nearly forgot about her. Theo couldn't fathom what the Monarch had in store for her. Knowing his twisted potential, it couldn't be good. Either way, the queen was right. He was a pawn delivering their fates.

Theo concaved. "What do I do?"

"Bow before a new master, a man who will soon battle the ancient hordes," she growled. "Serve him to dethrone the deceiver. But be warned, Raymond is ruthless and vengeful. His one goal may ultimately be for nothing, unreachable, but at least you will die doing the right thing."

Theo silently accepted.

"Good. Now disappear," she advised. Her hand opened, igniting the summoning slip. "Or this flame will be your guilty grave," she warned.

Time ticked against him. At the intersection of schemes, Theo rushed to his room to plant the fragile scroll for Ana to find. He broke his phone, then made his escape.

To this day, guilt struck the young guardian sickly. The lack of shadow vengeance forced Theo to repent the only way he knew how. The leather creaked beneath his reluctant grip. The high drone exuberating from the exhaust lowered to a tumbling bass and sung with each acceleration, headed to the last place a mutant servant should ever go.

As the pull on him grew, Theo craved the drive with every mile, pushing the engine to the max. He drove the vehicle how it was meant, the way Ana intended, and nobody stopped him. Perhaps foolish, he flew to the tower at the center of the Oasis, Joytech, to face his final verdict.

Geda, on the other hand, had a different experience.

Leaving the garages of Amora Roth, she turned right and drove past the cultivation Dunes and into the unknown outlands. The green faded into the dust of old colonies filled with metallic skeletons and jagged concrete teeth, sparse with vegetation and poisonous plants.

Skyscrapers became Brobdingnagian bridges. Houses were fossilized fragments of a different age. Desolate cities resembled spotted islands amongst rocks, and deep caverns. And smooth pavements quickly transitioned into hardened earth.

Beyond the Dunes was indeed nothing. The outlands was a deserted wasteland, a vile desecration of nature, and ultimately the result of Saltus blood drenching the earth. The world thirsted for a return nature did not claim; the spirit of earthly homeostasis was missing.

The Oasis was no longer in view when the Challenger slid to a stop. What seemed like an hour drive was only a few minutes. The environment drug on. The sands were endless, cusping the horizon, only stopping on jagged rocks and forgotten monuments.

Geda got a good look at the destruction. *To think, all of this happened suddenly. Within one week, roughly 90% of all humanity vanquished to smoother one man's soul. Him.*

The wind brisked her fingertips.

"Anastasius," she whispered.

Contrary to common belief, the Devil was gentle. He perched her life from monotony, gave her routine substance, and terribly, freedom. Moreover, he elevated her to a higher existence, a being with motivation, defiance, a sense of preservation, and intense justification; characteristics absent in modern society. He was a call to her natural mind.

If she could change, so too could the outlands. This land could be bustling with energy and excitement like the Oasis, but no, humanity herded into one congregation, leaving it all behind, to be eaten alive by the forces of time, and soon, the same plague will come for the Oasis.

However, within its emptiness, she found life in places deemed uninhabitable. She observed sparks of nature's reclaim, signs the desert was healing. A cottontail nibbled on the young buds of a *Rubus Sanctus* bramble. Insects crawled among erosion. And one lonely bird jumped limb to limb, searching for the next meal.

The land wasn't as barren as many presumed. Those that deemed it as such had never been neglected in a way that influences appreciation for little things. The outlands had life. It thrived with survivors and had the potential for cultivation, all the things advocates like Sasha have been preaching but no one took seriously.

Hope overlooked a persistent detail, the Malum.

As she turned, she found one feet away.

She froze, body and breath. How could she have forgotten their invasion, their conquering of nature from man? That said, the shadow did not advance against her. Instead, it stood tall, and basked in the sun. It seemed to know peace or at least found comfort in anguish.

With wisps of curl-ridden hair, a part of her wanted to believe this no-faced entity was him, the fallen king or that he was watching over her, escorting her travel beyond the safety of the Dunes. Still, she cautiously refrained from greeting the entity. Recognition of a Malum soul could endanger her, summoning the creature's instinct to devour her, rip her asunder, or worse. The thought shivered her. For now, they coexisted, human and shadow.

Their calmness got her thinking, *Could humans, mutants, and Malum coexist?* If the Malus Saltus were survivable, humanity could expand outwards, farm the outlands, and even chase the waves again. But there was only so much the Lord Raymond could do with his soldiers.

The idea brought back a youthful memory of when she saw the Dunes for the first time. From the tallest building, the size of the irregular hill was astronomical. Six in total, one Dune spanned the entire crescent quadrant. At age ten, Raymond introduced her to them.

"One day, we will return to the sea," he promised, kneeling to her tiny figure. The goal seemed unreasonable but she always possessed an ambitious trait.

"When?" Little Geda asked, excited.

A hopeless notion ruined his smile. "When the True King falls from his immortal throne. Don't fret. It will be hard work, but we will succeed."

"How?" she squeaked.

"I have you," he said confidently.

At the time, she didn't know what he meant but now she was positive her efforts would fulfill Raymond's dream.

Ana, please hear me, prayed Geda.

She took a breath and turned to the shadow, risking possession to get a message to him. "Ana, I need you. But… you need to be the dark commander for a bit longer until I can save you." Plans were stirring in her head, along with all the outcomes. She knew what to do but did not know where to begin.

"What do I do?" she whispered.

Suddenly a voice called forth, using her memories as a guide. "In the deepest portions of C.O.V. hell." Was it a response from the spectral being? It came again. This time using the heavenly recollection of Ana's confirmation, "It is the only place our Lord cannot go. There you will find the answers you seek."

Supporting this, Romulus did warn, "Do not go past level B." There must be something there, and there she would start.

"Thank you," she whispered to the Malum creature, who bent with a bow-like stretch upon her departure.

With sights set on the future, both children curved through the city, back to Joytech. The devil-embellished Challenger parked at a safe distance while the Superbird flew into the hanger unsuspectingly.

Multiple weapons pointed at Theo.

"Step out of the vehicle!" a guard yelled, locked and loaded.

Theo did. His hands rested atop his head, clearly human.

"It's just a kid, sir," the lieutenant called to the commanding officer, Captain Percival Nevan.

Percival disagreed, "With a tigerous engine? I don't think so. A mere mortal cannot operate such things."

Suspicious, he analyzed the young man as he approached. *Darkness has drained the vibrancy from his eyes but not in the way of a mutant's grief. And the vehicle, Plymouth Superbird, is a design I've not seen.* Then he saw the emblem and his eyes widened. *A soaring raven!*

"Take me to Raymond!" demanded Theo.

"And why would I do that?" Percival barked back. Nose to nose, the captain searched for a specific glisten in the boy's eyes. There were only splinters of allegiance.

"I killed a king." His firm demeanor evident of the truth.

In disbelief, the captain snatched Theo by the back of his neck and tossed him forward. "Take him to the Lord!" he ordered. Soldiers surrounded Theo, shackled him, and escorted him at gunpoint to the highest point of Joytech Tower.

To reach the lowest point, Geda needed exclusive access to the Order's most secret location. She called the only person who could help. "Sasha," she greeted through the phone.

"Geda? Is everything okay?" asked Sasha, discerning a hint of nervousness.

"I… I need your help."

"Just say the word, and I'm there."

"I need to get to the Royal Nest."

The Lioness froze and nearly stumbled down the spiral core.

Leo witnessed her misstep, an unusual miscalculation for the athletic creature. *What's got her so worked up?* he wondered. His interests piqued.

Before Sasha could ask Geda why or even how she knew about the nest, her radio blared, "2133 to Raven's Nest. Guardian in hand. Stand by."

Percival with a guardian? she thought. *What is going on?* Whatever the reason, it provided the perfect diversion. The treasonous task touched her impatient itch. She smiled. "Very well," she agreed. "Just step into the elevator, and I'll handle the rest."

Havoc had officially returned to Joytech. Under the excitement of the guardian's arrest, Sasha could sabotage undetected, sending Raymond's most precious into the heart of iniquitous practice. She hurried to the nearest control panel. Below her, the maintenance door opened. The escort could be heard scampering the steps, rushing, just as she was.

"399, 98, 7, 6, 5, 4, 3, 2, 1, 89…" Counting, Sasha focused. At step 361, their paths crossed. Followed by eight armed men, Captain Percival drug the stumbling young man by the arm.

Sasha recognized him. "Theo?" She didn't expect it to be him. However, there was no time for pleasantries. Barely a quarter of the way, the escort drove harder.

Unbelievable! simmered Percival. *How could this boy uncrown a king? It was nearly impossible for the trained to take down a royal, let alone a civilian.* Aggravated, he growled and grumbled. With that said, the growing rumble of prisoners overshadowed his frustration.

The very name of the guardian energized the tanks.

As he flew by, caged beasts came alive, fighting rage at the sight of him. The king was dead. They felt it in the dark essence commanding their equilibrium. Their ferocity blind to the acidic pain and dissolved state. Some possessed smiles knowing, too, the monarch bleed.

Tanks flew by so fast. Theo couldn't recognize their faces, intently searching for one prisoner, one companion Ana trusted. About halfway, he found him. "Leo!" yelled Theo, thankful he was there. However, the convoy didn't slow for conversation.

"Keep moving," pushed Percival.

"Wait!" Theo fought. He anchored his feet and dropped all his body weight to gain a few milliseconds with the advisory, but the soldiers increased their restraint. Percival was determined to deliver the liar to the Lord but not many could move a decider.

Leo's eyes met the struggle and Theo started to slid. *Is that Ana's guardian? Here?* Cold then shot through his blood. His instinct told him before the boy could.

Enduring, the tension had little room for words. "Er! Ana's… dead!" Despite the pain, he still fought. "Ah! Let me go! He needs to know."

After a second, a soldier cracked open his cast and they found the leverage to dislodge his resistance and carried him up the rest of the way.

"Tell it to Raymond, kid."

Theo shouted louder, "Bog! It was all Bog's doing!" Tears flooded his screams. Never did he think he would say such a thing.

Bog, their loving father; how could this happen?

No longer in sight, Leo still heard the boy's fight, registering what he said. "Ana's dead and it was Bog's doing," he repeated. "Ana is dead." He had an inkling but for the boy to confirm it. His whispers felt like spells. They settled in his heart and for the first time since his imprisonment, Leo choked on the green liquid.

Splicing into the mainframe, Sasha overheard everything. *Dead? The king? That means….* As her mind wondered, her hands developed a shake. *Focus!* she summoned. The keyboard clinked viciously, rushing to complete Geda's request.

Bloop! sounded the system, indicating the alarm override.

As Geda descended, Theo ascended.

The double doors of the Raven's nest rudely opened, interrupting Raymond's business. The Lord peered over his glasses as several men filled the room with a tense aura. "What is this?" he questioned.

Percival tossed the guardian to the floor. "This boy has requested an audience with you. He claims to have killed a king."

Interested, Raymond closed his work. "Is that true?" he asked, fully aware of the circumstances surrounding King Ana's demise, but unaware of how exactly his guardian was involved. Why did Theo feel responsible? What did Bog have him do?

Regardless, the young guardian held his ground. Bearing a tear-stained face, his eyes swirled with betrayal, vengeance, and even suicide. It was clear he sought to find one of those in this room.

"Speak up, young man!" ordered Raymond. "Which king has fallen? Was it the deceiving Casimir?" He tested his honesty.

"Anastasius." The name sent a breeze down everyone's spine. "I made the call that set his fate in motion. Ana's death was dealt by my hands but ultimately orchestrated by Bog."

"Bogu," corrected Raymond, standing from his throne. "His name is Bogu, and you have simply captured a glimpse of his true nature. Congratulations. Why should I reward you for committing an atrocity?"

Theo bowed his head. Gracefully, he lowered. "My master serves no higher purpose. He plays his game. I am but a pawn on his board. It is a place I do not wish to be. If you would allow me —"

"Allow you to what? To serve the Order?" Raymond scoffed. "There is something you must understand: We all play his game. We are all toy soldiers bound to die in the end. You were Anastas's guardian, servant to the most clever, a mutant closest to the True King, and still you couldn't see through the simplest of schemes. Even I knew of the trap before it was set. Why should I accept your surrender? What can you do? What would I even do with someone like you?"

Theo refuted with the same energy, "You can kill me, break me, stop me from fulfilling the Monarch's wishes again. I am afraid to discover what he has in store for Geda."

That got Raymond's attention.

"What makes you say that? Did he mention anything about her?" He asked hastily.

"No. It's just... Sarolt made me think."

Raymond smiled. "Ah, I see. So, you come to me to escape Bogu's meddling and to avoid leading Geda to her doom."

"I have," Theo admitted, pure heartedly.

"Hmm." Raymond judged him again, specifically the metal reinforcing him. *It could use some strengthening,* he thought. "Funny," the young guardian amused him. After a moment, Raymond snagged a folder from the pile on his desk. "Then you should know who you bow to," he warned.

Addressing the audience, Raymond raised the folder for all to see. "This is all that remains of my son, Darin. I will admit I secretly contracted his death with the very king you 'killed', yet somehow, Darin knew it would be Ana the whole time. Did you tell him? You were there when Leo delivered the message."

"How could I?" defended Theo. "Hey, your father wants you dead, that's not something you can just tell your friend."

"No, perhaps not. It wasn't anyone but Darin. He knew his reign was over, probably when King Anastas crossed his path. My son drove himself to death, all for this." The folder opened and Raymond displayed a slip of paper, speckled with discoloration. "Darin's Will, handwritten just hours before his death. What astonishes me most is within the verses, he names you, Theo, as his successor and heir to the company."

Theo's jaw dropped. "What?" he asked in disbelief.

Raymond handed the evidence to him to read. Theo took it. The generic lined paper immortalized the last humane fragments of Darin's mind. Some words were illegible, smeared by the writer's blood.

The page read:

> Theo, my unforgettable friend, my death is imminent and on my own accord. Forgive me, but I cannot see this to the end as I have planned. There are enemies all around me. My Geda despises me and my pedagogy, the refinement of her mind. It takes a sharp knife to keep her aligned. My grip tightens, trying to hold onto her, but she continues to slip through my fingertips and into the snake's pit. If guided wrong, she will lead this world to devastation. See that it does not happen. DO NOT ALLOW ARMAGEDDON TO BE IN HER NAME!
>
> "I am aware Father does not see me clearly or how my actions support his goals. Parents never see how we bleed, and vice versa. In the end, know I died as a result of my valiant actions. With that said, Raymond must have an heir, a beacon for the apocalypse they are creating, a reason for our warriors to push on when things go dark. I name you, Theon Bastille, heir to Joytech, the Order, and the Central Organization of Venators to stand in my place. Take the name Sambuca, and lead in my absence. I know you have what it takes to lead the Order. Follow as the 73rd heir and take charge of your destiny. Let my last action be the best.
>
> Darin Lee Sambuca

"What do you say?" Raymond posed.

There was nothing he could say. Shock replaced the weight on Theo's shoulders. The reality of the opportunity was complex and heavy. Reading Darin's last words and knowing he died with them in his pocket choked him. And 73rd heir? Theo had so many questions. With a deep breath, the young guardian held his emotions in. Theo could see the headlines now, "A Protector of Mutanity Finds Security with the Enemy.' Ironic as it was, this might be his only chance at redemption.

"Do you accept Darin's wishes? Will you become my son, the 73rd heir?" Raymond offered again.

"I will not consider you a father figure," Theo defined after careful consideration.

"No. You will be Theon Bastille Sambuca, adopted son and Shield Guardian of the late Devil King Anastasius, 73rd Prince of the Order."

"That is my title?"

"So long as you accept the name Sambuca, you can be whomever you want within the direction of the organization."

"Then I accept," he whispered.

"Very well —"

"Sir!" called a frantic voice as surveillance popped up behind the large desk. "Someone is in the Nest," reported Lion Tuwile.

"Show me," ordered Raymond.

"We are trying, but the system — it's fighting us." The screen flashed with multiple recordings until finally footage of the Nest came through, and they saw who trespassed.

Percival gasped. "Geda?"

"Should we interfere, sir?" Tuwile nervously asked.

"No. Leave her be."

"But, sir?" the agent persisted. Though fresh, he knew the cardinal rule: one was allowed in the Royal Nest.

"She is there for a reason," assured the Lord. "In fact, grant her full administrative access."

"Yes, sir," Tuwile obliged, ticking the keyboard. As the feed continued, they all held their breaths for the pivotal awakening.

The elevator stopped. The level indication did not appear on the counter but Geda was certain this was level E based on Romulus's instruction. To others, this floor did not exist. So far, no one stood in her way. Returning to the surface, however, is going to be a different story. *Thank you, Sasha,* she blessed. From here on, she was on her own.

The doors opened, blinding her with medical-grade aesthetics. A synthetic white radiated from every surface, including the chairs and tables. "Em," she grimaced.

A door to the left advertised relief. She quickly took it but found it led to a room identical to the previous. More spacious, the shade was a symptom of empty ambiance, which directed her to a mezzanine overlooking the space named Nest; the words Nimbus for Eternal Slumber and Technology (N.E.S.T.) was written on the far wall.

Capped with thirty foot ceilings, a monolith-like structure protruding up through the floor interrupted the bland consistency though it, too, carried a stark design. Overall, the unnatural futurism left her in awe.

What is this place? she wondered.

Even the air possessed unique qualities. Descending the steps made noise, but negative echoes damped the percussion. She paused at the lowest level and listened. Again, no sound, nothing nullified her mind beyond her own heartbeat. Unsteady, she could almost hear the blood pumping within.

Adjusting, the monolith pressed against her awareness. It easily towered over her by three feet and seemingly grew in size as she drew near.

Wow! It looked so much smaller from above, she thought. Upon closer inspection, every side was solid but one. A glass pane provided a view of the interior chamber; filled with more emptiness.

Hmm. It's like a sarcophagus, she connected. *Or like the vertical prisons.* Only this one was different, squarer and more spacious. Geda combed the frame. Like the tanks, a number was etched into the top, 7541; the same digits tattooed on her hand. Outstretched, she compared the two.

Weird. I don't remember ever seeing this. She flipped through the portfolio of memories but nothing like this stood out. Curious, her finger kissed the glass. Digital numbers shot across the surface, outwards from her touch and converged in the center to form the message, "7541. Geda Sambuca."

Suddenly, a female voice emerged. "Welcome back, subject 7541, codename: Geda. I'm afraid your nest is not ready. Is there anything else I can assist with?"

"Subject?" questioned Geda. She knew she was always a part of the research team but never like this. "My nest? Is this my tank?" Was she a prisoner? What did any of this mean? Of all his honesty, Raymond failed to mention this part. With no recollection of this place, she hoped whomever was speaking could bring her up to speed.

"I… I'm sorry," she spoke up. "I seem to have some lingering amnesia. What is this place?"

A light turned on in an adjacent room. "Here, you will find files regarding the Nest, its functions, and any personal records. All are up to date," said the voice.

"Thank you."

"Should you need anything else, just call my name."

"What *is* your name?" asked Geda.

The voice paused, deciding if it was okay to give the occupant restricted information. (Raymond manually keyed in the passphrase after Percival cleared the room.) The system replied with, "My name is Zarin."

As if a switch had been flipped, Geda's eyes widened.

"Zarin?" It had been ages since she heard that name. Triggered, her eyes tangled, deciphering locked memories. An overbearing weight squeezed her chest, and all her strength drained from her body.

"How do I know you?" she whispered breathlessly. She felt it upon reconnecting with the tablet, among the fire, now. What is this sensation? And why was it killing her? Faint, she slid to the base. "Zarin?"

"Yes?" the A.I. chimed in.

"Zarin was the name of the True Queen," Geda remembered. She once repeated the name in prayer before being burned by hypocrites.

"Yes," the A.I. confirmed. "The True Queen acquired many names throughout history. She was seen as divine, a mother in some religions and the harbinger of end in others."

"Do you know everything?"

"I know everything Raymond knows."

"What caused the Mutant War?" Geda demanded, testing the system's limitations.

"The conflict's origins can be traced back to the True Queen's rebellion against her King, disappearing upon the True King's request of her power. The culprit for her absence and keeper of her location is Raymond Sambuca."

So, the True King fights to secure her, but cannot dispatch Raymond without her location, Geda pieced together. *If Raymond has the power to end the war, why doesn't he?*

"Why does the True King need her power?"

"Historical sources indicate the Monarch's obsession with queen's blood, the source of mutant power, and his unethical tendencies of harvesting royals for their abilities. Zarin rebelled to smother this influence, frequently sweeping the medieval lands with Malum, led by her dark generals and royal harpies."

Like Sarolt, Geda recognized.

A.I. Zarin continued, "The rebellion's last attempt was recorded in the 4th century, etched into the Gammal Tablet. Shortly after, the resistance died but was revived around the 11th century with the claim of Queen Sarolt. With the assistance of the new royal, Queen Zarin made one last effort, ultimately sealing herself away forever. Her location remains a secret."

"I knew Zarin," said Geda, recalling her face as if it was yesterday. "She was winter in spring. The twisting dandelions of her regime, I remember the devotion." Her hands retraced the rhythm of her ancient ritual. "I carved my name in the stone tablet for future resurgence, should it be possible, one final seed of defiance before time culled our efforts."

Geda once waved the queen's banner with pride, but her memory only went so far. Her mind closed with the fire that took her from Ana and opened to a new fire that unknowingly saved him during the fall of Joytech tower 10 years ago.

More memories came to mind. *Fire? I think I remember... I remember being inside the glass,* she considered, stepping inside the monolithic sarcophagus.

Odd, it feels like Ana. A comforting smother influenced slumber, but when she closed her eyes, the memory was not as comforting.

It's dark and hot. And!

Silver-piercing diamond eyes squeezed life into her heart.

Ariel? She saw him. His eyes so full of hate.

Coughing, ironized phlegm surrounded her tongue.

Lightheadedness bubbled her brain once more, filling her sight with stars. *It's getting worse,* she reluctantly addressed.

"The tablet," she hurried. "Tell me about Gammal —"

"Gammal was a religious refugee colony established in the mid-4th century —"

"No," Geda corrected. "Give me a report on the Gammal tablet."

A.I. Zarin provided, "D.N.A. was identified and extracted from the crevices of the ancient tablet." What followed was not suitable for retelling. The facts numbed her reality. Hearing the truth behind her recreation made her gag.

Previously described as a test tube baby, the project for artificial incubation became a realization of desecration. If Sarolt gave her blood and Casimir, his seed, the combination of royalty could give Geda another chance to fulfill the True Queen's goal, kill the True King. And so they did.

The A.I. explained, "Resurrection, a nonce power of queen's blood, used wisely can undo time. Using the extracted DNA, Queen Sarolt made the sacrifice and used her sacred power to revive Zarin's dark general. It was a success but the specimen was very weak. The monolith was built as a maternal biome for project 7541. To my record, the monolith malfunctioned during Joytech's collapse, interrupting the incubation process and awakening you early."

Geda swallowed hard, extinguishing the need to vomit. "Sarolt," she ruminated, dazed. They were yoked. *No wonder I felt a way around her.*

Her gears spun faster. *If queen's blood has the power of resurrection, can it be used to save Ana? And if I was a dark general, would the Malum affect me? Can I pull him directly from the waters? If I did, would someone have to take his place?*

"Tell me what we know about the Malum Saltus."

The system answered, "Not much is known about the Malum Saltus, the dark figures commanded by nature. Studies have been done on how Malum affects society, specifically beaconing, recruiting generals for Malum control, and how to combat the dark hordes."

So, this is my mission? Geda considered. *Find the connection, follow the philosophy of Zarin, conquer the Malum, and destroy the True King, all to free him, Ana. Until my end, I will not stop. Ana, I will save you!*

The light blinked in the side room. "For more information, official reports are located here," reminded A.I. Zarin.

Before I confront the unknown, I must know everything. Geda cleaned her face with sleeve and followed the light into the other room.

There, a structure similar to her coffin occupied the small space. Horizontal, the bed bore the name, "1141 King Anastasius." Her heart shook, *He rested here.*

Another memory filtered across her brain's eye. Wooden toys of many shapes (trucks, trains, and airplanes) and ammunition from an agent's clip surrounded young Geda with play. On the floor, she was entertained by Lord Raymond's most loyal, a young agent with a scar on her face, Sasha. Her childish amusement made the warrior smile.

"Shall I make another one?" Sasha offered. Grabbing a lettered block, she started carving a shape with the king's blade.

Swiftly, the double doors opened. "My Lord! I have excellent news," stated the white coat running in.

"Dr. Jakobi?"

"Sir! Sir, look." The scientist slammed a file on Raymond's desk. "The D.N.A. extracted from subject 1141 contains the genomes we seek. We may have just unlocked the secret to mutant royalty, sir!"

Raymond gave Jakobi a look that then went to the child. "Sasha, please remove Geda from this conversation," he ordered.

"Yes, sir." The Lioness sheathed her blade, scooped Geda from the floor, and left.

1141, Ana. He bore a mark just as she did, she saw it once on his wrist. Geda looked at her mark and back to the royal bed. *What did they do to you?* she thought.

"A.I Zarin, I want all the files on King Ana."

"I could not find any information for King Ana," answered A.I. Zarin.

"Ana is the modern name for King Anastasius."

The computer chimed. "I have updated the information in my system. File number 1141 has all the information regarding King Ana. It would seem we have a lot to learn from each other."

Rummaging through the file cabinet, Geda found his file. "Yes, we do."

CHAPTER 29

Quartz Sanctuary

A month passed since the fatal fire, and the world carried on without King Ana. Word of his demise spread fast among the Separatists. With the Devil indisposed, the Oasis blindly prospered. Citizens felt safe. They could not be more wrong.

After graduation, Geda's reputation within the Order grew, as did her knowledge of the mutant world. In the Nest, she dove deeper and deeper into their history and all things Malum related, further than any human dared to go. Intensive research elevated her work. Now a curator of mutant history, she scoured documents and artefacts for answers to questions along the way.

Seeking redemption, Theo bowed to Raymond, accepting the position as heir and satisfying Darin's last wish. In Ana's absence, he extended the utilization of his training, guarding humanity and mutanity with high authority. Thankfully, he did not have to do it alone.

Sasha showed him the ropes of the organization, instructed him on the Order's philosophy, and inducted him in Venator training. After removing his tag, she guided him to proper management as a mutant sympathizer instead of the usual authoritative enforcer, forging his mindset for a better future, and he gracefully implemented her suggestions. After all, the only people in the Order who understood mutant suffering were the ones who walked alongside them.

From there, Theo devised ways to lessen hunger and aggression across the nation. The rationing system was reworked to incorporate everyone, mutant and human, without battle. He converted the Decider Games into a multifunctional tool for entertainment, C.O.V. training, and mutant medical exercise.

Theo then made a corporate allegiance with Romulus, making the Body Shop the leading distributor of quality meats; supplied by additional Joytech grow farms, prices dropped. Businesses were booming, and citizens no longer prowled the streets like feral cats. Upon Geda's request, Theo also abolished mutant experimentation, ultimately unplugging the chambers in the Royal Nest.

When presented to Lord Raymond, his reasoning was to unite the divided. "Today, many see the place of rest as a trap for experimentation," presented Theo. "Originally, the opportunity for mutants to sleep peacefully under Order protection reflected our reliability. We built a trust with our citizens that was eventually betrayed. The safe haven symbolized danger, ruining the Order's image. The Order became a regime instead of servants. By advertising the project's destruction, citizens will begin to favor the Order more freely, eventually restoring the trust we lost."

"But the claiming!" cried Dr. Jakobi.

"If you don't have it by now, it will never come to us," Theo pointed out. "Its time to put some power back in the people. Funding for the Nest will be redirected to Seperatist organizations to develop public havens for mutant slumber."

Impressed, Raymond sided with the new prince.

Within a month of his reign, Theo's popularity skyrocketed. The Oasis was well supplied. With natural resources and amenities prioritized, no human died from a mutant's hunger. Everyone was happy except the Central Organization of Venators, who pined for a hunt. For the first time in a long time, the Oasis was a paradise.

Reconstruction of Marcy Joans's restaurant started two weeks after the dorm burned. Locals contributed to rebuilding it in time for her release. For all she had done for others, this was the least they could do. Of course, some volunteers required encouragement.

Every day, the Peacekeeper oversaw their efforts from the rooftops, patiently waiting and watching for something to stand in the project's way. If every worker was there on time, Ariel would listen to the radio broadcasting among the streets, ready to jump at the next signal for help.

"Onto other news," said Reporter John, "investigators have uncovered more information surrounding Prince Darin Sambuca's death. On June 1st, the heir of Joytech's Raymond Sambuca was deemed responsible for the attack on Marcy Joans but new sources say otherwise."

"That's right, John. A new report from Joytech states Darin received threatening messages from the felonious mutant, Ammon Rajeeve. Still wanted for a crime he committed years ago, Darin's team hunted the mutant, but unfortunately, fell victim to Ammon's explosives," added Reporter Wyatt.

"What?" expelled Ariel.

John continued, "The video store owner was detained this morning by C.O.V. officials for further questioning."

As the news moved on, Ariel remained dumbstruck. *What are they trying to pull? Why are they changing their story now?* he scoffed. *How many times do I have to save that man?*

As one man was taken into custody, what happened to those already in custody? What of Leo? Three months have passed since his capture and hundreds long for his return, waiting for the Rose Garden to reopen and neon roses to bloom. Like most, Breanna anticipates the lights to ignite every time she walks by, itching for the next wave of Nostalgia, but that was impossible without his flowering companion.

Until then, no music played, no lights conceived waves, nor did blood rain. Only blood-splattered remained, traumatized by the substitute Separatist leader. Many have begun to wonder if the dealer would ever resurface.

As for the Lioness Sasha, life teetered on the edge of discipline. As the True King bent to harvest Sarolt, her purpose was revitalized. "You will destroy the True King," Raymond once promised. Timing, however, was not on her side, especially not with the Malum army now under the monarch's control. Though she tasted opportunity, she was forced to swallow motivation to maintain obedience.

"Here are the files you requested, sir." Sasha laid a folder on Raymond's desk.

"Thank you," he replied softly.

Raymond hid it well, but she detected the sorrow he felt. He mourned his son's passing. Less of regret and more the grief of a failed parent, Raymond kept a small picture of Darin on his desk.

She understood how he felt and in leaving, struggled to bury the sorrows of her youth. With uncomfortable thoughts of the mutant monarch, she forcibly extinguished the catalyst that conscribed her to a lifetime of service. It was like swallowing a knife. The endless calling felt unnatural; the anxiety turned her skin inside out. Even her subconscious fought her, resurfacing any justification to the contrary.

"It is *we* who will deliver the killing blow to the True king. Not Raymond," Sarolt once said. The usher rationalized all reasoning.

After all, it was Sasha's duty to hunt the self-proclaimed deity. Under Raymond, her vengeance had been confined to babysitting for the past ten years. Meanwhile, neglecting to secure the True King cost many lives. With Raymond in the lead of the political game, all she could do was follow. What was she to do when nothing came of their collective efforts?

Her easy influence over Theo was evidence of the Lord's singular focus, his obsessive preparation for retaliation. Otherwise, he would have tailored the new prince more carefully.

I am tired of waiting, Sasha huffed. No longer could she rely on the Lord's signal to dethrone the monarch knowing it would never come. While the charade commences between powers, it is time for the lesser beings to scheme. It was a revolution of one's control, a call to the army of the living and for that to happen, the Oasis needed to be united; a soul would need to be released from the Order's tree, a life thousands relied on.

Instantly, a name came into mind. Descending the spiral core, Sasha counted the tanks. *874. 873. 872.*

With each step, her determination grew, devouring the satisfaction of free will. She had followed command for so long, she forgot how it felt to act on her own. She smiled, crafting a multitude of excuses should she need them.

Raymond, you were always there for me. You took me in at my lowest and gave me the strength to be who I am. You entrusted the death of the True King to me. I will kill him. You just have to let me.

669. 668. 667.

Finally, she stopped. "Leo. Leo, wake up."

Name called, the mutant slowly opened his eyes and materialized. "Lioness?" he answered somberly. His speech gravely and pitted from the acid he submitted to.

"Come with me," she demanded, prepping a key to his prison.

"To where?" asked Leo sarcastically as if he had a choice.

Sasha didn't say. From a case, she procured a clean syringe, uncapped it, and plunged the tip into her vein, retrieving contents to flush his prison. Full of blood, the syringe pierced the nutrient line of his tank. Impurities defiled the sterile system, immediately triggering a safety breach. The acid drained, leaving him in an oddly pressurized space.

Hurling and gasping, Leo released the acid from his lungs. Then the door to his cage fell open and fresh air swept over him. "Ah," he sighed, relieved. Though, with the touch of new air a came damaging sting, slicing through every layer of sloughed skin. His stomach instinctively started to ache. Teeth clenched, stripes melanated.

"Are you poisoned?" he growled, groveling for control. The scent of the syringe told him she wasn't, and without hesitation, he lunged at her, desiring a bite but in his state, even a mortal could apprehend him.

Sasha stepped out of the way, grabbed the back of his neck and subdued his attack. She wasn't going to let him have the satisfaction of sinking his teeth into her, let alone suffer the potential repercussions. Instead, the syringe stabbed his vein and delivered the remnants of her collection; barely enough to drive the itch away but it allowed some security for Leo.

She slapped cuffs on his arms. "Let's go," she said, leading him down the spiral. With his hands bound, she escorted him to freedom, acting as a transfer. However, when they got through the maintenance door leading to the lobby, they were stopped by a one-man army.

The Lioness hit a brick wall. Leo saw what held them in place.

It's Ariel, he praised.

Their eyes met.

There for Ammon, Ariel locked up at the sight of her. He had been caught. Disguised as a delivery man, Sasha saw right through his cover. She saw his scars, his true face, and the unfamiliar burns blanketing his skin. Nobody saw him, not like they did. Ultimately, the two souls froze, immobilized by each other's presence, leaving Leo uncomfortably sandwiched in their war zone.

Acid ate at her flesh but the pain was nothing compared to seeing him. *Ariel,* Sasha couldn't believe it was him. For the first time in ten years, there were signs of him all over the city. CCTV caught every angle of his community outreach.

Now, he was here, physically before her. She could touch him. She could kill him. She could…

Sasha huffed. "Ariel," she growled, acknowledging him.

Before air could vocalize from his chest, flashing red lights cauterized his mind. Sirens blared as warnings popped up on the global monitors behind the receptionist's desk with the fatal words, "Arnireth Collapse."

Sasha's firm grip vanished.

"What's going on?" Percival yelled, rushing to desk controls.

The receptionist worked frantically to find out. "It's the pits, sir," she said, accessing local cameras. Live footage popped up on screen. "They've opened," she confirmed, horrified.

Shadows claimed the souls of the unsuspected. Bullets sliced the horizon, struggling to keep the sudden horde contained while more soldiers rushed to the stations unprepared.

"Ana," mumbled Ariel.

"Do what you can to keep this quiet until we can rally more troops," Percival ordered reception.

"Yes, sir." The alarms went silent, but the screens were still red. The flashing hazard altered any motivation, expression, disguise, or admiration of all who set their eyes upon it.

For Sasha, a fear swelled in her eyes; fear being a proper term for the general public. Ariel knew better. He knew the emotions stirring within her. He witnessed anxiety flourish, the tearing feeling of the potential of if she stayed, the dread of leaving without confronting the opportunity before her now. It was surrendering so that her enemy could live another day. The emotion had no name, but he knew she wanted to stay.

"Take him!" she yelled, pushing the prisoner to him. Leo fell into his arms, clutching a set of keys in his hands, the keys to his beasty. Watching her leave, Ariel clenched his teeth, resisting the urge to call out to her. He swallowed everything he wished to say, if anything could be said, and saved it for later. In some way, he knew he would see her again. He always did. He had to see her again, his greatest enemy and guardian.

Sasha, Ariel simmered.

"When Death embraces our Devil, life will wage war with shadows," Leo recited the prophecy under cycling lights.

"Heed ye, the words of Mother," acknowledged Ariel.

As hell opened, Geda sought to be closer to God, arriving at the Heavenly Springs Community Church of God. Compared to before, the atmosphere was somehow sickening. Previously accentual, red now covered everything. The Christian idol hung lower; the settling weight amplified the sacrificial pain.

Geda slid into one of the pews hoping someone would notice. They did. A priest sat in the row behind her. "You're here? At a time like this?" welcomed Yara Currant.

"Times certainly have changed, Currant. It's evident in your décor."

He snickered. "It is not by choice. Our master dictates all decisions. Color influences the masses."

"He's not wrong."

The two sat silently under God's presence. The hums of the high ceilings rang throughout the space, and the candles remained stable without the drain of nearby hunger.

The room was full of nothingness yet possessed an overwhelming welcomeness, an acceptance without judgment and cleanliness; safety. At that moment, she understood what Ana meant. It reflected an inner sense of what you needed most and pulled you in.

She smiled. "Mmm. He was right. I hate it."

Currant fumbled over the random expression. "Excuse me?"

"A friend once told me he hated churches. He could easily fall asleep in one. I think I now understand what he meant."

"I'm sure your friend had far worse things to be afraid of than falling asleep in a church."

"Perhaps," she said, giving him a side-eye.

The priest leaned in closer. "Geda, may I ask, why are you here? It is not safe," he whispered.

Geda sighed. "Yes. I felt the ground quake. But, I don't have much time left. I need to see him."

Currant shook his head. "Doing so is a trap. You will not be able to walk away," he begged her to listen to reason.

"You are the gatekeeper. Take me to him, or I will find my own way," threatened Geda.

Currant's brow raised. At this point, he had no choice but to assist. It was best for everyone. By complying, he could at least control the tide she wade in. *I hope she has a plan,* he prayed.

"There's no need for force," said Currant. "You could end up in a dangerous position. After all, patience is a virtue."

Standing, the priest gave her a wide-eyed look, and walked in the direction of a nearby door.

Was that a yes? she debated, rushing after him.

Currant speechlessly allowed her follow. In fact, he waited

for her to keep up. He even held the door open for her. However, his stare silently commanded her to keep everything she saw a secret.

Together, they passed through passages of time, traversing through hall after hall to get to the oldest part of the cathedral. From there, they descended a spiral stair leading to the ancient catacombs, navigated a labyrinth, cut corners sharply, then arrived at a door freshly cut into the dirt.

Currant paused, tousled his pocket, and pulled out a collection of keys. "Very few people have access to this door."

"What's behind it?" she asked.

The keys jumped as he pulled them apart, looking for the right one in the poor lighting. *Come on. There,* he found it. One key entered the lock. Its twin fell into her hand.

"This is a royal nest," he answered.

Her heart fluttered. "And you are giving me access?" Though generic, the key was the only thing securing the sanctuary from clergy intricacies.

"It may be necessary," he said, turning the latch.

Geda followed him down a narrow stairwell. Recalling the schematics presented during her last visit, the structure was a perfect copy. *We are far below the surface,* she identified. *The air is vastly different from before, like the nests of Joytech, only darker.*

The level continued to go deeper. They traveled down another long, descending hallway but as she progressed, she lost sense of the world around her. With no light in sight, her eyes became useless. Her nose detected no smell and her ears deafened at the absence of atmospheric chatter. The only sense was the ground beneath her feet, but even then, she trudged the cliff's edge looking into the void. Vertigo started to set in when she collided with the priest.

"Ohm!" she exclaimed.

"Sorry. I had to make sure you were still there," said Yara. "Grab onto me. The Malum can be difficult to navigate."

Her hand found his clothing. "Malum? Is that what this is?" she asked.

"Just essence," he assured. "Harmless unless you lose your way in it. Just stay straight, trust your step, and walk with your heart. You'll find your way." She did as instructed and eventually a light shone before them, signifying an archway.

"We're here," said Currant. Geda was relieved.

The archway transported them to an ancient Roman temple, littered with artifacts. Capped with a dome ceiling, classical oil paintings colored the walls. Ornate medallions and motifs textured stucco. At the center of the quartz room stood a stone coffin.

"It's a crypt," she gasped, lost for words.

"Yes," confirmed Yara.

"Of whom?"

The priest did not answer. Instead, he motioned for her to see for herself. Hesitant, she stepped forward. Her shoes blemished the virgin floor. The pools of water rippled her approach. As she ascended the steps to the crypt, God's most loyal servant remained in the shadows.

Deep down, she already knew the answer but seeing it for herself was something else entirely. And when her sight met the individual resting in the open stone, she nearly fell out of joy. "Ana!" Miraculously, his body was intact. His flesh untouched by the flaming grave. It was him, her king! Somehow, he survived.

Gently, her fingers caressed his face. Firm, he was as she remembered, but unnaturally cold. "I thought... I saw his body —"

"Burned? Yes. He was, severely," said Currant. "Most die enduring such heat, yet he survived, most likely due to his royal blood. Preparations for his slumber were barely done when Bogu called, informing me of his demise."

Bogu? How did she know that name?

Currant continued, "Built upon the royal wells, here King Ana can heal in his slumber, safe from the organization's clutches."

"Safe from all, except you," an unfamiliar voice added, pulling her attention away. Limping, a young child approached the crypt with a prideful smile, an expression she had seen before.

Goosebumps prickled her skin. *This child!* Alarms went off in her head. *This is the child Leo warned about? Is this Bogu? This is the True King?* The statement that did not correlate with her memory. However, within his waistband, the king's blade was securely tucked; the blade Casimir took. Whoever he was, her instincts were screaming and she listened.

Currant bowed to him as he passed and shot her a quick glance. *I see. So, this was the trap Currant mentioned,* Geda recognized. *I must fall for it to save Ana.* She swallowed.

The boy's dance tilted to a swagger climbing the subtle steps. "'Buried from God's eyes but cradled in his embrace,' that was Anastasius's request." Inconsiderately, Bogu sat on the seal of Ana's coffin and admired his knight. "Wouldn't you say I fulfilled it well?" he asked, peering up at her through his brow. She was still not convinced.

"Oh, Geda. How I've longed for this! Do you know how hard it is to keep a tiger on a leash? How about a child who will not sleep?" The more he talked, the more wickedness spilled from his innocent disguise.

Again, she didn't have a response fast enough to satisfy his excitement, an annoyance on his part. The boy's gaze combed her up and down. "Hmm. You don't seem to understand. Very well then," he said. Hopping off the edge of the sarcophagus, he twirled and morphed into a shadowy mist, which expanded into a taller figure before mutating into a fleshy existence. In his true form, she immediately recognized him.

Contrary to the title of divine, Bogu was rugged and scruffy. He possessed a wiry beard, peppered and long. His hair unkempt and wild, like a lion's mane. And his eyes, his eyes grew sharp and green. No longer youthful and pretty, the True King became seasoned by time and carried a physique representative of his strength.

This must be Bogu's royal form, Currant cheered. *Finally, a weak point.*

"Now, you are Bogu," Geda nodded. Undoubtedly, this being deserved her revenge, ancient and modern. Bogu, the Gammal Chief and God of Mutanity, twisted Ana to become his commander when he prayed for salvation.

"It has been a long time, Geda," greeted Bogu. "Our reunion would have been sooner if not for Anastas's resistance. Sometimes they have to die to learn their place."

"How can you say that? You are their father. You were supposed to help him!" As emotions rose, blood dripped from her nose. *Ah, not again,* she quickly caught the flow with her handkerchief.

Bogu spoke in her place. "Mutanity revolves around the hierarchy of survival and the one who has survived it all is me. You seem to have forgotten that now as you did ages ago," he growled. "Anastas is beneath me, a servant and numerous times, he has failed. So, I gave him one last trial which he, too, failed. In the end, Ana's only usefulness was in death."

"The dark army," she guessed confidently.

"No. You."

Me? Breath escaped her brace. This was beyond anything she anticipated.

Bogu carried on, "Though I could not capture her, the confrontation with Sarolt was not a waste. The ancient force I regained will allow me to reshape this desolate land. However," he looked down at Ana, "he is still my heir. His sacrifice is not meant to be permanent."

His cold gaze collided with hers. "I need Sarolt to take his place. With her blood, I can subside the Malum Saltus and save him. The world will finally be free. Until then, Ana retains their thirst. I need someone strong enough to bring her in. Do you think you can?"

Geda retracted as he neared. "Me? I was told not to trust you."

"Trust me or not, you are on death's door, and the Devil is not here to greet you."

Only God is, a terrifying thought but she could not deny what he said was true. After removing her tag, her symptoms grew progressively worse.

Currant nervously watched as Bogu grabbed her chin as if to deliver a kiss. The one planted by Ana barely survived despite her efforts to preserve it. Thankfully, the man went no further than to grab her attention.

"Now," he said. "It's your turn to serve me, forbidden being."

To be continue

About the Author

Salem Haskins, a Tennessee native, began writing in 2017 as a method to improve her communication skills; what started as a fan-fiction hobby ultimately turned into a compulsive form of therapy, and in 2024, her hard work paid off with her first indie publication, Forbidden Being, with endless plans to create more. When she isn't spending her time working a day job, you can always find her at home world-building